MW00777230

# A Christmas Boyfriend Recipe

## LISA H. CATMULL

SEASONS OF SC SUGAR CREEK

*To Sydnee,*
*And twins everywhere who are*
*born together and best friends forever*

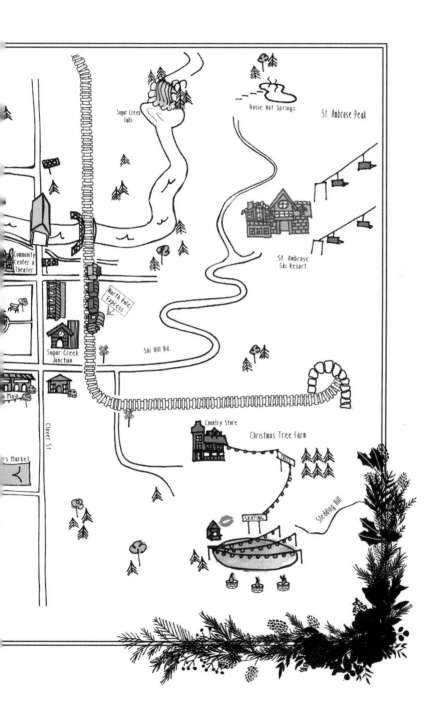

# Chapter One

JONAH DID IT AGAIN. It has to be him. I'm standing in the break room and there's no one else in the entire office building.

I lean my head against the wall and groan as I wait for my tea to steep. Of course, he has to be thoughtful. If he's off-limits, naturally, he's perfect.

"Brie?"

I whirl around. "Hey, Jonah." I brush my hands down the front of my business-casual slacks. He has no right to start the electric kettle for me every morning, so I'll have hot water when I get to work.

"You okay?" The deep brown eyes squint adorably until I can't breathe.

I whirl around. "Great. Thanks."

He glances at my "Shrimply Amazing" mug. "Tea again? You know the hot cocoa is free. On the house. Tarragon, lavender, cracked pepper, chili-cinnamon..."

I don't have the heart to tell him that I don't like his signature flavor combinations. "I never drink before noon."

A tiny grin lifts one side of his mouth, and something tickles my ribs. "Alright."

He jams his hands into his pockets.

This is my favorite part of the morning, and the reason why I'm early every day. "How did your barbecue beef turn out last night?"

Dimples appear in his cheeks. "Good."

It's also the most awkward part of the morning when I'm not sure if he wants to talk to me or not. Jonah glances at me. "I tried mesquite this time."

I shrug. "I'm telling you. I lived in Texas for six months, and you're never going to regret mesquite."

Jonah leans against the doorframe, a challenge twinkling in his eye. "Those are fighting words to any Southerner."

"But you live in Boston."

His mouth ticks up on one side. "I'll try Kansas-City style next."

"You'll go back to mesquite."

We grin at each other. "What about you? What did you make last night?"

I take a wax-paper covered square out of my bag and hand it to him. "Cheddar scones."

Our fingers brush, and I don't know if he even notices. His grin widens to a smile, though, when he unwraps the scone and tries a bite. "Wow. Thanks."

"Sure." I pick up my mug. "This should be ready now."

He pushes up the sleeves of his suit. A hint of skin shows below the cuffs. He didn't take the hint that I'm about to leave. I'm not complaining. Some mornings are like this. I take what I can get and ask a personal question this time. "So, did you always want to be a chef?"

He glances up from staring at the cheddar scone. "No. Everyone expected me to join the family business. I'm the oldest, so I had to rebel."

I settle into my seat. "And what wild, rebellious thing did you do?" I eye his button-up shirt and carefully groomed brown waves. His face is absolutely smooth, and I get a whiff of some pine cologne.

His mouth lifts in a half-grin. "I went to art school for a few months."

I take a sip of my tea before it cools too much.

Jonah continues. "But I spent all my free time cooking or thinking about food, so I quit and joined Jake in a culinary arts program."

This is one of the rare mornings where he opens up. "Do you ever regret it?"

Jonah straightens, and I know he's about to leave. I've gotten too personal. He shakes his head. "Never. I decided that cooking is a creative act, and every dish would be my work of art."

I bite my lip. Are we done talking?

"What about you?" Jonah asks. "Did you always want to be an accountant?"

I laugh. "I trained as a sous chef in your grandpa's kitchen, then I was a head chef in the Air Force. They sent me to culinary school, actually, even though I was just an airman and a sergeant, and you know. I was enlisted in the Air Force before I cross-trained and learned accounting." I take a huge breath.

"You trained as a chef?" Something sparks in his eyes.

"I did."

We stare awkwardly at each other, and wow. Those eyes of his.

But that's way too much information for Jonah to process, and sure enough. He's out of there.

"That explains why these scones are so good." Jonah grins at me. "Why all your treats are... Well, thanks." He waves and leaves the workroom. As soon as he's in the hallway, he takes another bite of scone.

Not that I'm watching his mouth.

I call after him. "See ya, Chef," but I think that very attractive mouth of his is too full to answer.

He certainly doesn't flinch at my nickname, like he did when I first met him. He simply wanders down the deserted hall to his glass-walled office. His perfectly tailored suit hits him just right everywhere. He's like a model walking down a fluorescent-lit runway, and I'm the only one who arrives early enough for the show.

I drop my head on the slick surface of a shiny melamine table. It's not fair. Some people have money and looks and manage not to be total idiots. Unlike me. *See ya, Chef?* What was I thinking?

"Yo, Brie."

Also, unlike Jonah's twin, who's also a morning guy. Unfortunately.

I pull my head off the table and stir some sugar into my tea. "Jake."

He fills an oversized travel mug with pebble ice, then fills it with Mountain Dew. It's snowing outside, and he's drinking fountain soda? I don't get this guy.

"How's life?" He settles at my table without asking.

I pick up my cup. "Great. I'm going to drink this at my desk."

He pops back up to walk with me. "Where are you going for Thanksgiving?"

I shrug. "Don't know." I point to my cubicle. "This is me." I slip into my office chair and focus on my laptop and extra monitor. Jake has that kind of Ken-doll attractiveness that is so beautiful it's hard to look at. He wears polo shirts and more casual attire than his brother, but he still smells like money.

He lounges with his arm on the top of the upholstered gray office divider. "How can you not know? It's tomorrow."

"I'm just that spontaneous." I wait for him to leave.

He doesn't.

I turn to him and smile. "Well, Happy Thanksgiving. Have a great time, wherever you go."

He starts to tell me a long story about his family's traditions, and I turn back around to my laptop. "Un-hunh. Sorry, I've got work to do before the break. I don't mean to be rude." Except that I do.

I didn't arrive early so I could spend my time listening to him talk. A lot.

Jonah yells from the other end of the hall. "Jake!"

The story stops midsentence. "I'll catch you up later."

"Mmm," I mutter indistinctly, and scroll through my Inbox.

I don't even work for Jake, but his dad has all of his companies in the same building, so I'm stuck with him and his perfectly tousled blond waves. If only his personality matched his chiseled jaw and piercing green eyes.

At least I also get to see his twin. His dark-haired, broad-shouldered, broody twin. I shake my head to clear the image of both Butler boys and force myself to focus on the computer screen.

I'm halfway through emptying my Inbox when my coworker arrives. Lindsay has a blush pink travel mug, also filled with pebble ice, but she has Diet Coke instead of Mountain Dew. Who are these people, and don't they know that it's winter?

She refuses to drink the free cocoa or anything without copious amounts of caffeine. Lindsay eyes my mug. "You didn't cave? The first sample is always free," she warns as she sits at the desk beside me. "Just like drug dealers."

"So, the Butler Food Group has some secret agenda? That's why they supply their employees with this mysterious powder in the break room?"

Lindsay changes out of her tennis shoes and slips into three-inch heels. "Yep. Once you start, you can never quit your job. Trust me."

I take a sip of my fruity hibiscus tea blend. "No worries. I can quit anytime. This is tea."

Lindsay's eyes widen. "Don't quit. We just hired you."

She is the most put-together looking person I know and the smartest woman on staff, but her inability to understand sarcasm still surprises me. "I'm joking."

She shrugs out of her black wool coat. "Right. Well, they will never pay you enough to maintain that kind of habit. Have you seen how much we sell their cocoa for?"

"Yep. We're both in accounting. I see the prices of everything." Her outfit is perfect, again, and I have to fight off my daily wave of insecurity. Not a wrinkle. I don't know how she does it. I manage to look disheveled before I get out the door.

Then again, I don't even know the brand names she buys or where she shops or how she affords those labels on the same salary that I make. I just know that those initials dancing backward with each other mean that her purse cost more than I make in a month.

I hand her a scone wrapped in wax paper. "Don't get used to these, if you don't want to get addicted to anything. You'll have to stay friends with me for life."

Lindsay moans. "Oh, which kind did you make? Blueberry or cranberry-orange?"

I brush the crumbs from my fingers. "Cheddar."

Lindsay squeals and breaks off a piece. "You're my new best friend."

I'm touched, and I smile at her as I delete another company email. "You saw this. right? They're encouraging work from home for everyone in the office in December?"

"Great!" Lindsay says. "You have to teach me how to make these scones. Maybe during the break?"

"I'm heading up to Vermont." I don't miss the look of disappointment on her face. I haven't been in Boston long, and I could use a friend. "I'm already planning on a girls' night out with you in January instead."

Lindsay's as transparent as they come. Her whole face shuts down, and she deflates. "You're going to be gone for the whole month?"

"Yeah. Work from home for December, right? Where are you going?"

Lindsay glances around the office. "Nowhere, unless they kick us out. I mean, my sister offered to let me accompany her and the nephews to Disney World. *Again*. Not my thing, you know, at this age."

Jonah and Jake head toward my desk. I admire the sight while I'm thinking, then I make a quick decision. I'm spontaneous, after all, and I do need to find friends here. "You want to come to

Vermont with me, Linz? Maybe we can switch to a two-bedroom cabin."

Her face lights up. "Really?"

"For sure. My friend is going to be busy. He works nights, so I'd love someone to hang out with."

"Text me the name of the place, and I'll pay half." She opens a tab in her browser. I can tell the exact moment when Lindsay notices Jake and Jonah. She stiffens, closes the tab, and swivels away from me.

I don't care if they're hovering beside us. "Cabins by the Bay in Sugar Creek, Vermont," I say.

Jonah clears his throat, and I smile at Lindsay. "If you can find us something, grab it and I'll cancel my reservation."

Jake is the one who interrupts our conversation, of course. "Hey, Ms. Santoro, J-Dog says I owe you an apology."

*J-Dog?* I turn to enjoy the tall drink of dark-haired hotness with his light-haired brother. The sight never gets old. "Thanks, Mr. Butler." I nod at Jonah. "And Mr. Butler."

Jonah won't meet my eyes. "Call me Jonah. I'm serious about that. But my brother"—he hits Jake in the shoulder—"is going to pay you a dollar for every time he says 'Yo'—"

"—like I'm some college-age frat boy." Jake grins and whacks his brother back. "Yeah, yeah."

Jonah shakes his head. "Be professional, dude."

Jake laughs. "Dude? You started it. Now who owes her a dollar?"

I don't have time for this, so I jump in. "No worries. I know how to handle bro culture. I was in the Air Force, remember?" I hold out my hand. "I'll start the collection now."

They probably think I'm bluffing for a minute, but I'm not. I didn't stay enlisted for ten years by going easy on the guys around me.

They each pull out their wallets. Jonah gives me a dollar bill, and Jake holds up a twenty. "Got change?"

"Nope." I stuff Jonah's money into my drawer and wait for Jake's.

He stares at Jonah's one-dollar bill. "Yes, you do. Come on."

I shake my head. *No mercy.* I know his type.

Jake hands me the twenty. "I should at least get credit for future—"

Jonah whacks him in the chest again. "No credits."

Jake rubs his chest. "Please?" I wonder how much his parents paid for that perfect row of gleaming whites. My mom never could afford braces for me, so I had to scrape together parts of my salary for two years to save up for Invisalign.

I've gotten lost staring at Jake when I realize Jonah is still talking. "—phone call."

But I didn't hear him. It's that Ken-doll effect. Jake is *too* pretty. I wonder if Jonah's used to people staring at his brother and ignoring him, so I train my gaze on Jonah. I like his look better anyway.

Jonah's brow furrows. "Brie?"

Now all I can think about is the color of Jonah's eyes. Dark brown. So dark. But nuanced. The brown is darker around the rim and lighter at the center. I blink. "What?"

"Jake got a call that we need to return. We've got to run. Are we good here?"

"Thanks, br—" He catches himself, then flashes another blinding smile. "I didn't say it, I don't have to pay for it. Right, Brie?"

I bite my lip. "Right." These twins don't play fair with their dimples and grins. "Thanks for stopping by, and thanks for the apology." But I'm feeling way out of my league.

Lindsay isn't flustered. She jumps right into the conversation. "If it's about the year-end reports, those calls come to me."

Jake is a peacock, and he changes as soon as Lindsay looks at him. A lazy grin slides onto his face, and he puffs out his chest. He folds his arms strategically, so we can't help but notice his biceps.

Lindsay is unaffected, if she even notices. She stares him down. "What was the call about?"

"Another TV competition." Jake seems like he's trying too hard to be casual about it. "One of those celebrity chef cookoff things."

I hold out my hand. "No humble brags. Rule number two of the Bro Fund."

Jake groans and gives me a dark look. "You're making these rules up as we go. Besides, I'm not bragg—"

Jonah's almost smiling. "Celebrity isn't bragging?"

"Accountants," Jake mutters, and he hands me another twenty. "Almost as bad as brothers."

"I heard that," someone says as he walks past. I look up. It's my boss, the twins' brother, Nick, and the head of the accounting department. "What's up?"

"TV show." Jonah shifts his weight to the other foot.

"With celebrity chefs," Jake repeats.

Lindsay nods and returns her gaze to her laptop. "So, not anything in our department." It's a clear dismissal of Jake, even though he's the CEO's son, and we're just cogs in the accounting department wheel. She might as well be the vice-president of accounting instead of Nick, but he just laughs.

I still haven't figured out why there's such a weird dynamic between Jake and Lindsay, but no one else seems worried about it.

Jake leans a hand on Lindsay's desk. "We get to give half of the money to a charity when we win."

She doesn't look up. "Can Brie take this one, Nick? I'm working on those reports."

Nick nods. "Sounds good." He claps Jonah on the shoulder. "Congrats, guys. See you tomorrow."

Jake tips his chin up in a total frat boy bro-nod, and I hold out my hand.

"Oh, come on, Brie. I didn't even say anything."

"I'll let you off with a warning this time." I'm not sure why Jonah appointed me the Bro-Police, but it's way too much fun.

LISA H. CATMULL

I catch Jonah's eye. "What do you need from me?"

He stares at me for a second, then swallows. "Lunch," he manages to get out.

"I don't run errands or fetch coffee. Sorry." I swivel back to my laptop and stare at my spreadsheets as disappointment washes over me.

Why are the hot guys always like that?

"I mean, I'll know after lunch. We have to clear this with my dad. It's really short notice."

I glance up. He's looking at the ceiling over my shoulder. I'm going to need a lot more information, which probably means talking to Jake instead of Jonah. I try not to sigh.

"Sure. You guys usually go around eleven-thirty, right?" I shouldn't admit that I know his schedule so well, but yeah, after three months of working here, I do. It's kinda hard not to notice the hottest guy in the office every time he walks past my desk. I wrap my sweater around myself and try to backpedal. "So, you'll be back around twelve-thirty or one? Or whatever time is good."

Jonah nods and jerks his head to his brother. "We'll have the details for you by then."

Jake scoffs. "No, we won't. I have two other meetings about the new restaurant, and I want to eat a decent lunch. The company already has a Nice Guy image. Does it matter who we give the money to?"

I open the drawer and point to the crumpled dollar bills. "Pay up, *bro*." I'm kinda hoping he never changes the way he talks. It's like getting a raise every time Jake opens his mouth.

He groans. "What?"

Jonah flicks a quick glance at me. I don't think he knows what triggered the bro-penalty, but then he answers his twin. *"Nice Guy image?"*

Jake scowls at his brother. "Speech police. Are you serious?"

We both nod. Jake hands me another twenty.

Jonah doesn't crack a smile. "Serious as a heart attack." His eyes catch mine and his mouth twitches, and I'm left wondering if he has a dry sense of humor or if he ever laughs or what a real smile looks like on him.

Jake grumbles, "You're such a dork," as they return to their shared office. I see Jonah wrap his arm around his brother's shoulder. Something melts inside me, even if I'm still annoyed with Jake.

I shut my new, overflowing Bro-Fund drawer. "The twins seem really close."

Lindsay laughs. "And you'd like to get in on that closeness?"

"Who wouldn't?" Of course I would, but I'll never admit it. I'll never admit any of the things I've been thinking about the Butler twins since I started working here. "Why? Do you?"

"Of course not." Lindsay turns back to her monitor with a slight flush to her cheeks.

I start crunching numbers. I know exactly which charity is on brand for the Butler Food Group, because it's my own passion.

I want to provide meals for thousands of hungry children on Christmas Eve, and I want their dad's company to pay for it even if the twins lose the cooking competition. Maybe we can get someone to match their donation and double it. I start outlining a proposal, and the morning flies.

If the twins win and get to donate their winnings to any charitable cause, then I want them to pick mine. I just have to talk them into it.

And I think I know how.

# Chapter Two

My plan falls apart as soon as I reach their glass-walled office. Jonah glances over and beckons me inside, but I stop at the door.

"Hey, Brie," Jake says, his voice strained. "Just finishing some negotiations."

An older man, who must be their dad, the head of the entire Butler Food Group and the owner of at least twelve restaurants in the Boston area alone, has Jake in a headlock. He's got the same deep brown eyes as Jonah and the same muscular build as the twins.

When he sees me, he doesn't let up. Grunts punctuate his words as he wrestles with his son. "Manners, boys. *Uh*. Introduce me. *Uh*. To my employee."

Jonah elbows his dad in the ribs to distract him while his brother spins out of the headlock. Jake's blond hair is disheveled, and I see a sliver of skin where his shirt's pulled up, but then I notice Jonah watching me.

I glance over at him, and he looks away.

Jake tugs at his polo shirt and twists the sleeves back into place. "Fine, but I still don't like the restaurant name. *Thirteen*. Completely unoriginal."

Meanwhile, Jonah calmly says, "Brie Santoro, this is my dad."
I smile at them both, but Jonah's got a question in his eyes when he finally meets my gaze.

My eyes dart to his loose button-up shirt, tucked into his waist, and the jacket covering everything, and I can't help wondering how similar these two twins are. I mean, are those abs identical, even if the twins aren't?

"Nice to meet you." The guy extends his hand. "Jim Butler."

My eyes snap to his. I'm hoping he didn't notice me checking out either of his sons. Jim Butler is a legend in the restaurant world. A celebrity chef before there were celebrity chefs. I can't believe I'm meeting him, so I play it cool, or try to, but I blurt out the first thought in my mind. "You look just like Pappy."

Jonah's staring at me with a weird expression, but I keep calm. I took off a gas mask in a room full of fumes during basic training. I can handle their dad, even if he's restaurant royalty.

Mr. Butler bends over and grabs a water bottle from the mini fridge behind him, totally playing it cool, too. "You know him?"

"I worked in his kitchen in New York."

Mr. Butler unscrews the water bottle. "You can't be old enough. That was, what? Ten years ago? You must have been a kid."

I smile. He's smooth. "I started washing dishes before I could walk."

Mr. Butler grins back at me with dimples in both cheeks. He's got laugh lines instead of worry lines around his eyes, and he reminds me of Jonah. I decide I like him.

Mr. Butler must like me, too, because he settles into an uphol-stered chair across from his boys. "So, you work with these two goons?"

Jake rests on the edge of his desk and crosses his legs at the ankle. "Seriously, Pops? A little respect."

Mr. Butler takes a long swig of his water. "Sorry. You work with these two... knuckleheads?"

Jake turns to Jonah. "How come Dad doesn't have to pay

when he talks like that?" He doesn't seem to expect an answer as Jonah shrugs and comes around his desk to lean against the edge, mirroring his brother's pose.

Jake almost has the tone of a child telling on his brother. "Jonah's taking the new harassment policy too far. He's hired an enforcer, and it's cost me almost a hundred bucks so far."

Mr. Butler just laughs. "Cheaper than a lawsuit. So, Brie, what do you do here?"

"I run the Bro-Fund to rehabilitate Jake."

I get a huge laugh this time from Mr. Butler. He's wiping the tears from his eyes as I continue, "I also work with one of your sons."

"Everyone works for one of my sons." Mr. Butler draws a deep breath as he stops laughing.

"Nick. Accounting."

Mr. Butler nods and looks at me expectantly, so I launch into my proposal. It seems a lot more implausible when I'm looking him in the eye. "Jonah and Jake are competing again, so I'm here to pin down the amount your company is going to match when they win and which charities we're supporting. I've decided that we'll donate the winnings to the local food banks."

It's not a question. I learned some psychology in the Air Force, and one of the first things my mentor, my Chief Master Sergeant, taught me was that people don't want to correct you. I suspect Jonah's not a confrontational guy. Maybe his dad isn't, either.

Except for that headlock.

"I'm matching their winnings?" I see the twinkle in his eye, and it's not as cocky as Jake's. He's more thoughtful, like Jonah, but playful, too. He's the perfect mix of his twins' personalities. "I've never done that before." He motions toward a chair.

I sit next to him and mirror his casual pose. "Yep. First time for everything. You're donating the same amount if they lose. Marketing will love it."

He offers me a water bottle, and I accept it. Jake's about to explode and object, but I only have to convince their dad right now. "Pappy would do it."

Mr. Butler shifts into focus mode, and I can see why he's the CEO of a restaurant empire. He leans forward, fingers steepled together. "Would he?"

It's been ten years since I worked for his father, but I'm confident that Pappy never changes. If Mr. Butler's trying to intimidate me, I won't cave. "Yes." I take a long swig of my water.

Mr. Butler waits until I'm done. A smile flits across his face before the dark brown eyes bore into me again. "Convince me."

So, I try. "The charitable donation from the cooking competition is a chance to feed hungry kids. That's completely on brand for you."

"On brand," Jake mutters.

I level a gaze at him, and he shuts up. *Fast.* There wasn't much left last time he opened his wallet, and I'm guessing he won't risk any disrespect.

I flick my gaze back to Mr. Butler. "You're donating to the local food banks with in-kind donations like eggs, milk, and produce that are about to expire in a couple days, the things that you overbought, or extras from those days when the customer count is low. You're going to create a working partnership that extends beyond this one-time win and use the twins' appearance to promote your new image: the restaurants that care and give back to their community."

Mr. Butler doesn't flinch. I glance at Jonah. His face is just as impassive. *Like father, like son* seems a little cliché, but these matching expressions are almost comical. The drawn eyebrows, the dimpled cheeks, the warm brown hair and eyes.

Well, I'm not intimidated. I think Jonah's on board, despite that look on his face, and I rehearsed that speech all morning. It's a good pitch, and it's a good plan.

Jake is shaking his head, so I launch into the next part. "I was hungry when I was a kid. Believe me, you don't want to eat expired canned goods and the weird selection people donate to food banks. They need cash and in-kind donations year-round—"

"Boys?" Mr. Butler cuts me off, even as he settles back in his chair. I was just launching into my sob story, and he seemed to sense it. He's as allergic to emotions as Jonah seems to be.

Jake's right. Their dad could use some Bro-Fund tutoring, too.

"No." Jake stands abruptly. "We've got slim margins, we know how to order without over-ordering, and we already have a —" He glances at me. "A *good* reputation."

My work is already paying off. Jake managed not to use "Nice Guy" as a put-down this time. I'm going to miss his payouts.

Jonah doesn't move. He's still while Jake is pacing. The calm in the center of the storm. Or a thinking machine. A robot. I haven't decided which yet.

Mr. Butler doesn't immediately shoot down the idea, so I'm going to bluff and see if I can win this one. "Come on, Chef. You know how much food gets wasted. Think how much good you could do."

Jonah nods. "Corporations as large as ours should give back to the community." That's it. One sentence, and he's done. He doesn't acknowledge my emotional pitch.

I'm leaning toward *robot* right now.

Jake opens his mouth to argue, but Mr. Butler's watch buzzes. He holds up a hand and reads a text, then groans. "Can you do this without setting foot in your brother's restaurant or Pappy's kitchen or this office?"

Jonah's brow furrows. "No."

Jake nods. "We're already working overtime to prep the new restaurant concept."

I can almost see the wheels turning in Jonah's mind. "Only four months until it opens—"

"—and we have six months of work." Jake returns to his desk and blows out a long breath.

This is slipping away from me. "But I can take this on. I'll need to have your sons look it over and approve it, but I can manage the logistics and coordinate with the restaurant managers. I don't mind some overtime. I won't charge you. It's for charity."

It's an insane offer, but that's how passionate I am about this cause.

Mr. Butler pushes out of his chair. He screws the lid on his water bottle and starts flipping it. Up and down. *Catch.* The water sloshes in the silence of the room. Up and down. *Slosh. Catch.* "No."

I expect Jake to be glad, but he's not. Jonah folds his arms across his chest and doesn't say anything, but Jake challenges his dad. "Why?"

I'm thinking it's the money or the logistics or he doesn't want to add more work for his restaurant managers, but then I catch the look of embarrassment on Mr. Butler's face.

He glances between his two sons and grimaces. "Because I just got a text from the staff psychologist. Neither of you have taken the minimum number of vacation days this year, and she's banning you from the office for the entire month of December."

# Chapter Three

JAKE GROANS and collapses in his chair. "Oh, come on, man. Can she even do that? Why do you listen to Mom?"

It takes a second for his comment to register, but as soon as it does, I hold out my hand. "Pay up, bro."

Mr. Butler's brow furrows, and he frowns at Jonah. "She wasn't joking about the fund thing?"

Jonah shakes his head, and Mr. Butler grins. Jake hands me the money without complaining. "Sorry." Even Jake seems to know that insulting mothers is not cool.

The embarrassment is gone. Mr. Butler is back to blustering now. "Your mom can do anything she wants. You're taking the month of December off. No discussion."

I'm trying to decide whether to leave quietly or fight this. Evidently "no discussion" is meaningless because Jonah starts arguing. "We just got invited to compete on a Christmas Eve cooking show. Since when is there a minimum?"

Maybe I'll stay and fight, too.

"Since Patty lost the baby, and Danny got divorced, and we still don't have any grandkids."

Or not. This is getting way too personal for me.

I'm barely on a first name basis with the twins after three

months of working here, and I just met Mr. Butler. I certainly don't want to know about Patty's miscarriage, because no one's pain should be public, or Danny's divorce, whichever brother he is, and I'm sure he doesn't want me to hear all about how he disappointed his dad.

Because the look on Mr. Butler's face is tearing at my heart. It's raw and real, and I'm super uncomfortable.

But he's standing between me and the door.

"Twenty-seven days isn't a lot to ask, and let's see, you've got *zero*. Both of you." Mr. Butler turns to me to settle his argument. "How many days have you taken?"

Oh, no. I am not getting involved. "I only started a few months ago, sir."

He narrows his eyes.

There's no way around it. I'm a workaholic, too. "So, uh. None."

"Welcome to the Butler Food Group family. Take your vacation days." Their dad turns his attention back to the twins. His voice is even stronger and surer now. "I'm deactivating your key cards tomorrow. Luke is changing the password on your laptops. Everything will work again on January third."

"What? My own brother wouldn't betray me." Jake's standing with his hands on his desk to steady himself.

"It's not technically December yet," Jonah says.

Leave it to the robot to be technical.

"I pay his salary, so yep. Your brother is loyal to no one." Mr. Butler smiles and stretches. "If you have any complaints, take it up with your mother. Something about you never having time to date and dying old and alone." He shrugs. "She's not wrong."

Both boys collapse into their desk chairs, obviously defeated, and it's clear who really runs this company. Pappy's told me about his daughter-in-law, and I have no doubts she would comb through human resource records to find a way to marry her sons off.

And Mr. Butler's fine with that.

But then a wave of emotion crosses Mr. Butler's face again. "I just want some grandbabies to spoil on Christmas morning." The laugh lines are worry lines now, and I'm surprised how much pain those endless brown eyes can hold.

Jake and Jonah seem to know they're beaten. I certainly do. Thousands of faceless hungry kids can't compete with the idea of Mr. Butler's unborn grandbabies.

"It was nice to meet you." I try to slip past him in the doorway. I'm gutted at the idea of losing so many meals for the food bank, but I'm surprised to feel such a sharp pang of disappointment when I realize I won't be working with the twins.

And that's just wrong. Those two things don't even compare. *World hunger. Hot celebrity chefs.* Nope. I've got to get out of here and back to the safety of my desk, where I can merely nod at the twins, and they say "Hi," and that's as well as we know each other.

Except on those mornings when Jonah tells me that every meal is a work of art, and I catch glimpses of his soul.

Mr. Butler stops me on my way out. "Sure, sure. Glad to have you on the team."

I glance at the hallway. *Freedom.*

His attention locks onto me. He's had one eye on his boys, but now he's focused on me. *Too focused.* It's unnerving, because he smiles broadly. *Too broadly.* "You know Pappy?"

I nod warily. I still haven't told my old employer that I've moved to Boston, and I'll be in massive trouble when he finds out that I haven't visited him. It's clear that his son is just as smart as he is.

And I can see something behind his eyes.

I'm hoping it's not unborn grandbabies, but judging by the quick glance down at my left hand, I think it is.

Mr. Butler nods sharply. "Then you're coming to Thanksgiving dinner. The boys will give you the address."

"Uh. Thanks for the offer. I..."

I don't have an excuse, and Jake knows it. I don't have plans, because it's not worth buying that much food for one person, and I don't have any friends in Boston yet. Not really.

I don't need this kind of pressure. The entire happiness of Mr. and Mrs. Butler's future is riding on my answer. Oh, and every Christmas morning for the rest of eternity.

But I go through boyfriends like crossword puzzles.

Jonah's watching me, too, now, and I catch his eye. This is beyond awkward, and I want him to give me some hint of what to do. There's no way he wants me to come, and I need him to shake his head or glare or something.

Jonah doesn't. I don't see any emotions there, but he holds my gaze long enough that Jake answers for me. "Of course she'll come. Brie doesn't have anywhere else to go. I'll give her a ride."

Jonah's gaze narrows now, and I wonder if he's upset about Jake making that call. No one wants a total stranger at Thanksgiving dinner.

But I really don't get this guy. I'm about to look at Jake and tell him not to answer for me and that he owes me that last twenty that I saw in his wallet when something flares in Jonah's eyes.

And now I can't look away. I can't breathe.

Jonah's voice is low and gruff as he says, "No. I will."

# Chapter Four

I'M STILL SHAKING the snow off my boots when Pappy sees me, but he gets the wrong idea.

Jonah likes to arrive early, and so do I, so we're the first ones to walk into his restaurant. I dust the snow off my hair and try to shrug out of my coat, but Jonah has some idea that he has to be a gentleman.

I get it.

I worked with Pappy long enough to know that Jonah's grandfather would disown him if he didn't treat me like a queen, so I stop and wait for him. Shivers run through me as he lifts the wool jacket off my shoulders. His fingers brush the woven fabric of my sweater, but I feel his touch all the way down to my toes.

I glance at Jonah, and his eyes lock onto mine. Now I'm sweltering with heat.

I'm probably imagining it. Jonah doesn't really talk, after all, so I have no idea what's going on with these looks.

Pappy yells across the dark, upscale restaurant lobby. "Shrimp? You kidding me? I thought Jimmy was pulling my leg." He takes a long look at me, then crushes me in a hug.

"Yep, it's me."

My ears start ringing as he yells into the kitchen for his wife.

"Mary! Come meet Jonah's new girlfriend. You're going to like this one."

I'm still wondering what Mr. Butler told him when Mary bustles out of the kitchen, wiping her hands on the apron around her waist. "James doesn't joke. No sense of humor." She grabs my face between her hands. "My little Brie." She kisses one cheek and then the other. "Finally, you date a Butler boy. I told you for years." She points her finger at Jonah. "Don't mess this up like the others."

"Why would he mess this up? He's my grandson," Pappy says.

"Because he's a stubborn and competitive workaholic, like you." She pats my face. "But she loves him, and this is Brie, so she can handle him." Mary disappears back into the kitchen.

I'm trying to hide my laugh, but it doesn't really work. I love the way a tiny, five-foot powerhouse intimidates her six-foot grandson. The sheepish look on Jonah's face is still killing me, but now I'm off in my own world, wondering how many girlfriends he's had and how he always messes things up.

Because who wouldn't want to date—*him*. I tear my eyes away as he slips out of his suit jacket and fiddles with the sleeves of his turtleneck, exposing corded forearms. He's been hiding some serious muscles.

So, this is how he unwinds. No jeans, just pushed-up sleeves.

I'm not complaining.

Before I can correct Pappy, Jake arrives with Mr. and Mrs. Butler. A cold blast of wind chills me as the door closes. Pappy skips the greetings and goes straight for the gossip. "You didn't tell me she was his girlfriend."

"I didn't know." Mr. Butler looks more amused than confused.

Jonah steps closer, so he's right behind me. We almost look like a couple now.

"Really?" A red-haired woman gives me the up and down. "How convenient for you, Jonah."

The twins look more like her than their dad. I can see now

that Jake's hair is closer to strawberry-blond than beach-blond, and she must be the reason that her husband and sons all dress so well.

I'm as plain as coal, and they're all shiny diamonds. I tug at my sweater and wish I'd worn a dress instead of jeans.

Jonah glances down at me, and I stop pulling at my sweater. He looks back to his mom. "What's convenient?"

The woman who must be his mother holds up her hand, as if he's going to argue. "I tell you yesterday to get a girlfriend or stop working, and now today you're dating someone I've never heard of?" She smiles at me. "You're still welcome to stay for dinner, of course, but I don't buy it. No offense, sweetie, whoever you are."

"None taken," I say quickly. "I'm not selling anything."

Mrs. Butler arches an eyebrow at my statement.

*What?* I say to myself. *I don't feel very welcome, and I'm hungry.*

Pappy laughs. "No, Maggie, it's fine. This is Brie, the girl I told you about. Her mom worked for me. She's family."

Mrs. Butler crosses the restaurant's entrance and extends her hand. "Welcome."

I take it, and her grip is firm, not one of those limp fish handshakes that usually come with air kisses. I'm definitely not getting any hugs or family vibes from her. No "make yourself at home with us," like Pappy always says.

I return the firm handshake. "I'm Brie Santoro, and—"

"—and she works with Nick. Yeah, yeah. I can't believe you didn't tell me you two were dating, Joe. You tell me everything." Apparently Jake's been quiet longer than he can stand.

I can tell that bugs Jonah, and I'm right. Instead of correcting his brother, Jonah says, "Not everything."

A shadow passes over Jake's face. "I'm your twin, man. You're breaking the code."

Jonah shrugs. "*You* don't tell me everything."

Jake's face clears. "Nah, but I know what you're thinking

before you do." Jake grins. "No wonder it took you so long to do your hair tonight. I knew it was Brie. Didn't I say so?"

Jonah whacks him in the chest, near the shoulder, and mutters, "Shut up."

"Called it." Jake nods at me. "What am I missing when you two are alone every morning at work?"

I can't stand the self-satisfied smirk on Jake's face, like Jonah can't ever have an original thought. "Innuendo is a no-go, bro." I hold out my hand, and Jake gives me the last twenty in his wallet.

In fact, he hands over his entire wallet. "I'm out. Guess you're stuck with the real me tonight."

I return the empty wallet, but I slip out his credit card. "Oh, you can go into debt with me. I accept I.O.U.s."

Jake grabs his credit card. "How much does *Feminazi* cost if I say it?"

I'm guessing that Jake just likes to push buttons, and he doesn't mean any of the stuff he says, but his brother is literal and the button-pushing works. Jonah whacks him again. "Fifty push-ups, and you owe me, not Brie."

Jake winces and rubs his chest. "It was a joke."

"That kind of joke isn't funny." Jonah points at the restaurant floor. "Fifty now or later?"

Jake elbows him. "Tomorrow morning, you bully."

Their dad laughs, but their mom narrows her eyes. She's watching me but talking to Jonah. "How long have you known each other? When did you start dating? Yesterday around, say, noon?"

Pappy pushes her into the dining area. "It's Thanksgiving. Save the interrogation for tomorrow. Brie is our guest."

Mr. Butler glances between Jonah and me, winks at Jonah, and mouths, "Way to work around Mom."

I hold out my hand. Mr. Butler stares at me and slaps my hand, like I'm giving him a high-five or something.

I can't help it. I laugh. "No, sir. You work at Butler Food Group, too. You're part of the Bro-Fund."

He rifles through his wallet. "The only cash I've got is a hundred. Can you break it?"

I tuck Jake's twenty into my pocket.

"No change," Jonah says. "I'm not trying to disrespect Mom or work around her rules."

Mr. Butler winks at us. "Sure." He hands me the hundred-dollar bill. "Do I get credit for the—"

"No," Jake and Jonah say at the same time. They turn to each other and grin.

Jake stares at his twin. "Seriously. I can't believe you kept this secret. I'm hurt, bro, hurt. That cuts deep." He claps Jonah on the back, and then I'm left alone with Jonah in the restaurant's lobby.

"So." Jonah rubs the back of his neck. "Sorry."

"I won't sue, Mr. Harassment-Lawsuit-Waiting-To-Happen. It's fine. Just a misunderstanding."

He doesn't laugh at my attempt to tease him. "Why am I a walking lawsuit?"

He's so much more than a suit, but my gaze drops to his perfectly fitted trousers and shirt anyway before I shake myself. I don't want to say it out loud. "Come on. You know."

He's baffled. *Clueless.* His legs fill out the suit, and that turtle-neck stretches across his arms in a way I couldn't see when he wore his jacket.

He looks like he's trying to think of something he said or did, but it's not his fault that he's hot. And nice. And intelligent.

And starts the water kettle every morning, so I can have a cup of tea when I come to work.

"You're *you.*" I wave vaguely at his body. "Your dad owns the company. You and your brothers are off-limits, right, and I'm sure you have women getting the wrong idea all the time."

I really want him to buy this, so I don't have to explain what else I'm thinking.

Jonah clears his throat. "Hence my memorization of the harassment policy." He still seems like he doesn't understand. "But what did I do?"

"Nothing." He didn't do anything. He just—*is*. And that's enough to make any woman lose her common sense and want to do something extreme.

Like, say, flirt with the boss's son, even though I really need this job, and I just got out of the Air Force, and I'm saving up earnest money for a pending loan on my townhouse, and I really, really can't take any risks right now.

*Hypothetically.*

His face finally clears. "Oh. I should have said *something*, not *nothing*."

This is a lost cause. "That's not what I meant, but yeah, that, too. We're good now. You can tell them that we're not dating, and..."

The look on his face stops me, so I clarify. "We're not dating, right? Or is this a date?"

He suddenly feels too close. I step back and lean against the custom wooden counter where the hostess usually stands.

Jonah approaches the counter and pushes some menus aside. He eyes me for a long moment, then leans a hand on the counter next to me. "I wouldn't mind if it was a date. I'm not your boss."

The rest of his extended family could arrive any moment. I take a mint from the bowl on the counter and unwrap it to stall for time.

But Jonah isn't like his brother. He doesn't talk to fill the air. He watches me with that steady gaze. We're even closer to each other now that he has me trapped here.

I smooth my shirt and try to take a deep breath. "I wasn't begging for a date."

Jonah's kind of bending over to talk to me, since I'm so short. Well, we would be talking, if he said anything.

"I don't have to beg for dates. Really. Guys ask me out. All the time."

Ack. Now I'm babbling like his brother. Maybe that's why Jake talks so much—because Jonah doesn't. I should hand Jonah the hundred-dollar bill for bragging, because that was a top-grade boast.

"Like now?" Is it my imagination or is Jonah leaning closer to me? I catch a whiff of some pine-scented soap or cologne, so I'm already distracted when he says, "Dating isn't against any rules. Technically. For us."

Now I'm going to melt. I don't care if it's November and seventeen degrees outside.

But he still hasn't asked me out. Not *technically*. "Such a romantic." I pat his cheek, and of course, his mom comes into the lobby right then.

She stops cold. "Jonah?"

I drop my hand, and the guilty look on his face is priceless when he turns around. I slip out from beneath Jonah. "I'm sorry, ma'am. We're on our way in."

"Pappy asked for help in the kitchen." Her eyes cut to mine, then back to Jonah. "No walk-in refrigerator, no making out. You know the rules."

She pushes her way back into the dining area, and I'm still laughing at his mom. First, she doesn't believe him, but now she doesn't want him to embarrass her by making out and getting caught. Who does she think I am?

Oh, yeah. The girl she caught caressing Jonah's cheek, totally wanting to kiss him while he hovered over her.

Fair point. Other families are arriving, so she's probably right about not making out.

Not that I've imagined slipping into the huge refrigerator to kiss her son.

But I am thinking about it now. A lot.

Jonah opens the door to the kitchen for me, and the smell of Thanksgiving dinner hits me all at once. He grabs an apron and slips it over his head, and it's not like I've never seen a man wear an apron before.

But Jonah picks an all-black apron and cinches it around his hips, and for some reason, it's the hottest thing I've ever seen when he starts washing his hands and forearms. I can see every vein in his arm now, covered with soap suds, and the heat of the kitchen is already getting to me.

"What can I do?"

Jonah glances over. "I've got this. Mary doesn't let guests help in the kitchen."

Pappy hands me an apron. "She's not a guest. She's your girlfriend, and she knows how to work with Mary."

I am a guest, and I'm not Jonah's girlfriend, but I'm not even going to correct Pappy or Mary while they're cooking. I value my meal too much. Pappy adopts the people who work in his kitchen, so I'm never going to be a guest at any meal he cooks. I'm always family to him.

Besides, Jonah's had two chances to correct Pappy, and he's chickened out both times.

Pappy points to the sink. I slip the apron over my head, and Jonah's eyes follow the movement.

"What?" I nudge him out of the way with my hip. It's ridiculous because I'm barely two inches taller than Mary, and Jonah towers over me by almost a foot. Still, he stumbles over and dries his hands on a towel.

"You want to help?" His gaze darts down to the oversized apron and the strings wrapped twice around my waist.

"I'd rather be in here than out there." I finish washing and whip the towel out of his hands. "Where do you want me, Pappy?"

"Plate."

I understand his shorthand. Pretty soon, Jonah and I are working side by side plating appetizers, and Pappy is talking to me as if the last ten years hadn't happened.

Pappy comes and goes, so we have to talk in bursts, but I'm hearing about all the awards for his new restaurant in Boston, how I should have moved with him from New York, and all the reasons I shouldn't have joined the Air Force. Nothing new. I've read it in every Christmas letter for the last ten years.

But Pappy needs to reiterate it all to my face, while looking deeply wounded that I abandoned him.

I try to end the guilt trip. "No, the Air Force was good. I'm glad I went in, and I'm glad I got out."

"But you could've married Jonah ten years ago."

I snort a laugh, and Jonah stiffens. Pappy wanders to another part of the kitchen.

I nudge Jonah. "Sorry. I wasn't laughing at the idea of marrying you."

He nods.

But I still feel like I hurt his feelings. "It's not like you would have wanted to get married ten years ago, either. Who gets married when they're eighteen?"

"Twenty."

I look over.

"I'm thirty. Ten years ago, I was twenty."

"Okay." I have no idea if he's been pining away to get married for ten years, or if he just wants to be precise about his age.

Pappy comes back. "Look at Mary and me. We met. Dated a week. Boom. Engaged. Married. Eight kids. Still together fifty plus years later." He brushes something off his hands, then waves a hand between me and Jonah. "You're both old. How you gonna have eight kids?"

"Yeah, I don't know. It might have to only be four, or maybe four sets of twins. That'll still add up to eight."

Pappy throws back his head and roars with laughter. "You could handle them. If anyone could, you could."

I grin at Jonah as Pappy walks away. "You *are* ancient. Thirty. Wow."

"Well seasoned." His mouth twitches with the tiniest smile before I see the worry wrinkles around his eyes.

"Hey, Chef, no worries. I know what your grandpa's like. I'm not gonna sue."

But Jonah's still giving me weird looks every time he hands me a plate. He's not as easy to read as his brother.

I make a guess. "I was joking about marrying you and having your babies. You know that, right?"

He coughs and glances over. "Oh, is *that* what you said? You want to have *my* babies?"

I was wrong. That wasn't what he was thinking, and the word "babies" sends him into full robot mode. No eye contact. No words.

Plate. *Slide.* Plate. *Slide.*

"Is that the kind of joke that isn't funny? Should I drop and give you fifty push-ups?"

Jonah's brow furrows. "For what?"

"Joking about grandkids."

Jonah's mouth tilts in a half-smile. "Pappy dishes it out. He can take it." His eyes sparkle with humor and burn with heat at the same time. "But can *you* handle it?"

My pulse quickens. I'm pretty sure that *I'm* the one who didn't get *his* joke earlier. He's got a dry sense of humor, I guess, and I'm the one who froze and went weird, not him.

I nudge him with my shoulder. "I can handle anything, Chef, even your babies."

He coughs again and a plate almost slips out of his hands. I love the way I get under his skin, because he's got me completely flustered. I hope we settle into a comfortable routine now that I cleared the air, but we don't. I'm pretty sure he was flirting, and I'm freaked out about it.

Maybe he still is. I'm even more aware every time our shoulders brush or our fingers touch each other's or I inhale another whiff of his aftershave, and it seems like it's happening a lot.

The tension between us is killing me. Are we *technically* on a date or not? He picked me up. We arrived together.

Did he really get dressed tonight for me, or does he always look this good at family dinners?

I'll never know. Robots don't talk. We probably won't *ever* finish that dating conversation.

Unless I start it again.

## Chapter Five

CHRISTMAS COMES EARLY for the prankster in me. No way am I letting Jonah off the hook when Pappy takes a full plate from me and asks, "Didn't I tell you about my grandsons? What took you so long to remember that I'm always right and marry one?"

Pappy winks at me and walks away. He thinks we're only dating, and he's teasing me about marriage. Mr. Butler must've learned that wink from his dad, but Pappy isn't being ironic. He's one-hundred-percent on board with this Jonah-Brie idea. Does that make us Bronah? Or Joey? Jo-ie? Yeah, couple names are the worst anyway.

But visions of unborn grandbabies are swirling in Pappy's eyes, now, too.

Jonah is really interested in the appetizers that he's plating, but one still slides off and hits the counter. Our hands brush as I wipe the counter in front of him, and he swallows. "You don't have to answer."

"I can handle it, remember, Chef?" This is Jonah's party. His family. It's his job to set things straight, not mine. When Pappy heads back toward us, I throw back the kind of answer he loves. "You did tell me about your *seventeen* grandsons when I worked for you, Pappy, but how could I choose just *one*? They compete on cooking shows, not on *The Bachelor*."

He laughs at that, and I think we're done, but nope. Pappy stops and gives me this intense, serious look. "So, you really like Jonah better than his twin? Most girls like Jake."

"You *really* don't have to answer that," Jonah mutters.

"Oh, but I want to." I shrug to lighten the mood again. "I like the dark, mysterious type. Blond is boring." I slide a squash blossom onto the rectangular white plate alongside the corn fritter, add a dollop of cranberry and chile relish, and hand the plate to Pappy.

He's still serious. "Good girl. You always were. Head on your shoulders." He walks away, and I really hope he's not crying.

Jonah shoots me a glance from beneath his wavy brown hair. He repeats what Pappy said. "Most girls like Jake."

Except this time, it's a question, even though, technically, it sounds like a statement. An irrefutable fact. I hear it in his voice, and I see the worry lines around his eyes. I actually understand Mr. Technical for once.

He's asking which twin I like. It's the same question that Pappy asked, and it bugs me, as if it's unthinkable that anyone could find Jonah more attractive or compelling than his annoying, frat-boy brother.

"Jake's fine, but I like you better." That's true. Let Jonah take it however he wants.

A tiny grin lifts one side of his mouth, and a dimple pops in that cheek.

Mary comes over. "I told you Jonah would get married first. The girls date Jake, but no one wants to marry him."

I bite my lip and try not to laugh, but a snort escapes me. I meet Jonah's eyes, and I'm relieved to see that he's laughing, too. Not out loud. Jonah's not really the laugh out loud type, but I can see that he's laughing on the inside.

But those eyes. When he smiles there are little crinkle lines around the corners, just like his dad, and it makes something dance inside my chest.

Mary and Pappy head to the other side of the kitchen, and I lower my voice to whisper, "So, are we dating or engaged? Or *not* on a date? Or do we secretly have a child together?"

Jonah's hand freezes on the plate he's holding.

"I didn't even say *babies*. I said *child*." I nudge him with my hip. "I want to get the story straight for your grandparents."

He flashes me a quick smile. I didn't know he could do that— smile like that. Now I'm frozen in place.

"Up to you." Jonah hands me a plate with a stuffed squash blossom already on it. The goat cheese and herb mixture smells amazing. "It'll be more efficient if we do it this way."

So, he doesn't want to talk about it. He's that kind of all-logic, no-emotion, conflict-avoiding guy. Yeah, been there, dated Spock. Check please.

But I still want to see if I can get him to break.

I slide a corn fritter on the plate and add a dollop of the cranberry relish. He's right. I've been out of the kitchen too long. "So, if we've secretly been engaged for, let's say, two months, should I call you 'boyfriend' or 'sweetie' or..."

He hands me another plate. "Jonah is fine."

This is too much fun. If he's not going to correct Pappy and Mary, I'm not going to, and If Mr. Technicality himself thinks we can flirt, then I'm not holding back. "Are you sure, honey butter?"

Mary slides another tray of fresh corn fritters in front of me. "Oh, don't call him that. Hasn't he told you his family nicknames?"

His eyes fill with panic, and I'm loving this. "Nope. We haven't had time."

Mary loves a joke, too, so she'll forgive me for teasing Jonah when I tell her the truth. Which I will. Any minute. As soon as he stops smelling so good and being so—*him*.

Mary comes back with another tray. "Let's see, there's Joe, Joey."

Pappy comes over. "J-Dog."

I'm barely holding it together while I plate the appetizers. I can't look at Jonah, but our arms brush as we work side by side.

Mary keeps going. "Lou, Killer, Blubby."

My shoulders are shaking with laughter as I set down the next plate. Pappy and Mary are over on the other side of the kitchen again, and I wait for Jonah.

Nothing. I glance over, and he's watching me. I nudge him with my shoulder this time. "Lou?"

"Short for Beluga."

I bite my lip.

"What? They're the cutest species of whale."

"So, Jonah and the whale? Your family really went there?"

He sets down his serving utensil. "I'm not sure someone with the nickname *Shrimp* has room to tease me."

"Whatever you say, *Killer.*"

We're actually flirting. I'm sure this time. Jonah is capable of humor after all, and it looks good on him. Everything does.

We're still standing side by side. The white plates for the appetizers are stacked by Jonah. Pappy's been bringing the squash blossoms and placing them in front of us. I've got the corn fritters in front of me, and the finished plates are on another counter. Jonah turns to look me in the eye, and I'm struck again by how rarely he does this.

He's tall. Like, really, really tall. Then again, I'm just that short, and everyone is taller than me.

And his eyes are still warm and deep and swirling with secrets. Pappy slams more squash blossoms in front of us. "Stop with the staring. Either kiss her or don't, but we've got dinner in five minutes, and I need help with the soup."

I'm about to laugh when I see a flash of interest in Jonah's eyes. The laugh dies in my throat, and I'm wondering again what it'd be like to kiss him. Not in the walk-in fridge. *Here.* Now.

Jonah clears his throat. "Soup."

My stomach does a flip-flop. This caveman grunting isn't

really my style, but I grunt back because his gaze drops to my lips. "Yeah."

We plate the rest of the appetizers in a hurry, and Jonah goes over to help Pappy with the soup. Mary gives me a bottle, and I squeeze a swirl of pesto crema into the tomato bisque. Jake and a few random cousins are taking the appetizers out to the tables, and the time flies by. The soup is served before I know it, and Jonah is escorting me out to the dining room.

I underestimated Pappy. There must be closer to eighty or a hundred people here. How many children and grandchildren does he have? I lost track, but it's been a while.

I know he has eight children. If they each had four kids, and they all married, and then half of them had kids... I give up on the math. It's a lot. The Butler clan is a lot to handle for an only child who grew up without a dad.

I understand Mr. Butler's complaint about not having grand-babies, though. All his brothers and sisters must have them except him. Little kids terrorize the restaurant. Babies crawl between tables, teenagers throw wadded napkins at each other, and the whole room buzzes with the energy of children.

Except at Jonah's table. He puts a hand on the small of my back, then drops it a second later. "Hey, Mom, Pops, thanks for saving a couple chairs for us. This is Brie." He points around at his brothers. "Also, Danny, Matt, and Nick. Luke's in Colorado."

"What about me?" Jake folds his arms across his chest.

Nick scoffs. "She knows you."

I also know Nick from work, since he's my boss, but I don't know the others. They're different enough that I think I can remember them. "Hi...Matt." I look across the table.

He nods.

"Danny, nice to meet you." He stares back without smiling.

Mrs. Butler also stares at me like I'm a curiosity from a museum. "Brie. Jonah hasn't mentioned you." She narrows her eyes and trains a laser-sharp gaze on him.

Do those two hate me? Or do they think I'm not good

enough for their family? Maybe I should have worn something nicer.

At least Mr. Butler likes me. "This is Jonah's *girlfriend*." He arches an eyebrow at me, then winks at Matt, and I'm starting to feel bad. Doesn't anyone believe that Jonah is capable of landing a girl as awesome as me?

Jake pulls out a chair, and I sit between him and Jonah. I shift my chair closer to Jonah, and he grins at me.

Take that, Danny and Matt and all the doubters. I'd be Jonah's girlfriend for real in a heartbeat, if he only had a heart.

Mrs. Butler is still assessing me unashamedly, so I wave. She blinks and leans back in her chair.

Pappy hits a glass with a spoon, and the room quiets. "Welcome family and friends. I always start Thanksgiving with my own thanks for all of you."

Mary blows kisses toward all the packed tables in the restaurant. I glance around, and a lot of curious stares greet me.

"Today we're extra thankful to have one particular person with us."

The appetizers look really good, so I'm not really paying attention to his speech. I'm just here to eat.

"You might remember when I lost a member of my restaurant crew twelve years ago to a drunk driver."

I drop my gaze to the napkin in my lap. *Please, no.*

"She finished the night shift and never returned to her daughter."

Murmurs sweep through the crowded dining room. "I'm thankful tonight to have her daughter here, and even more thankful that she's a part of our family now. Jonah? Where are you and Brie?"

Oh, I should have corrected Pappy. I'm not a liar, and now everyone in this room has the wrong idea. *Part of their family?*

"He's pushing it," I mutter to Jonah.

"You have no idea. Mom's tame compared to him." Jonah

37

takes my hand. We stand, and he waves to the room. We sit down as quickly as we can.

But it's nice to have his warm hand cover mine right now, and I don't drop it immediately.

My stomach is hollow. I don't need reminders of the past. I still can't talk about that night or explain what happened or answer questions.

I don't want to think about my mom, and what kind of daughter does that make me?

Jonah's fingers shift in mine. He rubs the top of my hand with a thumb.

"To life," Pappy says.

Jonah drops my hand to pick up his glass. I can't toast to this.

Mrs. Butler eyes me, and I'm not sure whether it's compassion or suspicion or understanding.

Everyone else raises a glass. "To life."

I lean over and whisper in Jonah's ear. "Can we talk, *boyfriend*?"

"Sure, but the corn fritters are best when they're hot."

I stare at him. "You're choosing food over public humiliation?"

"Are you embarrassed by me?"

"No." I glance around the table to make sure no one is listening. "I meant—you would be..."

Jonah shrugs and picks up a squash blossom. "People hear what they want to hear. Food wins every time."

He always surprises me when he speaks in full sentences, and this is almost a paragraph. I'm staring at him, like I just understood part of the Jonah puzzle.

He doesn't talk because he doesn't want his ideas misinterpreted? How often does this happen? Who misunderstands him?

Well, Pappy sure does.

But did Jonah really just lick the sauce off his finger?

"Napkin," I whisper, but my eyes are riveted on his mouth.

Jake's voice has an edge to it. "Hey, lovebirds. Save it for the walk-in."

We turn toward the others. I didn't realize how close I'm sitting or how this conversation looks. I scrape my chair further away so I can eat, but I'm jarred by Jake.

He buys this, and he's hurt.

Mrs. Butler glares around the table. "No walk-in make-outs."

Matt is sitting on Jonah's other side. "J-Dog. I can't believe you." He tugs Jonah into a side-arm hug. "Keeping this secret from us."

I load on the cranberry-chile relish and bite into a corn fritter before glancing at Jonah. He's nearly done. The guy really loves his food.

Jake can't let this go. "Man, I had no idea. I offered to pick Brie up, but he wouldn't let me." He looks around at his family. "I told Jonah I would ask her out if he didn't, and he didn't tell me not to."

I turn to Jonah, surprised. "Really?" I guess I've been reading his signals wrong all night.

He shrugs. "I knew you'd turn him down."

Everyone at the table laughs, but it's a good-natured laugh, like an inside joke. I feel a pang. I don't have a family. I don't have inside jokes.

I'm about to explain that this isn't real. I can't let Pappy get his hopes up or let Jake feel squeezed out, but I catch Jonah's eye.

He's not worried.

A conversation has started at the table. A friendly argument about Jake micromanaging Matt at a new restaurant or something. I can tell they've had this argument a thousand times.

Fine. It's Jonah's family. I'll never see them again. If he wants to prank them, I am happy to watch this play out. I'm all for it. Jonah deserves some respect from his brothers, and I'm not going to call him out.

Not if Jake will ask me out instead.

I pick up my squash blossom, and Pappy's cooking is even

better than I remembered. This food would be worth massive amounts of humiliation.

I finish and set my napkin on the table. "I'll see if Mary needs any help serving the soup."

His mother demands more details from Jonah as I leave the table, and a part of me feels guilty for leaving him with that mess. Just then, a hand touches the small of my back and a deep voice whispers in my ear. "I'll help you, Shrimp."

*Jonah.*

He almost has his arm around me as we enter the kitchen together.

We're nowhere near the soup, but I brace my hands on the edge of a counter and lean back. "Hi, Chef."

He slips a hand into the pocket of his suit pants. "Hi."

Why is he so handsome? And so quiet?

"You have no intention of telling them, do you?"

He shrugs. "At the right time."

"Which is when? Our golden anniversary?"

A full smile breaks over Jonah's face, and I can't look away.

Jake stumbles into the kitchen. "Break it up, you two. I knew it was an excuse to—"

"Stop it." Jonah slides beside me, so we're standing side by side. One hand rests behind me, and our bodies are almost touching.

Jake grins. "What? I'm out of twenties. I can tease you."

"Just don't." Jonah doesn't elaborate.

Jake glances between us, but his gaze lands on his brother. "You two were sparking yesterday, and you don't want me to ask Brie out, and you spent extra time on your hair, and then you were stressing about whether to wear the button down or the turtleneck tonight..." He laughs. "Is this why you suddenly started going to work so early every morning?"

I grin at Jonah. "Your hair looks great, and I like the turtleneck. The color goes well with your eyes."

He doesn't meet my gaze, though. "Seriously, Jake. Can you give us a minute alone? Or do you owe me a hundred push-ups?"

Jake mutters something under his breath that sounds a lot like "King Nazi," which doesn't even make sense historically. Or politically.

Whatever. He's still mad, but Jonah's not putting up with anything tonight. I'm surprised and impressed.

But Jake never lets up. Never. "No, listen, Joey, if you have a girlfriend, does this mean Ma will let us out of jail?"

Pappy slams the door as he enters the kitchen. "Soup!" he bellows.

We all spring into action. Jake heads out the door first. "Bye, lovebirds. I'm never going to forgive you for keeping this a secret, bro."

We're about to grab a tray covered with bowls of soup when Jonah stops me. "Jake's right."

"Okay." I load bowls of soup onto a second tray. "Can you be more specific?"

He looks around the kitchen, and I'm worried that the soup will get cold. I inch toward the door. Jonah stops me with a hand on my arm. "What if you *were* my girlfriend?"

I almost drop the tray, but I catch myself. I don't know what to do, so I tell the truth. "That would be awesome."

No one believes me when I tell the truth. Jonah closes his eyes and tilts his head back. "Be serious for a minute."

"I am."

His eyes snap open.

I smile at him and hoist the tray onto my shoulder. I've never had a confidence problem when it comes to dating.

I'm about to leave the kitchen when Jonah says, "No, really, think about it. Get of jail free card. *Girlfriend.*"

It's like some secret code. I'm not his twin, so it takes me a minute to put together what Jake said and what Jonah is saying now, but I finally get it. "So, you could prep for that cooking show, and I could continue with the proposal for the charitable donations."

"If I had a girlfriend."

"This might be taking the joke too far." I turn around so I can push the door open with my back.

"They already believe it, kind of, even Jake." Jonah picks up the other tray and walks toward me. "Could you keep being my girlfriend tonight? Or even better, for the whole month of December?"

I'm actually disappointed when he asks me, because I want him to mean it. I check, just to make sure. Maybe he wants dates for holiday parties, but I don't think so. "Like, fake date?"

He nods, then shakes his head. "Yeah, no."

That's right. He likes precision with his words. "A fake girlfriend, so you can keep working? Like a girlfriend of convenience instead of a marriage of convenience?" I clarify.

"Exactly. A girlfriend, not dating." He smiles again, looking relieved.

I nailed it.

His smile is dazzling this time, but my heart falls anyway. He doesn't want to date me, but I'm tempted to take the crumbs he offers. I have to steel myself for what I say next, since I have too much self-respect for what he's asking. "No. I don't lie."

I bump the door open and head into the dining area. Alone.

# Chapter Six

JONAH'S A STEP BEHIND ME. "BRIE."

I shake my head and paste on a smile as I place a bowl of steaming tomato bisque in front of his aunt or cousin or someone.

Now Jonah's shadowing me. He leans in close when I straighten. "You don't have to lie."

I tip my head to gaze at him. "When I give my word, I keep it."

I take another ceramic bowl off the tray, smile at someone else, and set the soup in front of them. It smells amazing, smoky and warm, and I just want to eat my Thanksgiving dinner and go home.

I step around the table. Edison lights dangle from the ceiling, and one entire wall is nothing but herbs growing in containers.

Jonah follows me. "So, keep your word."

Another bowl and another bowl. I like the rough wood panels. It almost looks like a posh barn in here.

Another table. He's still beside me.

He doesn't get it.

My mom made promises and never kept them. I won't be her.

My tray is empty. I hand it to him and take his full tray. I drop my voice to a whisper as we approach the next table. "I'm not going to fake anything, not for all the homeless kids in Boston." But that's a punch to my gut. I remember what it felt like to be hungry and eat food I didn't like.

And now I'm choked up.

Jonah gently spins me to face him. "So, make it real."

His hand is warm and gentle on my arm, and I wish things were that simple. I tamp down my emotions and force myself to look at him. Jonah's neck is red and blotchy. If men could blush, I would think that he's embarrassed.

Jonah follows me as I weave through the crowded tables and try not to step on any toddlers or toys. Mrs. Butler's eyes follow us, and I swerve away from their table to serve someone else.

The chatter of happy voices fills the air, and I barely hear Jonah when he talks to me. His voice is low and gravelly. "I've wanted to ask you out for months."

I turn and wait for him to explain, but it's like he's used all his words for the whole day. Jonah takes my elbow and guides me back into the kitchen, where he sets the trays down on a gleaming counter. He faces me in here, where we both feel at home. It's quiet, and it's only us and the stoves and ovens and countertops.

Jonah gestures to the kitchen. "Pops owns ten restaurants in Boston, three in New York, and two in Boulder."

I nod.

"I've opened three restaurants. Two here and the one in Boulder." He swallows. "But I've never wanted to date anyone that worked for my dad before."

I'm trying to see where he's going with this, so I go with a joke. "Is that why you memorized the harassment policy?"

"Yes." He answers me immediately, and he's serious.

I am teasing. I'm trying to lighten things again, but his answer knocks me off my feet.

"You read the entire policy to make sure you could...we could..."

"I wanted to ask you out tonight before Jake could." Jonah scrubs a hand over his face. "That came out wrong. I don't want you not to date me because my dad owns the company. Sorry. Double negative."

He blows out a breath. "One more try. I want to ask you out. On a date. Date you."

Except that he said he didn't. And even though he's the cutest thing I've ever seen, I can't say *yes* to that earnest, flustered face, even if the jaw is chiseled.

"Are you a zero to sixty guy? Because it sounds like you want to skip the dating and go straight to girlfriend."

Jonah tosses a nervous glance at the door to the dining room. "Would that be so bad?"

I laugh. "You're serious."

"Dating is awkward." Jonah shoves off the counter. "Never mind." He arranges bowls on another tray. "The soup's best when it's hot, too."

I bite my lip, and Jonah glances over. "What?"

I'm standing still. "Thinking."

He fills the last tray. "It was stupid. I'm sorry. Forget I said anything. It was Jake's idea, and I shouldn't listen to him."

"No, I get it. Jake's been needling you all night, and no matter what we do, he's right. You would have told him if we were dating, but you didn't."

"Because we aren't."

"But if we're dating just so you can work, it was his idea, sort of, so he's still right."

Jonah hefts the tray. "He thinks he knows me, and he doesn't. I want to surprise him."

"That's it? I'm not going to lie for a grudge between you and Bro Boy or go out with you to settle some bet."

Jonah walks toward the dining room. "That's not why I wanted to ask you out."

I trail beside him, stunned, and smile automatically at the random strangers who are his closest family.

"I'll tell them we broke up, and you don't have to say anything." Jonah pushes out into the dining area.

"Fastest breakup ever. That's a record, even for me."

Jonah flashes me a quick smile, but there's no humor in it. I'm not happy or relieved either. I'm disappointed because this pretty much ensures Jonah will *never* ask me out, not even in January or after he comes back to work.

We serve the bowls of soup to his family, and they all look a little impatient. I've avoided their table so carefully that they're the last ones to be served.

"Took long enough," Jake finally says and winks at Jonah.

"Everything okay?" Mrs. Butler asks.

"We were fighting, not making out." Jonah slides the last bowl of soup onto the table and heads back to the kitchen.

I sit down slowly. A sea of shocked faces greets me.

"Sorry we took so long." I'm impressed. Jonah managed to tell the truth about what happened and still convey the idea that we broke up. No lying required.

To my surprise, it's Danny who breaks the tense silence. "I get it. Couple years ago, it was me and Patty. Last year, it was Nick and his high-maintenance girlfriend. The holidays are a great time to break up. You okay? Need a ride?"

I'm actually kind of emotional, and I'm surprised, since I thought Danny hated me. "I'd love one after I finish my soup. You sure?"

Danny nods. "Anything, kid."

"Kid?" I gape at him. "How old are *you*?"

"Twenty-eight."

"Yeah, I'm the same age. I might be five foot two, but I'm an adult." I smile to let him know there are no hard feelings.

He smiles back at me. "Sorry."

Jonah glances between us as he sits down. "What's going on?"

"Danny's trying to pick up on your ex-girlfriend." Jake takes a big bite of soup. "Beat me to it."

Jonah clenches his jaw. "No."

Danny shakes his head at Jake. "Not funny." He turns to Jonah. "Easy. I'm just taking her home."

Jonah's jaw tightens even further. "Definitely *no*. I'll take you, Brie, whenever you want to go."

Nick speaks up. "What if she doesn't want to go with you? I'll take her."

I don't even care about the tomato bisque. I just want to leave. "Thanks, Boss."

Now Jonah glares at all of his brothers. "I've got this." He reaches out and puts a hand on my arm. "Stay and finish dinner."

I shake my head. "I'm not hungry anymore."

Mrs. Butler sighs in obvious exasperation. "Danny's right. Every year. I'd like just one Thanksgiving dinner without drama."

"Hey, Ma, she already apologized." Jake's face is tight with anger, too, now. "You know it's Joe, not her, if they broke up."

All my former frustrations come rushing back. Jake always thinking he knows what's going on with Jonah. No one thinking Jonah can keep a girlfriend. I know I have a temper, and before I can think, I speak. "It was me."

But now I have to give a reason. The soup's almost gone. "I'm not ready to commit like Jonah wants me to."

That's the truth.

"So, no grandbabies?" Mr. Butler asks.

Mrs. Butler whacks him in the shoulder. "There never were going to be any, Jim."

He rubs his arm. "A guy can hope."

Jonah looks at his dad, back at me, and then grins. "Yeah." He should be sad or something, if he wants to sell this breakup, but he isn't. I'm just as confused as everyone else at the table by his grin.

Because I'm honestly feeling it.

Someone removes our soup bowls, and Nick stands. "Ready, Brie?"

"Sure." I push back my chair to leave.

Jonah grabs my hand. "Hang on. It didn't come out right

when we were talking before." He darts a nervous glance around the table. "Let me try one more time?"

I stand anyway. "Here?"

He nods. He's still holding onto my hand. "Yeah."

"In front of your family?"

He swallows. "A guy can hope."

"There are, like, eighty people in this restaurant, Jonah. I don't think this is the time or place for this conversation."

"Please."

I'm really curious what he can possibly say or do, so I ignore my gut instinct. Something about Jonah makes me throw all the usual rules out the window. "You've got one shot."

His grip tightens. The grin widens to a smile, and I catch my breath. Jonah slips off his chair and down onto one knee. The dim lighting of the restaurant reflects in his warm eyes, and my heart stutters.

I gasp and cover my mouth with a hand. "If you're trying to surprise me, it's working."

"*Would* you marry me, Brie?" Jonah's eyes twinkle, like there's a secret between us.

# Chapter Seven

I'M TOO stunned to answer Jonah's marriage proposal. Voices drift to me through my shock.

"Too much, Joey."

"She said she's not ready to commit."

"Way to go big," Jake taunts on my other side.

Mrs. Butler's voice is the softest, but it carries across the table and cuts through the noise of the dining room. "No means no, baby. Let her go."

Jonah doesn't beg or repeat himself. He just grins at me, waiting with one side of his smile tugging up in a self-satisfied smirk. He's got me, and he knows it. He's worded his proposal so I can accept him without lying.

*Would you.*

Not *Will you*, but *Would you*. It's just a hypothetical question, not a promise to marry him someday.

And he surprised me and Jake and everyone, and maybe even himself.

The biggest part of the surprise, though? He wants this. He's waiting like his life depends on my answer, and his eyes are softer now, but still glinting with humor and heat and a million other emotions that he won't put into words.

Or can't.

A surge of emotion rushes through me, and I don't even understand them, because my mouth blurts out an answer before my brain can engage. "Yeah. Yes. I *would*."

I let out a deep breath, and Jonah laughs. Our eyes meet, and we understand each other. I tug him to his feet. Jonah crashes into me and wraps me in a huge hug.

*What did I just do?*

The brothers start whooping and shouting, and pretty soon the whole room knows what happened. Jonah spins me in a circle, and my feet fly off the ground.

My heart pounds like this is real.

Jonah sets me down and our eyes lock. He grins, and his eyes crinkle in laugh lines. "That's a rush. Whew. I've never proposed before."

In a crazy way, it does feel amazing to see a guy look at me like that and say those words. "I've never accepted anyone before."

Jake laughs. "How many have you turned down?"

I whack him in the chest. I'm family now, and I guess that's a family thing. "None. Jonah's the only one who's ever asked."

Mrs. Butler rushes over and hugs me. All of a sudden, she buys this. She tugs me away from Jonah and falls on my neck. "Welcome to the family."

"Thank you."

Mr. Butler joins the hug and pretty soon I'm engulfed by all his brothers. We're a mosh pit of emotions.

"Kiss her, kiss her, kiss her." Jake starts the chant, and his brothers join in. Well, all except Danny. He's watching us thoughtfully, and it's disconcerting.

Jonah barely touches my chin, and I startle. He glances at Danny and back to me. "You okay?"

I nod.

Jonah drops his hand from my face. "Sorry," he apologizes. "Mom has this thing about the Gottman's Six-Second kiss."

"It's a kiss with *potential*," Mrs. Butler interrupts.

"Ew," Danny says.

She persists. "That's what Dr. Gottman says."

"Ma," Jake complains. "Gross."

She turns to Mr. Butler and raises an eyebrow. "Let's demonstrate."

"No, no, no," Matt says. He's the quietest brother, quieter even than Jonah. He's the youngest and also a chef, and he's gotten lost in the mix tonight. "No need to demonstrate your *potential* with Dad and ruin Thanksgiving dinner for everyone."

Pappy comes over. He waves as he raises his voice. "Hush, everybody." The room slowly quiets. "Every engaged couple kisses in front of the family. It's tradition."

Almost a hundred sets of eyes are watching us, and the reality of what I just did hits me. Every one of these people believes me, and a technicality won't matter to them when we break up.

"What? You don't want to kiss him?" Mrs. Butler glances between me and Jonah. "You shouldn't have asked her in public. She isn't ready to commit."

Her accusation rings out in the silence. The same one that every ex-boyfriend has hurled at me. *Why won't you commit? Can't you stick to anything?*

My mom's face smirks at me in my memory. *You're just like me, Brie. You say you aren't, but you are.*

His family moves back to their chairs, and I'm left standing with Jonah in front of a very quiet restaurant full of nearly one hundred tense people, who all seem convinced that I lied, which feels ironic.

But I keep my word. Always and no matter what.

*Unlike you, Mom. I don't break promises.*

I reach up and wrap my arms around Jonah's neck, and his huge, six-foot frame leans over me. "You don't have to..." he whispers.

"Oh, I want to," I respond loud enough for Mrs. Butler and the whole restaurant to hear. I slowly cup his face with one hand

and press my mouth to his. The room fades as soon as our lips meet. *One, two.* I count in my mind.

Jonah's arm slips around my waist. *Three, four.* His fingers brush my cheek as he draws me close with the other. The scent of pine washes over me, and his embrace is the warmth I didn't know I needed. His chest is solid beneath me, and I'm not ready for this to end. *Five. Five and a half? Five and three quarters?*

"Hey," Jake interrupts. "Ten seconds is plenty!"

My eyes snap open, and Jonah looks at me in wonder.

"Come on," Matt complains. "Why'd you have to go and spoil my appetite when we haven't had the main course yet?"

I'm a little shell-shocked. I have to hand it to Mrs. Butler. There's something to that Six-Second rule, because I'm feeling all kinds of *potential* and wanting to see where things with Jonah could lead. *Theoretically.* I mean, we have a theoretical engagement.

But my lips are still tingling.

Maybe I meant *literally*. People always use that word wrong.

Thunderous shouts and clapping greet us. Hands push him away as everyone in his entire extended family surround me at once. It's a bit much.

His father smiles at me, then I catch a glimpse of Pappy with his arm around Mary, and I feel something foreign.

*Shame.* I've never lied, not since I was seven years old and told the fib about Tony Russo's birthmark to get even. Even though I told the truth, technically, I still feel like a fraud.

But this is for a good cause. *Hungry kids. Helping Jonah.*

And yet, our hypothetical engagement feels like a lie of omission. Is it truthful if I know I'm not going to follow through? I give my word, and I do what I say.

I'm not used to living in gray areas.

This engagement will only last a month. Jonah started it, and he'll end it as soon as he needs to. If he plans to call it quits, then I'm not the one lying. He is.

Jonah grabs my hand and pulls us back into our chairs at the table. I'm left-handed, so it's easy to rest my right hand on his leg.

His mom gives me another one of her skeptical looks. I can't keep up with her and Danny. Hot, cold, love, hate. What is it with them?

"I'm sorry I doubted you," Mrs. Butler apologizes to Jonah.

He nods and tugs my hand further onto his rock-solid leg. I'm fine with that.

"You know I'm a licensed marriage and family therapist."

Jake snorts. "Here it comes."

Jonah stills beside me, then drops my hand. He waves his hands, like he's warding something off. "No, Mom. Just, no."

"Yes, Joey. I want to meet with you and Brie tomorrow, in my office." She smiles at me. Now she likes me again? "To plan the wedding."

# Chapter Eight

"So." Jonah answers his mom.

"So." She echoes.

The silence stretches between them.

"So," I say.

Mrs. Butler and Jonah both turn to me.

I know how to talk to therapists and paraphrase the other person's comments, but there haven't been any, and I can't stay serious for long. "If I'm hearing you both, I'd say this conversation is only going so-so."

Mrs. Butler's mouth twitches, like she's repressing a smile. "I asked my son if he really thinks you're going to follow through with this engagement."

"So," I say, "what I hear you saying is that you don't think I will actually marry Jonah."

Jonah shifts uncomfortably in the seat beside me. His mother's office is plush and inviting with warm tones and plenty of throw pillows and homey sayings and PhD certificates on the wall.

This is not the way I imagined spending Black Friday or the rest of my Thanksgiving break.

"What I'm saying is that a Hail Mary pass to save a failing relationship will usually fail, too. I still want Jonah to take a month off work. In fact, maybe he should take a month off from his relationship with you. Things seem like they're going way too fast."

"Mom, Brie is going to be in Vermont. I've got to go up there. We just got engaged. You can't ask me to leave her."

I smile at him. He talks a lot more when he's one-on-one and away from Jake and his brothers.

"Are you going to Sugar Creek alone, Brie?"

I check my email again. "Lindsay booked us a room with two bedrooms, so I can cancel this other reservation. I also have a friend from the Air Force who lives up there. I'm going to see him."

"*Him?*" She picks up the phone and dials a number. "Danny, I'm ready for you."

Jonah tilts back his head. "You're kidding. We've already been here a half an hour, Mom. We told you everything you wanted to know."

It's the first time I've heard irritation creep into Jonah's voice. "Careful, bro. That might cost you a dollar."

"Sorry, Mom. Brie's right. I love Danny." Jonah dimples a smile at her, and then at me, and something flutters in my chest.

I've been on edge all day. Answering questions from my CEO's wife about how I met her son (*at work*) or how long I've been seeing him (*most days*) has been nerve-wracking, especially because it's her son, and it's meant a lot of very careful *not lying* on my part about the particulars.

I mean, technically, I see Jonah every day I go to work.

Yes, Jonah is rubbing off on me, and I'm unapologetically parsing language. Who's the robot now?

Danny slowly lumbers into the office. "Do I really have to do this?"

Mrs. Butler points to a chair. "I don't want another one of my sons to get a divorce. One was enough."

Danny slumps into his seat. "Hey, Brie, I'm the black sheep."

I smile. "We met last night. I remember."

He scrubs a hand over his face. "Let's get the confession over with. Here's the deal, J-Dog. I got married too fast. Everything was awesome. Things unraveled slowly, then the divorce took me by surprise."

Mrs. Butler sinks her head into her hands. "Two years of therapy, and that's all you understand?"

Danny groans. "I don't even know Brie, and none of my brothers want to hear about how much I messed up."

"I do." Jonah leans forward. "You know I'm a train wreck with women."

"True." Danny drops his elbows onto his knees and stares at the floor. "I'm only going through this once, and no questions."

We both nod.

"And I'm just giving advice. No personal details."

"Thanks," I say.

Danny's eyes shoot to mine.

I try to show him that I'm listening. "I'm serious. I bet this is hard." It is for me. I thought I would agree to be Jonah's fake fiancée and maybe text once or twice while he worked in Boston, and I worked from home in Sugar Creek.

Ha.

Danny shrugs. He takes a deep breath. "First, enjoy the bliss stage."

"Easy," Jonah says. "We're going to spend the month together in Vermont."

I reach over and take his hand. I love the way he keeps pushing his agenda, but only because it's also my agenda. If we ever disagreed about something, I'm pretty sure I'd be annoyed by this same trait.

Mrs. Butler motions to us both. "No interrupting."

Danny takes a deep breath. "Second, slow down. Patricia and I got engaged pretty fast. We all know Pappy's story, so I thought the rules didn't apply."

A ball of doubt wriggles around in my stomach. That sounds familiar.

"Then we got married quickly and tried for kids too soon. The babies wouldn't come, so we turned to some doctors for help. That didn't work either."

Danny is sharing plenty of personal details, but I'm not going to interrupt. There's something almost sacred about this moment, and I'm pretty sure Jonah's never heard any of this.

"Patty pulled away, and I felt like a failure, and nothing I did helped, so I stopped trying. So, third, talk. And fourth, don't stop trying. Next thing I knew, Patty moved out and I was divorced, and all I had left was my job and an empty apartment."

He looks up. "Anyone who thinks you stop loving your wife when you get divorced is crazy. I never stopped loving her; I just stopped showing her how much I loved her."

The silence that hangs in the room is holy.

"So, slow down. Make sure you can handle hard times together and learn how to show your love. Loving each other isn't enough."

He scrubs a hand over his face again, and it's clear that he's done talking.

"Thanks," Jonah says quietly, and I drop his hand.

Danny nods, but Jonah shoots me a concerned glance.

"It's awkward to stretch our arms across the chairs," I say.

Jonah pulls his chair closer to me and takes my hand again. He's determined to put on a good show for his mom, I guess.

"We aren't going to set a date or get me a ring or anything," I say. "We'll take things slow and just enjoy the next month during the holidays."

Like, we'll go so slow that it never happens. Danny's story fits our narrative perfectly.

But Mrs. Butler doesn't think so. "You're avoiding commitment, Brie. You don't want this engagement. If you did, you'd be eager to set a date and wear a ring. Instead, you're making arrangements to play and spend time with friends and other men. You're scared of anything serious."

"Yes, I'm terrified." She's too good. She knows what I'm

thinking, and I hate that, but I can own it.

Jonah sits back in his chair. "Can you go easy on Brie? First you tell her to commit, then you bring in Danny and he tells us to slow down and not commit. Which is it?"

He's challenging his mother for me, and I get the feeling that this doesn't happen very often.

Mrs. Butler arches an eyebrow. "You haven't dated long enough to make a commitment of this kind."

"But they did, Ma." Danny stands. "So, either support them or tell them to break up. No fence-sitting." He salutes us and stops in the doorway. "You can break your engagement. It doesn't mean you have to break up."

Then he's gone.

Hypothetical dating is a lot more work than I'd imagined. It was supposed to be easy. A little flirting. A kiss here or there. Maybe even some real dates. No *real* commitment.

Not a full-on therapy session with a licensed marriage counselor for our second date.

Mrs. Butler leans forward, but Jonah beats her to it.

"Which is it, Mom?" Jonah presses his point. "Are you asking me to break off this engagement or are you asking me to spend more time with Brie to make sure this is right?"

I can't help it. I actually love Jonah just a little bit right then— or at least crush hardcore on him. His face is intense, and I get a glimpse of what he must be like in business negotiations.

He's calling his mom's bluff. He's still got the grandbaby card in his back pocket, and he seems to be betting that his mom doesn't want to be the reason our relationship ends. Mr. Butler will never forgive her if he doesn't have grandbabies to spoil for the rest of their Christmases together for eternity.

But Mrs. Butler is a fierce negotiator, too. "Would you break this off if I advised you to?"

I glance at him, but he's locked eyes with his mom. "Yes. I trust you, Mom, and I know Brie does, too."

That hurts. I know she's the one he has to convince, if he's going to be allowed to work next month, but I still feel betrayed.

"And how do you feel when he says that?" Mrs. Butler turns to me.

I stand. I can't believe I'm blinking back tears or that I've had two fake breakups in two days. "You're the licensed marriage and family therapist. Jonah and I both have pretty bad track records. So." I have to clench my jaw to keep back my emotions. "So, maybe my first instincts were right, Jonah. Or maybe we're both workaholics who need to listen to your mom and take some time off separately, and I'll head up to Vermont alone…"

I can't risk my job over this. It's all gotten out of hand, and I still have to qualify for my townhouse loan in a few weeks. I head toward the door. "Thanks, Mrs. Butler. You saved us from a huge mistake. Saved me."

Jonah pushes out of his chair and intercepts me in front of the door. "Hey, hey, Brie. Hold on. I didn't finish. I trust you, Mom, but I'm doing the right thing. *We're* doing the right thing." His voices drops, and it's deep and gravelly now. He reaches a hand toward me. "This isn't a mistake."

He's taking this act too far. He doesn't even know me. He can't be willing to risk his relationship with his mom just to compete on a cooking show or win a prize to donate to charity, or even to work on his restaurant concept that's two months behind schedule… But he is trying to prove a point to his twin. He's more stubborn and independent than I realized. Or is it something else? "I'm really confused, Jonah, so I'm going to go now. Have a great holiday season, and good luck with…everything."

Jonah collapses in a chair. "No, I get it. That's fine. Thanks."

Mrs. Butler sighs. "Stop."

I have my hand on the doorknob.

"I sense Brie's hesitation and confusion, and I see your commitment, Jonah, and I like the way you respect her decisions. Those worries don't mean this engagement is wrong." She takes a deep breath. "My worries or yours. Danny is right. You need to slow down and spend more time *together*, not with other men."

I turn around. "No, I'm pretty sure it means it's time to break up. That's usually what I do, and Chief isn't *other men*. He's just a friend."

Mrs. Butler closes her eyes. "Wow. We could spend weeks unpacking that. Months. Years. I don't even know where to start."

"Lay off her." Jonah comes over and peels my hand off the doorknob. He stands beside me, so close that I can smell that woodsy soap or aftershave again.

"Thanks. It was a nice idea, J-Dog, but we both know it's not going to work." I'm trying to tell him with all my subtext that he needs to get over this. I mean, he already said *he* did and accepted my answer, but I feel like he's fighting it by just standing beside me, his hip tucked up beside mine, and smelling good.

And it's not fair to look at me like that when this is all just theoretical to begin with.

Or is it just me that's having a hard time letting go of this idea?

"That's the thing." Mrs. Butler comes around her desk and sits on the edge. "I like what I see between you two. Brie committed, even though she was scared. Jonah put himself out there, when he's usually afraid to try. You're both pushing yourselves to be better for each other."

I glance at him. "You're giving us too much credit."

"Probably. I don't know if you can make it." Mrs. Butler doesn't mince words. "But I'm willing to throw everything I've got at this and see if you fail or set a wedding date. Or run off with this *Chief* guy."

I am terrified of this woman who sees through me. She's fierce, and I don't know what she would do to me if I hurt Jonah or broke his heart.

But Jonah reaches out and grabs my hand. "I stand by my word, Brie."

"That's not playing fair," I mutter. "I keep my promises, too."

Mrs. Butler smiles at me. "Then we have a wedding to plan, and we'll set the date a long, long time away."

"No wedding plans," Jonah says quickly. "We're going to give it a month, then reevaluate. Right?"

I hesitate. Jonah edges closer to me.

I can't believe he's still trying to talk his mom into this. "Do you ever give up, Jonah?"

He locks eyes with me. "Not when I'm right."

And feeding hungry children at Christmas seems like a good thing to do. I cave. "Okay. If you'll let Jonah and Jake come to Sugar Creek with me, Mrs. Butler, I'll give it a month."

"Why Jake?" Mrs. Butler has a whole new set of worries now.

Why does everyone like Jake better?

I rest my hand on Jonah's chest like a girlfriend would, and then I'm all kinds of distracted, but I try to finish my argument.

*Jake.*

Jonah can't work on a restaurant concept alone.

"This is going to be hard on Jake, and the twins need a lot of brother time together. In fact, they need that almost more than I need time with Jonah. I mean, I do need time with Jonah, but Jake needs him, too."

Jonah relaxes a little. "And Brie needs time with her friend. I can't wait to meet Chief. That was his name, right?"

I nod again.

Mrs. Butler narrows her eyes. "How old is this guy?"

"Forty."

"Hunh." She holds out her hand. "Do you have a picture?"

I take my hand off Jonah's chest reluctantly and grab my phone from my pocket. I scroll through some old photos until I find the ones she wants. "Chief is my best friend. We were stationed together twice in the Air Force. He mentored me, and we grew close." I pull up his picture on my phone and wait for his mom to freak out.

No one understands my relationship with Chief.

What I don't expect is for Jonah to react so strongly. He stiffens as he takes the phone and passes it to his mom.

Mrs. Butler's eyes widen. "Oh, my."

I lean across Jonah and swipe through a few photos. "That was the last time we worked out together in the gym. He wanted before and after photos."

Jonah's jaw sets. I turn to look at him, but a frown greets me. His brow is furrowed, and he's staring at the phone in his mom's hand.

Mrs. Butler swipes through my photos. "Is that why he doesn't have a shirt on?"

I glance at Jonah. "Uh, yeah."

"Is this before or after?"

"Before."

"Hunh." Mrs. Butler hands the phone back to me. "I thought that was *after*. He looks good for forty."

I slip the phone into my pocket. "I don't have an answer for that, ma'am. Yes, he does? But Jonah looks good for thirty. Better, even, than Chief?"

I've never worked so hard for anything in my life, and those homeless kids better appreciate the meals when they get them. If they get them. If we pull this off.

Jonah's mouth ticks up in a half-smile, and he slips an arm around my waist. "Are we good here, Mom?"

She drops her head into both hands and sighs. When she looks at us, I'm still scared of her. "You know what you're doing, son?"

"I trust Brie one hundred percent. She's not Patty, and she'd never cheat on me."

I guess Danny left something out of the story.

Mrs. Butler's eyes flick to mine. "You want to marry my son? *My* son, not Chief or anyone else."

Now I'm on the spot. I scramble for a way out of this. "I told him *yes* yesterday, and I don't lie, ma'am."

Even though I'm pretty much using yesterday's truth to lie today.

She smiles. "You'd better call me Maggie, or Mom. Up to you. We're going to be talking a lot for the next month."

# Chapter Nine

I HEAD to Vermont on Saturday. I meant to spend a month alone and see Chief every now and then, but now I have Lindsay as a roommate and Jonah and Jake in the cabin across the way.

So much for a quiet holiday season.

Lindsay talks all the way up to Vermont. I learn a lot about her in the three hours it takes to reach the Cabins by the Bay. She's serious about becoming my new BFF. I know about her sister (*they were never close—too far apart in age*) and her parents (*they were never close—too interested in keeping up social appearances*) and her dating life (*she's never been close to a guy—she doesn't know why*).

This is the perfect time for me to tell her that I'm engaged, so I take a deep breath. If Mrs. Butler is going to buy it, I can't tell anyone it's fake. I mean, *hypothetical*. "Speaking of dating..."

"You went to dinner with the Butlers, right? How did that go? Everyone wants to go out with one of the brothers, but they never date anyone at the office. I had my eye on the twins when I started, and I even kissed one of them, but it didn't go anywhere." She only pauses for a moment before asking, "How was the food?"

"You kissed one of them?" I'm not sure how to handle this, if it's Jonah, and she's still crushing on him.

"Yeah. Not sure which one, to be honest. It was kinda dark in the closet. Christmas party the first year I was here. Long story. That sounds bad, and I'm not that kind of girl. It was this spontaneous thing, and I thought it would go somewhere, but it didn't."

She's sad for one second, but then starts talking immediately again. "We didn't have Christmas parties because of Covid for the next two years, so even if I was hoping for a repeat, it couldn't happen, but yeah, no. I gave up on him a long time ago. Them. Whichever twin it was."

"Oh." My heart sinks. I didn't think Jonah was that kind of guy.

Good thing this is temporary.

I go for it. I'm not sure if Lindsay and I are ever going to be close, even though she swears she is my new best friend. "Must be something about holiday parties, because I kissed Jonah at Thanksgiving dinner."

She's quiet a long time—for her—then she squeals, maybe a little too happy for me. "Yay! Good for you. Guess that rules him out. Jake's still single, though. Not that I want to date him, because I don't. I'm so over whatever happened."

"Good, because Jonah and I are actually engaged."

Lindsay goes truly quiet for the first time in our three-hour drive. It lasts ten seconds, and we're almost at the cabins now. "I didn't even know you were dating."

I use her own words. "Long story." I try to come up with something else. "Love at first sight, that kind of thing." I mean, I did feel a zing the first time I saw him. "We're taking it slow, and we haven't set a date for the wedding."

Lindsay squeals again, back to being my new bestie. "I'm so happy for you. Teach me everything you know! I want to get engaged. My parents say I should be married by now, and my sister has three kids, but I've never had a boyfriend."

We pull into the parking lot, and gravel crunches beneath the tires. "*Never?*"

A gleaming lake extends across the horizon. It's cold, but sunny, and a thrill of excitement races through me, like it does every time I visit a new place.

"Never." She pops open her car door, and her long legs are the first thing out of the car. She stretches and shakes her head, and her straight blond hair falls to her waist. Her ultra-thin, supermodel frame is obvious, even beneath her leggings and the cashmere sweater.

"I don't get it." I walk around my beat-up car and meet her at the trunk. We each heft our luggage and roll the suitcases across the parking lot to the Aspen Grove cabin. I punch in the code from the email and push open the door.

"We'll talk later, girl. I have tips and tricks for you. Boyfriend 101. We'll talk all night, every night." I wink at her, then wince. I've been around the Butlers too long. "Have you ever been to Vermont?"

"Every summer. I love the lake in June and July." Lindsay whips open the curtains and looks across the water. "But my parents go south for the winter, so this snow scene is new for me."

Our cabin is adorable. I'm blown away by the wooden beams, the woodburning stove, the custom carved rocking chair, and the granite countertops in the kitchen. There's a loft overlooking the living space, and everything is made of knotty wood: the bar stools, the ceiling, and the cabinets. Nautically themed pillows and pictures decorate the space. "This is nicer than I thought. How much did you pay, Lindsay?"

She reddens. "I upgraded us. My parents insisted."

"For an entire month? I can't pay half of this. It's larger than my townhouse."

"They're paying the whole month. Merry Christmas to my new bestie."

"Thanks."

I didn't realize how much my small gestures of friendship meant to her.

We've barely settled in when Chief shows up. I called him when we were half an hour away, and he followed my progress in the text app. Yeah, we share locations, and he might be ultra-protective.

He's just as tall as Jonah, but a lot thicker. He looks like he could be the same age as the twins. He's got the trim face of an athlete, but the solid frame of a guy who lives in the gym.

I run as soon as I see him, and he squeezes me in a hug. His first words aren't even hello. They're so predictable that I feel warm and happy and at peace for the first time in a year. "You've gone soft, Sergeant."

I punch him in the arm. "Hello to you, too. I've missed you so much."

"Hey." He pulls me into another hug. "I'll show you the gym."

I laugh. "Fine." I yell over to Lindsay's room, "Want a workout?"

"Sure. Let me change."

I can't believe I've finally made it to Sugar Creek, after everything I've heard from my friend. "It's great to see you."

Chief looks around our rented cabin. "How long has it been?"

I'm already in my workout clothes. I drive in Lycra and old t-shirts. *Hello, comfort.* "Almost a year exactly since I saw you. I got discharged from active duty last December. You retired three months ago, right?"

"Then we'll do three sets of everything." Chief tosses his keys up and down. It's like no time has passed, and we're back on the base. "Unless you'd rather do twelve."

"Three is good."

Lindsay hurries out of her bedroom. She stops dead when she sees Chief.

"Who are you?"

"Brie's old boss and your worst nightmare in the gym." He flashes the smile that most women can't resist.

Lindsay grabs a water bottle. "Lead the way."

We find the clubhouse with a roaring fireplace, couches, ping pong and pool tables, and another oversized plasma TV. There's a gym off to one side.

As soon as we walk inside, the smell of pain hits me, and my adrenaline notches up. Technically, it's probably the smell of foam and sweat and treadmill grease, but it's my favorite thing in the world.

The windows overlook the lake on one side. The treadmills, exercise bike, and stair stepper face the windows. There's a rack of dumbbell weights along another wall, and I balance on the Bosu while Chief loads weights up for me. I pick up a remote and flip to a cooking show.

He goes over to the television in the corner and turns it off. "Pull-ups," he grunts.

Lindsay rolls out a yoga mat and starts stretching. "This feels good after that drive. What kind of workout do you usually do?"

Chief blinks at her. "The hard kind." He doesn't like to talk, but Lindsay keeps trying anyway.

He also shows no mercy, and I'm grinning ear to ear through the crunches and V-ups. "I've missed you so much."

"Hold that longer. Less talk, more pain." He spots me on the weight lift without cracking a smile, and I feel like I'm home.

I don't really know what home is. I've moved so often that a gym feels more like home than anywhere else. I don't have a family anymore. Gram passed right after I graduated from high school, so I don't have anywhere to go for holidays.

I lean into the burn as I hold the weight longer this time. Chief nods his approval, and I move out of the way for Lindsay to try her luck.

"You're up, Lindsay."

She rolls her neck. "I don't lift."

"You do today." Chief lightens the weight for her. She's not used to Chief's tough love motivational approach, but she doesn't flinch.

"I got this," she says through gritted teeth, and she does.

Chief glances at me, and I can tell that he approves of my new friend because he's not scowling.

We finish up with our usual push-up contest, and I lose, like I always do, but I surprise him. "You're getting better, Sergeant."

"I haven't gone soft. You're getting old." I'm lying. My arms feel like spaghetti, and my stomach is in spasms.

He's a Michelangelo statue, every muscle chiseled and defined. Chief stares me down, then pulls me into a sweaty hug. "You're soft, Sergeant, but you're not half bad."

Even though it's freezing outside, I take off my t-shirt to use as a sweat towel. It's hanging around my neck, and the crisp air feels great on my overheated skin. I don't care if Chief sees me in my grubbies and a natty old exercise bra.

He keeps a sticky arm around my shoulders as we walk back to my cabin. I've missed this camaraderie with him more than I realized. Lindsay continues to interrogate him until we reach our door. Gravel crunches, and we turn as a sleek, black SUV pulls into the parking lot.

The twins have arrived early.

# Chapter Ten

JAKE HOPS out of the driver's side and slams his door. "Hey!" He glares at my bare midriff and Chief's arm across my shoulders, then strides across the parking lot.

With his long legs, it doesn't take long. Jonah follows behind at a slower pace. "It's fine, Jake," he mutters. Jonah wears a pair of Ray-Bans with very expensively distressed jeans and a Red Sox hoodie. Not the Old Navy or Gap kind—the one you actually buy at the stadium or a player gives to you, the kind I can't afford. It's a deep, dark navy color with a crimson "B" on the front.

He does have a casual look, and I can't help staring.

I can't see Jonah's expression behind the dark tinted glasses, but his brows furrow. When I don't move or do anything, he says, "Hi, Brie."

I haven't thought this through. How am I supposed to greet him? Do we hug? Kiss? High five? I don't do anything. "Hi, Jonah. Jake. Guys."

Jonah shifts his gaze over to Chief and holds out his hand. "I'm the fiancé."

Chief's arm slides off my shoulders so he can shake Jonah's hand. "Are you? Whose? Lindsay's?"

I'm in so much trouble for not telling my closest friend. We've known each other for almost six years. "No, he's mine. This is Jonah Butler. We're engaged."

Chief narrows his eyes.

"Yep, Jonah's my man. I'd hug him except I'm sweaty, and he's all..." I wave at his hoodie and dark jeans, and my pulse ratchets up a beat. "Clean."

I am not selling this. Jake and Lindsay are both staring at me. "You didn't tell your oldest friend?" Jake asks. He grabs his phone and starts texting. Now I'm in trouble with his mom, too.

"It's a Christmas surprise." Yeah, I didn't think this through at all. I want to hide behind Jonah or something, but we haven't discussed what we're going to do in public. We haven't talked or texted, really, since we left his mother's office, and there's a lot more nuance to this situation than I thought. I don't even know whether Jonah likes PDA.

I kinda hope he does.

I shiver. This conversation is taking way too long. I don't really want to put my sweaty t-shirt on, but it's starting to get cold out here.

Jonah takes off the Ray-Bans, slips out of his Red Sox sweatshirt, and tosses the still-warm clothing to me. He's wearing a snug black t-shirt underneath, and he looks just as ripped as Jake.

Who knew.

The sleeves of the sweatshirt hang several inches past my fingertips, and I tug the fabric around myself. "Thanks."

Jonah is matter-of-fact. "It's freezing out here." He's not complaining. He's explaining.

I smile. "Thanks, boyfriend."

Jonah nods at me and jams his hands into his pockets. "It's good to finally meet you, Chief."

Jake looks up from his phone. "Hey, man. Sorry. I'm Jonah's twin, Jake."

"Hey." Chief's face is impassive.

"Linz. I didn't know you were up here." Jake's whole persona shifts as soon as he sees her. He takes in the workout clothes, and

I'm about ready to cash in on the Bro Fund, but he's a perfect gentleman. "Are you cold? Do you need my sweatshirt? I have one in the car."

"I'm good." Lindsay's voice is tight, and I cut a quick glance at her. She's angry. No, nervous? Something's wrong, and I don't know her well enough yet to know what it is, but I've got to help her.

I point to my workout pants. "I'm sweaty, and it's thirty degrees. We'll see you inside after you drop your luggage."

"Not so fast." Chief points between me and Jonah. "How long has this been going on?"

I head toward my cabin. "It's too cold to argue out here. Jonah's whole family is already hating on the idea of us engaged. I need some support."

Chief follows me. "You'd get more support if you didn't spring this on me as a surprise. How long has his family known you're engaged?"

Jake laughs. "Not much longer than you, man. Jonah proposed to her the day she met my parents, which was just last week."

"No wonder they're not on board." Chief holds open the door to my cabin for everyone. He stops Jake as he enters. "You're part of the family. Do you hate the idea of Brie engaged to your brother?"

Jake's shock is obvious. He runs a hand through his perfectly styled blond waves. "I wouldn't say *hate*."

"But you don't love it. Is your brother as impulsive as Brie?"

Jake snorts. "He wasn't until he met her."

We're all inside the cabin now, and Chief turns to Jonah. "Why am I only hearing from Jake? Is he your appointed spokesman, or do you talk, fiancé?"

Jonah shrugs. "I talk."

Then there is a long, awkward silence.

"Thanks for the workout, Chief. I'm going to clean up." Lindsay disappears into the bathroom, and the shower turns on a minute later. I walk over to the kitchen counter and rest against the edge to wait for her to finish. No one needs to smell me right now.

Chief stiffens into command mode. Legs at shoulder width. Hands behind his back. Game face on. "Have you set a date yet?" He's talking to Jonah, not me, so I'm not going to answer.

The twins are both standing in the middle of the open space. I haven't asked them to sit, so the three men are grouped around the entrance and the back of the sectional couch.

"Not yet. No."

Chief stares at him. "I don't see a ring on Brie's finger."

Jonah fires back right away. "I proposed without planning it."

Chief folds his arms across his chest, and it's a totally alpha move. I know he's trying to intimidate Jonah.

Jonah casually walks over to the kitchen. He rests against the edge of the counter next to me. We're almost shoulder to shoulder, but he doesn't touch me. A thrill races through me anyway at his nearness and the obvious show of support.

Jonah's arm brushes mine as he kicks out his legs and crosses them at the ankle, then glances over at Chief. "I'm not going to rush Brie. She'll wear a ring when she's ready to choose one."

Chief is skeptical, and he has good reason. "You know how indecisive she is. She'll never set a date."

I'm counting on that, on never setting a date for the wedding, but Chief's questioning look makes me feel like I have to defend myself. "I have my grandma's ring somewhere, and I'm sentimental. I could wear that anytime I'm ready."

"Would you?" Jonah's gaze shoots down to mine. When our eyes meet, his gaze softens like velvet. Or warm butter. "You wouldn't want your own ring?"

I'm melting. This man is too good for me. I shake my head. "Grammy's ring is simple. No diamond, just a band. A chef doesn't need a diamond. Besides, her ring has a cool paisley etching from the Seventies. Very retro."

Chief snorts. "She says her grammy's ring is fine now, but

then when you don't buy her a giant diamond, watch out. She'll call off the wedding." We haven't even started working, and Chief is already warning Jonah that I'll break up with him.

Jonah doesn't flinch. "Brie can take as long as she wants to make up her mind about a ring. That's why we haven't set a date. I'm not going to pressure her."

Even though this is a *hypothetical* engagement, I still appreciate Jonah's trust in me. "I'm not going to call things off because I change my mind."

Chief stares at Jonah like he's a unicorn, except he's a man. Does that make him a Pegasus? "Props to you, man. Never thought I'd see Brie engaged. Most guys don't have that kind of patience for her indecisiveness."

What? Is he trying to talk Jonah into breaking up with me now?

"He's not most guys," I say.

Jonah straightens beside me. "Thanks." Our shoulders brush, and I wonder whether it's accidental.

Jake laughs and looks up from his phone. "Hey, Ma wants a picture. Chief, will you jump in? She specifically asked about you."

"Now? I'm still wearing my exercise clothes, and the lighting in this kitchen is too bright." Plus, this is going to look wrong to Mrs. Butler. Chief and me in workout gear while Jonah's wearing jeans and his t-shirt and Ray-Bans and being—perfect as usual.

Chief opens the door, and a blast of cold air rushes into the cabin. "Better lighting outside."

I groan. "Fine. Let's get this picture and get back inside. Lindsay?" I yell.

She pokes her head out of the bathroom.

"Photo."

"I don't have any makeup and my hair is wet."

"Perfect. Group shot."

Lindsay nods and shuts the bathroom door.

I hate to admit that I'm intimidated by my fake future

mother-in-law, but I do want her to like me. I slip off Jonah's navy-blue hoodie and toss it on the back of the sectional. Jonah's eyes zip to my torso and take in the exercise bra. "You work out with Chief in that?"

I open my suitcase and grab a sweater. "Yep. Is there a problem, boyfriend?"

"No." Jonah eyes his sweatshirt on the back of the couch.

I slip on my thrift-store sweater and take my hair out of its practically permanent ponytail. I toss him the Red Sox hoodie. "Here you go. It's cold out there."

He tosses it back. "Hang on to it."

"I'll wash it." I toss it back on the couch with a note to treat it like it's gold. There's a story there.

"I wouldn't mind working out with you and Lindsay," Jake says.

"You can't handle our workout," I tease.

Chief eyes Jake as we file out the door and into the sunlight. The lake is behind us, and there are mountains off to one side. I wrap one arm around Jonah's waist and the other around Chief. They drape their arms around my shoulders. It's the first time I've touched Jonah since Thanksgiving, and I'm smelly from my workout. I shift my weight away from him.

Lindsay rushes out of the cabin with a fresh set of clothes. She stopped to put on mascara and gloss, and I feel even more out of place with Jonah's designer clothes and Lindsay's supermodel looks.

But she's the one who hesitates.

"Join us, roomie?"

Lindsay stands next to Chief instead of Jonah. I can't blame her, since I'm not sure if I'm engaged to someone she kissed three years ago. Evidently, neither is she.

As soon as we're done, Chief lets go, but Jonah's arm stays on my shoulder a little longer before it slides off.

I hug the sweater to myself. "Text the pictures to me, too?"

"Already on it." Jake smirks. "Oh, Mom loves this."

"Yeah, the lake and scenery are gorgeous." I shiver and drop my arms, even though I love the warmth of being sandwiched between Chief and Jonah.

"That's not what she loves." Jake smirks.

I'm not going to ask. "Let's head inside."

Chief looks between me and Jonah. "Don't mind me. I'm used to Brie and her PDA. I'll wait for the goodbye kiss."

He's worse than actually having a brother or a dad.

"I'm too short for PDA." My head is level with Jonah's shoulder. Well, his armpit, really.

Chief smirks. "That's never stopped you before."

I'm not sure why, but this feels like some kind of power play. I'm not going to kiss Jonah because Chief told me to, but it would be weird not to kiss him when everyone's expecting it.

Gah. Chief's just as bad as Jake. He thinks he knows me. He thinks I can never surprise him.

Jake grins and throws Chief a wink. "You should have seen them making out at the family dinner, man. Disgusting. Kissing in front of everyone for, like, ten seconds."

"It was only six," Jonah says. "Maybe eight."

"I stopped counting." I catch Jonah's eye. "After four or five."

"So did I."

A smile passes between us, and something flutters in my stomach. Lindsay watches me, and a surge of compassion surprises me. I want to learn her story, and I have to help her.

Chief cracks a smile. "I'm not surprised. That's Brie. She burns fast and hot and then she's done."

"Not this time," I say. That's completely honest.

"Sure." He grabs a set of keys from his pocket. "I've got to head home and shower, too. Work out again tomorrow morning? Five-thirty?"

"I don't think I'll be able to walk tomorrow."

Chief scoffs. "We only did abs and arms today."

"Fine," I say. "As long as you go easy on me. You're in, too, Lindsay, right?"

She nods. "As long as Chief goes easy on us."

He puts a finger in his ear and shakes it, like he can't hear us. "I'm sorry. I don't know those words. Go easy?"

Jonah interrupts our banter. "Hey, Chief?"

Here it comes. The part where my jealous boyfriend gets stupid and overreacts. This happens every time one of them meets Chief. I tried to include Lindsay in the workout, so he'd know there was no reason to worry.

But Jonah surprises me. "I'm looking for some romantic places to take Brie. Do you know if there's anything special going on for Christmas?"

He acts like he's not jealous of Chief, like he's secure or confident, or something I've never seen in a boyfriend before.

"Sure." Chief takes in Jonah, head to toe, like it's a military inspection. "You're really going to marry Brie?"

"That's the plan," Jonah says.

Chief scoffs.

It's almost a half-truth, but it's not really a lie. We have a plan.

"That'd be a Christmas miracle. You realize her longest relationship lasted three weeks, and that was only because she didn't have the heart to break up with the guy until after the season finale of some show ended."

"He didn't have a TV, and I did. I'm not heartless."

Jonah looks down at me with one of those glittering gazes, the kind where he seems serious, but I can see the joke in his eyes. "I saw that plasma TV in your cabin. We'll have to start watching *The Great British Baking Show*—all the seasons. You wouldn't break our engagement without knowing who's star baker, would you?"

"Celebrity chefs and cooking competitions? I avoid those shows." I bite my lip, and Jonah almost grins at me.

Chief actually laughs. "I'll have to hand it to you. You do know the way to Brie's heart. She's watched every episode of Tommy Fuller's *Smack Downs* that he's ever made."

Jonah arches an eyebrow at me. "All of them?"

Chief rats me out. "Multiple times."

Jonah grins.

"We're on those shows." Jake turns to Lindsay. "I can show you, if you haven't seen them."

She frowns. "I don't know."

"Not really the way she wants to spend Christmas." Chief snaps back into command mode. "Follow me to my apartment, Joe, and I'll point you toward Main Street, if you're still sure about this romance thing. They've got brochures and a schedule of holiday events at Town Hall. It's across from the shops."

Jake perks up. "Shops? Is there anywhere we can grab lunch?"

"Yep. There's a deli with great meatball subs."

"You want one, Linz?" Jake asks.

She looks like a deer in the headlights. "Okay." She heads back inside the cabin.

"Perfect." Jonah nods back. "Thanks, man. Meatball subs all around."

"Don't thank me." Chief waves and walks toward his chair. "Heaven have mercy on your soul," he mutters.

"Hey!" I yell. "I heard that! Say it to my face!" Even though I know why he is so cynical about marriage, I'm not going to let him get away with it. "You better be talking about heartburn from meatball sandwiches."

"You know I'm not." Chief turns around and walks backward toward his car. "You really want me to repeat that?"

I throw up both arms, like I'm a rockstar or a rapper or a dorky girl trying to trash talk. "Who are you loyal to—me or Jonah?"

"Easy choice—Joe." Chief turns back around and disappears into his car.

I'm a little surprised. Chief doesn't usually like my boyfriends. I thought he'd hate the idea of me having a fiancé, but he's already got an annoying nickname for him.

"Hurry, Joey. I'm hungry," Jake yells at us as he jogs over to the SUV. "I'll warm up the car while you make out."

Doesn't anyone ever just call the man Jonah?

He and I should have made some sort of make-out plan. I yell back. "No need, Jake."

Jonah leans down, and his dark eyes lock onto mine.

I drop my voice. "I still haven't showered."

"I told you, I'm not afraid of that." His lips are right there, only a few inches away. His eyes search my face, and his voice is low. "We need to talk when I get back."

I'm scared of his intensity, but I nod. "I should tell Chief the truth."

"I didn't lie to him." Jonah steps closer. I shiver, and it has nothing to do with the temperature outside. "Did you?"

I shake my head. I was careful with the way I worded everything. "I didn't lie, but he thinks you're my boyfriend, and you're not."

"I'm not?" Jonah cups my face with one hand. He's touching me—on purpose. My heart races. I feel like a kid cheating on a test, and I'm waiting for the teacher to catch me. I can't enjoy this, because I'm lying.

He leans down. "Too bad, because if I were your boyfriend, I'd kiss you now, before I go eat a meatball sandwich with onions and peppers."

I catch my breath, then I do what I always do when I'm nervous. I make a joke. "You're the only one I know who bases his kisses on his meals."

But Jonah closes the distance, and his hand caresses my cheek. "Where do you think the phrase *Kiss the Chef* comes from?"

For a second I think he might kiss me, and my skin burns beneath his touch, but Jake honks the horn.

Jonah blows out an exasperated breath and drops his hand. We stare at each other. "Jake's hungry," I say.

Jonah gazes down at me, and his eyes glitter. "I'm starving, too." He reaches out and grabs a couple of my fingers with his. "Famished. Like I haven't eaten since Thanksgiving Day." His gaze drops to my lips.

I swallow. I'm not used to this side of him.

Jake honks again. Jonah drops my hand and turns to walk backward toward Jake's SUV. He slips on his Ray-Bans and tugs his Red Sox beanie over his ears. A grin tugs at one side of his mouth. "We definitely need to talk when I get back."

# Chapter Eleven

WHEN I GET inside I'm still thinking about Jonah and sandwiches and kissing, so I grab my phone to scroll reels. Instead, I see that my phone has blown up in the two minutes it took to say an awkward goodbye to the twins and Chief in the frigid Vermont air.

Jake texted the picture of me with Jonah, Chief, and Lindsay to his mom, who then sent it to all the aunties and cousins.

**Rosemary**: Who's the hottie?
**Olivia**: Is he with Jonah's fiancée?
**Emily**: Looks like Jonah's getting dumped. Any bets on how soon?
**Sue**: Dibs on the hot guy if he's not with the fiancée. What is her name anyway?
**Rosemary**: Didn't bother to ask her name. If she's with Jonah, we won't see her again.

*Harsh.* I decide to chime in, so they know I'm part of this thread.

**Me**: My name is Brie. Still engaged, FYI. Just arrived in Sugar Creek. Gorgeous lake.

By the time I look up, I'm at my cabin. I grab some clean clothes, and I've already turned on the water when I hear my phone chime.

I grab it off the counter, and there are twenty-seven notifications from the family text thread.

**Rosemary**: Gorgeous lake? Gorgeous guy.
**Olivia**: Is he with that other girl or single?
**Aunt Sarah**: Glad you made it safe, sweetie. I'm Jonah's favorite aunt.
**Emily**: Brie, is Hot Guy single?
**Rosemary**: We need *his* name
**Olivia**: And address
**Sue**: Leaving now (car emoji)
**Aunt Doyle**: Looks lovely. I'm Jonah's favorite aunt. Don't listen to Sarah.
**Anna**: Can I crash on your couch?

The phone keeps buzzing. How many cousins and cousins-in-law does Jonah have? Do I need to say anything? Then his mom texts the entire family.

**Mrs. Butler**: Chief is even bigger than I thought. Taller. Built.

I sigh. I know it's a good cause—hungry children—but I have to win Mrs. Butler over. She's not on board with this engagement, and I don't need an online couples' therapy visit with her. She's a Mama Bear, and if I cross her, it could be my job on the line.

**Me**: Jonah is grabbing me a sandwich in town, because he's the best boyfriend ever.

I even add a heart emoji. That starts a whole new set of responses.

I shut off the shower and sit on the counter in my grubby workout clothes. I'm going to have to add an hour into my day for these family text threads, and I'm going to have to get more pictures with Jonah.

> **Mrs. Butler**: Boyfriend? You're engaged. Think that way.
> **Aunt Sarah**: Butler men make the best husbands.
> **Rosemary**: Fiancé is such an awkward word. Boyfriend is better.
> **Emily**: I repeat, is your friend single? You didn't answer.
> **Aunt Doyle**: I thought you were dating Vincent Murphy's boy.
> **Emily**: We broke up.
> **Olivia**: Called it.
> **Mrs. Butler**: What happened? I like the Murphy boys.
> **Anna**: Brie has room on her couch for you, Em. I'll give up my spot.
> **Mrs. Butler**: You broke up with Todd? I'm going to see his mom tomorrow, and we'll talk.
> **Emily**: Todd "needs his space," Aunt Maggie, so please don't talk to them.
> **Mrs. Butler**: Space? I never liked the Murphy boys.

I put down my phone. I'm not even going to imagine what the text thread will be like when Jonah and I end our engagement.

I start the water again and slip into the shower. I think of ways to break up with Jonah without making his family hate me. I can't come up with anything.

That's Jonah's job anyway. He'll have to dump me, and maybe they'll all feel sorry for me. Yes, I like that storyline better, but then he looks bad, and that's not fair.

I lather my hair with a new peppermint shampoo. I could try "emotionally unavailable." They've probably heard that from his other girlfriends. Or "works too hard" or "intimidated by strong women"? I've used those before. I have a long menu of breakup reasons, and I'll serve up the right one for this order.

It's a long shower. I have a month to find something wrong with Jonah, because I know Mrs. Butler is going to call me and demand my side of any story that he spins. I haven't found any reasons so far, but I've never had trouble breaking up with boyfriends before. I go through the list of my old boyfriends and the reasons I broke things off, and I condition my hair twice because I'm so distracted.

I sing "Jingle Bells" at the top of my lungs instead, the Batman/Robin version, to get Jonah off my mind and force myself to stop thinking about the impossible. There's no way to end the engagement and still have his family like me.

They all seem to hate Patty, and Mary and Pappy will never forgive me if they think I broke Jonah's heart.

The song doesn't work. I open the bathroom door, wearing my track pants and a sloppy t-shirt, and Jonah's sitting at the table with a sandwich. It's like I summoned him instead. How long was I texting his family in there, and how long was that shower?

And how many verses did I sing?

"Hey."

Jonah's pensive, but his face changes when he sees me. The dimples in his cheeks pop even more when he smiles. "Nice voice."

Can I tell his family I broke up because he eavesdrops while I shower? Probably not. "Thanks."

"Hungry?"

I slip onto a barstool beneath the kitchen counter and take the towel off my head. I run a few fingers through my hair to make sure it doesn't look like a complete disaster, then grab my sandwich. "What are you up to?"

"Planning my month." His eyes give me a quick once-over, then return to his computer screen.

"The entire month?" He has a spreadsheet open on his laptop. Color-coded boxes fill his screen.

"Well, until I leave to tape the show. I don't know the exact date yet, so I'm planning the first three weeks, and Pappy's planning on you for Christmas dinner."

"Of course you're a planner." I take a bite, then the sandwich hits my taste buds. "What kind of sauce is that on the meatballs?"

Jonah's eye flick to my sub. "It's good, whatever it is."

I close my eyes as I eat a perfect sandwich. "This is totally worth not kissing you." I open my eyes in time to catch Jonah's reaction.

His eyes are locked onto my mouth. He's the one who brought up garlic and peppers and onions and kissing—or not kissing. He closes the screen of his laptop, and I have his full attention.

Jonah slides a pile of brochures across the table in between my napkins and the paper bag the sandwich rests on. "So."

I shake my head. "You go plan your month. We don't need to do anything together, if we're not actually engaged."

Jonah glances over his shoulder. "Is that what you meant earlier when you said that I'm not your boyfriend?"

I follow his eyes to the door. Is he worried someone will walk in? "Where's Lindsay?"

"Jake." It's a one-word explanation. He takes a bite of his meatball sub.

"She's eating in your cabin with Jake?"

He nods. "I asked them if I could have a few minutes alone with you so you could break up with me."

Jonah's really cute when he's nervous. Sometimes his neck flushes bright red. Other times he won't meet my eyes. Right now he takes another bite of his sandwich and plays with the wax-paper wrapper.

"You told them that?" He's right that these sandwiches are the least sexy meal a couple could eat. My mouth is on fire.

"You didn't want to hug me when I arrived, and you moved

away from me when we took the picture." Jonah shrugs. "Then you didn't want to kiss me, and you said I'm not your boyfriend... But thanks for trying. It's me, not you."

"You didn't do anything."

"It's always me." Jonah fiddles with the edge of the paper bag. "Most women dump me after a few weeks, and that's when you break up with guys. At least it's believable."

I unwrap the sandwich a little more, so I can take another bite. "Hey, we only have to last three weeks. We can do it." I lean over and lift the screen of his laptop to see how his mind works, but then I'm distracted. Our shoulders brush, and I'm in his space. He's warm and smells like pine. I glance at an open spreadsheet. "It's less than a month until your competition."

"Twenty-eight days until it airs, I think," Jonah says, sounding almost hopeful. He hasn't pulled away from me.

I teeter on my barstool and slide back to my own part of the kitchen counter. "I can manage to put up with almost anything for four weeks."

Jonah clicks between different tabs in the spreadsheet. He's serious about his plans. He glances over. "Can you? We're hiding something from your oldest friend and my twin and your new BFF."

Now it's my turn to take an oversized bite and stall for time while I think. "That's true, but telling them the truth makes us look like liars, too. How long do we have, anyway, before Jake bursts in here and decides we're done talking?"

Jonah glances over his shoulder again. "Any second."

"Then talk fast, boyfriend. I know you don't talk, as a rule, but it's time to get out of your comfort zone."

He wipes his hands on a napkin. "I don't see any other way to get the restaurant open, but I don't know how to be the kind of boyfriend you deserve."

I'm trying to reconcile this vulnerable version of Jonah with the other ones I've seen. "Do you always give up this easily?"

"Only with women." Jonah stares at the glossy brochures

instead of me. "Dating is harder than a cooking competition. There are clear rules to win on a TV show. I don't know where I stand with women. Should I hug you or not hug you? Do you want me to kiss you or not kiss you? Are you going to sue my dad's company for sexual harassment after all, or sell this story to a tabloid if I say or do the wrong thing?" He shrugs. "It's not like there's a recipe for being your boyfriend."

He's opening up to me, so I'm going to build on that. "But you want to win that show. You want to donate that money to charity, and you really want to work with Jake on your restaurant concept. Are you seriously saying that you're so afraid of dating that you would give all of that up?"

Jonah looks at me with a shredded napkin in his hand. His eyes flash with the steely determination that was lacking one moment ago. "I would give up anything rather than ask you to compromise your beliefs. If you don't lie for anyone else, I won't ask you to lie for me."

My heart hammers in my chest. "I'm not breaking the engagement, Jonah, so you're still my boyfriend. I'm trying to figure out how to make it work, like you are. If you win, we could help thousands of hungry children have a real Christmas dinner instead of SpaghettiOs."

Jonah's brow furrows. "You want this to work?"

"You keep giving me a way out, but I want to fight for this like it's one of Tommy Fuller's *Smack Downs*. Fight for this fake relationship like it's real." My voice hitches. "Like you care."

"I care," Jonah says gruffly.

"About what?" I can't let myself get emotional. "I was hungry, and I was almost homeless. We moved every year, and I never had Christmas in the same apartment twice. The only good meals I ever had were in Pappy's kitchen when I was old enough to work for him."

"I care about food, too. I think about flavors all the time, but I also care about my twin and my dad and opening the restaurant and not failing with my family's money." Jonah crumples his waxed paper.

I take another bite of my sandwich. "So, are you in or out?"

Jonah tosses his paper and napkin in the trash. "I don't like talking, and this engagement takes more work than a real relationship but without any of the...benefits."

I laugh. "That's the most honest thing you've said all day."

Jonah turns around to lean on the counter and takes a deep breath. His eyes are fixed on the door. "I don't know how to act around you, and we always have an audience. When are we going to get to know each other?"

"My hands are committed to a messy meatball sub, or we could start right now."

Jonah doesn't seem to know if I'm joking or serious, so I wink. That's what his family does, after all.

"We'll figure it out." That's my style, and I don't know what else to do. "I don't have to know everything before it happens to go with the flow. I'm passionate enough about this cause to see this through."

Jonah does not improvise. He needs exact answers. "But can you be passionate about me?"

His question hangs in the air, and the echoes of every failed relationship ping between us. I've never fallen in love, no matter how many times I thought I might have. I've never tried very hard or been anything except casual and afraid, and I'm pretty sure Jonah is the same way.

We're both terrified that the other person will see what a mess we really are. We might be awesome when we're on our own, but being in a relationship brings out a whole new level of insecurity in even the most stable people.

"You're taking a long time to answer." Jonah jams his hands in his pockets.

"I've always looked for the exit sign after a few weeks, if I'm honest."

He nods. "Me, too."

I'm already trying to find a way out of this engagement with him. I just spent my entire shower thinking of ways to break up. "But I made you a promise." I dig deep. *I'm not my mom.* "There's only one way this is going to work. If you're going to open your restaurant on time and compete, and if we're going to get that money for the food bank, then I'm going to treat you completely unlike any other boyfriend I've ever had."

"It's not passion," Jonah says with a wince, "but I can't ask more from you than I'm willing to give."

It's the least romantic conversation I can imagine, in fact. I flip my wet hair over my shoulder, and it's also the least sexy way possible. "Oh, I'll give back as much passion as you give me."

And there's the embarrassed look I love on Jonah. He leans over the sink to wash the meatball sub off his hands, then grabs a towel to dry them.

What is it about a man's arms? Jonah's muscles flex as he turns the towel in his hands, and it's better than any TikTok I've ever watched. I want to watch this on repeat, over and over, seven seconds of the corded veins in his arms as he dries the droplets of water from his hand.

Jonah catches me staring. "Brie?"

I push the glossy papers and printed schedules back toward him. "So, you wanted to plan our month?" I've lost my train of thought, and I'm trying to ignore the attraction I'm feeling.

Jonah goes to the refrigerator, grabs a bottled water, and pushes it toward me. "We should probably figure out what kind of couple we are, so you don't sue me." He pushes his sleeves up, and it doesn't help my concentration.

"Thanks." I take a sip of the chilled drink. "I want to do as little as possible during the holidays." Then I'm open with him, because he was open with me. "I can't develop real feelings in a relationship with an expiration date."

He gathers the brochures. "Right. No hugging, no hands, no public kissing."

"Is *private* kissing still okay?" I'm almost done with my sandwich, and he's still too serious.

Jonah's neck splotches red halfway up. "As little private kissing as possible, too. It's too easy to think I'm in love when the other person doesn't ever feel the same..." He trails off and glances nervously at the door. "I didn't think Jake had this much self-restraint."

"He might actually buy this. Too bad about the kissing, though." I have to be literal with him now, because he's not getting it. "I was talking about the brochures, Jonah, not the PDA, when I said I didn't want to do a lot of extra-curricular activities. It wasn't a euphemism." I grin at him. "We're going to have to hold hands and...stuff."

He smiles hesitantly and heads toward the door. "Okay. Can I ask one favor?"

I crumple my sandwich wrapper and toss everything in the trash. "Sure."

Jonah looks earnestly at me across the empty space of the cabin. There's a dining table and a couch between us, but it feels like a lot more distance than that. I'm not sure we've actually decided to do anything that'll make us look engaged. "Promise you'll tell me what I'm doing wrong, so I can change before you break up with me."

My heart hurts for him. He still thinks I won't be able to last four weeks. Who are these other women in his past, and how did they treat him?

Probably the same way I treated my old boyfriends. One strike, and you're out. *Just like I treated my boyfriends*, Mom's voice gloats in my head.

"Sure. I'll complain all the time, Jonah, if that's what you want. I'll even give you a recipe to be my boyfriend." I want to hug him, but I have meatball sauce all over my fingers and it's still weird between us. I wash my hands and dry them, and it's not sexy like Jonah's suds were. "I promise I'll give you step-by-step instructions, if you'll answer one question first."

This is so bizarre. I've never had such a deep, honest conversation with any of my real boyfriends, and I'm not intending to stay in this relationship.

Jonah hunches his shoulders. He slips on his Ray-Bans and slides closer to the door. "What?"

"Did you kiss Lindsay at the Christmas party before Covid?"

# Chapter Twelve

JONAH SLOWLY SLIDES off his sunglasses. "Why would I kiss Lindsay? We've never been on a date."

"That's not a direct answer. Yes or no."

He steps away from the door, then crosses the room to me. "No. Is that why you don't want to kiss me again?"

"I don't know where you got the idea that I don't want to kiss you again."

Jonah reddens.

"Lindsay told me she kissed one of you, though, and I'd like to know who my fiancé has kissed."

"Must have been Jake."

I fold my arms across my chest. My hair is half-wet, half-dry, and my neck feels clammy, so I can't hold the pose very long. I go over to the couch and grab his hoodie. It smells like pine soap and manliness, but I slip it over my head anyway. It's hard to stay mad at him when everything about him smells like Christmas. I'm still going to try.

*They're always lying*, Mom's voice warns me.

"How would I know if you were lying?" I hate that I'm listening to my mom's voice, but I watched her get hurt too many times. I won't be naïve like she was.

Jonah eyes me warily. "I already told you."

"I have trust issues." I tug at the bottom of the sweatshirt and try to straighten the hood, so it will lay flat on my back. I'm short, though, and it's tangled.

He approaches me slowly. "I don't lie, Brie." He reaches out and straightens the fabric. His hand lingers on my shoulder for a moment, then he pulls away. "I swear on my favorite Red Sox hoodie."

It is soft and worn in. I hug the sweatshirt close and wrap my arms around my middle. "Asking me to marry you? Kissing me? Pretending to be attracted to me? I can't handle cheating, and if I find you kissing Lindsay behind my back while we're engaged..."

Jonah's eyes rake over my body, and heat flares in his eyes. "PDA isn't pretending for me. What about you?"

I drink in his tall form from head to toe, his solid chest, his wide shoulders, and his thick, dark hair. "No..." I whisper. "I won't have to lie about that."

The door slams open and hides us from view. I see Jake and Lindsay before they notice us standing in the kitchen. I put my hands on Jonah's stomach and lean into him. His muscles contract and harden beneath my touch, and our eyes lock.

No way am I going to let Jake think this is anything but real. The engagement might be fake or tentative or whatever technical word, but the chemistry between me and Jonah is legit. I'm on fire right now.

I flex on my tiptoes and whisper in Jonah's ear. "Hug me."

But he doesn't.

I put my head on his shoulder, just in time. Jake slams the door shut, and we're not hidden anymore.

Lindsay notices us first. "Brie!"

I'm exploring my boss's son's stomach muscles and wondering what I got myself into this time. It's not the weirdest thing I've done, but maybe one of the stupidest. I leave one hand on Jonah's stomach, kind of possessive.

"Hey. Great sandwich. We'll have to remember that place." I

smile at Jonah. Hopefully, I look natural to Lindsay and Jake, but Jonah's a statue right now.

I'm just trying to help him open his restaurant. That's what I keep telling myself, but I might also be enjoying myself too much now that I've discovered his stomach muscles. I casually remove my hand.

"You never knock," Jonah says.

"Sorry, bro." Jake winks at me. "I thought I gave you enough time to talk Brie off the ledge again." He looks at Jonah, who's not touching me. "Or did you break up?"

I slip an arm around Jonah's waist. "I wasn't on a ledge. Just onions and peppers and a little misunderstanding about not kissing when we have bad breath."

Jonah rests his head on my damp hair, takes a deep breath, and I swear he sighs and mutters, "Peppermint," under his breath.

Jake raises his eyebrows. "You were going to break up over bad breath?"

I rest my other hand on Jonah's chest. "Do you want to kiss your girlfriend after a meatball sub?" This is the perfect excuse. "Sorry, J-Dog. No kisses until the onions wear off."

Jonah grins. "Then we are *not* going back to that shop."

Jake rolls his eyes. "It's a sandwich."

"Haven't you ever heard of the food of love?" Jonah grabs his laptop and walks over to the couch. "You're a chef. You ought to understand that garlic kills the vibe."

Lindsay looks embarrassed.

I catch her eye. "Are we too much for you? We can back off if we make you uncomfortable."

Lindsay grabs her laptop and settles at the far end of the sectional couch, away from Jonah. "You're adorable. I told you they were fine, Jake. He was worried about Jonah getting dumped."

Jake looks at us, then over at Lindsay. "No, I wasn't."

"It was kind of cute." Lindsay starts typing.

Jake goes completely still and stares at Lindsay's back from the kitchen where he and I are still standing. "Yeah, I was a *little* worried."

Jonah looks over his shoulder from the couch, and Jake motions with his head toward Lindsay.

"I just want my twin to be happy," Jake says. "It makes me want to fall in love, too."

Jonah shrugs, and Jake points toward Lindsay's back.

Jake must be the twin that kissed her. He's desperate for her attention. Suddenly, it's easier to believe Jonah's denials.

I grab a cloth to wipe the kitchen counter. I can still see sandwich crumbs, and it's the chef in me. I can't leave them there. "That's our plan, Jake. Show you how good love is."

Jonah holds up the brochures he showed me earlier. "In fact, Brie and I want to include you in the many ways we nurture our fledgling romance."

Jake shakes his head. "You have to stop saying that. You're killing the vibe, man, not the garlic or meatball sub."

Jonah doesn't flush. He's not even embarrassed. "What? That's what Mom said to do."

"Mom's a therapist. No one talks like her." Jake flops on the couch next to Lindsay, and she has to scoot over to make room for him.

"Which ones look most promising?" Jonah asks.

Jake leans across Lindsay to reach for the brochures. Jonah tries to throw them, but they're paper. They flutter to the carpet.

I plant myself in the middle of the sectional couch, collect the brochures, and flip through them. "I'm planning to ride the North Pole Express when Chief works."

Jonah twists his head to look at me from his end of the couch. We could seat ten people on this thing. "He got us four V.I.P. tickets for Monday."

I don't want my friend to get stuck with Jake all the time, just because I'm the fiancée-of-convenience of his twin. "Is that okay, Lindsay?"

She nods. I thumb through the brochures. "Skiing might be nice."

Jonah pushes off his cushion and comes to the middle of the sectional. He pulls his computer onto his lap, and our shoulders brush as he settles beside me. I want to snuggle into him, but he's all business right now.

And he already shot me down. Twice. I tried to hug him, and I put my arm around him, and he did nothing. He might look like a Michelangelo, but he's also about that huggable.

Jonah leans over to read the brochures in my lap. His shoulder slips behind mine, and the bare skin of his cheek hovers near me. My pulse ratchets up a few notches. I glance at him, but he stares at my lap. I would only have to turn a fraction of an inch to kiss his cheek. If I were his girlfriend, I would. *Thank you, garlic and onions, for stopping me.*

His fingers skim my legs as he flips through the glossy ads spread all over my lap. I can't take much more. I hand him the skiing brochure, and he reads the dates. "Looks like they're open all week. Chief is off Thursdays. I'll put us down for a night he can come."

I'm a little surprised that Jonah knows his schedule and wants to include him, but I won't complain. Most of my boyfriends go out of their way to avoid Chief.

Jonah's typing on his spreadsheet, so I gather the papers in my lap. "What do you want to do, Lindsay?" I stretch to hand the glossy holiday advertisements to her, and I'm almost flat on the sofa before I can reach her.

Jonah's eyes follow my movement as I pull myself up, but his eyes snap to his computer screen as soon as I right myself.

Lindsay sets her laptop on the couch, as if trying to make space between herself and Jake. "Is it weird if I want to visit Santa? I go with my nephews every year, and we always get a picture. They're really worried I won't get presents if I don't come to Florida with them to see Santa."

Jake moves Lindsay's laptop to his other side and scoots closer to her so he can see the brochure. "I love Santa. He has candy canes."

Jonah scans his laptop screen. "How about tonight after the tree lighting?"

Jake tips his head against the back of the couch and stretches his legs at an angle to reach the ottoman. His knee touches Lindsay's leg. "Nice. Throw in some ice skating or sledding or something." He closes his eyes.

Lindsay stares at the brochures in front of her. Jake's thigh touches her leg now, and she shifts on the couch. Closer, not farther. Just barely, but I hide a grin.

I hand Jonah an advertisement for a Christmas tree farm. "They have sleds."

Jake grabs a pillow and jams it behind his head. "When are we going to finish our relaxing, so we can start working?"

"Almost there." Jonah turns his screen to show me a spreadsheet titled "Christmas Season Events." It's color-coded and looks way too complicated for someone as spontaneous as me.

"The blue events are with Jake. The pink are with you. The yellow are with you and Lindsay and me and Jake. The red is my work schedule, but I won't send that version to my mom."

I shake my head. "You're the only person I know who spends an hour making a spreadsheet to prove how chill and easygoing he is."

"You don't know my mom. She needs a plan for everything."

Jake nods, his eyes still shut, from the far end of the couch. "She's pretty freaked out about Chief, and Dad's been texting nonstop for updates today."

"They haven't been texting me." Jonah takes his phone out of his pocket. "Oh. It was on silent."

I laugh. "Go ahead and take care of that. It might be a while."

Jonah scrolls through some texts for ten or fifteen minutes while I scroll reels. Lindsay's relaxed into the couch cushions, and her shoulder barely touches Jake's, who looks like he's asleep.

Jonah holds up his phone to show me the screen. "You know that picture Jake sent to my mom?"

"Yeah. The one with Chief and Lindsay by the lake."

Jonah looks like the phone has betrayed him. "My mom loved that picture of us."

"And that's a problem?"

Jake sits up and groans. "She's going to want one *every day*." As he sits, Lindsay goes flying into his lap. She must have been leaning on him more than she realized.

She recovers quickly and reaches over him to get her laptop, acting like she was doing that all along. Her entire torso and chest are splayed across his knees and lap. Jake grins at her as she rights herself and scoots away from him.

Jonah slips his phone in the front pocket of his jeans, and now I'm staring at the outline of his leg. I like these jeans.

"How long until Mom texts us and demands photo proof of your relaxing?" Jake asks.

"Counting the seconds..." Jonah stares at his phone, then glances up. "Oh, there it is. Mom texted the ultimatum an hour ago."

"Request," I say. "If it's your mother, it's a request."

Jonah digs a dollar out of his wallet and hands it to me. Correction, I love those jeans.

"I'm relaxed. Send a picture of me." Jake stretches, and Lindsay's eyes follow his movement as it exposes a thin band of taut skin between his jeans and t-shirt. He hands his phone to Lindsay.

Maybe she's not as impervious to the twins as she says she is. Her eyes dart between Jake and the image on his phone. Jake folds his arms behind his head so his arm muscles pop. He rests his cheek on the pillow behind his head and gives her a sultry look.

Lindsay hands the phone back to Jake. "You have an interesting relationship with your mother, if that's the kind of picture you want to send her."

Jake grins. "Oh, I told her they were for you. Want me to airdrop them to you, Linz?"

Her phone dings over and over.

"There's your new lock screen."

Lindsay doesn't pick up her phone.

Jonah's phone pings at the same time as Jake's. He turns to me. "My mom is so helpful that she's already bought tickets for *everything* on my agenda."

I groan. "Doesn't she understand the color code?"

Jonah shifts so his knee touches mine and rests an arm on the couch behind me. I'm cocooned in his tallness. His dark eyes spark as he gazes down and practically growls, "That is the sexiest thing a woman has ever said to me."

I feel the heat. "We speak different love languages, Jonah. If all it takes is a few highlighter pens and a spreadsheet..."

A crooked smile lifts one side of his mouth. "Stop talking like that in front of Jake and save it for our alone time, or I won't be able to control myself, onions or not."

I flush, and Jake and Jonah both laugh. Lindsay picks up her phone while Jake isn't looking.

"*Alone time*? You're talking like Mom again." Jake checks his phone. "Four tickets, Linz." He drops to his knees dramatically.

She throws her phone onto the couch. "What?"

"My mom expects me to go, and I need a date. I'm begging."

"You're ridiculous."

Jake grabs her hands. "But you have to help me. Jonah and I are trying to open this restaurant in four months, and my mom barely let me come here with Jonah and Brie, and I can't lose an entire month of work if she makes me go back to Boston." His arms land on her knees. He's practically hugging her legs, and now it's his chest and torso that are splayed across her lap. "Please. It's the Christmas season."

Lindsay's mouth barely lifts in a smile.

Jonah meets my eyes. "Sorry. My mom goes overboard sometimes."

Jake is still begging Lindsay. "My dad will lock the laptops. My brother can change our passwords remotely, because that's how evil of a genius he is. If we don't have access, Jonah can't approve funds for the starving children." He widens his bright green eyes. "Please, please, please." He lowers his voice to a whisper. "Don't let me be the lonely loser at all the Christmas parties without a date."

It wouldn't work on me, but Lindsay bites her lip. "Let me get this straight. You're addicted to work, and you're going to use hungry kids as an excuse to continue your workaholic ways?"

Jake grins at her. "Exactly."

Lindsay laughs. "You're pathetic. I'll go with you to a play, Jake, as long as it's *The Christmas Carol*, and you learn something from it. You can be my service project."

She taps Jake on the head. He groans and collapses fully into her lap, then grins up at her and whoops. "Put us down for everything on your sexy spreadsheet, brother."

She peels his arms off her lap.

"You're an accountant, babe." Jake stands and dances like a dad in front of the fireplace. "Do you like spreadsheets, Lindsay? I'll make you a spreadsheet for Christmas."

She shakes her head and doesn't answer him.

Jonah is changing boxes on his spreadsheet from blue to yellow. "Now who looks like an old man?"

Jake leans over his brother's screen. "The play is *White Christmas*, not *The Christmas Carol*. Is that okay?"

Lindsay nods.

I tuck my phone into my pocket. "Same lesson. Stop working and live life."

Jake does another embarrassing dad dance. "I'm living. Text Mom a video of me." He squints and points at Jonah's screen. "Change that square to yellow, too. Lindsay's coming."

None of us take a video of his victory dance.

Jonah snaps his laptop shut. He turns his body toward me, and we sink into the cushion together. "Thanks, girlfriend."

I don't know what I'm supposed to do. I get the feeling that he isn't very affectionate in public with his other girlfriends. I put a hand on his knee. "Anything for the starving children."

Jonah locks eyes with me. "We'll dial it back for you, Jake, so you don't feel like such a loser when you're with us." He leaves the couch without a goodbye kiss, and I'm not sure if the knee groping was too much.

Jonah opens the door, and Jake groans. "Are we going?"

Jonah nods. "We can work now that Mom's got her picture and my spreadsheet. Bye, Brie."

I wave from the couch. Jake follows his twin out the door, and Lindsay's eyes follow him the entire way.

I'm still not sure what I'm supposed to do for the next month. There's plenty of attraction between Jonah and me, but I can't read him. We can't use garlic and onions as an excuse to avoid kissing every day, and I'm not sure I can pull this off if Jonah doesn't want me to touch him.

Jake might buy it, but Chief will never believe me if I'm not crawling all over my boyfriend. He knows what I'm really like when I think I'm in love.

Let's just say, there's usually a lot more PDA, and Jonah's going to have to up his game.

Time to come up with step one of our Recipe for a Fake Fiancé.

# Chapter Thirteen

JONAH'S already got us scheduled for tonight. We pile into Jake's SUV and drive a few miles to the center of town. "Everything is so close," I say to break the ice. "Sugar Creek is so much smaller than Boston."

"Do you like your apartment?" Lindsay seems genuinely curious as she looks over her shoulder from the front seat.

"Enough to buy it. It's an old townhouse, and my landlords are selling."

Jake whips into a parking spot. "You said the community center, right?"

Jonah glances at his phone. "Christmas carols before the tree lighting."

"Sir, yes, sir." I salute Jonah.

We're in the back seat together. He shifts to look at me. "Why do I feel like you're mocking me every time you say *Chef* or *Sir* or something that should sound respectful?"

"Because she is." Jake puts the car in park. "Classic feminist appropriation of male power structures to mock the existing authority."

Lindsay laughs. "I thought you went to culinary school, *Chef*."

"See." Jonah scoots forward on his seat. "Lindsay is making fun of us, too."

Jake grins. "She wouldn't tease me if she didn't care. We have our own pet names for each other now, right, Linz?"

"No, *Chef*." But she glances back at me as the twins get out of the car to open our doors.

She has been paying attention to me, and she's trying to tease Jake. Hunh.

It's colder than I expected tonight. I'm not really sure what our dates entail. If the engagement is hypothetical, what does that make our dates? Experiments? A test batch before we bake the final product?

We've just arrived at the entrance to the Shops on Main. Life-size nutcrackers guard Santa's hut. We wander past the stores, and the scent of woodsmoke drifts through the air. Firepits dot the sidewalk, and families huddle around with long skewers and flaming marshmallows. We find an unoccupied firepit and stop.

Jonah leans down. "Am I supposed to have a pet name for you?"

His voice is close to my ear, and it startles me. "No, we're good, Killer."

His eyebrows furrow. "Are you joking or serious? Because you just said we don't need nicknames, but then you used one."

I hold my hands out to warm on the flames. "We're good."

Jake's restless. "Should we find the Christmas tree?"

We cross the street to the town square where an enormous evergreen towers over us. It's dark over here, since the tree isn't lit yet. Unlike the Shops on Main, there's nowhere to take a picture and nothing to take a picture of. I'm going to have to wait until the lights turn on.

"But..." Jonah's voice makes me jump again. He's beside me, but not really. I'm not sure what he's trying to do. "I should know more about you than anyone else."

I nudge him with my shoulder. "You already do, Jonah. I'm not hard to get to know."

We head to a domed performance area. Crowds are singing carols, and I can see the stars in the night sky. Jonah stands next to Jake, so I go and stand by Lindsay. Jonah catches my eye. "Do you want to sing with the crowd? I know you've got a good voice."

He does this thing with his mouth, where he's almost smiling. I guess he does have a sense of humor.

I stand on tiptoe and lean around Lindsay to answer him without shouting. "You know it."

He grins.

I nod at him. "Tell me when they start 'Jingle Bells.'"

Jake tightens the plaid scarf around his neck. It's probably Burberry or something. "You want a cocoa?" He leaves before we answer.

Jonah glances at me. "Should I get you a tea instead? I wonder if they have any."

Something warms inside me without drinking anything at all. "I doubt they have tea, but thanks for thinking of it."

Jake's back a few minutes later holding insulated cups with *Marshmallow* scrawled across them. "They had flavor shots. Four bucks each. Not bad. I think it's a syrup."

He hands the first cup to Lindsay.

Jonah accepts one and takes a sip. "Too hot."

I can't resist the chance to tease Jake. "What flavors do they have?"

"Mint, caramel, or marshmallow."

"No cracked pepper or tarragon?" He and Jonah sell a few gourmet products in the grocery stores, because that's the kind of celebrity chefs they are—the ones with their own line of custom mixes and sauces. Mostly, though, their hot cocoa line is placed in high-end boutique hotels, because tarragon hot cocoa is more of a one-time experience.

Jake rolls his eyes at me. "You're welcome."

But Jonah's tiny smile widens, and I can't help pushing his twin a little more. "Thanks for the super bland milk chocolate marshmallow drink. It seems really popular with the children."

Jake's just taken a long sip of his cocoa. "Are you calling me a kid?"

"Nope. Let's go get your picture with Santa now, big guy."

He laughs. "Not until they turn on the lights."

The music drifts over us, and I wrap my hands around the warm cup. I do want to sing along, but not here, where people might hear me. I content myself with listening to the voices around us.

Jonah watches me with a weird expression. I leave Lindsay and stand next to him. "What?"

He darts a glance at his twin, then whispers, "You and Jake would make a better couple."

I tug him slightly apart from Jake and Lindsay. "Step number one for your boyfriend recipe."

He swirls the cocoa in his cup. "I'm listening." But he's not even looking at me.

"Confidence. I chose *you*. Own it."

His hand stills, and his eyes dart to mine. "I don't like to brag."

Talking about feelings with Jonah is going to be more work than I realized. "You're not boasting about yourself. You're showing me off. You're completely secure because I'm crazy about you, and you can't believe you're lucky enough that you landed someone as amazing as me."

He still looks skeptical.

"Think of this as preheating the oven, if you know what I mean." I run my free hand up his arm and across the sculpted length of his shoulder. "The other part of this step: *emotional* intimacy before physical intimacy."

Jonah's lopsided smile breaks across his face. "Now you're talking my language."

"What?" I bite my lip. "Benefits?"

"No." Jonah's eyes flare. "Ovens. I know how to preheat."

And I don't doubt he does, because every part of me is on fire despite the dewy frost in the air.

A group of women march onto the stage, and I stare. They must be Mary and Pappy's age, but they're wearing evening gowns and tiaras and look like slightly aged beauty queens. One of them has the most blinged-out snow parka that I've ever seen over her dress, and another has ski pants beneath her flowing gown. Someone introduces them as the "Sugar Mamas," and everyone cheers loudly.

"It's a shame Chief had to miss this," Jonah whispers. His arm brushes my shoulder as he bends down, but it doesn't linger.

"He's part of the Christmas magic. His train lights up when the tree does." I point over to the train depot across the street.

"We could have watched the lighting there with him." Jonah seems determined to show me how *not* jealous and secure he is now, I guess.

Or does he want to know if I'd rather be with Chief?

"Shhh," Jake says. "They're counting down."

One of the Sugar Mamas adjusts her tiara. The counting continues. "Five, four, three, two, one." The mayor presses something and lights flare everywhere. Colors cascade up and down the Christmas tree. The train blows its whistle, and the train depot lights up.

Across the street, the Shops on Main glow with life. Thousands of strands of lights decorate the buildings. Splashes of red, gold, green, and blue hit my eyes. The trees are wrapped with thousands of sparkling stars, and the entire town square glitters magically.

Now, my boyfriend should wrap his arms around me while the Christmas carols float in the night air. "I'm cold." I shiver.

Jonah looks at my coat. "I'm okay. The cocoa warmed me up, and I've got my Red Sox beanie." He tugs at the hat covering his hair and ears.

We're at Clueless DEFCON 5, nowhere near a nuclear 1. He's a total fade out, no idea what I'm trying to do. Most guys are on high alert all the time, trying to find a way to touch me. Not Jonah.

I hold out my cup. "My cocoa's gone." I shiver again, but Jonah just takes my cup and wanders away and finds a trash can.

He's truly clueless. Bonus points for being thoughtful, even if he's hardly touched me all evening.

Jonah talks to his twin instead of me when he returns. "Let's get a selfie."

"I got this." Jake grabs his phone, which is the latest model, of course. He and Lindsay squish into the frame with us. The moment feels like a vignette of someone else's life, complete with the bokeh lens on Jake's phone. Lights blur on the ornament-bedecked evergreen in the background, and Jonah even puts his arm around me for a moment.

"How about a picture of me and Jonah for your mom?" I trap Jonah's muscled arm around my shoulders to keep it there. "Relax." I tuck myself into his side and even rest my head on his chest/shoulder/arm. It's a little awkward.

But he unstiffens a little. "Are you sure you got it?" Jonah asks. "Check before we go."

We stay kind of cuddled together until Jake texts a picture to his mom, then Jake hands the phone to me. "Linz, our turn."

She's as stiff as cardboard beside him—worse than Jonah—and I can't figure her out. I doubt Jake can, either. Ten minutes ago she was flirting, and now she doesn't want to touch him. She and I need a long heart-to-heart, and she needs to know which twin kissed her.

I look across the street. "Where's Santa's hut?"

Jake rubs his hands. "That's what I'm talking about. Candy canes. Hang on, let me post a picture to my social media."

I forget that he's a celebrity of sorts and has thousands of followers. So does Jonah. Jake posts a picture of himself alone, but Jonah posts a picture of the two of us together.

We cross the street and I'm shivering for real now. I know how to dress for New England, but I didn't wear enough layers beneath my coat.

Jonah stops in front of a shop. "Hang on, Jake. Christmas tradition."

Jake grins. "Yeah." He pushes open the door. "Dad will be so proud."

The store is full of gear, sweaters and scarves and everything a person might need in cold weather. Jonah heads straight to a rack of bright Christmas sweaters. "What should we get this year?"

"Something with a tree that lights up, obviously." Jake flips through the sweaters and holds one up. It's got two Victorian men boxing and says, "Deck the Halls." The men are wearing Santa hats and have the name "Hall Bros" on the back of their jerseys. There's mistletoe, and it looks like a Victorian greeting card with boxers.

Jonah looks closely at the image. "There's a Christmas tree on this one."

A teenager appears out of nowhere. "Do you have more of these?" Jake asks.

"Let me check. What size?"

"Large."

"Hang on." Jonah holds a Christmas sweater up to me. "What size are you?"

"Women's small."

Jonah turns to the teenager. "What's the smallest size you have?"

"I'll see what we got." The teenager disappears.

Lindsay's grown quiet.

"What about you?" I ask. "Do you have a collection?"

"I'm good." Lindsay goes back over to the scarves.

The teenager brings back a bunch of sweaters. Jake grabs two men's and two women's sweaters, all matching. The twins disappear to the cash register, and I go find Lindsay.

"What's up?"

She glances over at Jake and Jonah. "Long story."

"Give me the short version."

"Butler Food Group always had a Christmas party every year before Covid. Everyone wore ugly Christmas sweaters."

I already know this, but she clearly wants to tell me the whole story. "And?"

"The first year I was hired, in 2019, I ended up in a closet with mistletoe kissing a guy."

I still can't tell why she wants to talk about it here. Now. "Right. You told me."

"The thing is, I'm not sure who I kissed, because...." She glances at the twins again.

I get it. "Because the twins were wearing matching sweaters."

She nods. "They match every year, and neither of them ever asked me out or even acknowledged the kiss afterward. It was dark in the closet, and they were both wearing Santa hats, so I couldn't tell what color his hair was."

"And their voices sound exactly alike." This is my new best friend, and she's still hurting, three years later. I'll risk talking about it in the store and hope the twins don't hear. "It was Jake."

"How do you know?"

I can't tell her that I asked Jonah. She'll be mortified. "I have a guy-dar. Like radar." I pull her deeper into the store to be sure the twins can't hear us. "Jake is really into you, and Jonah's not."

Lindsay still looks confused, and the twins are almost done buying their sweaters. "How do I know if a guy is into me?" She seems embarrassed to ask.

I pretend to look at coats on a rack. "Which one gives you a second glance and which one doesn't? Jake stops to talk to you, and Jonah doesn't when we're at work."

Lindsay stares at the twins. "Jake talks to you, too."

I follow her gaze over to the twins. Fair point. Jake was thinking of asking me out, too, but I don't tell her that. "But Jake sits on your desk and interrupts you. Jonah walks right by and doesn't stop."

Lindsay tilts her head to one side. "Oh. So, Jake rearranging the files on my desk means he likes me?"

I smile. "Yes."

She shakes her head. "I'm so confused. It's just annoying."

"Yes." I tug her away from the coat rack and further away from the twins. "He knows you have a precise system, and he comes over on purpose to mess it up. He knows it will get your attention."

She blinks. "That's so seventh grade."

I laugh. "Do you trust me, bestie?"

Her face clears. "Absolutely. You got engaged to one of the hottest guys at work in three months. You're a rockstar."

"Test out my theory, as long as you don't mind that he's a thirty-year-old man with the social skills of an adolescent boy."

She laughs, but then she's agonized again. Lindsay rifles mindlessly through clearance-priced sets of snow gloves. "What if I kissed Jonah on accident?"

I take the gloves out of her hands. "It doesn't matter to me or him now, if you did."

The guys are pulling the tags off the sweaters and unbuttoning their coats. I want her to enjoy the next month. I understand her better now—all the times she sneaks glances at Jake, the way she's angry at him, but also totally crushing on him. I'm curious, though. "Was it a good kiss?"

Her face softens. "Amazing."

The twins are heading back to us. I whisper, "So, you're confused because this guy, whoever it was, walked away from a life-changing kiss and never asked you out. You assume Jake is a player, but what if *you* never sent *him* any *interested* vibes?"

Lindsay looks like I'm speaking a foreign language. "I don't know what *interested* vibes are or how to send them."

"Improvise," I murmur, as the twins approach us.

Jonah holds up a sweater in my size. "I bought you something."

"An ugly engagement sweater?"

"We can wear them on our golden anniversary."

We have our own inside joke now. I hold up the knit sweater

with two men boxing in front of a fireplace and unbutton my jacket. Jonah takes it out of my hand for me, and I slip the sweater over my Henley. "It's just what I wanted."

"I already know you that well." Jonah opens his wool coat and flashes the sweater he's wearing over his collared shirt. He's confident right now, but he's not even trying. It's natural, and that warms me more than the sweater.

The thing is, I was shivering, and Jonah noticed. He bought me a sweater when I was cold. Sure, he jokes about it, but I'm still touched that he paid that much attention to me. He's thoughtful and kind and confident.

Recipe step one—check. He senses my emotions and meets my needs. I'm successfully preheated and ready to move on, but Jonah moves at a different pace than I do. I hug him. "Thanks."

He gives me a quick hug and lets go. I was ready to enjoy a few of the *benefits*, as Jonah calls them, of being engaged, but he's not. I don't mean anything crazy. I wanted a longer hug. Maybe rub a few circles on my back?

Nope. I might as well have hugged a stranger or the Christmas tree. He's that bristly and stand off-ish—as cuddly as pine needles that haven't been watered for a week.

Jake and Lindsay slip their sweaters on, I hand my phone to the teenager, and we get an awkward picture. I put my arm around Jonah's waist for a split second, then we drift apart. After we get our coats on and head outside, Jake heads straight for Santa's hut. "Candy cane time."

He's wearing two-hundred-dollar distressed jeans, a thousand-dollar wool coat, and I don't even know what shoes like that cost, but Jake is willing to stand in line for half an hour in the cold for a fifty-cent candy cane.

He annoys me half of the time, but he's got a good heart like his brother. I wish I knew why he never acknowledged his kiss with Lindsay, but I mean to find out.

I'm sending a text with the Christmas sweater to Mrs. Butler, who insists that I call her "Mom" or "Maggie," and then she texts photos of every ugly Christmas sweater the twins have ever worn, and before you know it, we are next in line to see Santa.

"I'm sorry." I slip the phone back in my pocket. "Your mom managed to patch things up with Ellen and that Murphy boy."

"Why did she need to patch things up?" Jonah asks.

Jake splutters. "That Murphy boy?"

"The one Ellen was dating, but they broke up, but he was feeling insecure, so your mom talked to his mom, and they're back together." I smile at everyone. "His older brother likes her, too, so it's complicated, but they're the better match. Liam needs to ask Anna out and get over Ellen. High school was a long time ago."

Jonah gapes at me.

Lindsay smiles. "I know the Murphys. Liam and I went out a few times. Is he back in town?"

Jake grabs for my phone. "Don't let Lindsay into the secret family text chain. Brie clearly knows too much."

I hold it away from him and show Lindsay some pictures of the twins at their worst during their teenage years. "How much damage would this do? Your mom sent it just now."

We step forward as an elf beckons to us. Lindsay giggles and swipes across the screen.

Jake steps behind Lindsay to see the pictures, but he's clearly taking advantage of the moment to stand close to her. "Mom did that? No one's loyal to me anymore."

"Which pictures are they? I can't see." Jonah wraps his fingers around my wrist and tugs me to him. I fall into his chest, and he pins me inside his arms. He gazes down at me with his warm, intense eyes. "Oh, not those. You know too much. You can't ever leave the family," Jonah says. His voice lowers until I'm the only one who can hear it. "You have to marry me now."

And I can't tell whether he's joking.

# Chapter Fourteen

"It's our turn to see Santa." Jake whacks his brother on the shoulder. "Have your *alone time* later."

My pulse races as Jonah lets go. I've never had a boyfriend look at me like I was the air he breathed, but Jonah nearly makes my heart stop. He puts a hand on the small of my back as we walk toward Santa, and I can barely feel it through my thick coat and new sweater.

But I still feel it, and my pulse ratchets even higher.

"Ladies first." Jake flashes a dazzling smile at Lindsay.

I glance over my shoulder at the long line of waiting children. "Let's go as a group."

Santa greets us with a deep laugh and turns a kind eye to us in turn. "Let's see." He hands a candy cane to Lindsay. "Ladies first. What do you want for Christmas?"

She perches on his knee but smiles at me. "A new best friend."

Jonah's hand falls away from my back as I sit on Santa's other knee. "Awww. Back atcha, bestie. I want a townhouse, Santa. I'll even pay for it, if you can get the loan approved."

He laughs and hands me a candy cane, then gives another to Jake. "And you?"

"A new restaurant."

Finally, Santa hands Jonah a candy cane. "And you, young man?"

"Cheese."

We all stare at him. His neck splotches red above the coat. "I mean, a cheese *board*. A charcuterie board."

Santa's only off his game for a minute, and then he laughs. "Ho, ho, ho. That's the spirit. Merry Christmas." The twins stand on either side of Santa. One of his elves uses Jake's phone to take a few pictures, then they escort us out of the hut.

We wander back to our parking spot through the twinkling lights. Jonah and Jake hang back together, and Lindsay and I walk ahead. Jake turns to his twin and mutters, "Charcuterie?"

"Later," Jonah says.

"You want a cheese board?" Jake's eyes widen, then he grins. "What?"

"*Brie.*"

They're doing their twin thing again when they don't use sentences and barely use words. Jake understands something and Jonah doesn't want him to elaborate, but he obviously means me.

Jonah holds open the door for me when we reach the car. I'm still trying to make sense of the abrupt change of conversation topic when Lindsay giggles.

"Santa asked him what he wanted for Christmas, and he said *cheese.*"

Jake looks over at her, one hand on the steering wheel as he pulls out of the parking spot. "He wants a *cheese board*. Any particular kind of cheese you want, J-Dog?"

"Drop it." Jonah's voice is the closest thing to a growl that I've ever heard from him. "See you tomorrow, Brie?"

When he says my name, Jake and Lindsay look at each and start laughing all over again.

Yep, Jonah is definitely talking about me. *I'm* his Christmas wish. I bite my lip to hold back a laugh, but it's so cute that I slide closer to him on the back bench of the SUV.

It's Saturday night, so I can chill tomorrow. I'll check out the cute community church in the center of town or something. I need some space. "Sure. Maybe we can all have dinner."

Jake's voice interrupts from the front. "We should work out with them on Monday morning, too."

"You can't handle our workout," Lindsay challenges him. "Brie already told you."

Jake grins at her. "I'd like to see you try to keep up with me."

My phone buzzes like crazy, and I ignore it. "You'd just like to *see* us. Rule number one with Chief is no drama during workouts. Sorry, Jake."

Jonah leans over. "Do you need to get those texts? Maybe Chief is finished with work."

I leave my phone in my pocket. "It's your mom. I sent her the Santa picture. We should be good for a few days now."

Jonah leans back in his seat. "Right."

I forget how literal he is. I have to be specific with him. "I mean, we're good with the pictures and the dates. We can still hang out."

Jake gives Jonah a funny look. *Right*. If I'm engaged, they wouldn't be dates. Or I would want to go on them.

I put a hand on Jonah's shoulder. "I feel like our fledgling romance has legs, now that we nurtured it tonight. It can limp along for a few days until our next amorous encounter."

Jonah flashes a quick smile. "Sure." But I know something's off.

We're back at the cabins, and Jake and Lindsay stand outside in the cold with us.

"We need some *alone time*," I say. "Wanna wander down to the firepits by the lake?"

Jonah nods. Jake and Lindsay disappear inside their cabins, and I'm alone with my fiancé. Jonah jams his hands inside his jean pockets, and I'm distracted and curious about whether he had the jeans tailored to fit him that well.

"Thanks for the date and the sweater."

Jonah shifts his weight from one foot to the other. "So..."

I wait. I'm learning his tells. It takes him a minute to get his ideas out. He swallows. "I'm wondering."

Those crinkle lines are out in full force around his eyes. He'd look so much better with laugh lines. I mean, he's hot. But he's so careful, and I'm not.

"Yeah?"

"Am I okay to put my arm around you? Only when it's crucial, of course. I'm really confused about when PDA is okay or necessary or when should I be hands off."

He's so nervous that he's rambling. I try to help him. "I was thinking about that tonight, too." I don't tell him that I am frustrated or that I think he's clueless. We're working on his confidence.

Jonah scrubs a hand down his face. "Tonight was awful. I tried to improvise, but it didn't work."

Oh. *This* is him improvising? "You're doing fine with Step One, boyfriend."

We arrive at the lake shore. A light breeze carries the smell of woodsmoke, and flames crackle in the winter air. A few families stand by the closest bonfire, so we wander along the lake until we find another firepit.

We're standing in the dark, and it's much quieter over here. A nearly full moon reflects on the lake. A few clouds drift by, but it's not stormy tonight. Porch lights gleam in the distance, and it's hard to make out his expression.

Jonah's voice is low and gravelly. "I want to do better than *fine.*"

"If you're ready for Step Two of your fake fiancé recipe—"

"I'm ready." He interrupts me as he steps closer. "But I like boyfriend recipe better. Leave the fake part out."

"Now that you've preheated the oven, gather the ingredients." He stares blankly.

"Me." I open my arms. "I can't hug you. You're too tall. *You* have to be the one to hug me, or I look like a terrier dog attacking its owner."

Jonah laughs, and I wish I could see him better, but the night is even more magical out here by the lake. The stars twinkle between the clouds, and the flames reach for our hands.

Jonah bends down and wraps me in his arms. His lips press against my hair, and I can barely hear him. "Goodnight, girlfriend."

We stand that way for a couple minutes. This is what I wanted when we were at the Christmas tree lighting. Here, in the privacy of darkness, Jonah is braver. It seems pointless to put on a display of PDA that no one will see.

I stay in his arms as long as he holds the hug. My stomach is a mess as he walks me to my cabin. Somehow, Jonah's tender hug did more to me than any of my other boyfriends' octopus-like holds.

I feel cherished, and that scares me. "Goodnight." We give each other a quick hug this time and go into our own cabins.

Jake wolf-whistles when Jonah opens his door.

I slip inside and glance around. Lindsay's already disappeared into her room. No long heart-to-heart tonight. I flop on the couch and pull out my phone. Thirty-eight notifications.

Jake's right. I've been inducted into their secret cousin cult, and I never want to leave. I look at the picture of me with Jonah and our ugly sweaters. He knew I was cold, so now I'm wearing "Deck the Halls."

But I've got a townhouse loan pending, and I can't mess anything up. I need a letter from his brother to verify my employment, and I can't let things get real with Jonah. Whenever things get real, I panic and then I break up. The only reason things are going well with Jonah is because it's short-term, so neither of us is emotionally invested.

*Liar!* The memory of that hug screams at me. I let down my guard and let someone else be my strength for two minutes. I can't get used to that. I stand alone, and I don't rely on anyone.

I silence my phone and put on my candy cane pajamas. I've got a day to detox from that hug and remind myself that this is business, not personal. It's not even for the food bank. My home loan is on the line here.

I can't lose my loan. I can't move again. *Because then I'm no different from you, Mom.* I'd be moving every year, and I'd be having Christmas in a new place every time.

I need this loan to prove to myself that I've matured. *I can have Christmas in the same place two years in a row, which you never let us do, Mom, and I can stay in one place for longer than six months.*

But Mom's boyfriends never lasted long, either. Her voice drifts into my head in the same taunting tone I remember from my childhood.

*If you were really different from me, you'd stay with Jonah. That would prove me wrong. I never married anyone. You'd marry him.*

I stop arguing with the voice of my deceased mother. Even though she's been gone twelve years, I can't get her out of my head.

Because only a bad daughter would enjoy herself and forget to mourn her mother on the anniversary of her death.

# Chapter Fifteen

I HARDLY SEE the twins on Monday. Jonah and I email when I have questions, and Jake stops by briefly to drop off some lunch—club sandwiches with no onions or peppers. They're bland and tasteless, and Jonah isn't around for a kiss anyway. I'm asking for extra garlic next time.

Lindsay and I work on our usual accounts all afternoon, and I don't see either twin until it's time to take a ride on the North Pole Express, Chief's train.

It's not the job I would have expected my former Chief Master Sergeant to take after leaving the Air Force, but he didn't expect to leave the service so quickly.

I grab my coat without changing my Henley or doing my hair, but Lindsay is still digging through her haute couture outfits.

I flop on the couch. "Your clothes don't matter. Your personality does."

The door to Lindsay's bedroom is open. She digs more frantically through the pile of overpriced sweaters and tops.

"People don't like my personality. That's why I have to wear this."

It's like someone punched me in the gut. "I like you, and I'm your relationship coach, remember? Wear something comfortable so you're not even thinking about it."

Lindsay stops. "I always worry about what I'm wearing."

I shrug. "Try a new approach."

She grabs a faded sweatshirt. The letters of her college are peeling and falling off.

I nod. "You don't care what Jake thinks, anyway, right? Who cares if he likes your personality or your shirt or your breath or your hair?"

She slips it over her t-shirt. "Right. He's only going to see my coat anyway."

I groan. "No. We do not care if Jake likes our coat. Repeat after me."

Lindsay puts back her wool coat and grabs her puffy parka. "We don't care."

"You don't care." I smile at her and toss her a pack of spearmint gum. "But you do have some serious morning breath going on tonight. Freshen up."

We head out to Jake's SUV. It's freezing, and the twins are already inside the car, warming up the heater. I slide into the back seat with Jonah and Lindsay rides shotgun.

"You look great," Jake says to her.

Lindsay laughs and looks at me, then turns back to him. "Thanks. Want a piece of gum?"

He looks worried. "Do I need one?"

She smiles and shrugs. Jake takes a piece of gum from her.

Jonah looks like a model for a men's catalog, and I can't believe he's sitting by me or that we're engaged. Maybe he's not used to this either, because he's fiddling with his gloves. "Hey, Brie."

"Hey. Good day of work?"

"Jake and I made some progress on the new restaurant. You?"

"I updated some spreadsheets." I catch his eye. "Or should I tell you about it when we're alone?"

He grins, and some of the tension dissipates, but we still sit on separate sides of the back seat while Jake talks the rest of the short drive to the train depot. When we tumble out of the toasty warm car into the winter air, Chief is waiting outside the lobby of the train museum. I rush over, and he wraps me in a hug. He rests his head on mine so he can talk over me, because I'm that short. He nods at the twins. "Good to see you again, guys."

I look up as Jonah and Jake nod back at him. Jonah studies me with a closed expression.

Jake stares at our affection with outright hostility, then pulls out his phone. He's still glaring at me as he says, "Hang on. I've got a call coming in, and I've got to take it."

Chief lets go of me to open the door. "Lindsay, you're still walking. I didn't work you hard enough."

She can barely move. "No way. I'm taking tomorrow off."

Jonah's arm lands abruptly on my shoulders from behind. I didn't even see him coming. He improvised.

"Hey, boyfriend." I slip my arm around Jonah's waist to try to make this look more casual. I don't want Chief to suspect anything, because he's the only family I have. He, of all people, deserves the truth, and I will tell him. When this is over.

Jonah steers me through the tables covered with model train tracks and tiny plastic evergreens. "How often do you and Chief work out together?"

Chief answers. "Every morning at five-thirty."

I smile at him as we weave our way through the displays and find our way to the train depot outside. "Just like old times."

Lindsay looks around the decorated train station. Strands of lights hang from every post. "That is your idea of holiday magic? Abs all day?"

"Sounds magical to me," I mutter and pat Jonah's rock-hard stomach.

He flinches, and I instantly remove my hand.

"Work off that turkey before your gut knows what hit it." Chief hands Lindsay a ticket and hands the others to me. "V.I.P.

You get the whole car to yourselves. Our little red caboose, Rosie, is a good girl. You'll have fun back there."

For a minute I think he's joking, but there really is a red caboose at the back of the train. "Thanks."

Jonah's arm tugs me closer to him. "I should work out with you sometime."

"Nah, three of us are enough to fill that tiny gym." Chief folds his arms so his biceps bulge. "But I've got a haircut coming up."

"Haircut?"

"Yeah. You should come to that."

My boyfriends all fall for this. Sure, enough, Jonah thinks it's a harmless invitation. He runs a hand through those beautiful, soft waves. "My hair could use a trim."

Chief smiles. That should be the first clue that it's a trap. Chief doesn't smile, but Jonah doesn't know him like I do. "Thursday. Colleen's. Call her and tell her you're with me."

Jake nods, like he's listening to us as well as his phone call.

I shake my head.

"You, too, Sarge."

"Oh, I wouldn't miss one of your haircuts." I'm already mourning the loss of Jonah's beautiful hair, because I know what's about to happen.

Jonah's looking between us, but I can't say anything. Rules are rules, and I'm going to let the haircut play out without any interference from me. I hand him a ticket. "North Pole, here we come."

Chief waves to us. We wander down the tracks toward the last car, and Jake follows us. I loop my arm through Lindsay's, so we're walking three across.

"I'm ticklish."

Lindsay and I both look at Jonah.

He places a hand on the flat of my abdomen, and I suck in a breath. His fingers splay across my stomach, sliding over to my ribs. Lindsay's eyes widen.

"I'm ticklish. That's why I flinch when you touch me there."

My answer comes out on a breath. "Oh."

He has no idea what he's doing to me, but then his hand drops, and I can breathe again.

"Good to know." I barely manage to get out. "I'll remember that next time we have a tickle fight."

We're halfway down the railway track. His eyes dart to my ribs, and a grin tugs at one corner of his mouth. "Is that an invitation?"

"No." We reach the end of the track. A set of metal steps leads into the caboose.

Jonah's eyes flare as he reaches for my waist. "Let me help you in."

Jake shakes his head and moves in front of the train steps. He holds out a hand, and we all stop to listen. "I gotta go, man. Thanks. Yeah, later." He slips his phone in his pocket and locks eyes with us. "You're not helping Lindsay up those stairs, J-Dog." He takes her arm. "May I?" They climb the steps close together, and Jake grins the whole way.

I put one foot on the first rung, and Jonah wraps his hands around my waist. "Need help?" he asks innocently. His fingers dig into my ribs as he helps me up the first stair, tickling me in the most vulnerable spot.

Then his hands still on my ribcage. He leans forward and murmurs in a husky voice, "Still up for that tickle fight?"

"You know you'd lose." I whip my head over my shoulder, and that's all the challenge Jonah needs. His fingers find my ribs again. I bite my lip until I can't stand it anymore. I giggle and move up a step.

He steps behind me on the stairs, his stomach pressed against my back, and his hands drop to my hips as he helps me up the next step. His breath tickles my ear. "Oh, I think I won."

I don't trust myself to say anything, so I climb the final stair, and we enter the luxury car together.

Brass tacks, red upholstery, and strings of rope lights decorate the top all around. Jonah rests a hand on my shoulder to escort me into the caboose. As soon as Jake sees him, he lets out a whoop. "Dude! That was Tommy Fuller *himself*, not an assistant."

My heart stops. Why does it have to be him? Out of all the celebrity chefs, he's the only one I have to avoid.

Jonah chooses the velvet-lined seat closest to me. "Great. What's up?"

I'm glad we have the luxury caboose to ourselves. I stand and cross the train car to sit on the opposite side, where Jonah and Jake can't see my reaction to their news.

"*Santa Snack Smack Down*. He wants to make sure we're in."

Jonah's brow furrows when he notices where I am. I angle my body away from him, but he shoots me a worried glance. His face doesn't match his tone of voice. "Awesome."

Jake drops beside his twin. "He gave me all the details, probably more than he's giving everyone else. I got the inside scoop."

Jonah tries to catch my eye. "Tommy gave us our big break."

I nod across the caboose. "I saw that episode." I've watched that particular one more times than the rest.

Lindsay sits near me. There are hand warmers on the seat. "This should boost sales. I'll update the projections for the restaurants."

I welcome the subject change. "Will it affect the projections for the grocery store product line?"

Jonah nods. "It might. We see a bump in reservations at the restaurants every time we compete on a show. Can we get Luke on a call tomorrow? We'll want to update the website. When does the show air?"

Jake laughs. "Christmas Eve. It's crazy, right? We'll have to leave here on the tenth to tape on the twelfth."

"Dad will have a coronary." Jonah looks at me. "You'll come and watch the taping, right, Brie?"

The train jerks and pulls out of the station. Lights flash by on either side. I stare out the dark windows as I scramble for an excuse. "I close on my townhouse that day."

The crease on Jonah's brow deepens. "Which day? The tenth or the twelfth?"

He's caught me. I glance at him. "The tenth."

Jonah's smart, and he thinks quickly. "So, you can close and still make it on the twelfth. You don't need to be there early."

"It might have been the twelfth. I'm not sure."

Jake snorts. "Don't you already live there?"

Now I'm getting interrogated by both of them. "Yeah."

The heaters kick on, and warm air blows on me from slits in the brass vent above my head. Tinny speakers begin to play Christmas songs.

Jonah shifts on his seat. He leans forward and puts his elbows on his knees. "You don't need to move any boxes."

He's not buying it, but I try again. "No."

Jake glares at me, and Lindsay is uncharacteristically quiet. Jonah is calm, like he's solving a logic puzzle. Water probably doesn't dare to boil if he watches it. He uses his *Let's be reasonable voice* with me. "The closing shouldn't take too long, and you can do it before or after the show."

"It's not scheduled, though, so I'd have to be free all day."

The expression in Jonah's dark eyes is unreadable in the dimly lit caboose. "You love Tommy Fuller's shows. I'm sure you can get the bank to schedule if you call."

We're at an impasse. We're sitting on different sides of the caboose, and it feels tense, even to me. To my surprise, it's Jake who makes the next move.

"It's so much fun to be in the audience." He leaves his seat and crosses the caboose toward us. "You're going to love it, Brie. You, too, Linz."

"Am I invited?" she asks.

"I have a ticket with your name on it. The view is great on this side of the train." He pushes himself between us and drapes an arm behind each of us. "I can see the lights in town."

Jonah crosses the cozy caboose and sits on my other side. His hip is snug against mine. He rests an arm awkwardly on the metal rim of the window ledge behind me, pushing his brother's arm away from me.

I hate fighting with Jonah. I used to look for ways to prove someone was wrong for me, but I already know he is temporary. I want to enjoy the little time we have, and I don't want to hurt him.

His other girlfriends have damaged him enough. I'm not going to pile on.

I lean my head on his shoulder, and his arm pulls me closer.

Musical elves burst into the caboose, and we hardly have a minute to talk for the next half an hour. A conductor comes in and tells a story, then Mrs. Santa brings us mediocre hot cocoa that makes Jake grumpy. "Too bland," he mutters to Lindsay.

Jonah moves his arm away from my shoulder. "It's gone numb, anyway." He accepts a cup of cocoa. "Snuggling is supposed to be romantic, but nothing's romantic about pins and needles shooting up my arm."

I hide a smile as I sip my cocoa. Once again, he's all logic and no emotion, but his logic has its own charm.

Soon enough, we've arrived at the North Pole. Really, I think we've gone halfway around the St. Ambrose loop or something, but I'm willing to pretend it's the North Pole. The musical elves hand out shortbread cookies and candy canes, which cheers Jake up.

Lights shimmer in the distance, and the lake is a dark emerald crescent on the other side of the train. Snow reflects on St. Ambrose Peak. Bells ring over the intercom, and the conductor gives us a lovely speech about Christmas and believing as he gives us each our own bell to take home.

It's quieter on the return ride. Jake and Lindsay move to the other side of the train car. Jake makes a big deal about how the view is better on that side, but really, I think he wants to give us some space.

I can't tell if he likes the idea of me with Jonah or not, but tonight he's definitely playing the wingman for his brother. Jake keeps up a steady stream of conversation to entertain Lindsay, and she has no trouble keeping up. Lindsay's a talker.

There's less conversation on our side of the train car. I toss the bell in my hand, over and over, and listen to its tinkle. Jonah's eyes drop to the noisy ornament. "Good speech."

I nod. I don't want to admit that the cheesy acting got to me.

The outline of the mountain flashes by as we round a corner. He rests his arm behind me on the window ledge again, inches away from my shoulder. "I wish it were as easy as the conductor says."

My hand stills, and I slip the bell into my pocket. "What do you have trouble believing in?"

Jonah turns to the dark window. "Myself. Santa Claus. The idea that I can ever marry. It all seems mythical." He flashes a humorless smile. "Having a successful relationship seems about as likely as an old man flying around the globe in a few hours to deliver millions of toys to children he doesn't know without getting caught."

Jake's happily eating his candy cane on the other side, and it's quiet for once in the caboose. A ukulele plays a holiday song in the background on a speaker.

I nudge him with my shoulder. "I believe in you."

He nudges me back. "I'm real." He seems most comfortable when he treats me like I'm on a football team with him, instead of his girlfriend or fiancée. "But we're not."

I tilt my head to look at Jonah. "You're doing great with Step One, boyfriend. Look at you, being all emotionally intimate with me right now. You're even willing to risk a numb arm again."

Jonah drops his voice. "I know you'd have to leave Sugar Creek early, but I wish you would come."

Now I feel worse. "I can't come. I'm sorry." I can't tell him the real reason. I'm the one who isn't willing to take Step One to make this relationship work.

But he doesn't call me on it. "When are we breaking up?"

"Jingle Bells" is playing, but I don't feel like singing along. "That's your job. You decide when to end it."

"My job?" Jonah thinks hard, so I stare at his dimples instead of the view out the window. He shifts closer to me, and his leg brushes against mine. "If you're not coming to the show, it should be a few days earlier, at least."

I nod. "That makes sense."

Jonah's arm cages me between the window and his body. His endlessly deep eyes swirl with emotion, but his voice is still pure logic and reason. "Can I break our engagement December tenth, so I can clear my head before the show and focus on competing?"

*Two weeks.* My head tilts toward him. We're sitting with a perfect view of the mountain and the lights in the distance. Anyone else would kiss me, but Jonah's trying to coordinate our schedules for a breakup. "Yes, Chef."

"I know what *Yes, Chef* means when it comes out of your mouth." Jonah pushes a stray lock of hair behind my ear. "It means *I say that you're in charge, but really I am.*"

I tug the bell out of my pocket. "On the contrary. I believe you can do anything you set your mind to." I jingle the bell in his face, and Jonah grabs my hand. "I believe you can break up with me on December tenth."

I love the feel of his warm fingers around mine, and I don't pull away.

Jonah keeps a firm grip on my hand, so I can't ring the bell. His voice is husky and low in my ear. "Can we talk about something else?"

But I can't let go of the topic. I have to keep pushing him. "Instead of scheduling our breakup ahead of time? How about noon? I'll bring the meatball subs..."

Jonah ignores me. "Yes, instead of that." His fingers caress the silver bell in my grip, and his touch feathers against the edge of my hand. A new Christmas song starts playing, and it's way too peppy and upbeat. We're only going to be engaged for two weeks now, instead of four.

And I'll be spending Christmas Day alone, again, as usual.

Jake's watching us. His eyes dart to our hands, but he can't hear our conversation over the music, and I'm glad that the train car is wide enough for some privacy.

I drop my head on Jonah's shoulder. "How's your arm?"

Jonah laughs. "That's not what I want to talk about."

"Okay. You told me what you don't believe. Tell me what you do." I jingle the bell in his face and slip it back into my pocket. "The conductor said belief is magical and makes anything possible. What's the hardest thing you do?"

I'm really pushing Jonah. This isn't the kind of conversation I have with my friends, but he feels safe. The heater blows warm air, the cocoa and cookies filled me, and the cheesy songs feel like the happy parts of my childhood.

*I did some things right*, Mom says wistfully in my head. *I did my best.*

I fight back tears, and Jonah's gaze drops to mine. Something changes, and he starts talking.

"When I'm competing, I can't describe it..." He shakes his head. "I'm in the zone. I can do anything. I push harder, I work better, and I can plate the meal faster than seems possible."

I'm afraid to move and break the spell we just created. Jonah talks so rarely, but he's opening up in the peace of our little Rosie caboose. It's like one of those early mornings we used to have at work, except better, because we get to cuddle, too.

I shift a little so that my shoulder nestles into his side. "When I was in the Air Force, I knew everything that was happening in my kitchen, and even though a million things were going on, I was on top of it all."

Jonah nods. "Yeah. I work well under pressure. I don't need the pressure to do my best, but I love the cooking competitions. I love a good fight." He smiles wolfishly at me, and it's a look I've never seen.

I'm completely lost. I want this guy to fight for me, but he gives up so easily. I gather myself. "I've been there. I don't cook on

TV, but I had to produce complex meals under extreme pressure in busy, overcrowded kitchens."

Jonah's arm drops naturally onto my shoulders as he relaxes. He's somewhere else now. "When I hear those voices in the audience, and I know people believe in me, I can do anything."

The train slowly winds its way back down the mountain toward Sugar Creek. Jonah's embrace is warm, and his thumb traces circles on the back of my hand. Christmas carols play in the background, and I tip my head onto his shoulder. The stillness of the night washes over me, but not even the peace of the evening can calm my racing pulse.

He wants that voice to be mine. Jonah won't say it, but he wishes I believed in him enough to show up. I wish he would fight for me the same way he competes to win on TV.

But he won't, and I can't show up for him.

What hurts the most is that I can't tell him why. I've never told anyone, and it's another reason I'm always alone. No matter how close I get to friends, no one knows my secret.

My eyes flutter shut, and Jonah's head rests against mine. I wish I could go back to that world. I loved cooking with Pappy and everything I did in the Air Force, but that life is over for me. I can't risk it, but I can help him understand.

There's a reason I returned to Boston instead of New York when I left the Air Force. There's a reason I'm buying a townhouse and putting down roots there instead of choosing the place where I grew up.

I look at Jonah. "My mom and I worked together in Pappy's kitchen. Those cooking shows bring up too many memories of New York and professional kitchens for me, especially at Christmas. I can't ever go back to New York."

Jonah pulls back to look at me. "Never?"

"Never. I'll watch you win from my couch, but I can't head down to the Manhattan studio. Too close to my old home."

Jonah's gaze snaps to me. "How do you know which studio Tommy films in?"

I still. I shouldn't have let that slip. "Everyone knows."

He sits up, and his arm drops away. "Nobody knows. He's obsessed with security. You'd have to know Tommy personally to know that. Have you met him?"

"No." I close my eyes to end the conversation as a flood of memories fills my mind.

My mom went to the Manhattan studio once when I was eleven. She wanted to get some child support from him or something. It didn't work, and she almost got arrested.

She didn't come home for hours because of the scene she made at his studio, and I nearly went into the foster care system that night. That terrified me more than living with Mom's ups and downs and unreasonable demands.

She was so mad when she got home that she didn't speak to me for three days. It was my fault because she had done it for me, and she needed the money because of me. We spent the night packing, and we moved again the next day.

I didn't care, because it was better than foster care, and at least I had Grammy.

So, yeah, I'm not going to risk an encounter with Tommy Fuller, because even though he's my dad, I'd probably get the same welcome. A night in jail. I'm pretty sure I'm on the Do Not Allow list for his security detail.

After all, my mom and I are the *reason* he's obsessed with security now—to keep us out. My parents were only married for a few months, and he's a big celebrity now. I guess I'm an embarrassment or something. I don't know what his deal is, but I know this.

My dad definitely does not want to meet me.

# Chapter Sixteen

I TRY to talk to Lindsay the next morning at the gym, but Chief cuts me off.

"What are my two rules?"

I grunt as I lunge. "No." *Lunge.* "Complaints." *Lunge.*

He watches my form and corrects it. "And?"

I take a long sip from my gallon-sized water bottle. "No drama."

He refuses to talk about my boyfriends while we work out. *Ever.*

I try to ask Lindsay about her Christmas kiss with Jake, or whichever twin it was, again during breakfast, but Jonah comes over early with his laptop and a breakfast casserole that Jake made.

"I heated some water for tea," Jonah says. He rummages around in our cupboard for the cream-speckled mugs that every resort seems to use and looks at me. "Where are your tea bags?"

Something warm trickles through my veins. "Thanks. The cupboard on the other side of the sink."

Jonah runs back for the electric kettle, then he's in the cabin again, and we can't talk in front of him while the casserole bakes in our oven. It's got chiles and Monterey Jack cheese and eggs and potatoes, and our cabin smells amazing.

And I have my morning tea.

Jonah texts Jake when the casserole is done baking, and we break for brunch. The twins decide to stay and work. Jonah and I work side-by-side, and Jake and Lindsay spread out on opposite ends of the couch, so again, no talking about The Mistletoe Incident of 2019.

Also, not as much work as yesterday. Jake leaves to take a phone call, and all of us get a lot more work done with him gone. I line up more donations for the food banks.

When the sun starts to drop in the sky, I start chopping garlic and onions and peppers. I warm some olive oil and toss everything in a pan. Jonah leaves the couch a couple minutes later when the aromatics start smelling good.

He walks up behind me, and his voice rumbles in my ear. "No kissing tonight?"

I add a can of crushed San Marzano tomatoes. "It's homemade lasagna or kissing. Your choice."

He groans and rests his head on top of mine, like Chief did yesterday. "You're killing me. No man should have to make that choice."

But I don't think he's serious. Jonah watches me push the vegetables around the pan, then takes the spoon. One arm rests on the counter and the other arm brushes my waist as he stirs the sauce. The heat from the gas stove feels like a thousand flames. "If we both eat garlic..."

He has me trapped between the stove and his arms. I shift so I'm facing him. "Then it still tastes like a marinara kiss." I reach around him to grab some torn basil leaves off the counter.

Jonah's dark eyes never leave mine as I drop the basil into the sauce. He folds the leaves into the bubbling marinara, and it's me that's wilting instead of the basil. I duck under his arms and gather the ingredients to layer the lasagna while Jonah stirs the simmering sauce.

My emotions are on slow boil. Sitting next to Jonah all day

was hard enough, but I can't handle having him almost hug me now, too, not after he opened up to me last night.

It might have been okay when we had a month together, but the clock is ticking. We have twelve days now. Yes, I checked his color-coded calendar, and he has "Break Up" written on his private version that his mom and Jake can't see.

I grate some aged parmesan, stir it into some ricotta, crack some eggs, and shred some spinach leaves. There's not much else to do.

"Thanks, Jonah. It smells ready." I take the sauce off the stove and let it cool for a second, then use it to assemble the lasagna. I keep myself busy by making breadsticks, and he watches me every now and then from the couch.

I add extra garlic butter to the breadsticks, then choose the garlic ranch salad dressing when I toss the lettuce.

Yes, we're moving backward on the intimacy scale, but he's the one who just cut the timeline in half. We only have two more weeks of this, so I'm not sure it's worth training him after all.

An hour later, I take the lasagna out of the oven and throw in the breadsticks. Jonah must've texted his brother, because Jake walks in without knocking fifteen minutes later, right as the garlic breadsticks come out of the oven.

I point at two plates on the counter. "Girls' night. I love you boys, but don't come back tonight."

Jake hugs me and fills his plate. "I can hug you, right? You're practically my twin's wife. We're family."

It's kind of uncomfortable, but it's better than the death glares last night. "Of course, we're family. Get outta here. The lasagna is getting cold."

But it's going to be weird if we get close.

Jake gazes at the lasagna. "This smells so good, I could kiss you."

Jonah slams his laptop shut and leaves the couch. "Don't touch her."

"Your girlfriend made us lasagna. I'm going to marry her if you don't."

Jonah scrambles over to the counter. "You know the rule." He shoves Jake out of the way, slides a generous square of the lasagna onto his plate, and grabs a breadstick.

I serve him some salad and add a second breadstick. "What rule?"

Jonah grabs a fork from the counter. "You don't kiss your brother's girl. No exceptions. The first one to kiss her gets to date her. Dibs. No poaching."

Lindsay and I exchange a glance. "That's so seventh grade," she says.

"It's like licking a plate so you can sit somewhere," I add. "Shouldn't it be the other way around? The first one to date her gets to kiss her?"

Jake sighs dramatically. "It's juvenile, but it's the twin code. We were probably in third grade when we swore to it, and neither of us has ever broken it."

"Spit promise," Jonah shovels a bite in his mouth and groans. "I love you, Brie. Jake is never going to marry you."

I know he doesn't really love me, but it feels good to hear the words. "That's the lasagna talking. You love my sauce."

"I love you and your sauce." Jonah gives me a one-armed hug. He takes his plate and walks slowly to the door. "Goodnight, girlfriend."

I smile at him. "Goodnight, garlic breath."

Jonah juggles his laptop under one arm and holds his plate and fork with the other hand while Jake holds the door for both of them. "I love you, too, Brie," Jake says. "Keep me in mind if things don't work out with J-Dog."

Jonah nudges him hard, and Jake's plate nearly falls out of his hand. Jonah steadies the plate for him. "Stop it. We're engaged."

Jake holds his plate protectively. "I'm still cooking for you tomorrow!" he yells as they leave. He turns to Jonah, and I barely hear him as they walk away. "What? Rules are made to be broken, bro, and she can cook."

"You owe me your entire life savings," I yell back to Jake. "Just transfer it all to the Bro Fund."

He laughs, and I wait until the door closes all the way.

"Okay, Lindsay. If Jonah kissed you, he would never let Jake flirt with you like that." I offer her a plate, and we serve ourselves dinner. "Twin code."

Lindsay and I settle onto barstools at the counter. She pours us glasses of water. "You and Jonah are so cute."

I shrug that off. "I want to hear the Jake and Lindsay story. The long version this time."

She pushes the lasagna around her plate. "There isn't a Jake and Lindsay story."

"Liar." I take a huge bite.

She grins. "It was the end of the Christmas party, and I was putting decorations away. I didn't bother to turn on the light in the closet, because I could see well enough. Someone surprised me. I realized it was one of the twins wearing a Christmas sweater and a Santa hat. I was holding mistletoe, and he suggested we use it, so we did, then someone opened the closet door."

"You left out the part where it was awesome."

Lindsay bites her lip. "It was amazing."

I load a bite onto my fork. "We don't need to discuss how long it lasted..."

She's blushing now. "I left the closet a minute later and grabbed my purse to go home."

"A minute?"

"Or two." She grins. "Or five."

I sip my water. "First of all, Jonah would never randomly suggest to a stranger that they use mistletoe. That's more of a Jake thing. And Jonah is not a five-minute-make-out-with-a-stranger kind of guy."

At least I hope he's not. He did spring the fake engagement and six-second kiss on me, so I could be wrong.

I shake off the thought. "What happened when you got back from the holiday break?"

Lindsay finally takes a bite of the lasagna. She answers me after she swallows. "I found out Jake had a girlfriend."

I put down my fork.

"That's why I thought it was Jonah, but he never looked at me or talked to me. I was really confused."

My guy-dar is pinging. "Did Jake pay attention to you? How long did he date that girlfriend?"

Lindsay tugs at her breadstick, untwisting the golden-brown pieces. "Actually, he broke up with her over the holiday break. I only found out about her afterward when they got back together."

I nod with my mouth full of salad. *Target acquired.* Definitely Jake.

"What?"

I point to my full mouth. After I finish, I explain. "He broke up *for* you, then you ignored him, so he got back together with her."

"No way." Lindsay cuts a petite bite of lasagna, and I wonder how we're friends. "He never asked me out."

"And we're back to those vibes. You shot him down, so he thought you were just kissing him for fun at the party."

Lindsay cocks her head to one side. "I never shot him down."

I stare at my supermodel friend. "Painful truth time. I think you did, sweetie. You probably shoot guys down all the time without knowing."

She sets down her fork.

"Is something wrong with the lasagna?"

Lindsay shakes her head. She's honestly crying. I didn't put that many red pepper flakes in the sauce. I think.

She pushes her plate away. "I never date, and I don't have close friends. Usually, if one of my friends knows I have a crush on someone, she goes out of her way to get a date with him. I've been blaming other people, but it's me, isn't it?"

I finish my bite. "It's you. All you. But your friends are messed up, too. Who would do that?"

"Pretty much everyone I know. I can't believe how lucky I am that you're engaged. I don't have to worry about you going after the guys I like."

I'm going to let that comment slide and hope we're still friends in two weeks when Jonah breaks up with me.

"The twins have their twin code, and we have our girl code. I would never do that. Friends first. You don't have to worry about that with me, I promise. I don't have a family, so my friends are everything. You're the only one stopping you from a lifetime of bliss right now."

"I like you. You eat carbs." Lindsay crams an enormous piece of breadstick into her mouth this time.

I laugh. Lindsay is tall, thin, and blonde. The opposite of me. "Did you go to prep school and some insanely expensive college or something?"

She nods.

"So, everyone's been jealous of you? Your whole life?"

She nods again. "I didn't go to Senior Prom or any of the dances in high school. The boys all thought I had a date or that I'd turn them down. None of the girls wanted me to go with them in their friend group."

"You'd outshine them." I'm still processing this. Lindsay needs to date. She needs a boyfriend and some confidence.

"This is the first time I've had a best friend. Pathetic, right? Even my sister seems jealous of me. She's married and I'm not, but she's always complaining about how good my life is. Do I just not know how to have friends?"

I push her plate back toward her. "You're fine. Those jealous lame-sauce friends robbed you of your confidence. Don't let them take lasagna from you, too."

Lindsay laughs and takes another bite. "Have you dated a lot?"

I shrug and shove more comfort food in my mouth. I'm lucky

that my tiny frame can handle it. "I always have a boyfriend. It's pathological. I'm afraid to be on my own. I have my own issues, but it's never a lack of friends or dating."

"What is it, then?"

I really don't want to dig into it. I'll scrape the surface. "I can't choose just one man. They're all too delicious. Dating is like the ultimate boyfriend buffet." I spear a bite of salad. "There's always someone or something or somewhere better, so why settle down?"

Something like panic flits across her face. "But you're buying a townhouse and you're engaged to Jonah."

I smile. "I always tell myself it's different this time, but in the end, it never is."

Lindsay picks up her plate. "That's so sad. I want things to work for you and him."

"I know." And it is sad. "Me, too. I want things to work out this time. I've never been engaged before." And that's not a lie.

"You'll make it. I can tell." Lindsay takes her plate over to the sink. "I might not have your guy-dar or whatever, but I know love when I see it."

At least we're fooling her. Then again, she doesn't always pick up on subtle social cues.

I should coach her on the emotional IQ part to help her with Jake, just not enough that she sees through Jonah and me.

Lindsay yanks on the faucet handle, and water blasts all over her. She slams it off and carefully pulls on the knob in tiny increments until it trickles on. "I'll do the dishes. You cooked."

"You're not my slave. You're my friend. You don't have to buy my friendship by paying for the cabin or doing all the work." I join her by the counter. "You wash, I'll dry?"

She puts her hands on the counter and drops her head as the sink fills with water. "Wow. Do I do that?"

I put a hand on her shoulder. "You're generous. I love that about you, but you don't have to earn your place with me."

Lindsay blows out a breath and pours some soap in the sink. "I'm sorry I'm so pathetic."

"No, you're not." But now I'm determined that she needs more than just me as a friend. She needs a boyfriend, and Jake seems to like her a lot. "You're kind and caring and you love to share." We finish washing and drying the dishes in silence, and I can tell she's thinking hard.

I'm about one hundred percent certain Jake kissed her and has been crushing on her for three years since then.

But how can she date him, when he's going to hate me in two weeks? What if she falls in love with my ex-fiancé's brother, and I have to see Jonah all the time after we break up? Even worse, what if we have to double date after Jonah dumps me?

But it's the Girl Code. It's what's best for Lindsay. I'm going to do everything I can to help her, even if it means heartbreak for me in the future.

# Chapter Seventeen

JONAH'S PHONE buzzes while we're driving to the Christmas tree farm. "Hey, Ma."

We haven't sent Mrs. Butler a photo for two days. The North Pole Express train ride was on Monday night, and it's Wednesday.

The sledding is on the far side of town, so the drive will take five or ten minutes instead of two. That means we have time to talk. *Unfortunately.*

"She's right here."

Jonah talks to his mom *every* day. I guess I'm supposed to call or text that often, too, and I can't wrap my head around the idea of a mother who's actually involved in my life.

Immediately I feel guilty for thinking ill of the dead.

*No offense, Mom. I like my independence. Mrs. Butler is smothering me.*

"She wasn't on the call with Luke because she works in accounting. No. Yeah."

I whisper to Jake, "Was I supposed to join the Zoom call?"

He shrugs, and we turn right past the Shops on Main to head toward the Christmas tree farm.

"Yes, she works out with Chief every day. Yes, I work out, too. No, it's fine. We go at different times."

I wonder if it bothers Jonah. I don't mind if his mom is suspicious of Chief, because it ensures that he and Jake can stay up here and work. We've barely started to line up donations for the food bank and coordinate with the restaurants.

The twins are trying to prep for their competition and work on opening their restaurant. We can't afford any interruptions. We've only got eleven days left, but if Jonah's jealous, we need to talk.

"We worked together in her cabin yesterday, but uh." He glances at me. "We get more done if we're in separate cabins."

He shouldn't have said that. Jake turns around from the driver's seat, and he's signaling with a hand across his throat. "Stop."

"We're working on the *Santa Snack Smack Down*."

"Let me talk to Mom." Jake holds out his hand. "Actually, Linz, can you grab that for me?"

Lindsay holds the phone so Jake can talk to Mrs. Butler. *Maggie*. I'm never calling her *Mom*.

I ache to have a mother again, no matter how functional or dysfunctional, and I can't allow myself to pretend, not even for one moment.

Jonah and I sit together in the back seat, and I feel like a toddler in trouble. I nudge him and quietly mouth my question. "What's up?"

He glances over. "Nothing."

Mrs. Butler's voice is on speakerphone now. "Jake? Which twin is this now?"

"Yeah, it's me. Listen, Ma. You can't butt in, even if you are a marriage therapist."

"I don't want another Patricia situation."

Jonah talks over his brother's shoulder. "Mom, it's Jonah again. Brie is nothing like Patricia."

"Alone. Moves a lot. New to the area. Sounds like it to me, and—"

Jake interrupts. "Jonah is nothing like Danny. Danny's got too much swagger."

Jonah looks indignantly at Jake. "I have swagger."

"No, you don't," Jake says. "Not with women. Just with food."

Jonah shrugs. "Fair point."

Mrs. Butler sighs. "Jonah is just like his father in all the ways that Daniel is."

Jake glares at the phone. "Meaning what?"

"Dad has food swagger," Jonah mutters. "He's happily married."

Mrs. Butler's voice ratchets up a notch. "Jonah, you will let the right woman walk away if you're not careful, just like your brother did. Your dad is not great at expressing his feelings. None of you boys are. Swagger isn't emotion. You haven't set a date yet, and Brie still isn't wearing your ring because you aren't taking this fledgling romance seriously enough."

Jake and I both snicker. Jonah shoots me a glance. I mouth the words, "Fledgling romance."

It's strange to listen in the back seat while Jake and Jonah argue with the car's speakerphone. I guess it's another twin thing—taking on their mom together. Jake is the one to end the call. "We're at the Christmas tree farm. We're going sledding, and Jonah is going to hug his fledgling romance for all she's worth all the way down the hill. They're fine. Love you, Mom. Bye."

Jake nods and Lindsay hangs up. He grabs the phone and tosses it back to us. "Mom's freaking."

Jonah's jaw clenches. "You should have let me handle that."

Oh. It's not a twin thing. It's a Jake-Butting-In-Again thing.

We pile out of the car. The Christmas tree farm is a *far-see* past the country store. One of the people at the cabins told us to pass the Shops on Main, turn right after the railroad tracks, and then go as far as we could see. "It's a *far-see*," she said.

Evergreens dot the landscape, and families wander up and

down the rows. Strings of Edison lights hang around the edges and there's an ice skating pond on the far side.

Jake points at the phone. "You know what she was like with Danny. She can't go through that again—none of us can. You can't ever get divorced."

"We won't. I promise." Jonah grabs my hand. He tugs me over to him and whispers so that only I can hear him, "If we never get married, we won't ever get divorced."

We follow Jake over to a line for sleds. Someone's made a track that goes down a long, steep hill. I feel sick about the phone call, and I whisper back to Jonah, "She's going to take the breakup pretty hard."

Jake turns around and walks backward. His voice carries to all the couples and families around us. "Just set a wedding date and make Mom happy."

Jonah drapes an arm around my shoulder. "It's not that easy."

Jake says, "Go talk, and don't come back until you have a date. I'll let you know when it's our turn." He puts a hand on the small of Lindsay's back and steers her into the line for sleds.

Jonah and I step to the side. It's colder in the shadows. Jonah rubs the back of his neck. "What am I supposed to tell her?"

"She can't start buying things for a wedding that isn't going to happen." I curl into myself, and Jonah tugs me into a hug.

He calls his mom back with one hand. Her worried face fills the screen, but she smiles widely. "Hi, lovebirds! What took so long to call me back?"

"We were making out." Jonah shifts the phone so she can see both of us better. "I'm joking, Ma. We're going sledding. There are people everywhere. We have to pay and stand in line. It's not the best place for a therapy session."

"I haven't heard from you for two days. You're working during your vacation, Brie doesn't have a ring, and you haven't set a date." She stops to draw a deep, steadying breath. "One, two, three, four."

We breathe with her. There are firepits over by the ice skating pond, and we wander in that direction after our box-breathing. Four in, four out, all four sides of the box.

"Jake tells me you never kiss in front of him. When your father and I were engaged, we couldn't keep our hands off each other."

I slide my arm around Jonah's waist and drop my head on his chest. I'm already emotionally exhausted and the conversation has just begun. "We're not really into PDA."

"Hi, sweetie. Tough time of year for you."

I wave. I don't want to talk about my mom's death again. Not here. Not ever.

"Joey's never been affectionate with his girlfriends in public, but you're engaged, and Brie has different needs. If you're going to make this marriage work, Jonah, you have to be okay with more affection."

Is she shouting? Can everyone in line hear about my *needs* even from here? Jake grins at me and blows me a kiss.

Jonah turns us away from the curious eyes of the people in line and his gawking brother. He lowers his voice. "I try, but Brie likes her space."

Mrs. Butler's eyes are too sharp and knowing. "Does she? Because Patricia liked her *space*, too, and Daniel's divorced now. You're not going to make it to the altar at this rate."

Jonah and I glance at each other.

"I knew it." Mrs. Butler covers her eyes. Her voice shakes, and I can't tell if she's crying. "Jim! Your oldest son never listens to me."

Jonah tenses beside me. "Jake's waving us over. We gotta go."

We start walking through the twinkling lights. The smell of pine tickles my nose, and the lights reflect on the snow.

Mr. Butler's voice booms through the chill night air. "Jonah! Don't hang up on your mother."

"Take it off the speaker," I whisper. We stop before we get back to the line.

Jonah holds the phone between our ears, and our cheeks are

next to each other. Mr. Butler grins at us. "You promised me grandbabies."

"We never promised that," Jonah says.

"Tell Brie you love her every day. Don't let her get away. Promise me that, and I'll get my grandbabies."

Jonah doesn't answer, and we look at each other. We can't promise grandbabies, because that would be a lie.

Mr. and Mrs. Butler's faces fill the screen the way our faces fill their screen. "Or come home tomorrow morning."

Jonah glances sideways at me. "I told her I loved her yesterday."

"He did, and I told him I loved him." It's a good thing that it's always been easy for me to tell my friends I love them. I kiss his cheek for good measure. It's slightly stubbly, since it's almost eight o'clock at night. I want to explore his cheek, but I pull away.

Jonah stills. His face turns toward me, and his dark eyes deepen in the shadows. Maybe I went too far.

I shiver. "It's cold over here."

He eyes me instead of his parents. "We gotta go. It's our turn."

"Promise you'll do everything you can to keep her." Mr. Butler hugs his wife, and her face softens. For the first time, she reminds me of Jonah.

"Of course, Dad."

"Promise." Mrs. Butler smiles.

"Jonah! Now!" Jake yells.

"Gotta run." Jonah's about to hang up when his mom puts up her hand.

"And kiss her every night."

"We are not discussing our alone time with you. I draw the line there." Jonah kisses me on the cheek, and his lips linger. "Bye, Ma. Dad." He ends the call.

Jake waves us over frantically. There's some kind of shuttle to the top of the sledding hill, and the car doors pop open. Jonah grabs my hand, and we jog over to the SUV together.

Jake wolf whistles. "You were *almost* making out. Well done, bro. Hop in."

Everyone's watching us when we slide into the last two seats.

"What was all that about your needs?" Lindsay asks.

But Jonah's phone rings again. "Danny," he says by way of greeting. "I'm in a car with other people. Can I call you back?"

Everyone saw us in line, and they saw us leave. They probably heard half of the therapy session, and they saw the cheek kisses. Who knows what they thought they saw in the shadows, but we've already provided the evening's entertainment for the entire sledding hill.

And now we're entertaining the SUV occupants.

Jonah's voice carries in the quiet car. "No, we haven't set a date."

I slip my arm around his waist and lay my head on his shoulder. I thought this was going to be harmless, and the only person whose emotions would be involved would be Jonah, but no. He's the first brother to get married since Danny's divorce. He's their best hope for grandbabies, and I don't know what it's like to have a family that cares.

"I hear you, but she's not like Patricia."

I grab the phone. "Hi, Danny? It's Brie. It's good to talk again."

"Hey. My mom said to call and ask if Chief is the reason you won't set a date for the wedding."

I take a deep breath. The entire car is listening. I don't care.

"I do what I say I'll do. I saw enough of my buddies lose their marriages in the Air Force that I will never cheat *on* anybody or *with* anybody. If I make a promise to your brother, I'll keep it, so thanks for the call, but we're good."

I hang up and take a deep breath. I'm shaking.

Jonah takes the phone. "I didn't say anything to my mom about that." He glares at Jake. "If I don't have a problem with her friends, you shouldn't either. Don't cause problems between me and Brie."

146

The SUV winds up the hill through the Christmas tree farm. It couldn't be more picturesque, but my pulse is still pounding in my head. I take the phone out of Jonah's hand and hit the number. "Danny? I'm sorry I hung up on you."

"I'm sorry, too. I don't care if your best friend has a hot rock-star body. Jonah's got five celebrity brothers, so you're going to have to get used to hanging out with rockstars."

I laugh, and we sit in awkward silence while the rest of the people in the car stare at me. Someone whispers, "Is she really friends with a rockstar? Who are his brothers?"

I talk as quietly as I can. "So, give me your advice to make a relationship with your caveman brother work."

Jonah grunts. "I'm not a caveman."

Danny answers quickly. "Don't dump him every time you want to."

"Oh, that's going to be hard."

He laughs. "Just tell him how he messed up and let him try to fix it."

I'm holding the phone so Jonah can hear. I know he understands baseball analogies. "Three strikes before I toss the bum out?"

Danny's still serious. "Look, Patricia and I put up walls and then the silence became a weapon that no one could crack. Just fight and make up and make out."

Jonah grabs the phone. "Thanks for having my back, bro. Make out. Can do. Hey, we've gotta jump."

Danny's right. I broke up with my other boyfriends at the first sign of trouble, and I didn't always give them warning or reasons. It was just—on to the next.

I grab the phone back. "You know you're my favorite brother, and I love you, Dan Man."

"Hey!" Jake yells. "I thought you loved me best."

Danny laughs. "Sure, sis. You're not too bad. I'll tell Mom to chill out. Bye." He hangs up.

Jake grins. "Danny says I'm a hot rockstar celebrity." He puffs out his chest, then winks. "Did you hear that part, Linz?"

She rolls her eyes. We're nearly at the top of the hill. A couple young girls in front of us have turned around and are eying Jonah like he really is a rockstar. I smile at them. "How you doing?"

They giggle and turn around after stealing one last look at Jonah and Jake. "I think they're famous," one of the girls whispers.

The phone rings again, and I answer his FaceTime call. "Luke. Hey. Yeah. We're about to go sledding, so I'm going to make this quick. Thanks for relaying your concerns about my absence at the last meeting to your dad. I didn't think you were the type who liked a clingy woman."

Luke gapes at me. "I'm not, but sorry. If it doesn't look like a duck or act like a duck... If you don't have a wedding date set and you don't have a ring, then how are you engaged?"

This guy is way too smart, like the rest of his family. "I give Jonah space, and he lets me introvert. We don't spend every moment of every day together, and we're both fine with that. If you're not okay with the kind of relationship your brother needs, reexamine your life, and ask yourself why you're twenty-six and still single, and he is the one engaged. Hugs. See you at the wedding, *whenever* it happens. You're still my second-favorite brother." I blow kisses, hang up, and hand back the phone.

"That's just rude." Jake looks over his shoulder. "I'm his twin. How am I your third favorite?"

"I never said that you were."

Jonah's mouth tugs in a half-smile. "So, which one is he? Four? Five?"

I grin back. "I haven't decided yet. Let's see...five hot rockstar brothers, plus your parents, so technically, I have seven to choose from?"

Jake snorts.

Everyone in the SUV is listening to the Butler Twin Show, so lower my voice. "Jake, if you keep telling your mom that I'm in love with Chief, you're never going to be number one. Come on, dude. You're complaining about our lack of PDA, when really you should be grateful we're not making." I take a deep breath. "Or would you rather that I suck your brother's face all the time?"

The SUV comes to a stop, but none of the other passengers get out. The young girls turn around and take a picture of us. I pop the door and climb out. "Do you want a picture with Jonah? I can take one for you."

The girls giggle and scamper out of the car without answering.

Jake bumps me with his shoulder as he follows us out of the car. "I knew you loved me best."

I bump him back. "You're a gossip and you hate the fact that your brother is engaged."

He bumps me again. "Do not."

Jonah folds his arms across his chest. "Stop flirting with my fiancée."

Jake stops, and the other people walk around us. "I'm not."

We climb the rest of the way to the top of a steep hill, and someone hands Jonah a sled. He wraps his arms around me, and I fit perfectly in his embrace.

Jake grabs a sled, and he and Lindsay move past us. "Was I flirting with Brie?" he asks Lindsay. "Because I meant to flirt with you."

"You're asking the wrong person," Lindsay says. "I don't know how to flirt."

Jake's eyes light up. "Really? You don't know how?"

When he realizes it's not a come-on or an invitation, and that she's *actually* not flirting when she *says* she can't flirt, he grins. "Oh, you found the right person. I can teach you."

He puts his hand on the small of her back again and leads her away.

Jonah shakes his head. A light snow dusts our shoulders, and he rests his head on top of mine. "Is there a kiss involved somewhere in there with the *I Love Yous*?"

I look at him. "Now who's flirting?"

He flashes the same wolfish grin as his twin. "We need some alone time."

The moment would be perfect except for one thing—our audience.

"She's awesome, dude," a teenager says as his group of friends pass us and fist bump Jonah. They're the first ones down the hill, riding face first on their stomachs.

A few more kids line up behind us.

"Go ahead." Jonah waves them forward. I'm overwhelmed by his family's love and concern and involvement, but he doesn't press me to talk. I'm starting to appreciate his quietness and understatement.

A cute young couple passes us. The wife stops in front of us. "Don't let anyone pressure you into getting married before you're ready. Take your time."

Her husband wraps an arm around her. "Look at us. Took her two years to say yes. Now we have to get a babysitter to get a night to ourselves. Happily married for twelve years."

They cuddle on a sled and slide down the hill.

I'm starting to calm down. Jonah steps forward, but I tug on his arm. "I need a minute."

He leans down and scans my face. "I'm sorry about my family. All of them were out of line. It doesn't matter how many shows I win or how many restaurants I open. If I'm not married, I'm a disappointment."

"Hey. No." I can't believe that his parents would really think like that. "I'm sorry, too. I shouldn't have talked to any of them that way. I have a temper, if you can't tell."

And I freaked out when I saw how freaked out his mom was. I don't want to break her heart, and I'm not used to having anyone care so much about the particulars of my life.

He grins. "That kid is right. You were awesome, and I loved it. See, I can say it, too."

"You almost said you love me." I pat his cheek. I can't help it. I want to play with that stubble. "So, you almost get a kiss."

He actually laughs.

"I'm so embarrassed. I hate it when I lose my cool. Luke challenged my integrity, and that put my back up."

Jake and Lindsay wait at the front of the line. Jonah holds up a hand. "Be there in a sec."

I lower my voice. "I hung up on Danny. I invited Luke to a wedding that's never going to happen."

"You apologized, asked for advice, and told Luke you loved him. You fit right in, Brie. Families argue, and we make up." He lifts a hand to brush my cheek. "Then we make out?"

Something flutters in my stomach. Ever since I kissed him on the cheek, I've been hungry for more than that.

I bite my lip, and his eyes drop there. He inches forward. "I promised my parents...every night..."

I swallow. "We can't disappoint your parents. Let's talk during our *alone time*. There's no one else left at the top of the hill, and we'd better get down before the next car full of people arrives."

Jake waves us ahead. "You can go ahead of us, because I'm your favorite brother." He's enjoying his flirting lesson with Lindsay, so I help him out.

"Thanks, bro. You're number two right now." I climb awkwardly onto the sled. "Jonah's always going to be first." Jonah's arms wrap around me from behind, and before I can say or do anything, we're flying down the hill. His pine aftershave fills my senses, mingling with the fresh trees around us, and his legs trap me on either side.

Jonah tugs me to his chest, and his mouth brushes my right ear. His voice is husky and warm as the brisk night air whooshes past. "Thanks for having my back with my family, girlfriend."

We land in a heap at the bottom. Jonah tugs the sled out from beneath us, and I roll over. He traps me on the snow. I put a hand on his chest, and he covers my fingers with his.

"I promised my parents I wouldn't let you get away." He lifts me to his chest and shifts us to a sitting position. I'm practically in his lap when Jake and Lindsay's sled flies past us.

Jonah meets my gaze and tugs me closer. The snow burns cold beneath me, and he pulls me the rest of the way into his lap. I wrap my arms around his neck and play with the curls at the bottom, poking out beneath his Red Sox beanie. Jonah cups my cheek as his mouth moves toward mine.

He stops with his lips an inch away. "Am I ready for Step Three yet?"

I stare at him confused.

"Your boyfriend recipe. Which step is the kissing step?"

# Chapter Eighteen

ANOTHER COUPLE almost crashes into us. Teenagers zip past on either side, and Jake hollers, "S'mores! I got a firepit and two kits."

I'm frustrated because I wanted that kiss. "If you have to ask, you aren't ready. You act, Jonah, instead of asking. You already know my answer is *yes*."

I climb out of his lap and crawl to my feet ungracefully. The man knows more ways to kill a mood than I thought existed. I brush the snow off my pants.

He tugs the sled back to a shed and hands it to someone. I'm about to walk over to the firepit when he rests his forehead against the wall. I hate the defeated way he's slumped against the wooden slats of the building, so I thread my arm through his and tug him behind the shed. "Look, I'm making this up as I go. I improvise most of my recipes."

"So do I," Jonah mutters. "But I'm better at *that* kind of improvising than this."

"I'm sorry." I pull him onto a bench where we can see the ice skating on one side and the sledding hill on the other. I soften my voice, so he'll know I'm not angry or sarcastic. "Do you want me to spell this out?"

Jonah shrugs. "I read all that stuff about consent, and now I'm afraid to do anything without asking."

I take his hand. "You don't have to ask every single time. We're engaged. Trust your instincts. It's like knowing when a sauce is done. No one can tell you. You just get a feel for it."

He looks up. "Sauces usually come together at the last possible moment. That seems appropriate, since this is fake."

"No, this is hypothetical. That means we get to experiment." I arch an eyebrow.

Jonah lets out a deep breath.

More strands of lights hang around us here, giving off a gentle glow. "Okay, I thought I had trauma, but you have some serious girlfriend PTSD. Who have you dated?"

"No one like you." Jonah's eyes turn dull, and his shoulders droop. "Women who want me for my money or my hot celebrity body. Mostly my family connections." He grins and grimaces at the same time. "It's funny. Those relationships felt fake, and this one feels more real. You're real, and they were superficial."

"Oh, I want you for your hot celebrity body." I smile at him, and Jonah's head snaps up. He just won himself a kiss, and he doesn't even know it yet.

I hope that Lindsay will forgive me for stranding her with Jake. Hopefully their flirting lesson will continue while Jonah and I have a boyfriend training session. "If I had to come up with all of the steps for your boyfriend recipe, I'd say it goes like this. Step one. Preheat the oven. Emotional intimacy before physical intimacy. Open up and get to know each other."

Jonah nods and shifts closer to me.

"Step two. Gather the ingredients. Keep me close. Find ways to spend time together."

He nods again, and a small grin starts at one corner of his mouth. "I can do that."

"You are. You're doing great on those steps." I blow out a breath and rub my hands.

Jonah's brow furrows. "Are you cold?"

I rub the seat of my pants. "I should have worn something waterproof."

He starts to ask, "Can I—" Then he stops. He wraps an arm around my shoulders and pulls me close. "Let me warm you up."

I smile. "Step three. Mix the ingredients. Start with low-key affection. You're doing that right now." I snuggle into his side. "Now this is the tricky part. Steps four and five happen at the same time."

Jake wanders past the shed looking for us, but neither of us moves to join him. Jonah shifts on the bench so our legs are touching each other. *All* of us is touching: hip, shoulder, thigh. "I like the mixing step, but the relationship can go wrong a million ways from here."

"It's simple. Throw it in the oven, put it on broil, and don't walk away until it's done."

Jonah stares. "It's not that easy."

"It's that easy. Would you leave a boiling pot of water on the stove or a tray of garlic bread toasting in the oven?"

"Of course not."

"Most boyfriends walk away from relationships once the thrill of the chase is over. They get bored, or they fall into a routine, or they take the woman for granted."

Jonah stands and tugs me off the bench. He pulls me into a hug. "Step four is the kissing part?"

I am so ready for this. "Yes."

His warm brown eyes lock onto mine. "And step five is to keep doing it until it's perfected?"

I bite my lip. "Something like that. All the steps. The emotional part, too, not just the kissing and hugging and..." I swallow. "I've never lasted that long, to be honest."

Jonah's eyes drop to my lips. "I felt very emotionally intimate with you when you yelled at my brothers then almost cried." He leans against the shed again, but this time, he takes me with him. He tugs, and I fall onto his chest.

I try not to smile. "That was a deep bonding moment when I lost my temper."

He cups my cheek. "I've gathered you in my arms."

"Uh-huh. You don't have to narrate every step, Jonah."

He grins wolfishly. "I'm a rockstar celebrity chef, Brie. I'm used to narrating every step as I improvise a recipe, and right now, I'm going to kiss you."

I hold my breath as he slowly lowers his lips to cover mine. When our mouths finally meet, it's just as explosive as the first time. I wrap my arms around his neck and eagerly respond. He settles back against the shed and tugs me closer.

I drink in the scent of his aftershave and the evergreens and the woodsmoke. There's something safe and warm and comforting about this kiss. I relax into the embrace, enjoying the solid feel of his chest beneath me.

Finally, this relationship feels real. The awkwardness melts away as his mouth slants over mine thirstily, his hand behind my neck, and Jonah tilts my head to match his. We can't get enough of each other, and I trace a line up his chest. His puffy, parka-covered chest.

My fingers catch on the seams of his coat. There are muscles somewhere in there.

I tug at his zipper to get better access to his sculpted shoulders, and Jonah groans as my fingers slip inside his coat. "Why does it have to be winter?"

We've just started kissing again when Jake's voice cuts through the air. "Really, J-Dog? How cliché is this? Making out behind the shed."

I collapse on Jonah's chest and laugh, and he hugs me, resting his head on top of mine. "Sorry, Jake. Hey, Lindsay."

Jake's voice is muffled through Jonah's coat. "We ate your s'mores."

That's funny, too, and I giggle again. I try to stop laughing, but it doesn't work.

Jonah grabs my hand. "We're ready to go, if you're done."

Jake folds his arms across his chest. "The question is whether you're done."

Jonah and I exchange a look. "We won't be done for a long time," he says. "But we can leave."

We hold hands, even with our thick gloves on, and it finally feels like the holiday season.

I send Mrs. Butler a picture of us as often as I can. There is one of us with Jonah's arms wrapped around me at the top of the sledding hill. The next day I send a picture of us cooking lunch together. Jonah is testing a new sauce. He's holding up the spoon, and I'm kissing his cheek.

That afternoon, we're sitting with our laptops. Jonah and I are together, and Lindsay is on the far end of the sectional sofa. Jake is still annoyed with us, so he's not talking, and we're all getting a lot more work done.

Evidently, his flirting lesson with Lindsay last night didn't go as well as my boyfriend training with Jonah. S'mores aren't sexy. It's hard to seduce someone when you're burning marshmallows and have sticky goo on your fingers.

Lindsay snaps a photo of Jonah and me together on the couch, though, and I text that. When she sets her phone down, I see that she's changed her home screen photo to the picture that Jake sent her.

We call Luke a couple hours later, and I make sure to join the meeting from the couch beside Jonah. I even take a screenshot and send it to Mrs. Butler.

The best part of the Zoom call is when Luke's coworker drops a bag on his desk for Taco Tuesday, crosses her legs, and leans across his desk to see what the Zoom call is about. She's almost as short as I am, and she's totally affronted that he's sneaking a meeting while she's gone.

"What website redesign?" She turns the laptop toward her, and it's obvious that she's sat on his desk before. He's rearranging papers, but he's left enough space for her.

Jake and Jonah explain the changes they need, but I'm watching Luke, who is most decidedly *not* watching Andie, even though she's sprawled all over his desk and taking over his meeting.

She gets the gist of what we're doing and nods. "He can't work two jobs full-time."

"I agree." Jake is still a little grouchy. "But that's his choice."

Lindsay sits next to Jake. Their shoulders brush as she leans in, so her face appears on the screen. "He could use some help."

Luke shoots her a glare. "I'm fine."

"Hey, man." Jake's instantly on Lindsay's side. "It's a good idea."

"I'll help," Andie says. She opens the bag of tacos and picks the tomatoes off Luke's taco. "We can go axe-throwing with everyone if we finish this together."

"Lindsay can give you the information you need," Jake says. "She's been really on top of this for the last few years ever since she was hired."

Lindsay turns to him and blinks. "Thanks, Jake. I'm surprised you noticed."

He grins. "I've been watching." His eyes blaze, and none of us can mistake his interest, not even Lindsay. I think.

Luke clears his throat. "Thanks for touching base, guys." He reaches for a taco, and Andie takes a fry out of his bag.

"The tacos are getting cold." Andie puts her email and mobile number in the chat. "Lindsay, will you send me the info that you need on the website? Good meeting, everyone." She ends the call.

Jake shuts his laptop and relaxes into the couch. "That girl has got Luke on a tight leash." He looks meaningfully at Jonah.

Jonah meets his gaze without flinching. "Hey, man, I'm okay

with that. At least I belong to someone." He grins. "Would you rather be free-range?"

I shake my head. "You're mixing your metaphors. Leashes are for dogs. Free-range refers to chickens. You are neither, Jonah."

Lindsay leaves Jake's end of the couch and returns to the far end of the living room. She picks up her phone. "Jake is definitely the free-range type."

"I'm not a chicken." He follows Lindsay and stands in front of her, blocking the fireplace and TV. "Dare me to do anything."

Jonah and I look at each other. "Closet," he mouths, and I laugh. We've tried to figure out a way to get Jake to admit he's kissed Lindsay, but we're stuck.

"What?" Jake says aggressively. "What did you say to Brie?"

"Nothing." Jonah winks at me. He looks at me like he wants to find a dark closet for the two of us, and Jake looks away in disgust.

Lindsay glances at Jake. She might think she isn't crushing on him, but I know otherwise. She's totally checking him out, and I know when her eyes land on his signature feature. The one thing that every woman in the office, married or unmarried, loves about him.

His wavy, strawberry-blond hair. It looks blond from a distance, but then you get close, and you can't keep your eyes off it. The hint of red. The subtle curl. The green eyes beneath floppy bangs.

Lindsay's mouth curls into an evil smile. "Shave your head."

His eyes lock onto hers. "Anything but that."

"Free-range." Lindsay leaves the couch to grab a water bottle, and I hear chicken squawks as she disappears behind the refrigerator door. She closes the door. "Enjoy your haircut with Chief."

A muscle twitches in Jake's jaw.

Maybe Lindsay did learn something from her flirting lesson. The thing is, she forgot to lock her phone before she left to grab that water bottle. Jake leans over and picks up her phone from the couch.

He grins when he sees the wallpaper photo of himself. He runs a hand through his thick, wavy hair. "Yeah, I will enjoy my haircut. Do you want a picture of it?"

Lindsay squeals and runs back. Jake throws an arm around her shoulder. "Selfie first. You got one of Brie and Jonah." He takes a picture of them together, then hands her back the phone. "We look even better."

She jams it in her pocket. "Is this the before photo?"

"For what?" Jake flops on the couch next to Lindsay's laptop.

"For your haircut. For the shaved head."

He laughs. "Right." Jake casually throws an arm on the back of the sofa when Lindsay sits beside him.

She threw down the challenge. The question now is how far Jake is willing to go to impress her.

# Chapter Nineteen

JONAH AND JAKE quit work after the Zoom call and make us dinner. Again. They've fed Lindsay and me almost every meal for the last few days. They're prepping for the cooking competition, so they time themselves and only use limited ingredients.

Naturally, that includes garlic.

I spend the time making dessert in our cabin while they're cooking in theirs. I ask Lindsay about the flirting lesson. "Is Jake a good teacher?"

She bites back a smile. "He's persistent."

"And not subtle. Did you see the way he looked at you during the call with Luke?"

She scrapes back a barstool at the kitchen counter and sighs. "Yeah. Maybe he did kiss me."

"He's been watching you for years." She needs the same lesson I gave Jonah last night. Jake's trying to move Lindsay out of the colleague zone, skip the friend zone, and go straight to girlfriend. He's laying on the emotional bids thick and heavy now.

"It's so romantic." Her brow furrows. "But I'm still mad and confused about what happened."

Jake slams the door open without knocking. "Dinner!"

"Later," she whispers.

"Condemned man's last meal before his haircut," I mutter as we follow him across the crunchy snow to the twins' cabin. I carry my tray of cannoli as an offering.

We enter their cabin, and Jake's eyes narrow. "Is there a reason you're being extra nice to us tonight?"

He noticed.

"I can't make cannoli for my boyfriend and his brother?"

Jake brings a bowl of curry over to the table. "Back me up, J. Why does Brie suddenly like me?"

I go over and slip an arm around Jonah's waist. "I've always liked you, Jake. You're my favorite brother tonight."

Jonah looks down. "What about me?"

"I'm hugging you, boyfriend."

He pushes me into a chair and puts a plate in front of me. "I feel used."

"I wish someone would use me," Jake mutters. He serves a dish of Thai vegetables over fried rice. "Comfort food. Jonah's idea. What's up with you two? First, cannoli, and then this? Did you argue or something?"

I scoot my chair beneath the table. Short legs can't reach very far. "Nothing's wrong."

Jake sits, and we start eating. "But I'm your favorite brother? I don't buy it. Everyone likes Matt best."

Lindsay laughs. "I haven't met Matt."

"And you're not going to." Jake locks eyes with her, and her laugh fades as the tension between them grows.

Jonah hands me a water bottle. "Hello, Brie is engaged to me. Forget Matt. I'm her favorite."

I take a bite. "This meal is my favorite. Thanks for cooking, guys."

Lindsay studies the food on her plate, then takes a bite. Jake shakes his head. "Now Brie even likes my cooking."

"I helped, too." Jonah holds up a spoonful of sauce. "It's my part of the meal she likes."

"Boys, boys." I hold up my hands. "I'll come clean if you'll stop arguing."

The twins both laugh. "She sounds like Mom," Jonah says.

"I don't sound like anyone's mom." I take another bite. I don't want to ever sound like my mom, at least. "The truth is that I'm a little worried to let you hang out with Chief. He's my self-appointed big brother and dad all in one. He gets overprotective and thinks no guy is ever good enough for me."

Jake narrows his eyes. Jonah keeps eating and takes a long drink of water. "You aren't *letting us* hang out with Chief. He asked, and we agreed. Just a few guys hanging out."

"Well, Chief can be a dealbreaker for some guys when they meet him."

Jake snorts and takes another bite. He coughs, and his eyes start watering. "Too much heat in that bite, bro."

"No, I slipped an extra pepper in your bowl." Jonah grins at me. "Since you said I like things spicy."

I sense there was an argument that I missed, but I'm not going to ask for more details.

"Why would Chief be a problem?" Lindsay asks.

Jake's still wiping his eyes, and he can't talk. He shakes his head vigorously. "Too. Hot."

"Chief is pretty hot. Are you intimidated by his abs?" Lindsay asks. "Because they are delicious."

Jake coughs again, and his eyes are still streaming tears.

"Or is the food too hot?" Lindsay says innocently. "The fried rice is delicious, too."

I severely underestimated her flirting skills. The girl has potential.

I glance at Jonah. "I hope we're still engaged when the evening's over."

His fork freezes halfway to his mouth. "You're worried that *I'll* break up with *you* tonight?"

I shrug. "Most guys do, after they meet Chief."

Our eyes meet, and the intensity in his gaze rivets me. A grin lifts one side of his mouth. "We're good, girlfriend. I've already met him." His mouth closes on the forkful of food, and I'm fascinated by the movement of his lips.

I don't know what spice is in this food, but I'm feeling the heat, too.

We finish dinner and Jonah takes the dessert with us to the salon. He cradles the cannoli in one arm and drapes the other around me.

The salon looks like someone's garage converted into a beauty parlor. We stop a few feet from the entrance. Jonah's voice is low and gravelly. "Why would I break up with you tonight? I barely made it to Step Five, and this is my favorite part."

He leans in for a kiss, but it's awkward because he's holding a tray of cannoli between us. I step sideways and the tray jostles. It's too dangerous, and Lindsay's not around to hold the tray of dessert for us.

Colleen didn't have enough spots for her. Fitting three extra trims into an hour was pushing it.

Jake whistles sharply. "Hey, lover boy." He opens the door. "Let's go. Seven o'clock."

We enter the garage/beauty salon, and there's room for six salon chairs. A huge plasma screen TV dominates one end, and posters of One Direction members cover another wall.

Jonah gives the cannoli to a short woman with gray hair and reaches out to shake Chief's hand. "Good to see you again."

Chief nods.

Jonah's hand rests on my shoulder, and then this guy who supposedly can't stand PDA is running his hands up and down my back. He must be nervous despite what he said.

I still his hands. "Let's get a picture."

Chief takes off his coat. "Sure thing, Sarge."

Jake won't budge. He glances between me and Chief. "Why?"

"It's a tradition," I say, and push Jonah over toward Chief. Jake joins them. "Lindsay is right. We need a *before* picture."

I text the picture to Mrs. Butler. She doesn't reply, which is unusual.

The owner, Colleen, lets us sit in the unused chairs while we wait for our turns. A couple other women wander in. I recognize them from the Christmas tree lighting. They look different without their tiaras, but the Sugar Mamas are gathering at the salon. Every chair is filled as well as a worn couch near the plasma TV. A radio station plays Christmas music in the background.

It looks like potluck night. I see Chief's homemade hummus and a bag of pita bread. The Sugar Mamas are laying out veggies and dip and a fruit tray. My chocolate chip cannolis go quickly.

"Welcome, boys." Colleen switches on her hot pink clippers and buzzes the sides of Chief's head. She nods toward the women at the back of the room. "That's Deb. Rose. Ingrid. Dory."

I settle back for the show.

"Colleen made her famous gingersnaps," Deb says. "So, I brought some fruit. I get enough sweets during the day." She's tall and slender and doesn't look like she eats any desserts, but I guess she owns a bakery.

"And bread." Ingrid's version of bread is some intricate twist with cinnamon swirls, and I can't wait to try it.

"Don't be modest," Deb says. "It's Swedish cinnamon-cardamon bread with orange glaze."

Jake immediately goes over and rips off a piece.

"And vegetables." I think that one is Rose. She seems like the motherly type who would make sure we all get our celery before we eat the cannoli.

One of the women pulls some knitting needles out of her bag. She's got long white hair woven into a braid. "The apples are from the Palmers' orchard, just past the Christmas tree farm."

"Quite a crowd. How often do you come here?" Jake yells over the noise of the clippers.

Chief answers from the salon chair. "Every two weeks. When's the last time you got your hair cut?"

Jake looks at Jonah. "March?"

165

I meet Chief's eyes. This is going to be better than usual.

Colleen clicks her tongue. "You should be in here every four weeks. Six weeks at the most."

"They're not married." Chief folds his arms across his chest. "Bachelors."

I snort. "As if you're not also a bachelor."

"I'm a bachelor who builds model trains for a museum and runs a railroad and has a life," Chief replies. "I have to maintain my image."

"I maintain my image." Jake runs a hand through his curls. "Wild and free."

Colleen glances at him, then switches off the clippers and brushes them off. "Wild?" She scoffs. "Being a bachelor is no excuse for shaggy hair." She selects a pair of sharp scissors and begins to trim Chief's high top.

"High and tight," he says. "Fade a little on the edges."

Chief talks nonstop about various styles of flat tops, shaved heads, mohawks, and high tops. His haircut is over in fifteen minutes. The twins aren't nervous yet. *Rookies.* They don't know he is talking about those hairstyles for a reason.

When he's done, he turns to Jonah. "How about a little bet?"

Jonah leaves his chair. "Sure."

The Sugar Mamas settle into the couch to watch. "This should be good. My money's on Chief," Rose says.

Deb smiles. "I'll take that bet. The new guys might take him."

Dory keeps knitting, but her eyes are fixed on the show in front of her, not her needles.

Chief stands with his hands behind his back and his legs shoulder's width apart. His usual intimidation stance. "Push-ups. Winner picks the losers' hair style."

Jonah shrugs off his jacket and rolls up his sleeves. *Hello, muscles.* I haven't seen them since he lent me his hoodie. I need to talk to him about wearing t-shirts instead of collared shirts. *Curse you, Winter, and your long-sleeved shirts.*

Jake's got his coat off, and his t-shirt stretches across washboard abs, too. "Prepare to shave your head, bro."

The twins flank Chief. There's barely enough room in the middle of Colleen's salon for three men to do push-ups.

"Pass the popcorn," one of the Sugar Mamas says.

Colleen folds her arms and smiles expectantly, and I feel a twinge of guilt. It's so unfair. "Last chance to back out."

But they're holding their positions on the floor with their legs straight and arms perfectly bent. I start recording on my phone. "On your mark. Don't say I didn't warn you. Go!"

Chief barks out the numbers, and his push-ups are crisp. "One. Two. Three." He keeps going. Jake drops out at eighty-seven. Jonah's still with him at a hundred. They both slow down at a hundred and twenty-five. Most of my boyfriends were gone well before now.

*One hundred fifty.* Jonah's not watching Chief. He's hitting his mark on every number.

Now I'm *really* curious what kind of muscles are under that button-up shirt.

*One-hundred seventy-five.* They're both breathing hard, and their arms shake as they slowly push up. Chief's barely breathing out the numbers.

"One. Ninety. Eight." Down. Up.

"One. Ninety. Nine." Down. Up.

"Two. Hundred." Chief is down.

Jonah's up. His arms are jelly, but he's waiting for the count, so I say it for Chief.

"Two hundred and one."

Jonah does one more push-up.

And then it happens. Chief says the words I've never heard before. "I give."

# Chapter Twenty

Jonah drops to the floor, and the Sugar Mamas clap and cheer. I rush over to the table in the back and grab three water bottles. Jonah rolls onto his back, and I hand him the first water bottle. Chief gets the second, and Jake gets the third.

Jonah pushes off the floor and brushes off his hands. I grab his arm and lead him over to Colleen's chair. "Awesome job. You must be exhausted."

He nods and collapses into the hot pink salon chair. Chief staggers into another. "You put up a good fight. You, too, Jake."

He grunts. "Thanks."

Jonah wipes his brow with his t-shirt, and a sliver of washboard abs flashes above his jeans. I'm insanely proud of him because I know how hard Chief works to stay in shape.

Also, I want to kiss Jonah's face off, but he still hasn't caught his breath from the push-ups, so I don't.

Dory picks up a remote. "Almost time." The others fill their plates. Evidently the push-up show is over, and their other show is about to begin.

Colleen takes one of her hot pink towels and wipes his brow and neck. When he's not sweaty anymore, she looks at Chief. "So, what hairstyle?"

Chief takes a long drink of water. "He's the boss tonight, C."

"Right. Habit." Colleen runs her fingers through Jonah's hair. "I like it long, but not this long. Let's get it off the neck and go for the styled messy look."

Jonah glances at me. "Girlfriend?"

Colleen finger combs his hair. "I thought they were bachelors."

A smile breaks across Jonah's face. "I'm engaged. Jake's single."

"Hey." Jake grabs the towel that Colleen offers him and wipes his face and neck. "No need to rub it in."

I walk over and examine Jonah's dark hair. It only makes his brown eyes warmer and deeper. "I agree that the curls should come off the neck, but what if you keep the top a little long?"

Colleen nods and begins to trim Jonah's hair.

*The Bachelor* begins playing on the enormous TV. "Reruns," Collen whispers. "If you know what happens, don't tell Chief."

One of the other Sugar Mamas catches my eye. "He's got twenty more seasons to go."

No Drama Chief watches *Bachelor* reruns with a group of sixty-year-old women every week? He's just lost to Jonah, or I would tease him.

Jake leans over, and he's using his *Let's Make A Deal* voice. "So, how does this work?"

Chief grins. "Jonah picks your new hairstyle."

Jake relaxes into a chair. "Good save, bro."

Jonah meets Chief's eye across the room. His voice is low enough to be heard, but not loud enough to interrupt the show in the background. "Lindsay thought you'd look good bald."

Jake doesn't seem worried, and I wonder if he should be.

"Help yourself," Colleen says, so I get some hummus and carrots, and a couple gingerbread cookies. It's a weird combination, but the sesame-tahini and ginger kind of work together.

I load a plate and take it over to Jonah. I make sure the cannoli doesn't touch the hummus, and he eats it first.

I stand beside the salon chair while Colleen trims the curls at the bottom. She really knows what she's doing. She trims the hair at an angle, lifting each piece in her hot pink comb before chipping the edges. If he was good-looking before, he's in a whole new league now. He's going to look the part of a celebrity chef when he hits the show.

Jonah glances over at me and dips a cookie in the hummus. "Thanks."

I realize I'm staring. "Sure." I wander back to my own chair and sit next to Chief again.

He leans over. "I'm fine with it."

"With what?"

"With you marrying him."

I've got hummus breath, so I pull back a little. "Because of the push-ups?"

"Because he's cool." Chief steals a carrot off my plate. "You know we've been texting, right?"

I set down my plate. "No." I grab myself a water bottle and watch Colleen spritz Jonah's hair. She's an artist at work, and he's her masterpiece. "Jonah doesn't volunteer a lot of information. He's private."

Chief grins. "Need-to-know basis. What have I been telling you for years?"

"That you don't need to know about my love life."

Chief nods. "Exactly, but he's different than your other boyfriends. Not your usual type."

I take a long drink. I can't tell whether Jake and Jonah are listening, and it's weird to be talking like this with Chief. "We had a different start to our relationship than usual."

"Whatever you did, keep it up. It's working."

Chief never likes my boyfriends. "You like him because he doesn't talk."

"Exactly. You talk enough for both of you."

I'm disappointed because I finally found a boyfriend that Chief likes, and he's temporary.

Colleen runs her hands through Jonah's hair with some magical concoction of styling products. It's perfectly messy, but every hair is strategically placed. I take a picture for myself. That's going on *my* lock screen.

Chief raises his voice. "Alright. Jake's turn."

"You have to move to New York with us," he says to Colleen. "We need you for every show we're ever going to be on."

Colleen chuckles. "Charmer. Wait until you see *your* haircut before you say that."

I drag another carrot through the hummus. "New York?"

Jonah settles into the chair on the other side of me, and I wish there was a couch so he wasn't so far away. This is one of those moments when I'm happy to act like we're a couple. Be a couple. Whatever we are.

Jake perches on the chair that Jonah just vacated. "The new restaurant we're opening. New York."

"I thought it was in Boston."

Jake shakes his head. "Time to see if we can make it in the real world without Daddy's help."

"But he's still funding the whole thing?"

Jonah's mouth ticks up ironically. "We're going to prove how independent we are by using his money to open a restaurant that he co-owns with us—"

"—but not in the city where he lives." Jake grins as he finishes the sentence for his twin.

My heart drops. "I'm buying a townhome in Boston. I've already put down earnest money, and I close on the loan any day."

Jonah shakes his head. "You don't have to keep it."

Jake squirms in his chair across the parlor. "Stay there after you get married and come back to visit. Rent it out. Vrbo or something. No biggie. Real estate is a great investment."

But that's not the only reason I can't move to New York. Tommy Fuller lives there.

"Sorry to interrupt." Colleen looks at Jonah. "What cut for this guy?"

He shrugs. "I defer to Chief." But Chief is too engrossed in the show to notice.

Jake clamps his hands on his long hair and raises his voice. "Chief, you wouldn't ask her to shave these pretty curls."

"Flat top," Chief says without glancing over. "Blend it with his beard. Keep the curls on top."

Colleen wraps a hot pink cape around him and grabs the clippers, and Jake relents. His shoulder-length hair disappears in minutes. "I'll never forget this, Joey. Never."

"It's cleaner, Jakey. You won't need a hairnet." But Jonah shifts in his chair and I wonder if he's really okay with doing this to his brother.

Chief seems to notice the movement, too. He glances at Jonah, then jerks his head toward me. "How is she?"

I'm right between them. "I can hear you."

Jonah answers anyway. "She thought I'd break up with her tonight."

Chief settles back in his pink salon chair like it's a cotton candy throne. "She always expects the worst. At least you know the warning signs now."

"Cannoli."

"Lasagna."

They both laugh again. "Hey, am I that predictable?"

Jonah nods. "You were so nice today that even Jake picked up on it."

Chief laughs.

"I'm always nice." I've never heard either of these guys talk like this, and especially not about me. I'm used to the no-drama workout zone, not this bromance chatter.

"How about you?" Chief asks Jake. "Who are you dating?"

Jake sighs and tells Chief his entire dating history. "First there was Hannah. Then Julie, Scarlet, Cookie, Joann, and Tianna."

Chief stares at him. "And right now?"

"I wasn't done. Then there was Becky, then Riley. We were on and off for a couple years. Kennedy was the last one, and I haven't dated since..."

"Danny got divorced?" I guess.

He looks at his hands. "Yeah."

That explains why he hasn't been trying to get serious about asking Lindsay out.

The Sugar Mamas and I aren't even pretending to watch *The Bachelor* rerun anymore. I eat another gingerbread cookie and wipe the hummus off my plate with the last carrot, then I get a clean plate for the cannoli.

"Can't fault your reasoning," Chief says gruffly. "Divorce changes a man's perspective on love."

Colleen has cut the curls, shaved Jake's head all the way up to the crown, tapered the cut toward his neck, and blended the stubble into his beard. The curls are still long on top, and it works. It's fairly sexy, but I'm not going to tell Jonah that.

She's trimmed Jake's beard, too, so it's barely there, but has a nice sharp edge to it. The whole look is clean and tight, but a little wild, too, like Jake.

Jonah studies him for a minute. "It's got a Michael Voltaggio vibe."

"That's good," I reassure Jake.

"I'm not a bad boy," he complains. "No tattoos. I'm going for the nice guy image." His eyes narrow as he looks at his twin's haircut. "More like Jonah's."

I sense some tension, so I jump in. "It's hot. Women will like it."

Jonah runs his hand through his hair, tousling it on accident and making it look even better. "You think Jake is hot?"

I shift in my chair and give his new hairstyle my full attention. "Sure. You know you guys look a lot alike."

Jonah's brow furrows. Jake rubs the bare sides of his head and stares into the mirror, looking like someone killed his puppy.

I put a hand on Jonah's arm. "Jake is fine if you like blond hair, but I like dark hair."

Colleen runs her concoction of styling products through Jake's hair, and the cut looks amazing.

Chief is the one who helps the most. "Lindsay likes blond guys. She likes me, after all."

Jake takes in Chief's larger, more muscled chest and his taller frame. "Does she?"

Chief shrugs. "Yeah."

"We need an after picture." I motion to the twins and Chief. "Together."

"No." Jake tears the hot pink cape off his neck, then slips his phone out of his pocket. "One of me alone for Linz." He won't go anywhere near Jonah or Chief.

Colleen, Chief, and Jonah crowd together in front of the One Direction posters. I get a few pictures, and they settle back into their seats. Jake snaps a selfie on his own. "Hello, social media. Meet your new hairdo."

I'm sure he's also texting the picture to Lindsay. I text our picture to Mrs. Butler, and again, no reply.

"Mom loves my new look." Jake holds up the phone. "Lindsay didn't respond yet."

Chief holds up his phone. "She likes *my* haircut."

A muscle twitches in Jake's jaw.

"Why didn't your mom respond to my text?" I ask.

Jake smirks. "She's still weirded out that you're friends with Chief. We all are."

"I'm not," Jonah says aggressively. "He's cool."

"Thanks," Chief says. "I already gave her my blessing to marry you, so we're good. And just so you know, Jake, Lindsay's my friend. That's all. I'm not looking for anything more with anybody."

Jake scowls as Colleen sweeps up the remnants of his curls from the floor around him. "Cool."

Colleen motions to me. "Your turn, Brie."

I glance up from my phone. Still no text. "I didn't know I was getting a haircut."

Chief barks out the order. "Jonah's choice."

Colleen unwinds the space buns I usually wear. It's either that or a ponytail. My hair drops down to my shoulders and a little past it. "I didn't bet anyone."

Jonah stares at me with my hair down, and I realize he's never seen it like this. I've never worn a dress or tried to impress him. Have I even worn makeup?

His mouth lifts in a smile. "I wouldn't want to change anything about your hair anyway."

Chief points at Jake. "And that's why your brother is getting married, and you're still single."

I'm worried that Jake will get angrier when Chief compares him to his twin, but the opposite happens. Jake's shoulders droop, and he rubs his neck. "Yeah. No, you're right. Jonah's rocking this relationship, and I'm scared, man. My brother got divorced, and I'm not gonna lie. It was all on him. He totally neglected her. He thinks his wife cheated on him because he was gone so much, but he doesn't even know. I shut down after that. I can see that happening to me because I work such long hours. I'd come home from the restaurant some night at two a.m. and find another man in my wife's bed."

"I'm scared, too," Jonah admits. "Brie would never do that, but there are plenty of other ways it can go wrong."

"But you don't let your fears stop you." Jake fiddles with a loose leather strap on the edge of his chair. "Respect. Props to you and Brie. I know I'm a chicken. Free-range. Whatever. I like to flirt, but I never follow through. I don't want to end up divorced like Danny."

Someone's handing out roses on the screen, and I wonder if we've been at Colleen's salon that long. I chime in to steer the conversation away from cheating wives. I want to spare Chief some painful memories. "Who isn't scared? That's normal when you're dating."

But Chief has never given excuses or avoided hard conversations. He leans forward. "My wife found herself a new boyfriend while I was in Afghanistan. Brie went over and found her in bed with him. That's stopped me from dating for the last two years."

The room goes silent. The buzz of the TV plays quietly behind us. Someone shuts it off.

Chief's face shutters, and his emotions are locked tight behind a wall. "Call me crazy, but I thought marriage meant you stopped dating other people."

Jake's hand freezes on the armchair. "Sorry, man."

"Nope. Better this way. If she's like that, I don't want her."

Jake nods. "That's fair."

Chief looks at me. "I found my own family in the Air Force. I might not be married, but I have people I love, and we watch out for each other. Brie saved me that night."

I make a heart with my hands. "Love you, bro." But I lost a dear friend the night he lost his wife.

Chief flashes back a heart sign. "Right, sis." He's all business now. The master sergeant again. "I can't give you advice that I don't live, Jake, but maybe Jonah and Brie can."

I don't want that kind of pressure. I'm about to admit that I'm a huge liar and the whole thing is phony. "Jake doesn't need any more advice, especially not from us. We're not experts." I try to catch Jonah's eye.

But he jumps in anyway. "You're not Danny and you're not going to pick a Patricia."

Poor Danny. He wasn't joking when he said he was the black sheep in his family.

Jake is still staring into the mirror ahead of him. He runs his hands through the new, short hair and feels his beard. "It's arrogant to believe that I can be someone's whole world and mean everything to them." It seems like he's accusing Jonah, but also confessing his darkest fears, and I don't know what to do with this side of Jake that's both vulnerable and angry at the same time.

His defenses are crumbling. He's not the cocky flirt I've seen. He's as insecure as the rest of us.

It's my turn to be open and vulnerable, since Jonah has no response for his brother.

Colleen's done with my trim and heats the curling iron. Yeah. It's hot pink, like the rest of the salon. She's a combination of Barbie and Mrs. Claus, and this salon is like *Legally Blonde's* version of the North Pole.

I talk in theoretical terms. "Jonah wouldn't ever be my whole world. I would have you and Lindsay and my job, haircuts with Colleen, Luke and your aunties and cousins, and maybe I'd get a cat, and I would still work out with Chief. No one can fill all of your needs, and you don't have to be their whole world."

Jonah watches me intensely. I'm pretty sure he noticed my use of the hypothetical terms.

Jake didn't. He leans forward in his chair and grows animated. He still seems upset about his haircut, and now he's angry that anyone else is happy when he's not. "Then what's the point of having a relationship? Why fall in love? Why even try when it's so hard?"

Once again, my temper flares. "So you have someone to turn to, someone who will always listen to you, someone who knows you better than anyone else—"

Jake interrupts. "I have that."

I am paralyzed because Colleen is using the curling iron and I'm afraid to move, so I can't turn my head to look at him. I catch his smug expression in the mirror instead. "Someone who's not your mom or your dad or one of your brothers."

His face falls. "Touché."

"Hey, Jake, love means having someone who belongs to me and feels like my whole world, even though we both belong to other people, too. A healthy relationship would be an entire solar system. I'd be the earth, and they'd be the sun, pulling me into their orbit, and I'd have an entire galaxy of friends and family circling around us."

"Hovering." Jonah glances at me. "Family hovers more than it circles or orbits." When no one speaks, he adds, "Also, kissing is good."

Jake glances at him and grudgingly agrees. "Yeah. I like kissing."

Collen's curled my hair so that I look unusually feminine. One of the Sugar Mamas smiles and gives me a thumbs-up. Rose, maybe? Chief stands, and I know it's time to leave. He's past his ability to talk about relationships. "Thanks, Colleen."

Jonah stands and digs his wallet out of a pocket. "How much?" He thumbs through the bills. "Will a hundred cover me and Brie?"

Colleen's eyes widen. "I don't know what you pay in Boston, but we don't charge that much in Sugar Creek. Thanks. That's really generous."

I stand and reach for my jacket, but Jonah strides across the room in a few steps and grabs my coat. He stuffs his wallet into a back pocket with one hand, then faces me, holding open my coat.

"You're hovering," I say with a smile, as I slip my arms into the waiting warmth.

"Pulling you into my orbit." He wraps me into a hug and rests his chin on my head. "You look heavenly." He presses a kiss to the top of my head, and I turn and wrap my arms around his waist.

"Ugh," Jake complains. "I don't even know you anymore, bro. How cheesy can you be?"

Jonah grins. "I'm dating Brie."

Jake groans. "Stop with the dad jokes. You're not even married yet."

I turn my head to rest my cheek on Jonah's chest, and I catch sight of Jake and Chief both watching us with heavy expressions. "Do you hate us, or do you hate love?" I joke.

"You're blinding me with your sunshine." Jake slaps a hundred-dollar bill on the counter. "For me." He slams another hundred down. "For Chief."

Chief nods. "Thanks."

Colleen smiles at Jake. "You're a good kid. Come back anytime."

"Thanks for the haircut, Colleen." He grabs the empty tray we brought the cannoli on. "Can you two stop revolving around each other so we can go home?"

"Someone's a black hole," Jonah mutters. Jake slugs him in the chest.

We follow him out to the SUV and drive home in silence.

This engagement feels more and more real every day. I've stopped thinking of reasons to break up with Jonah and started enjoying our time together, but I'm buying a townhouse in Boston, and apparently, he is moving to New York. I've already started the loan and made a down payment. This will never work. I can't back out.

Neither can Jonah. He's worked on his new restaurant with Jake for months, and now this engagement is straining their relationship. Tension's been building between him and Jake—his brother, his best friend, and his business partner.

And somehow, it all culminated tonight.

I've jeopardized everything that matters most to Jonah with one haircut.

# Chapter Twenty-One

I NEED to apologize to Jake about that haircut. He stole Jonah's Red Sox beanie and hasn't stopped wearing it all day.

I don't think Lindsay has even seen Jake's new 'do, other than the photo he texted her. I can tell he's trying to be cool, but the tension between him and Jonah is obvious.

I mean, Jonah has no Red Sox gear left, so the man is a little cranky. I've been wearing his Red Sox hoodie anytime I get cold in the cabin, and now Jake decided that the beanie belongs to him.

I can tell Jake's not used to losing to his brother. He keeps throwing out comments like, "Two hundred and one, huh?" or "Are you working out without me?" but the laugh that accompanies it doesn't really make it funny.

By the time we leave for our Friday night date—Mrs. Butler's idea, ice skating—I don't think Jake and Jonah have done much more than grunt all day. Jake's backhanded compliments don't count. I mean, the man is trying, but it's falling flat.

They cook lunch and dinner for us, but they write lists and notes and use strict times, so there isn't much conversation.

Jake jams a black wool beanie on his head as we leave for the ice skating rink. "How long is your romance going to be fledgling?"

I smile at him. "Tired of helping us nurture it already?"

He jingles the keys in his palm. "I wouldn't mind a quiet night in front of the fireplace for a change."

I glance at Lindsay. Not only am I getting in between Jonah and his twin, now I'm killing her chances with the guy she's been crushing on for three years. "Let's make it quick, text your mom a photo, then come back and chill."

Jake shrugs. "You're the boss."

I ignore the barb in his tone. Jonah is smart enough not to respond, too, and his brother doesn't have anyone to needle. Jake pushes the door open and sighs. "Let's get this nurturing over with, lovebirds."

My legs are still exhausted from my morning workout with Chief as we drive through Sugar Creek. We turn right after the railroad tracks, drive a far-see, and arrive at the Christmas tree farm again. There are Edison lights strung around the rink and firepits around the edge. The pond is nestled among rows of neatly tended pine and spruce trees. The evergreens grow at different heights, waiting to be harvested another year.

The smell of fir trees tickles my nose again, and wood smoke rises from the firepits. I love this place. The scent on the winter air is like lumberjack cologne, except it's real. I grab Jonah. "Let's get a selfie here."

A grin tugs at one side of his mouth. "Sure thing, girlfriend."

He wraps his arm around my shoulders and snaps the shot with evergreens in the background and the frozen pond to one side.

Jake rubs his gloved hands together, and Lindsay shuffles her feet. "I can take the picture for you."

I hand her my phone. "Do you want a picture, too?"

Lindsay and Jake both shake their heads, and Jake tugs at the beanie on his practically bald head. I text the picture of me and Jonah to Mrs. Butler, who forwards it to the entire Butlers' pantry of aunts and cousins.

**Me**: Ice skating.
**Mrs. Butler**: (heart emojis) Miss you, sweetie. Have you set a date yet?
**Aunt Doyle**: Olivia's coming home for Christmas.
**Emily**: Can't wait to see you again, Brie. Bring Chief.

I realize that everyone still thinks I'm coming to the Christmas dinner, but Jonah still has "break up" scheduled on his personal calendar. I slip my phone in my coat pocket and zip it up without responding. No, we haven't set a date.

We're never going to set one.

Jake and Lindsay find a different bench, and Jonah slides next to me. He drops a pair of ice skates in front of me and starts lacing up his own. By the expert way he tugs the laces and the way his thumb automatically tugs at the strings, I'm pretty sure he played ice hockey in school.

I tug at my laces and tie a quick bow. Is that how people put on ice skates?

Jonah's hand wraps around my ankle. "Too loose." He kneels in front of me and tightens the laces until the skates feel like prison. My ankles have committed some offense, and Jonah is sentencing them to a night of torture.

His hand slides from the laces to the leather at the top of my skate. His thumb rubs my lower leg as his fingers feel the fit on my foot. "Have you ever skated before?"

"No."

His rich, brown eyes zip to mine. "Go ahead and stand."

I wobble on the plastic guards and drop a hand to his shoulder to steady myself. His fingers are still testing my foot and ankle inside the skate, but his thumb keeps skimming my calf.

"How's that?" he asks and looks up, eyes twinkling. "It feels good to me."

I grin back. "Thanks. It's great." Electricity shoots up my leg and makes my stomach do cartwheels. The good kind.

He stands, and I grab the nearby railing to keep my balance while I slip the plastic guards off the blades.

Jonah straightens on his skates and holds out his hands. "I got you."

We step onto the ice, and I'm clutching Jonah on one side and clinging to the railing on the other. We slowly make our way to the ice skating rink, and then there's nothing to do but let go.

Jonah glides on the ice and tugs me along with him. "My mom is a genius. Best date idea ever."

I grunt. "For you."

A smile breaks across his entire face. "Yep."

Jake and Lindsay skate around the rink effortlessly. Next time they pass us, Lindsay slows down.

I glance up from the ice for a second. "You're like a human Zamboni," I say. "Thanks for clearing a path in front of me."

Lindsay skates backward to face me. "I took ice skating lessons for a few years."

"Of course you did. You probably competed, didn't you?"

Lindsay blushes, then does a perfect double axel and returns to me. "Yeah."

I take tiny little steps on my skates. "I pity you rich people. You have no idea what it's like to suffer."

She laughs, but Jake's face darkens a little before they zip away.

"I've got to talk to him." I risk a look at Jonah. "Jake hates me, and it's eating at me."

I'm a little steadier now, but not by much. Jonah wraps an arm around my waist, and something delicious tingles up and down my spine as he says, "I don't want to share you yet."

He pulls me closer, and my stomach does more cartwheels. We slowly make our way around the rink. Rows of lights twinkle around the edges. My phone buzzes with texts from the cousins, and I ignore it. They know I'm on a date.

I won't set a date, but I'm on one. *That's as good as it gets, Mrs. Butler.*

Jonah slips his gloved fingers between mine. "Steady?"

I feel a little daring, so I nod and straighten. His hand is my only lifeline as we skate together. My ankles scream at me in the prison boots, and four-year-olds pass me, but I laugh. "This could be fun."

Jonah lets go. "It is when I'm with you."

My heart melts a little despite the cold.

He yells, "Jake," and his twin slows down. I didn't even see him coming behind us. "Switch partners?"

"Why?" Jake asks.

"Because we're all friends here," Jonah says. He bends down and says softly, "I'll give you two plenty of time to talk."

Jake holds out his hand, and I take it.

# Chapter Twenty-Two

JONAH PIVOTS so he's skating backward, and pretty soon he and Lindsay carve a path away from me. They look good together: people who grew up the same way—in private schools, with parents who took time to celebrate the holidays or go on trips.

*We never had the money*, Mom says. *It wasn't just the time.*

But my friends all went ice skating. Their parents had the time and the money, and they didn't have anything more than us. I think my mom didn't have the emotional energy for anyone other than herself, and that's what I haven't forgiven her for.

For not caring enough about me when I still miss her so much.

"Hey, earth to Brie. You okay?"

I'm standing still. "Sorry, Jake." I start skating, and I wobble.

His grip on my hand tightens. "First time?"

I almost go down. "Is it that obvious?" Jake's arm shoots out to catch me, then he leaves it around my shoulders to keep me upright. It's really awkward. I don't want to fall, but I don't want to put my arm around his waist.

Jake glances over. "You okay?"

I nod. "I'm fine. I'm also sorry about your haircut."

He blows out a long breath. "Wow. Yeah. Okay, I'm not going to lie. I'm still upset with Jonah."

"I know. I hate that our engagement is coming between you two."

We don't get very far around the rink because I'm new at this.

Jake pivots and cuts through the crowd. "Let's take a breather, yeah?"

"Yeah." The conversation is off to a rough start. It's about as successful as my attempts at ice skating, which is to say—not successful.

He lets go of my shoulders and skates ahead, toward the edge of the frozen pond. He shakes out his arm, and I wonder if he felt as weird as I did a second ago. I'm watching him from behind when I go down. *Hard.*

Jake turns around. "Brie!" He skates back and puts an arm beneath my shoulders. "Are you okay?"

"I don't know." I rub my bottom. The ice is hard. Really hard.

I catch Jonah's eye, and he and Lindsay slow down on the next pass. "Tough fall." Jonah straightens. "You're in good hands, girlfriend. Thanks, Jake." He smiles at Lindsay, and they skate away like pros.

But he looks back at his brother's arm around me, and his jaw flexes.

I accept Jake's hand and put my weight on him as he helps me to my feet. His arm steadies me, and this feels a lot like hugging. I have to wrap an arm around Jake's waist to stay upright. Once he's sure I'm standing, Jake practically carries me off the pond and back to the benches. He unlaces my boots, and he has one hand on my leg above the boot the whole time. Again, *awkward.* He's not looking at me when he asks in a gruff voice, "How are you?"

"Sore."

He shakes his head, and I think he's mad at himself.

"Hey, it's not your fault that I've never skated." I put a hand on his shoulder to steady myself as he tugs at the laces.

A movement catches my eye. I glance over, and Jonah and Lindsay wave from the rink. I take my hand off Jake's shoulder.

"I can do the rest."

He looks up as he tugs off the first skate. "You sure?"

I struggle with the knot on the second skate.

"I got this." Jake pushes my hand aside, and his fingers brush mine as he expertly unties the knot.

I tug at the too-tight skate. "Thanks."

"Sure." He slides onto the bench beside me. I loosen my skate and finally pull it off. We both put our shoes back on.

"It feels great to be on solid ground again," I say.

Jake rubs the back of his neck. "Want a hot chocolate while we wait for Jonah and Lindsay?"

I nod. "You sure love your bland milk chocolate for someone who sells gourmet dark chocolate basil lavender cracked pepper stuff."

He laughs. "Jonah comes up with the flavors. I'm the pretty face of our brand."

We get in line, and I'm glad that I fell, even though I really am sore. "I want to be your friend, Jake."

He smirks at me. "And I want to be your favorite brother."

Someone gives us cups of creamy milk chocolate cocoa, and we find a bench. I bump his shoulder. "Maybe you can tell me more about rich people who know how to suffer. Your life looks good from the outside."

Jake stretches beside me and kicks out his legs. "It's complicated."

I give him my best stare. "Try me." I kick out my tiny legs. They barely reach the ground.

He sets his cup on the frozen snow and considers me. "You really want to know?"

I spin my cup to dig a hole in the snow and set down my cocoa, too. "Yeah."

Jake shrugs. "Yeah, I know how to suffer. My twin is loyal to you instead of me, and he's lying to me. I can tell he's keeping secrets for you, and that bugs me. We've never had secrets between us." He arches an eyebrow, as if challenging me.

"That's the worst you've got? I've got a whole list of first world problems that could beat that."

Jake laughs. "Poor you. My life is way worse. Jonah chooses you over me *every* time. It's not just last night." He gets serious and his green eyes bore into me. "I'm mad that my brother is moving on without me, and I'm getting left behind. I'm scared of being alone when he gets married, and I'll have no one."

I drink my cocoa and set it down. Across the way, Jonah and Lindsay are getting off the rink. Neither of them looks happy.

Jake is sitting on the bench with his arm behind me, and we're really close. His eyes probe mine, waiting for an answer.

I shift a little to one side, but the benches are narrow. "I'm sorry. You're right. You don't know everything about Jonah. You have no idea what's been happening between me and Jonah for the last three months because he doesn't spend every single second with you, and he's not going to talk about our *alone time*. That's got to be hard, but it can't be the first time one of you had a girl-friend and the other didn't."

Jake bumps my shoulder. "So, those early mornings at the office?"

I grin. "Yeah."

"It's just that I'm usually the one with the girlfriend, and he's not. I'm not used to him being the one who's winning or has the upper hand or whatever. I mean, he's engaged, and Lindsay won't give me the time of day."

Finally, the whole truth. "It's not a competition. Your parents love you, too."

Jake's voice gets rough and soft at the same time. "I see what you and Jonah have, and I want that, too."

"So, go get it." I nod toward Lindsay. She has her skates unlaced. She pulls the boot off gracefully in one try. "All you have to do is get over yourself. Stop trying to be the sun and expecting her to fall at your feet and revolve around you. How about you let *your* world be rocked by *her*?"

Jake leans back on the bench. "I'm not talking about this with you. That pep talk last night with Chief was awkward enough."

Jonah's jamming his feet into his shoes as fast as he can, so our talk is almost over. "Look, there doesn't have to be any weirdness between us. I appreciate how open and vulnerable you were last night."

Jake actually grunts. "You want me to articulate? About emotions?"

I laugh. "Yeah. It's not impossible. Look, I don't care if you almost asked me out. Jonah doesn't either. I hate seeing you and your brother like this because of me."

*Especially because it's not real*, I think to myself. I glance at Lindsay, who looks betrayed by me. Every one of her girlfriends has gone after the guy she likes. "Lindsay would open up to you, if you'd take a chance and be real with her."

Jake grabs our cups and stands. I follow him over to a trash can. "You don't get it. Jonah always picks me, and for the first time in my life, he's choosing someone else. I'm losing my twin. It had to happen sometime, but I never expected it to hurt so much."

Jonah strides over, and Lindsay isn't far behind.

"You don't have to lose him. You can still be close, and you can still find your own happily ever after. Can we forget the haircut and be friends?"

"This is about way more than a haircut," Jake mutters, "but yeah. I hope I just permanently cemented *Most Favorite Brother* status with all that vulnerability crap."

Jonah arrives and glances between us. "You guys ready to go?"

Jake folds his arms across his chest. "Sure. Yep. Brie loves me best of all the brothers now, and we can't wait to get home for more bonding."

Jonah tucks me into his side protectively. "Except me, of course."

"Of course." Jake crumples the cups and tosses them in the trash.

"Enough sarcasm, Jake," I say.

He opens his wallet and hands me a twenty. "I didn't mean it like that."

I unfold the bill, running my fingers along its creases. "Give it to Lindsay. You graduated from my Bro Fund, and I'm promoting you to hers."

Jake shoves his wallet back in his pocket and laughs. "Or I flunked, and I'm hopeless."

Lindsay arrives. "I'm ready to go back and watch something on TV now."

I hand her the twenty, and she frowns at me.

"You're in charge of my Bro Fund now," he mutters.

She stares at the twenty with a slightly confused smile. "What did you do?"

I nod at him, like *This is your chance*, and he draws a deep breath, faces Lindsay, and unloads without warning. "I just bared my soul to Brie about all my emotional wounds, and how I feel bad that my twin is moving ahead with his life, blah blah, skip the sob story details. I called it a bunch of crap." Jake waves his hand around casually, but I know he's hurting.

Well, it was a good start.

He folds his arms across his chest, and of course that only turns him into this sexy, brooding hottie, but he has no idea. He glares at Lindsay. "I could really use some TV to distract me from sulking." He opens his wallet and hands her another twenty. "I probably owe you for that. For calling it *sulking*."

Lindsay accepts the twenty and slips both bills in her tiny purse. "Okay."

Not the smoothest flirting I've heard from him, if he's trying to set up some snuggling on the couch. Even Jonah feels bad. He puts an arm around his twin's shoulder. "Whoa, dude."

Jake shakes it off. "What? I mess everything up."

"Not everything." Jonah slugs him in the arm.

Jake glances at Lindsay. "Well?"

I shoot him a warning look, but he doesn't pay attention.

She holds out her hand. "I already answered you. I said, *Okay.*"

Jake turns on his smolder now. "I bare my soul, Linz, and all you say is, *Okay?*"

But Lindsay is impervious to smolder. She motions with her hand, and Jake slips another twenty out of his wallet. Lindsay rolls her eyes. "Okay, let's watch the *Great British Baking Show?* You're going to go broke, Jake, if you keep this up."

Jake turns to me with an accusing look. I get it. He opened up emotionally—kind of—and Lindsay didn't respond.

Plus, I resurrected the Bro Fund. Not his night.

I sigh. *Emotion coaching time.* "Lindsay, do you think Jake messes everything up?"

She considers him, and we spend several seconds watching her stare at him. I shiver, and Jonah pulls me closer. I know she doesn't answer questions quickly, so I smile at Lindsay. "Let's walk and talk?"

I loop my arm through hers and motion to Jonah, who nudges Jake. We all head toward the parking lot. I hope that things between me and Jake didn't look as bad as I'm sure they did. Lindsay has every right to be angry or confused right now.

The snow crunches beneath our feet as we weave through a field of evergreens to return to the parking lot. Christmas carols play in the distance. I repeat my question, "So, on a scale of one to always, Lindsay, how much of the time does Jake mess up?"

She glances at the twins behind us. "He doesn't mess anything up. Jake is a successful celebrity chef. He's got a great family. He's always nice to everyone at work. He's usually too hard on himself. Take his new haircut."

Jake unlocks the car with his key fob and opens Lindsay's door. He leans on the door frame. "Am I?"

"The new haircut is really hot, but you keep hiding it." She tugs the beanie off his head. "I get that it's cold tonight, but you shouldn't hide the best parts of yourself. I don't know why you do that. It's like you're afraid to let people see how great you really are, because what if they don't like you, after they know that?"

She runs her fingers through the curls on top, hands him the beanie, and slips in the car. Jake slams the door after her.

I'm standing on the same side of the car, and Jonah's already inside. It's just the two of us outside.

"She gets me." Jake's face contracts with emotion. "I didn't think..." He covers his eyes with one hand.

Jonah pops the door open from inside the car. He's leaning across the backseat bench from the other side, so he's almost flat on the seat. "Hey, girlfriend. I miss you."

Jake uncovers his eyes and scrubs a hand down his face.

"Brie?" Jonah slides across the bench.

"Thanks." I duck inside the car and cuddle next to him. My emotions are all over the place, more slippery than ice, and I can't pin them down.

Jonah tugs me close to him, and his voice tickles my ear. "How did your conversation go?"

"I don't know. Bad, I think."

Jake slides inside and starts the car. He puts the car in reverse, and our eyes meet for a moment. "You're my favorite."

"After me. That goes without saying." Jonah tucks a finger beneath my chin and tilts my face toward him. His voice lowers almost to a whisper. "I hated seeing his arms around you when you fell. That should have been me."

I've never seen jealousy in his eyes, but they flash with heat now. I was worried about Chief, but Jonah is fine with my friendship with my old master sergeant.

But he cares about the way his twin held me on the ice and shared his fears.

I can only think of one way to fix the tension between the brothers, so I put a hand on Jonah's shoulder and whisper in his ear, "We should tell him the truth."

Jonah turns on the bench so quickly that my hand slips onto

the seat. He grabs my fingers with his and cradles my cheek with his other hand. His dark eyes still dance with fire as he lowers his face toward mine. His lips almost move against my own as he whispers back, "I can't do that."

"Why?" I ask breathlessly. The answer is the cooking show. *Work.* Something like that.

"Because then he could date you." Jonah closes the distance between us and presses his lips to mine. He doesn't stop kissing me until we reach the cabins.

# Chapter Twenty-Three

LINDSAY and I talk late into the night and get up early for our workout, then wander through some boutiques on Sugar Creek's Main Street. She finds a hand-knitted scarf for her sister and some toys for her nephews, and I find apple-cider caramels, the world's eighth wonder.

We aren't home for five minutes before Jake slams open the door without knocking. "Hey, Shrimp, are you ready for our date?" He waves a bag of jumbo shrimp as he walks over to the refrigerator and jams various ingredients inside. "I brought dinner. Shrimp for the shrimp."

I roll my eyes. "Like no date has ever done that before."

Jonah pushes through the doorway behind him. "*I'm* her date, not you, and since when do *you* have a nickname for *my* girlfriend?"

There's some weird tension between the twins tonight, and I can't win. If I'm friends with Jake, then I'm disloyal to Jonah. This hypothetical thing is way more work than my real relationships.

"Double date." Jake settles on the couch and drapes an arm across the top. "Right, Linz?"

She freezes on the couch. "What are you talking about?"

Jake leans forward with his elbows on his knees. "Come on. We've watched half of this *Great British* season together. Doesn't that count for anything?"

Never mind. Lindsay *doesn't* know how to flirt. The girl is as gorgeous as they come, but also incredibly clueless. She rifles through the bags from our shopping trip. "You have to ask people out on dates."

Jake stares at her in disbelief. "I'm cooking you dinner, then I'm taking you to the hot springs. How is that *not* a date?"

Lindsay looks away from him and over at Jonah. "I thought you guys were practicing for your *Santa Smack Down* show, then going out to relax."

Jonah goes over to the refrigerator and pokes around. "We are. Head-to-head competition." He glares at Jake. "Come pick a protein, a vegetable, and a spice. We'll have dinner ready in half an hour."

"No. Forty-five minutes." Jake tips his head against the back of the couch. "We don't have sous chefs."

What's with the boys tonight? I shake my head. Lindsay and Jake are never, ever getting together. Jake is stubborn and proud and impossible, and Jonah is the world's worst wingman. If I don't step in, it's hopeless.

As hopeless as Jonah and me. I push away the thought. "What's for dinner?"

"Come and pick. Make it random and hard, like the TV show will be."

Jake snorts. "Not completely random."

Jonah closes his eyes. "Do you have to contradict everything I say today?"

Jake grins from the couch. "No."

Lindsay throws her shopping bags in her bedroom and wanders over to the kitchen. She stands shoulder to shoulder with Jonah. "Chicken, squash, and garlic."

Jake hops off the couch and grabs them from Jonah. "That's me."

"What?" Jonah protests. "You brought the shrimp."

"You snooze, you lose." Jake smirks. "Thanks, babe." He gives Lindsay a quick side-arm hug with the hand that isn't holding the ingredients.

I join them at the refrigerator. "Are you kidding? You made it too easy, Lindsay." I dig through the bags until I find the shrimp. "Have fun cleaning those, boyfriend." I pull out some gorgeous hake white fish filets, too, because I don't hate Jonah. "Or these."

But I do love to watch him squirm. I spy the worst vegetable I can imagine having to use. "Cauliflower, and...turmeric. Have fun with that."

Jonah's thinking. He's not laughing or glaring. He's already got his game face on, so I enjoy the dimpled cheeks and the crease lines around his eyes.

"Three, two, one...go!" I shout and set a timer on the microwave.

Jake grabs his ingredients, knocks Jonah out of the way, and starts working.

"Hey! Where am I supposed to cook?"

"Our cabin." Jake looks around. "Where's the cutting board?"

I hold up a hand. "No outside help."

Jonah frowns at his brother, tosses the ingredients in a Santa Claus tea towel, and bolts for the door.

Sure, it's not Kitchen Stadium, but there's enough room to cook a gourmet meal in the cabin's kitchen, which isn't too tiny, thanks to Lindsay's generous upgrade. She and I race back and forth between our cabin and theirs to watch the progress.

Pretty soon it smells amazing. The chicken sautés in some garlic-infused oil in our cabin, and Jonah uses the turmeric to make a curry in his.

Lindsay stops me before we enter our cabin. "I know we talked about this last night, but I'm still getting mixed signals from Jake. He flirts more with you than he does with me."

We didn't grab our coats for the short jog between buildings. "I'm safe, remember? Off the market. I'm like a sister. He's teasing me, not flirting. It seems the same, but the difference is that he knows I'm taken."

Lindsay shakes her head. "I wish I understood people."

I shiver and rub my arms. "Look, Lindsay. He told you he wants to take you out. He's not subtle. He likes you."

She bites her lip.

"So, flirt with him, however you know how." I smile at her, grab her arm, and tug her inside the cabin. I take her over to stand very, very close to Jake while he's cooking.

His knife slips on the squash he's cutting when Lindsay leans across him to pick up the herbs he's already minced. "That smells good." She flashes a smile and stands shoulder to shoulder with him.

He stops what he's doing and picks up an uncut piece of the herb. "It's tarragon." He rubs a little between his fingers and holds it below her nose.

She closes her eyes and inhales, and Jake's eyes never leave her face. Her eyes flutter open. "Wow. So fresh." Jake grins, picks up his knife, and starts cutting again.

Forty-five minutes later, Jonah's made a coconut korma with shrimp and hake fish filets. Jake's plated a chicken and tarragon pasta with a butternut squash puree on the side.

"So?" Jake asks. "Who wins for plating?"

"Um, no." I refuse to get drawn into this. "Don't answer that, Lindsay."

"She's my date. She has to like my dish better. Right, Linz?"

She glances at me. I shake my head because picking sides between twins is a bad idea, but she doesn't understand me. She answers, but not the way I expect. She tilts her head and studies the plates on the table. "I'm not your date because you never asked me out."

Jake turns to his brother. "Fine. Execution and taste."

Jonah tries a bite of Jake's pasta. "It's bland."

He's right. Jake turns to me and arches an eyebrow.

I shrug. "It could use more heat. The acid is nice, but you overdid the lemon."

Jake takes a bite and mutters something beneath his breath. I can't tell if he's mad at me or himself, but he's mad at someone, because it doesn't sound good.

Jonah goes back to eating his curry. "I have to be honest, since we're going to compete together. I'm hurting us both if I lie to you right now."

Jake looks at me. "Well?"

I gave him some notes, so it's only fair to comment on Jonah's dish. I taste the curry. The fish flakes beautifully, and the spices blend perfectly. The coconut milk tempers the hint of heat, and the vegetables are tender-crisp, as they should be. This dish is perfection. "The fish is cooked well, and there's a good balance of flavors."

Jonah's mouth ticks up in a grin. Jake grunts. "Of course it is."

I shouldn't have let myself get drawn into this competition, after the push-ups and the haircuts, and then especially after the ice skating.

"I like the pasta," Lindsay says. "The curry is too strong for me."

Jake grins. "You're not just saying that because you're my date?"

She picks up her glass. "No, it's true, and I wouldn't say that out of loyalty, because I'm not your date. Repeating that I'm your date won't make it true, Jake, so if you want to date me, you'll have to ask me out." She brings the cup to her lips and tips it delicately.

Water slides down her throat, and Jake watches the movement.

I stifle a laugh. I'm so proud of Lindsay for getting up her courage to try to flirt. It's all wrong, but it's a first step. Maybe this isn't flirting. Maybe this is just her brutal truth-telling.

The table goes silent, but Jake recovers quickly. He grins. No, smirks. It's slow and sexy and smoldering. "Hey, Linz, wanna go out with me tonight?"

"Depends. Do you have a girlfriend back in Boston I don't know about?"

*Whoa.* None of us were expecting that.

Jake looks at us, and he's completely bewildered. He runs his hand through his hair, but it's mostly not there, so he ends up rubbing the sides of his shaved head.

But he hardly misses a beat. "Nope, but if you'd rather skip dating and go straight to girlfriend, we can do that."

Jonah points his fork at me. "What did I tell you? No one *likes* dating. They like relationships."

Jake leans forward and smolders some more. "What do you say, babe? Am I your boyfriend? Or do *you* have one back in Boston?"

Lindsay stammers. "J-just making sure you're single. I don't want to...date...someone who has a girlfriend."

Jonah and I look at each other. Jonah frowns, so I'm pretty sure we're having the same thought. Lindsay must be remembering that Jake had a girlfriend the last time he kissed her.

"Ah, so that's the point of the background check?" Jake wets his lips. "I wondered about your intentions for me."

Lindsay's in way over her head. First, she can't tear her eyes away, then she pushes the food around her plate and won't look at Jake.

"Lindsay?" I prompt. "Are you good to go out with Jake tonight or would you rather stay home from the hot springs?"

There are so many tips I could give her on dating that I don't even know where to start, but Jake's already falling all over himself because of her. She doesn't need my help. She's doing fine, just being her super awkward, five-foot, nine-inch, supermodel self.

But I do sometimes have to help her with the basics, like making sure she answers Jake when he asks her out.

Her head shoots up. I smile encouragingly at her. "I mean, now that he's passed the background check. Right? Anything else we need to know?" I agree with Chief—some things should be on a need-to-know basis. This is one of them.

Jake smiles at Lindsay. "Nothing else, babe. What you see is what you get. If you want it." He arches an eyebrow suggestively.

She pushes back from the table. "It's a date. I'll go change."

Jake watches her leave. "Is that a *yes*?" he yells after her. He shakes his head and lowers his voice. "Lindsay is the most confusing woman I've ever dated, and that's saying a lot."

"Especially since you're not dating her yet." Jonah tosses his napkin on the table.

I set down my fork. "Thanks for two great dinners, guys. You're going to win that donation for the food banks for sure."

Jonah has his business face on, the one where he's intense and thinking and coiled and ready for action. "Dad is getting excited about your idea. I've forwarded your plan, and he loves it. We waste so much food."

"Thanks for making it a reality. It means everything to me."

We grin at each other. Jonah stands. "I'm ready to change. See you at the car in ten minutes?"

I nod.

Jake takes his plate over to the sink and scrapes his pasta into the trash. "It was bland. The curry was better. I can admit when I'm beaten."

"The magic of...salt." Jonah rinses his plate in the sink and nudges Jake with his shoulder.

Jake grabs the plate from him. "Shut up."

Jonah leaves our cabin. I clear my plate and put the leftovers in the refrigerator.

Jake finishes the dishes, then turns to look at me. "How did you do it?"

"Do what? You made dinner."

Jake grabs the towel from the refrigerator door handle and dries the cast iron skillet. "How did you turn my brother into a PDA-machine? You're the most disgusting couple I've ever seen. That ride home last night?" Jake digs into the pocket of his jeans and tosses his keys to me. "I don't ever want a repeat of that. J-Dog can drive tonight."

Lindsay pokes her head out of her bedroom. "What do I wear to the hot springs?"

Jake steps away from me. "Chief said to wear t-shirts and coats over our swimsuits."

"Thanks." She closes the door of her room.

Jake drops back against the counter. "I can't talk to her. I get these glimmers of possibility, like..." He gazes down at me. "Well, let's just say, I wish I could talk to her as easily as I do with you."

This is getting into *awkward* again. "You can. I gave Jonah a recipe."

Jake nods. "For the curry? That explains why it was so good."

I'm offended on Jonah's behalf. "No, that was all him. I gave him a recipe for the PDA, which, by the way, has also been all him."

Jake's all attention now. "Ugh, I know." He pushes off the counter. "I want your recipe."

I glance at Lindsay's door. "I already told you the basic idea. Get over yourself."

He rolls his eyes. "That is *not* what you told Joey." He pulls out a chair for himself and one for me.

"No. Jonah's waiting in the car, and I've got to change. I'll tell you more later, but step one is..." I don't want to have this conversation with him. It's too personal. I sigh. "I have to ask Jonah if it's okay to talk about this with you. This was just between him and me."

"Cliffhanger, seriously?" Jake pats the chair invitingly. "No offense, but I don't usually have trouble with women. Lindsay is killing me, here, Shrimp, and you have a recipe for some secret sauce. I need it."

I look at him. "She's worth it. She gets you, and she's amazing."

"I don't know." He shifts closer and drops his voice, probably so Lindsay won't hear us. "I'm not so sure she does get me. Does it have to be this hard?"

Now I'm coaching Lindsay and Jake both. This better pay off someday.

"No effort, no reward." I step away and put distance between us. "There are no shortcuts. Relationships require a lot of work. Make tonight all about Lindsay, not yourself, and I'll ask Jonah to give you the Boyfriend Recipe. He's the one who perfected it."

# Chapter Twenty-Four

SNOW FALLS LIGHTLY as we leave our cabins. It's a beautiful drive through Sugar Creek. Christmas lights glimmer on the rooflines of every house, and I can just make out the train rounding the corner of the mountain in the distance.

Jake is terrible at giving directions and even worse at letting anyone else drive.

He's got his phone out. "It's ahead on the right."

"Got it," Jonah says mildly, and starts to turn.

"Not here," Jake shouts in a panic. "That's the ski resort."

Jonah blows out a breath. "Then why did you say to turn?"

Jake's jaw clenches. "I said *ahead*, so you *wouldn't* turn at the ski resort."

There's a tense silence. We see the silhouette of a covered bridge on one side as we approach the Rosie Hot Springs.

Jake consults his phone. "Now you turn."

Jonah's grip on the steering wheel tightens. "I know."

"No, I meant back there," Jake yells.

Jonah swerves and barely makes the turn. "You should just drive, then both of us would be happy," he mutters.

I put a hand on Jonah's knee, and he glances over. "What?"

I smile. "Thanks for driving. I miss the back seat, too." I give him a Butler boy wink.

Jonah's shoulders untense. He grins and covers my hand on his leg until he pulls into the parking lot.

"Both hands on the wheel to back up," Jake mutters.

Jonah's shoulders hunch up again as he looks in the rearview mirror. "I've got this. I'm thirty years old."

He pulls into a space in the practically empty parking lot, and we walk up a set of wooden steps. The bubbling, sulphuric smell of natural hot springs greets us, but it's not bad, and the springs are almost deserted. We're probably the only ones crazy enough to come out here on a Saturday night in December.

Lindsay and I peel off layers of clothing, set them on wooden benches, and tiptoe across the ground to slip into the cascading pools of brilliantly green and blue water. It's perfectly warm.

Jake stretches slowly as he takes off his t-shirt. He stands at the side of the hot spring in his swimming trunks. He's perfectly framed by evergreens on all sides, and he's perched on the edge of a ragged granite rock. Lindsay and I are both staring like he's a chiseled statue, too, and he knows it. He grins and slowly enters the water, keeping himself halfway out, so we can still see his perfectly defined chest.

Jonah has his back to us. He peels off his jeans and t-shirt, then turns around and looks at the sky, awestruck. "It's still snowing."

If Jake's abs were awesome, Jonah's are a work of art. Did I already mention Michelangelo? Because Jonah is as still as a statue, staring up at the white-gray sky and the fluttering snowflakes. There's a gentle halo of light from the buildings behind him, and it's a beautiful sight. I am happy tonight, taking in his abs wonderland.

Jake glances at me and Lindsay, then grunts. "Dude, get in. You're going to freeze."

Jonah startles, then grins. He jumps in across from Jake, splashing us. The water is fairly clear, even though it's so vividly colored, and they've mounted some lights around the hot springs, so I can see every ripple of Jonah's muscles as he settles into the water.

The stars twinkle overhead, steam rises from the natural springs, and the temperature of the water is perfect. Everyone's quiet right now.

"So, Brie," Jake begins.

I trail my fingers through the water. "So, Jake?"

"I heard you were working on a new recipe." He pulls himself slightly out of the water and rests his arms on a granite rock at the edge of the spring.

"Not now."

Jonah turns to me. "What's he talking about?"

Lindsay floats in the pond, and the snow melts as it hits her skin.

I swim closer to Jonah and loop my arms around his neck. The water pushes our bodies together and apart, and he catches me the next time I float near him. I lift a dripping wet hand and tug his ear down to my mouth. "Jake wants to know the Boyfriend Recipe."

Jonah holds onto me while the water pushes and pulls me. *Toward him and away. Toward him and away.* Beads of water cascade down his chest. Steam rises as the snow falls gently onto the exposed skin of his shoulders. I glance down while I have this close proximity. Yep, it's a six pack. That tight t-shirt didn't lie.

Jonah glances over. "You want Brie's new recipe?"

Jake shrugs. "I hear it works." He looks meaningfully at me, wrapped in Jonah's arms.

Jonah grins and looks at Lindsay. "You sure? Because it does work, and it's dangerous."

Lindsay swims across one of the pools, climbs a rock, and settles into the smaller pool beside it. "Oooh. I want to hear it, if it's dangerous."

Jonah presses his cheek against mine. "It might make you lose control."

Jake snorts and mutters, "Backseat make-out, for example?"

Lindsay's brow contracts. "What?"

Jonah turns his head so quickly that I'm surprised and kisses my cheek. "I meant, it's dangerous to lose control of your heart. You might fall in love."

He's good. He almost has *me* believing that we're really engaged.

Lindsay sighs. "Aah. You two are hashtag couple goals. If that's what you're talking about, I definitely want that recipe. I want someone who adores me like that."

Jake meets my gaze. I don't have to say *I told you so*. He floats a little closer to her. "So, let's hear this famous recipe, bro."

Jonah can't talk without his hands, so I let go and float beside him. He counts the steps on his hand. "Number one. Feelings first. Small steps. Second, spend time together. Third thing, take it slow. Real affection isn't until step four, and step five is the most important. Maintain with mental energy."

I stare at Jonah. It's probably the longest speech I've ever heard him give, and judging by Jake's response, his brother is shocked, too.

Jonah's given this a lot of thought, and he's been putting it into action. I haven't given him enough credit for the intentional ways he's trying to nurture our fledgling romance.

But he is.

Lindsay sighs again. "Guys don't ever talk about feelings. They jump to step four." She gives Jake a pointed stare.

"What?" He holds up both hands, then floats over to Jonah and claps him on the back. "That was deep. You and Brie did that?"

Jonah looks at me. We skipped the first three steps, went straight to four, and have no intention of doing number five.

"Ish," I say. "We developed the recipe as we went."

"But step number one is the key." Jonah grabs my hand underwater and tugs me closer. "If you want to turn up the heat on step number four, you have to preheat with step one." His eyes rake over my face, and I feel the fire in his gaze. "The deeper the emotional connection, the hotter the kisses."

My cheeks flush bright red.

Jake laughs. "You sound like Mom."

"Yeah, well, your mom is right." Lindsay hops out of the hot spring and grabs her towel from a nearby bench. She huddles on a rock, tucking her knees up to her chest and cocooning herself in the towel. "As awesome as a kiss might be for a moment, it's nothing if the guy isn't honest. Or if, say, he has a girlfriend and doesn't tell you."

Jake pushes himself out of the water and grabs a towel. "Why are we back to that subject?"

Jonah and I look at each other. We can't say anything and betray Lindsay's trust, but Jake is really being obtuse.

Or he *didn't* kiss her.

And I'm being lied to, just like Scarlett lied to Chief.

I hop out and grab a towel. One or the other of the twins is being idiotic, and they are lumped together in my mind now. I need some space to figure out which one it is.

I dry off as quickly as I can. "Let's call an Uber, Linz."

She turns to me with huge eyes. "Why?"

"You and I need some private girl talk."

Jonah's face falls, and he finally notices my mood shift. Now he hops out of the hot spring, but he doesn't cover his perfectly sculpted body with a towel. No, I have to watch the beads of water trickle down every plane of his chest until they reach the V of his hips.

Well, I don't *have* to, but I do.

"Brie?" He wrinkles his forehead.

I level a gaze at him. "Lindsay's right. Kissing a dishonest guy isn't my thing, either."

He finally grabs a towel and dries his face. The water still drips from his swim trunks, so now I'm staring at the muscles of his legs.

"Are we talking theoretically?"

I stop drying myself with my towel. "Yes and no." We only kissed because of a theoretical engagement, but it's a literal kiss we're discussing.

Jonah approaches me. "Why are we talking about people with girlfriends kissing Lindsay? How is that both theoretical and not?"

Lindsay slips into her clothes and zips up her parka. She looks at me, emotions swirling in her eyes. I don't know how much to say here or what to talk about privately. Lindsay's eyes flash with anger when she looks back at Jake.

We need to sort this out, and I'll give Jonah a chance to tell me the truth. "Maybe that never happened. Maybe she never kissed *that* guy."

Jonah stares at me, stunned. He has no response.

I don't care if my clothes cling to me. I have to get away. Jake's confused, and Jonah's got this guilty silence going on, so maybe I've been wrong.

What if Jonah kissed Lindsay. What if he lied?

He and I are both lying to everyone around us right now.

I don't think Jake's ever lied to me.

My hands tremble as I try to zip up my coat. Jonah rushes to dry his hands, then helps with the stuck zipper. "Hey, hang on a second. This sounds pretty real, if you know what I mean." He jerks his head toward Lindsay. "Who do you think Lindsay kissed?"

Jake tosses his towel into a basket and slips one leg into his jeans. "When did she kiss someone?"

I'm shivering, but luckily Lindsay's already ordering an Uber on her app. Well, trying to. The cell phone reception is spotty right now. She rolls her eyes at Jake's question and mutters, "Like you don't know."

Jonah's got nothing but his swim trunks on. "This stops now. I'm done with theoretical." He rubs the towel on his face again. "Jake, bro, tell Brie you kissed Lindsay before she breaks up with me."

I freeze, and Jake does, too. He's stuck with his t-shirt halfway over his head. "Excuse me?" He tugs it over his head, so he can see.

Jonah shakes his head. "Please." He points at me. "Brie thinks I kissed her best friend."

"Which friend?"

Lindsay folds her arms across her chest. "Seriously?"

"Not winning any points for emotional honesty," I say to both twins.

Jake shrugs his t-shirt the rest of the way down his chest, covering the washboard abs. "We don't need a group conversation about a personal topic."

Jonah's going to turn into an icicle. "Yeah, well, if we don't have this conversation, I'm going to lose Brie." He advances on his brother. "Or is that what you want? Can't stand to see me with something you don't have? Do you *want* her to break up with me?"

A flash of guilt crosses Jake's face. "I'm happy for you."

"You've been complaining ever since I got engaged." Jonah shakes his head, and now he's drying off with a vengeance.

My heart is breaking, and I'm so confused. On one hand, I'm the cause of the brothers' argument, and on the other hand, I don't know if I even trust them. Either of them.

A maroon sedan enters the deserted parking lot, and I grab my mini backpack.

Jonah grabs his clothes and slips into his sneakers. "Wait, Brie. Don't leave like this."

I turn. "You said you were done with theoretical." I'm done with him and this whole fake engagement.

His face pales. "Not like that. No, I'm not."

Jake and Lindsay are confused, as they should be.

Jonah jogs toward me in the narrow space between the hot spring and a bench. He crosses a thin granite rock that separates two pools and jostles Jake to get past him. "Move."

Jake shoves him. "You move."

The shove sends Jonah stumbling. He trips, and he falls backward—all the way into the hot spring. Flailing.

It's horrible. It's not slow motion. It happens so fast that it's comical, and Jake laughs. Jonah's dry clothes are still in his arms, and he falls with his shoes still on. *Bam.* Back first.

He comes up, spluttering, after a long minute.

"Sorry," Jake says, still laughing.

Jonah throws everything on the cement. His wet t-shirt. His heavy jeans. He tugs off one shoe. Another. The last shoe hits Jake *hard* in the chest. I'm pretty sure Jonah wasn't aiming for his brother, but it hits him anyway.

Jake stops laughing. He rubs his chest. "You could've hit my face."

"That's what you care about? Your image?" Lindsay stalks down the wooden steps and across the parking lot, but I can't go. Not now. She slips inside the sedan, and I'm tugged both directions. Both of my friends need me.

"Hey, Linz, wait. No." Jake bolts across the parking lot, and I make my choice. I edge onto the thin sliver of rock, bend over, and offer Jonah a hand out of the water. He hesitates. "Get in with me?"

I don't move.

"I swear to you I didn't kiss Lindsay. I'm not a liar."

I glance at Jake's figure disappearing into the car. The door shuts, and the sedan leaves.

"Everything we've done for the last two weeks has been a lie. Why should I trust you?"

Jonah closes his eyes and rests against the edge of the hot spring. "Nothing I've said or done has been a lie. I really like you, and I need you to believe me, because..." He swallows. "I don't want to lose you."

I shimmy out of my soggy pants and unzip my coat. How many times am I going to ask him if he's lying? I have serious trust issues because of Chief's divorce, and my dad leaving us, but yeah. Jonah isn't Scarlett. He isn't my mom.

I'd rather live a life where I trust people. I won't let Scarlett— or my mom—ruin my relationships, too.

I slip back into the blissfully warm water. Jonah's eyes open when he feels the splash beside him.

"Does your brother have his wallet?" I ask.

"Nope." Jonah grins. "He didn't drive, so he didn't need his license, and I said I'd pay the hot springs entrance fee, so..."

The sedan disappears in the distance.

Jonah tugs me closer to him, and I float almost into his lap. His voice is low and gravelly in my ear. "Lindsay will have to pay."

"Some date." I bite my lip, then burst out laughing. "I'd love to see the conversation between them on the ride home."

Jonah wipes his face, which only makes more water drip down his chiseled features. I take advantage of the moment to look at his dripping wet torso. His trunks are slung low around his hips, and I can see why he beat his brother at push-ups.

He runs a hand through his hair, which is perfectly tousled now and completely wet. "I blew that."

"You did, but you love your brother and your friends. I like how loyal you are." I've seen a lot of his good qualities, and I need to remember that when I feel like running away.

He reaches for my hand, and I wrap my arms around his neck instead. He groans. "It was Lindsay's secret to tell, not mine, and I shouldn't have forced Jake's hand." He closes his eyes and holds me close. "Then I almost lost you. Stop trying to break up early with me."

We bob and float together in the current of the pools. My emotions have been on a roller coaster, but I feel peaceful now. Jake and Lindsay are gone, so it's just the two of us. The snow falls gently, and the flowing water warms us.

There aren't any other guests crazy enough to be out here. The covered bridge is nothing but a dark silhouette now, and the outline of the mountain is dotted with bright lights from the ski runs. Christmas lights from the town flicker in the distance, blurs of every color, and Jonah's skin is warm against my own.

But he's down. The fight with his brother gutted him. I can tell.

I nod. "Okay. We'll keep things theoretical." I nudge him. "After all, I like our *alone time*."

Jonah's hands slide down to my waist, and I'm slippery in the mineral-rich waters. "Me, too."

I lean back against him. "I like how hard you work when you want something. I like how deeply you think and how careful you are with people's emotions. I like the way you care about your family."

Jonah scoffs. "Like tonight?"

I laugh. "*Usually*. I like the way you treat me when your parents aren't around and no one else sees us. You put in as much effort as if this were a real relationship, and a lot more effort than any of my other boyfriends ever have."

He takes a deep shuddering breath. "You see that in me?"

A burst of ice lands on my face. I brush it off. "Yes, and lots more. I wouldn't be just anyone's fake girlfriend." And it's painful to know that I can't have him or be with him, when he's so amazing and not at all conceited.

His grip at my waist tightens. "I don't think anyone has ever seen me the way you do."

I relax against him. "Then no one's looked very hard. You're smart, sexy, driven, kind, gentle, thoughtful, funny, and nice. And humble."

"Thanks." Jonah laughs. "*Usually*, I'm those things. *Hopefully*."

I trail my fingers through the water, stirring up currents in the hot spring. "The stillness of the night makes it feel like we're the only two people in the universe. We can talk about anything, and no one will hear us. It's just us and the stars in the night sky."

Jonah tips his head back to look at the falling snow. "Are we getting deep tonight? *More* emotional intimacy? I don't think we can turn the heat up any higher."

I smile and let the stillness settle into me.

Jonah's voice grows pensive. "I'm not a rockstar celebrity chef right now. I'm the worst brother ever tonight." His deep tone rumbles in his chest behind me. He presses a kiss to the top of my head. "Do you know how many stars there are?"

I shake my head. The snowflakes blend into the cloudy night sky, and it's hard to see the stars through the snow.

The water swirls around us as Jonah's voice murmurs in my ears. "You're my universe now, and I want my moments with you to be as limitless as the stars in the sky. Each second we spend together is a memory in the constellation of my heart's sky. I only have six days—five hundred thousand seconds—until I lose your light, and I don't mean to waste a single one without you."

And now I can't see because of the tears in my eyes. I wipe my eyes and pretend like it's water from the hot spring. "And you're poetic," I say softly. "You keep surprising me."

The water flows between us, still pushing and pulling, like this dance we're doing, and I'm tiptoeing around the truth. "I'll cherish these moments and memories, too."

"I wish you would come to New York," Jonah whispers as he holds me tight. "It would mean the world to me if you would come watch the show. You're my world, and without you everything would feel off-balance."

I turn and cling to him, burying my head in his neck. "I wish I could."

"Why can't we live in our own little universe?" Jonah asks. He lifts a hand and wipes my cheek with his thumb. "Let's make this real."

His mouth inches nearer to mine, and I want more than anything to say *Yes* or explain my reason for saying *No*. I've been alone for so long.

So, I say the only thing I can, with his eyes blazing, and my heart thumping wildly. "Maybe."

# Chapter Twenty-Five

JONAH BRUSHES some snow off a nearby bush, and it melts in the hot spring's perfectly warm water. "That's not a *No*, so I'm calling this date a win."

I look at the snow-covered evergreens ringing the natural pools. "At least you didn't have to bum a rideshare from your date."

Steam rises off the bubbling surface of the ponds. "But I'm going to need you to drive us back."

We soak a while longer, then I dry off and change. I don't have any clothes that would remotely fit his tall, muscular body, and everything he owns is sopping wet—shoes, jeans, and shirt.

Jonah jams on his soggy shoes and tosses me the keys. He grabs my hand, and we run down the wooden steps and across the empty parking lot. He slips off his shoes as soon as we're in the SUV, then he cranks up the heat.

The car has barely warmed up by the time we reach the cabins. I leave the heater running when we pull up. "I'll go get you some shoes."

Jonah wraps his still-wet coat around himself and his swimming trunks. I steal one last peek at the calf muscles and hurry to his cabin, feeling a little guilty for being dry and warm.

Jake's not there. I rummage in Jonah's bedroom, grab a pair of boots, and rush back outside.

I hand him the boots and wrap my arms around myself as I wait for him. "Do you want my coat?" It's a ridiculous offer. It would never fit.

He grins. "Nah, I'm good, Shrimp. Go ahead. I'll change into dry clothes and come say *Goodnight*."

"Goodnight," I say, as I turn to leave.

His voice deepens. "I'm not ready to say that yet." Jonah hops out of Jake's SUV and locks it.

I wave as I scamper across the freezing parking lot and race toward my cabin. He raises his left hand. "Later." He's gripping a bundle of wet clothes in the other. "Love you," he shouts casually over his shoulder.

I freeze with my hand on the doorknob.

"Mom said to tell you every day." He drops his wet clothes in the entrance to his cabin and flips on the porch light switch.

"Right." It used to be easy to say that casually, but I can't force it now. "You're still my favorite brother." I wink and slip inside the cabin, then press a hand to my chest. Jonah is stealing my heart, piece by piece, and I don't know how I'll ever walk away.

"Brie?" Jake's deep voice rumbles from the kitchen.

I scream and drop my towel. "You startled me."

Lindsay pauses their baking show. "We've been waiting for you."

I guess this is why Jake wasn't in his cabin. "Awesome. Wait five more minutes." I kick off my shoes, run upstairs, rinse off in the shower, and change into some sweats and a t-shirt.

I flip on the fireplace switch when I head back downstairs. "I'm ready for you. What's up?"

There's a new aroma in the air. *Heaven*. And Jake's stirring something brown and chocolatey.

He glances at me when I peer over his shoulder. "How's Jonah?"

"Wet." I wander to the couch, grab Jonah's hoodie, and put it on. Some of the relaxation from the hot springs evaporates. "How are you?"

Jake takes the sauce off the stove. "Bruised and embarrassed. Look, I apologized to Lindsay, and I want to apologize to you. I haven't been my best self the last couple of weeks."

I grab a blanket and snuggle into the couch cushions. "Okay."

"We had a long talk in the grocery store." Lindsay plays with the edges of her own blanket. "You know me. Once I get started, I don't stop."

*The grocery store?* I tip my head against the back of the couch. "I'm glad you cleared the air. Can I go to bed? Your mom expects us to go skiing tomorrow, and I'm exhausted." And I really can't get in the middle of anything else between Jake and Jonah.

Jake groans and collapses on the couch. "I need a break. I'll tell her that you and Jonah are doing fine, and maybe we can all chill for a few days." He tips his head to rest on the sectional and rubs the back of his neck. "You and Joey *are* doing fine, right?"

"We're great." I could sleep right here, if they would leave. The perfect temperature of the hot springs made me drowsy, and I don't want to lose that cozy, warm feeling entirely. "Was there anything specific you wanted to talk to me about, or are we just going to eat Jake's chocolate concoction?"

Lindsay and Jake exchange a glance. He clears his throat. "So, I guess you know that I kissed Lindsay a few years ago."

Even though I trust Jonah, I'm surprised at the relief I feel when Jake admits it. I let out a long breath and close my eyes. "I'm listening."

"And we haven't been on the same, uh, wavelength again since then." Jake clears his throat again, and I flutter my eyes open.

"Sure. Is there a question?"

Lindsay answers. "How do you start Step One? How do you jump into sharing feelings with strangers? How do you go from being coworkers and colleagues to people with whom you trust the deepest thoughts of your heart when you've barely shared them with your best friend?"

I sit up. "Honestly, you're doing fine. *We* only met three months ago, and we're already best friends. You and Jake have known each other for three years."

"How did you and Jonah get together?" Jake asks. "I didn't see that one coming. I guess I should have, with the early mornings and all that, but I didn't."

I can't answer that truthfully, but I can validate his feelings. I sigh and turn to face him. "I know that bugs you because you feel like we snuck behind your back, and you still don't understand."

They look at each other and nod. Jake grabs a pillow and folds it onto itself. "How am I supposed to be all awesome like my brother if I don't know what he did?"

Lindsay nudges him with her shoulder. "You know how to ask girls out."

"But I want to marry someone this time." He turns and looks Lindsay full in the face. "I'm tired of having fun."

Her mouth curves in a sexy smile. "So, you don't think marriage would be fun?"

Jake swallows and lets go of the pillow. It springs up and hits him in the chest. He jumps off the couch and goes back to the kitchen.

"Alright, alright." I push out of the comfy couch cushions. I'm getting pulled into this, whether or not I want to, and evidently, I'm not getting any chocolate until we have this talk, either. "Jonah put himself out there. He asked. I'm not afraid to try and fail. That's all. We are honest with each other." *Even if we aren't honest with anyone else.*

Jake opens the freezer and rummages for something. "So, I just tell Lindsay that I want to marry her, and I've been secretly watching her for the last three years, and I might already be in love, and then she falls at my feet?"

Her eyes widen, and she stares at the refrigerator door that hides him.

But he's in earnest. This isn't the teasing or flirty Jake that I've encountered.

"No. Remember the part where your world revolves around her, not the other way?" I push aside my blanket and walk over to the kitchen. I open the cupboard and grab four bowls. "You tell Lindsay that you've been secretly in love with her for the last three years *and* that you'll do anything to be with her and make her happy, and then you do that. Make her happy."

Jake takes the bowls from me and sets them on the counter, then pulls me into a hug. "I love you, Brie."

Jonah yells from the doorway. "Hands off my girlfriend. Will you stop loving her already?"

I don't let go. "Good luck, bro." I pat his back and then break the hug. "Hey, boyfriend. Warmed up yet? You almost missed the party."

Jonah shuts the door and strides across the room. "I came over to apologize, Jake, for everything tonight." He and his brother exchange a meaningful glance, and I don't know what they argued about before dinner or the hot springs, but Jake nods, and the moment is over. Jonah slips an arm around my waist and pulls me close. "Now explain that hug."

Jake's nostrils flare. "I'm not going to apologize for wanting to be on good terms with my future sister-in-law." His eyes dart to Lindsay. "I *will* apologize for shoving you into the hot springs, though, and not owning up to my Christmas closet kiss."

Jonah leads me over to the couch. The fireplace blows warm air behind us, and my back is toasty warm. "Love and kisses all around. Can we have the chocolate now?"

Jake holds up his hands. "Fine."

Lindsay leaves the couch. "Did you mean anything you said, Jake, or were you just...?" She glances at me. "He likes to joke, right, or was he serious?"

"Hold that thought." Jake points at Jonah. "I made your nasty dark chocolate fudge sauce, no milk chocolate at all, and we found some peppermint ice cream at the county store. I even whipped some cream for you and crushed some candy canes with a rolling pin."

Jonah's mouth tips in a half-grin. "I bet that felt good."

Jake rubs the back of his neck, then grins. "It did."

"Apology accepted," Jonah says, and nods toward Lindsay. "Go ahead, man."

Jake grabs her hands and tugs her over to the doorway. "Come here, Lindsay." Even though they're standing in the dimly lit entrance, we can hear everything. "Look, I'll be honest. I'm tired of dating. I want to be happy like Jonah, and I can't imagine anyone I'd rather..."

I smile at Jonah during the awkward silence. "I'll fill you in tomorrow," I whisper. "Drama."

A muscle in Jonah's jaw ticks. "I don't like to see him hugging you."

I press a finger to his lips and tip my head toward the doorway. He scoops the peppermint ice cream into each bowl, tops it with Jake's heavenly hot fudge sauce, drops a dollop of whipped cream, and then sprinkles each bowl with a little of Jake's crushed cane.

Meanwhile, Jake's still pouring his heart out to Lindsay by the front door. "I'm thirty, and I ought to be married because my parents need grandchildren yesterday, besides, I want someone to come home to. I want someone to share my life with, and yeah. I want to be a dad with six kids, like my dad. If that doesn't terrify you, then maybe we can go out sometime."

Jonah's eyes widen in shock, and I press my lips together to hold back a laugh. He bends down, and his breath is warm on my ear. "Is Jake crazy?"

I shake my head, and now Jonah's holding back a laugh. "He took that note on emotional intimacy a little too far."

"Overachiever." I dip a spoon into the fudge sauce. "Oh, this is good."

"It's my recipe." Jonah arches an eyebrow suggestively.

We're giggling and whispering together, so we miss the rest of the extremely awkward conversation between Jake and Lindsay as we finish eating our hot fudge apology sundaes in the semi-lit kitchen. Only the lights beneath the cabinets are on now.

The front door slams, so Jake must have left.

"I'll put his bowl in the freezer and take it over when I go," Jonah says. "I ruined it with the fudge sauce, but he might bring himself to eat it anyway."

"Goodnight," Lindsay yells. She closes her bedroom door extra loud, so I know we're alone.

"I'll put hers in the freezer, too," I say. "She'll want it for breakfast. We'll eat leftovers while we gossip about you and Jake."

Jonah's dark brown eyes soften. He leans down and brushes his lips across mine. "You can gossip about a double wedding and lots of grandbabies for the parents. What do you say?"

"No pressure." Panic seizes me. *Maybe* is just a way of putting off *No* until later. It never turns into *Yes*. My mom taught me that. So, I repeat my answer from the hot springs. "I still say *Maybe*."

Jonah tilts my chin toward him. "I have one more question for you."

I'm so tired that I'll answer almost anything if it means I can go to sleep. "Sure, boyfriend."

He takes my fingers and rubs them gently. "Will you wear my ring while I change that *Maybe* into a *Yes*?"

# Chapter Twenty-Six

"No."

Jonah drops his head, and his shoulders droop.

"*No* to all of it."

His head whips up, and his eyebrows furrow. "What? How much is *all*?"

He's a competitive chef, and I forget how driven he is because he's so low-key about it. He's studying me with a gleam in his eye. A challenge.

So, I have to be brutally honest. "*All* is all, Jonah. I can't do this. I can't pretend like we have everything figured out when we aren't even dating. I can't have Jake and Lindsay and your whole family pin their hopes on us when you still have our breakup scheduled on your private calendar."

Jonah advances toward me and reaches out his arms to snag me in an embrace. "I'll delete that item."

"No." I back away. "Tell Jake whatever you need to." I'm pushing around the couch to get away from him. I shimmy out of his Red Sox hoodie and toss it to him.

He catches it automatically and sets it back on the sofa. "Brie."

"I'm buying a townhouse. I'm closing on a loan. I sunk all my savings into it, so I could put down roots and stay in Boston."

"I have money," Jonah says.

I swallow. "I'd make a terrible mom for those grandkids anyway."

"You were adorable with the kids on the sledding hill."

He's making this so hard. "I don't want to be anything like my mom."

"Then be like mine. Be yourself. Be the opposite of your mom." He scrubs a hand down his face. "We don't need to talk about having kids yet. Just don't break up with me."

I take a deep breath. "But I'm never going to be the person you need, so tell everybody you have to focus on prepping for your competition."

Jonah's whole body slumps. "There's no way I can think about that right now."

I round the sectional sofa, and he follows me. I blurt out the closest thing to the truth. "Tell them you pushed me for too much of a commitment again, and I freaked out because I'm still feeling PTSD about Chief's divorce."

Jonah stops. "You're running. You're scared." He nods. "Okay. I get that." He folds his arms across his chest and studies me with that contemplative gaze again.

My stomach flops, and I scramble to change the subject. "I have the paperwork in place for the nonprofit donations to the food banks."

Jonah's brow wrinkles. "I'll pay any amount to charity out of my own pocket if you'll wear my ring."

His offer stuns me into silence. He probably has that kind of money, but the fact that he cares enough to say that makes this choice a thousand times harder. He's going to fight for me. For us. I brace myself on the end of the sofa. "I love you, Jonah. I do. You're a great guy."

He scoffs. "Don't. Please. I've heard this so many times. I thought things were going well. Don't tell me it's you. I need the truth, because you were willing to give me a chance an hour ago."

I can't speak because of the lump in my throat. Jonah tries to wait me out, but I'm still struggling. He scrubs a hand down his face. "I feel like I'm dating the Dread Pirate Roberts." He cocks his head to one side. "Thank you for the wonderful date, Jonah. I'll most likely dump you in the morning."

I laugh, despite my hurt. Jonah is smart, and he understands me. He's a deep thinker, and he'll figure it out eventually. I love him and respect him enough to tell him the truth, after all the times he opened up to me.

"Fine. There is something else—something I've never told anyone." I slide onto the last piece of the couch and let out a deep breath. "Tommy Fuller is my father, and he won't acknowledge me."

Jonah stares. "So... That's how you know that he tapes in the Manhattan studio?"

I nod. "My mom tried to talk to him there and ask for child support, and he tried to get her arrested. Long story."

Jonah drops on the couch beside me. "Want to tell me?"

"No." I shake my head. "I've never told anyone." He tentatively puts an arm around me, and I bury my face in his neck. His grip on my shoulders tightens as he pulls me into a hug. The tears come fast and hard, and Jonah holds me until they stop.

"I can't ever meet Tommy. He doesn't want me, and I can't be anywhere near him. I don't even know what lies he believes about me or what's going on, but my mom has always said he's dangerous."

"That doesn't make sense." Jonah runs a hand up and down my back. "But that's why you think New York and the celebrity chef world is a hard *No*."

"That's why it's not safe." It's a relief to tell someone the truth. "If I go watch your cooking competition, Tommy will take one look at me and know I'm his daughter, and then I don't know what he'll do."

Jonah pulls back and tips my face up at him. His eyes widen. "Whoa. I don't know how I didn't see it."

I wipe my eyes. "Freaky, right? We have the same pale green eyes."

Jonah stares. "And the nose, and the sense of humor, and... Wow. Yeah." He tucks me into his side again. "Tommy would know in a second, but what could he do?"

"I don't know. My mom was so terrified of him that we had to move every year. Maybe he was violent." I sniff. "I have this stupid name, so it's not like I could ever pretend we're not related, if we met."

"I like your name." Jonah reaches over to grab a box of tissues that someone left on the couch. "I know Tommy. There's no way he was ever violent to a wife of his, and there's no way he wouldn't want to be your dad."

I scoff. "Yeah, agree to disagree on all of that, plus I'm not going to risk my safety or my career or my financial security on your hunch." I push away. I can't afford to enjoy his comfort anymore. "But thanks for trying."

"You're breaking up with me because of *him*?" Jonah presses his lips together, like he's holding back big emotions and trying not to cry. When he finally speaks, his voice is low and rough. "We can get through this together. He can't get you arrested for dating me."

I shake my head. "No one even knows about me. I'm nobody. Imagine what the headlines would be like if the news or social media found out that he has this secret daughter, and Tommy doesn't want anyone to know. He'd be furious. It could ruin his career, and then he'd ruin yours. And mine. And your family's business. He's powerful in this industry, and it could get really ugly really fast."

Jonah levels a gaze at me. "I can handle publicity. The attention from the paparazzi always dies down."

I push off the couch. Jonah follows me and reaches for my hands, but I tug them away. He tips his head toward the ceiling.

"My family has a lot of resources. Granted, Tommy has a lot more pull than we do. If we pulled out of his show now, I doubt Jake and I would ever compete on another show again." He blows out a breath. "You're right that he could hurt my career. I'm not helping my own argument."

My stomach sinks. "Right, and it's not just money or headlines or how much influence he has." I swallow. "You don't know what it's like to always have a parent choose someone or something else instead of you. I'm not used to being important to anyone. Not really. Not for long. I mean, he'd rather send my mom to jail than meet me or pay for my school clothes. I don't want to meet him and see that rejection and disgust on his face, too, and know that neither of my parents loved me."

*Because then no one will ever love me. Then I'm unlovable.*

As if he can read my mind, Jonah opens his arms and offers himself to me. "I love you, Brie. You're the light in my universe."

My breath catches at the sincerity in his voice, and it takes everything I have not to rush into his arms and hug him. "Thank you, Jonah. Truly. But I can never be in the same sphere as Tommy. He's an essential part of your world, so I can't be in your universe."

He reaches for my hands, and when I slowly place them in his palms, he tugs me to him. "Can we go back to that *Maybe* you gave me before? Give me a couple days to think about all of this. There's got to be a way."

"I don't know."

A half-smile tugs at the corner of Jonah's mouth. "That's the same thing as *Maybe*." He pulls me closer, and my defenses weaken. He lifts a hand and gently tucks a stray piece of hair behind my ear. "Don't give me an answer tonight when we're both tired, and it's been a weird day with Jake and the hot springs and everything."

It's a lame excuse, but I grasp at the straw he offers and lean into his embrace.

Jonah holds me for a minute. "Well?"

I gaze up at him. "You said not to give you an answer tonight."

Jonah pulls back and looks at me. I finally understand that phrase, *half-agony, half-hope*, because his eyes are swirling with so many emotions I can't breathe. Jonah's thumb grazes my cheek. "Will you answer me tonight about whether you're going to answer me about the ring and everything else later?"

He doesn't have to say *Please* or beg or plead. Everything's in the wrinkle lines around his worried eyes and the dimpled cheeks. Those dumb dimples.

"Yes, I'll give you a *Maybe*, and we can discuss the *Yes* or *No* tomorrow?"

I phrase it like a question, and I expect a huge grin in response, but instead Jonah's face crumples. He pulls me into a tight hug. "I thought I lost you." He rests his head on top of mine, and I feel his heart beating like he's had the scare of his life. He holds me like that, like I'm every Christmas wish come true, until it's time to say *Goodnight*.

But I know I won't sleep at all tonight, because what answer can I give Jonah in the morning?

# Chapter Twenty-Seven

IT's SUNDAY, so I have a plausible reason for avoiding Jonah all day. I find a worship service at the cute community church in the center of town, then I lay on my bed and read all afternoon.

I expect a flood of texts from Jonah or something to try to influence my decision, but nothing comes. He's thinking, too, after all, and I don't know what conclusions he's reached.

Lindsay knocks on my door and interrupts me. "Are you ready to go?"

"Go where?"

She pushes open my door. "Dinner."

I lock my phone. I'll finish the book later. "Where are we going? Do you want to try somewhere on Main Street?"

Lindsay sits cross-legged on the edge of my bed. "The twins have been working on sauces this afternoon. Dinner is almost ready."

I flop on the bed and unlock my phone. I don't have an answer for Jonah yet. "I'm not hungry. You go ahead."

The bed dips as she stands. "It smells amazing over there. I doubt Jake will leave you alone. He's been asking about your opinion all day."

She looks at me, but I don't answer the unspoken question, so she leaves.

I roll off the bed, grab my favorite worn-out hoodie, because no way am I wearing Jonah's right now, and wander downstairs to wait. It's a little chilly, but we're leaving soon. The fireplace takes a few minutes to warm up before the blower motor kicks on, so I grab a blanket to cover myself and start reading again.

Jake slams open the door a few minutes later. "I'm not eating without both of you."

Lindsay laughs. "Hi, Jake. Come on in."

"It's getting cold. What's the holdup?" He leaves one hand on the doorknob. "Let's go."

Jonah enters quietly behind him. I haven't seen him since last night, and it's like a knife through the heart. He's wearing a black apron over a button-down shirt. The cuffed sleeves are rolled up, exposing his forearms. Those beautiful, vein-popping forearms.

How could I ever walk away from that? "Hey, Jonah."

"Hi, Brie. Haven't heard from you all day." Jonah's expression is closed, and his dark eyes are lifeless. The new haircut fits his face perfectly, but he looks both handsome and haunted at the same time.

I did that. I put that pain there. What does that expression mean?

"Hang on." Jake enters the living room and grabs the Red Sox hoodie on the end of the sectional. "What's Brie's hoodie doing in my spot?"

Jonah's eyes shoot to mine. He reaches around him. "Sorry." He takes it and heads toward the door. My stomach drops into free-fall, like I've jumped off a glacier. Ice water fills my veins, and I tug the blanket tighter around myself.

Jake gapes at him. "Where are you going?"

"I'm putting it away." Jonah opens the door, like he's going back to their cabin.

Lindsay and Jake stare at me, and I slip my phone beneath my blanket and into my pocket.

Jake snatches the hoodie out of Jonah's hands. "That belongs to Brie now." He strides over and pulls my blanket off. He scowls when he sees what I'm wearing. "A Yankees hoodie?"

I snatch for the blanket, and Jake holds it just out of my reach. He shoves Jonah's Red Sox hoodie at me.

I set it on the couch. Jonah stares at me and my Yankees hoodie, and I've never felt more distance between us.

Jake narrows his eyes. "Did you two break up?"

I lock eyes with Jonah. "Maybe."

Lindsay sits cross-legged next to me. "What do you mean?"

Jonah arches an eyebrow. I burrow into the couch. "I don't feel like talking right now."

Jake glances frantically between me and his brother. "You're kidding, right? Was everything a lie between you two?"

Jonah's gaze snaps to his twin. "What do you mean?"

Jake scoffs. "How could you marry someone who likes the Yankees? And how could Brie possibly like the Yankees? How does *anyone* like the Yankees?"

I lean forward, tug the blanket out of his hands, and cover my chest. "I grew up in New York, and the Yankees are the greatest team that ever lived." It's ironic that Jake thinks I'm lying when I'm finally telling the complete truth. "Or whatever. Teams don't live, but you'll see when you move to New York."

Jake flops on my other side. "This is not okay. What hope do Lindsay and I have if you two can't make it?"

But I'm a chef, too, so I'm worried about ruining the meal. "Should we eat? We can argue about sports teams over dinner."

"It'll wait," Jonah says gruffly.

Jake waves a hand through the air. "Sure, sure. It'll hold. What happened? You were fine last night."

My gaze clashes with Jonah. How do we explain this? "I freaked. You know that Chief's wife cheated on him, so I have a hard time with commitment." That's my story, and I'm sticking to it.

Like his brother, though, Jake won't accept simple answers. "So, the boyfriend recipe doesn't work? Is that it?"

"She said *Maybe*," Jonah says.

Lindsay pulls the blanket onto her lap, too, and snuggles next to me. "We haven't even tried the recipe yet."

Jake looks expectantly at me. "There's more to the story."

I've never felt so much pressure. Jonah grabs his phone and starts texting someone, and my heart hammers in my chest. I don't want to hurt his parents, too. Is he telling them that we broke up? Will they know before I do?

Jake clears his throat. "Spill, Brie. The whole story."

Jonah's not looking at me, and I'm desperate to not cry, so I launch into Chief's story. "It's all about the fifth step of the recipe." They look like they have no idea what I'm talking about. "Commitment. I got off work and thought I would surprise my friend with some take-out for dinner, but I was the one who got the surprise." I pause to let them fill in the details for themselves. "I saw her wedding ring lying on the coffee table in the living room, along with, well, various articles of clothing, and I've never thought of wedding rings the same way. If it's so easily discarded, then what does it mean in the first place?"

Jake's going to make me tell the *whole* story. "I don't get it. How did you get inside their apartment? Where was Chief?"

"Keypad. Afghanistan."

It takes a moment, but he nods. Lindsay claps a hand to her mouth.

"I texted him and woke him up. Long story, but it was the middle of the night for him, and he asked me to stay there and take video of the guy coming out of the apartment to get proof. I had to testify against his wife, and she assaulted me. It was ugly."

Jonah glances up from his phone, and I know he's been listening to the whole story by the vein pulsing in his neck. He stands. "You two should get back to dinner." He leans over and grabs the Red Sox hoodie off the floor. "I can bring you a plate, if you want, Brie, or you and I can eat over here."

I nod. He's trying to get a moment to tell me that he knows I'm right. This will never work.

"No." Jake snatches the navy-blue hoodie once again. "Jonah would never, ever do that, and I know you wouldn't. He's not Danny, and you're not Patricia. Neither am I, and Lindsay isn't either. This is ridiculous. When are we going to stop being traumatized by our friends' stories?"

"And why did you freak out last night when things were going so well?" Lindsay asks. "I mean, if you don't mind my asking. I'm totally worried that Jake would cheat on me, too, since he was cheating on someone else the first time he kissed me. Never mind. You don't have to answer that. That was a completely fair freakout for you to have."

Jonah settles on the far end of the couch.

Lindsay smiles, and Jake stares at her. "I am never, ever going to gain your trust, am I?"

She shrugs. "Actions speak louder, and all that."

Jake holds out his hand. "I'm not giving up on you. Tell me how to earn your trust while we eat. Jonah's given up on dinner, and now his pork is getting cold. Tragic." He grins, but Jonah's face is still dead serious.

Jonah's shoulders are slumped, and I'm not sure whether he's more upset about dinner or me. The man does take his food seriously.

Lindsay takes Jake's hand. "Let's start by acknowledging the way you traumatized me by kissing me while you had a girlfriend and then walking away without acknowledging it for three years, oh yeah, and making me wonder if it was your brother."

Jake glances over his shoulder at me. "See what great communicators we are? We're having a breakthrough right now."

I sink into the couch. "So, what I'm hearing is that Lindsay thinks you're the worst."

Jake laughs. "She's not wrong. In fact, she's probably an excellent judge of character."

Lindsay laughs, too, and my *Maybe* breakup might actually

be helping them make progress. So, at least there's that. I had a theoretical engagement, and now I have a hypothetical breakup.

"Lindsay?" Jake yanks the blanket off me. "Let's fix this. If Joey and Brie won't, it's up to us."

I hold onto the cuff of my Yankees hoodie. "Hey! No intervention is necessary."

Lindsay pulls me to my feet and grabs one sleeve of my hoodie. "Yes, it is. I can't let you like the Yankees."

Lindsay slips my hoodie over my head, and Jake holds up the Red Sox hoodie. Lindsay crams my arms into it, and Jake pulls it over my head. "That's better," he says. "Now I can eat." He nods at Jonah on his way out. "You got this, bro. You're a Butler brother. You know how to fight. Talk her off the ledge."

They leave the cabin. I tug at the sweatshirt to unbunch it and flatten the hood. It smells like pine and woodsmoke, like someone made a man candle of Jonah's scent. I curl into it and pick up my Yankees hoodie from the floor. "I'm not on any ledge."

Jonah follows my movements with his gaze, watching me intently, then he pushes off the opposite end of the couch. He crosses the room and stands in front of me with his arms hanging awkwardly at his sides. His gaze drops to the hoodie. "That looks better."

I pull at the bottom of the oversized sweatshirt and smooth my hair. "They think your Red Sox shirt is more binding than an engagement ring."

Jonah approaches me like I'm a frightened deer, carefully, one step at a time. He slowly runs one hand along the frayed edge of my sleeve. "They think you have to marry me now that you put it back on, or something." Jake and Lindsay are gone, but he lowers his voice anyway. It's deep and rumbly. "I won't tell them your real reasons for breaking up with me."

I slip my hand in my pocket and pull out my grandmother's ring. "You mean, this? And who says I'm breaking up with you? I never gave you an answer."

He freezes, then steps even closer, and his dark eyes gleam with a piercing intensity. "You gave me back my hoodie."

"It has to get washed at some point." But I always wear a shirt under it, and I only wear it for a couple hours at a time. Washing it would ruin the Jonah-aroma, and I've never spilled anything on it yet.

"So, that wasn't your answer?" We're standing a breath apart now. Jonah's eyes rake over my face, searching for something I'm not ready to give him.

I swallow. "I don't have an answer yet."

Jonah's eyes drop to my grandmother's ring. "Okay. No rush." His hand cups my own. "May I see it?"

I drop the ring lightly into his palm, and his pinky finger skims the edge of my hand as I let go.

Jonah holds up the ring, then rolls it around and around. "Does it fit?"

Our eyes lock, and my heart races at his proximity. I've already cried myself to sleep and cried through the church services this morning. I should know better, but I hold out my left hand. "About as well as the hoodie. It's a little too big."

Jonah's tentative gaze grows more confident as his fingers brush against the sensitive skin on my palm. He takes his time exploring my outstretched hand, and every nerve tingles where he touches me. A crooked grin lifts one side of his mouth when I gasp at his touch. Jonah takes hold of my hand. "Let's see how the ring would look. Hypothetically."

He waits for my permission, and I nod.

The ring slides easily onto my fourth finger, as I know it will.

I already tried it on this morning.

# Chapter Twenty-Eight

A SLAMMING door interrupts the moment. "That's more like it." Jake wraps an arm around both of us and pushes us outside. "Come tell me that my dish is better."

"Knock," Jonah growls. "Seriously, how hard is it to learn to knock?"

Jake walks behind us until we're inside the twins' cabin, and then he pulls out a chair and pushes me into it. "I'm not eating without Brie."

Lindsay looks up from some thinly sliced steak. "There you are." She notices the ring. "Oh. They didn't break up. They were just *on* a break. That's different."

"Well, break time is over." Jake slides into a chair. He balances all the components of Jonah's dish on his fork, tastes a bite, and swears. "You beat me again." There are pureed potatoes and pickled vegetables, and the marinade on the meat has reduced to a glaze.

I lean over and pull out the chair beside me. Jonah shoots me a glance, then slowly sits.

"Seriously." Jake loads another bite on his fork. "If you and Jonah can't make it, no one can."

"I mean, right?" Lindsay sips her water. "What hope do I have if Brie breaks up with the man of her dreams?"

Jonah arches an eyebrow at me. A tiny smile plays on his lips. "Man of your dreams?"

I wrap my hand around the comforting chill of a smooth glass cup. "I might have said that at some point."

"Dream lover, right there." Jake can't stop eating his brother's dish. "Tell me about that ring."

Jonah sets down his fork. "It's just—"

"—it's just my grandmother's," I interrupt. I can't dash their hopes, not when they haven't been on a real date yet. "My grammy was married for twenty happy years, and she wore it until she died. It's my only heirloom and my good luck charm, even if Gramps died young."

Lindsay takes my hand and examines the golden band with its swirling paisley design. "I like it. It's simple, but it has a story."

Jake leans over to look as well. "Have you sent Ma a picture yet? That is pretty funky. I love the vibe."

Jonah holds up a hand. "Don't. We're just trying it out. Brie might be taking it off tonight, right?"

I push the food around my plate. "Maybe." I smile at him.

Jonah clears his throat. "I'll walk Brie back to her cabin, then come clean up." He catches my eye.

I'm pretty sure he senses my discomfort. We still haven't had a good conversation, and he obviously wants an answer, something more solid than a *Maybe*. We need some alone time.

Jake shakes his head violently. His mouth is too full to talk. After he swallows, he points at my chair. "Not when you and Joey just got back together. You can cuddle and read on the couch. I'll do the dishes and Lindsay can watch TV. Right, babe?"

She rolls her eyes. "*Babe?*"

"Who's in charge of the Bro Fund now?" Jonah asks innocently.

Lindsay grins. Jake mutters a few choice words beneath his breath and empties his wallet into her waiting hand. "Come on.

You know you want to. We can finish our season and find out who wins."

Lindsay looks at me. She's even more indecisive than I am. "Shouldn't I help with dishes?"

"I got this." Jake insists. He's working hard for his snuggle session.

I take a bite of pork tenderloin, pureed potatoes, and a creamy mushroom sauce. "The fresh herbs make this sing."

Jonah flashes me a tentative smile. "Thanks."

Neither of us knows what to do with an audience listening to us. I poke at the mushroom sauce that I didn't really taste. "Is that dill or tarragon?"

"Parsley and thyme."

Jake pushes the other plate away. "Don't try mine. Too much salt. I went with a barbecue rub on some ribs, and it failed epically."

"I don't mind the salt," Lindsay says. "You're too hard on yourself."

His face softens. "Thanks, Linz."

"Should've gone with mesquite," Jonah mutters and almost grins at me. "Beats Kansas City barbecue every time."

I grin back. "Now you're talking."

Jake glances between us. "Ah, nah. You're up in the night. I've got to nail my flavors. We can't let Tommy down, especially since he moved the show to Boston for us."

I cough, then try to cover my reaction by taking a long drink of water. "The show is in Boston?"

Jonah glares at his brother. "Confidentiality, man. We can't tell anyone where the show is. You know Tommy is hardcore about privacy."

Jake shrugs. "It's Brie, and you're engaged. Right, lovebirds, you're still on?"

Jonah catches my eye, then slowly nods his head. "Probably."

I bite my lip. *Probably* is better than *Maybe*. It's still somewhere in the vast wasteland of *Undecided* where I've taken up residence, but at least there's some hope there. I nod back at Jonah.

He looks at Lindsay. "But you're not. We signed a waiver."

Jake arches an eyebrow. "Not yet, bro. Not yet. I still have a week."

Lindsay laughs. "Do you boys compete for everything?"

The twins answer at the same time. "Yes."

Jake shovels another bite of the pork and mushroom sauce into his mouth. "Hang on." He finishes it, then continues talking. "Here's the deal, Brie, since Jonah won't tell you. Tommy is thinking of moving to Boston. He might open restaurants or start taping his shows there. He's coming to our house for Christmas Eve and Christmas Day to talk to Dad and Pappy."

I lock eyes with Jonah. This is why we can never be together. Panic rises in my chest, and my heart pounds in my ears. Every time I let a little hope into my heart, something crowds it out.

Jake turns on the TV. "Go. I'll do the dishes."

I can't look away from Jonah.

Guilt flashes in his eyes. "I signed a confidentiality agreement." He starts their fireplace, which is a mirror image of ours, and grabs a throw blanket. "Cuddle time?" he asks grimly, like it's his execution and I'm holding an axe.

I'm not that mad, but I feel betrayed that he kept that huge piece of information from me when he's knows I'm trying to gather my courage to make this huge decision.

We sit close to each other, but we're not touching beneath the blanket. Jake probably can't tell. After a couple minutes, I shift so my back leans against Jonah's shoulder, and I'm facing away from him. I kick out my legs the long way on the couch, and that gives us a reason not to snuggle. The blanket stretches at a weird angle and doesn't cover either of us.

It could be a metaphor for our relationship, but I push the thought away and shove the blanket onto Jonah's lap. I'm not getting deep. Not tonight.

My mind is still racing from Jake's information. New York isn't safe. What will I do if my dad moves to Boston?

I don't want to move again. I want to have Christmas in the same place twice.

*Now you understand me*, Mom says in my head. *I never wanted to move so often either.*

Jonah sacrifices the blanket and tucks it around my legs. *Martyr.* He leans across my lap, and I get a whiff of his pine after-shave as he straightens.

"Thanks," I say grudgingly.

He nods and stares at the TV.

I can't concentrate on my book because I'm left-handed. I ate dinner earlier with my left hand, and now I'm holding my phone with my right hand but swiping with my left hand. *Every. Single. Page.* I pull up the blanket when it slips—with my left hand.

Every time I do *anything*, I see a flash of gold and notice that band on my finger.

How long am I going to wear this? Somehow, I can't bring myself to break the fragile thread of hope that Lindsay and Jake have, even if it's erroneously based on me and Jonah. I also can't be the one to extinguish the tiny flame of hope that's flared to life in my own heart.

Part of me wants to wear Grammy's ring for the rest of the night, because it's like a hug from the past, even if it means that Jonah keeps glancing over at me with sad puppy dog eyes, like he wants to say, *That looks good on you.*

Or *You should keep that on.*

Or *Marry me tomorrow.*

Or *Probably* is a lot like *Yes.*

Or am I the only one thinking those thoughts?

A notification comes in that my loan has finally been approved. That's a week or two early, so I'm relieved. I'd better finish the paperwork. I have to get a letter from my current employer, and what if I break up with Jonah? Will Mr. Butler refuse to sign the notice, or worse yet, fire me?

But what if I keep this ring on? Jonah is moving to New York in a few months. What would I do with the townhouse then, and how can our fledgling romance survive long-distance?

I've already sunk so much money into the escrow for this loan that I can't afford to leave Boston. I already gave up my dream of working as a professional chef when I heard that Tommy had moved to New York. I decided it wasn't safe to return to the world I knew, and I extended my contract with the Air Force to cross-train as an accountant.

What choice do I have? Maybe Tommy will hate Boston and stay in New York. I can't keep moving to avoid him, if he opens restaurants in every major city.

I shift my weight on the couch to sit up, and Jonah glances at my phone screen, like he wants to know who I'm texting or what I'm doing.

He didn't warn me that Tommy is moving to Boston. I don't have to explain myself to him.

I click on the link and fill out the application—again. It looks just like the last one. Name, social, date of birth. Credit card, bank account, blah blah. It takes a while, and the episode is nearly over. I double check a few numbers on my bank app, but yeah, I have most of them memorized.

Jake comes over.

"Thanks for doing the dishes," Jonah says.

"Anything to buy you some *almost-alone time*." Jake winks at us and tosses Jonah another blanket for his lap. He settles next to Lindsay. "Hashtag couples' goals right there, babe. You're with me, right? You want something like that?"

Lindsay doesn't look away from the TV, but nods. "You know it. Love, marriage, kids, the whole deal."

Jake relaxes and drapes an arm across the back of the couch. He tosses a blanket over her lap and turns to look at her. "Is this okay?"

Lindsay stiffens. "Is what okay?"

I glance up from my loan approval form. "It's couples' cuddle time," I say. "Let's watch the finale."

"Oh." Lindsay arranges the blanket over both of them. "This is great." She slips her arm behind his back. Not in a cute way. In a really awkward way.

Jonah shifts on the couch. "Are you comfortable?"

"Yep."

He stretches his legs and kind of grunts.

I sigh. "Are you?"

He rolls his shoulder, the one I'm kind of leaning against. "Maybe. Maybe not. Mostly not." He gazes down at me, and I know we're not talking about his position on the couch right now.

"You're fine, boyfriend." I nudge his shoulder, then turn. Lindsay's watching me. Lindsay, who has never had a boyfriend and doesn't know how to cuddle. Lindsay, my new best friend, who I'd do almost anything for. Lindsay, whose arm is currently pinned behind Jake's back at an uncomfortable angle.

I swing my legs around. Jonah immediately opens his arms. I snuggle into his side and toss the other blanket on the couch. He leans down, and his low voice rumbles in my ear. "Much better."

His hand strokes my hair, and my head falls onto his chest. I close my eyes and tuck my feet under myself.

Jonah pulls me closer into the circle of his arms, and neither of us pretends to watch the show. It's been less than a day, and I've missed him so much that it's a physical pain. I didn't know until he held me, and the ache vanished.

Jonah presses a kiss to the top of my head, and I'm feeling drowsy. The fireplace blower kicks on. Jake hops up to turn off the overhead lights, so there's only a faint glow from the under-counter lights.

"Congratulate me," I say. My ring hand rests on Jonah's chest. "I closed on my townhome tonight."

Jonah tucks a finger beneath my chin and tips my head to face him. "You can't. It's Sunday."

"Well, I got a text that my loan was approved."

He's rubbing circles on my back now. "Weird."

But my eyes are closed again. "Why is that weird?"

"Shhh," Jake says. "They're judging the showstoppers."

"Sorry." Jonah lowers his voice. "It's Sunday. Who works at a loan office on Sunday night?"

Cold seeps through every part of me. I'm an accountant. I should be the one asking that question.

I sit up so quickly that I knock his chin with my head. "Sorry."

He keeps his arm locked tight around me. He laces his fingers through mine and spins the engagement ring on my finger. "Can I see the text?"

"Yeah." I grab the phone out of my pocket, and he has to let go because I'm scrolling frantically. Both hands are shaking. "This is so bad." I should have told him when I got the text. I should have shown it to him, but I was still mad at him for keeping secrets from me.

Secrets that he legally is not allowed to tell me, so yeah, it's not his fault that he has integrity.

He's holding me tight with one arm around my shoulders, and now his other hand is on my knee. "I'm sure it's fine. Probably some automatic message to fill out forms for your loan. Luke programs stuff like that."

"No. You're right." I find the text, and we read it together. "Look at the red flags. Typos. No mortgage company name. Urgent deadline." I collapse into the couch.

Jonah wraps me in a hug and holds me tight. "I'll call Nick, and he'll walk you through this. We'll set up new accounts and do whatever you need to protect you."

He's already got his phone out, but I put a hand over it.

Jonah traces the ring slowly. "What?"

"Nick's my boss, and I work in finance. I can't believe I fell for this. If he knows, he'll think I'm so dumb. I don't want to make extra work for him. He's already so busy, and I should have known better."

*You're a burden. If it wasn't for you, my life would be so much easier.* Echoes of Mom ring in my head. *Are you trying to make my life harder?* she asks.

Jonah pushes my hand aside and pierces me with the fiercest gaze I've ever seen. "It's never your fault when someone takes advantage of you, and no one takes advantage of my fiancée."

I lower my voice so Jake and Lindsay can't hear our conversation over the noise of the television. "I'm your fiancée again? Hypothetically?"

Jonah's already dialing, and he's holding his phone next to his ear. "You can decide how theoretical that ring is, but it looks pretty real to me, and it looks pretty good on your hand, girlfriend."

Something warmer than cocoa or Christmas fills me inside.

I hear Nick's voice. "Joey. What's up?"

Jonah looks at me, and I nod. He puts the call on speakerphone. "Hey. We have a situation, and I don't know how to salvage it."

Nick's voice booms across the living room. "Did Brie break up with you? *Beg.* That's all I've got."

Jake and Lindsay laugh.

"Nah, he's good, bro," Jake yells. "She broke up, but they're already back together. He's the real deal at this love and relationship thing."

Jonah takes Nick off speaker and lowers his voice. "Sorry, Nick. Don't listen to Jake. We didn't break up, and we're fine. Long story, but no need to tell Mom what Jake said." Jonah takes a deep breath. "I called because Brie got caught in a phishing scam and gave them..." He glances at me.

I take the phone. "Everything. I gave them everything. Hey, Nick, it's me."

"What was it?"

"An online loan application that looked identical to my original one. How bad is it?"

Nick's voice is low and deep, like his brother's, and just as gentle. "I'm so glad you called. I got caught in one of those a year ago, and I know how easy it is. No shame. I can walk you through this because I just did it. You're going to have to close your accounts, and you're going to lose your loan."

I can't speak.

Jonah presses his cheek against mine, so we can both speak into his phone. "There's no way she can still buy her townhome? She's supposed to close in a week."

Nick groans. "Nah, man. I had to close my account last year and open a new one for this exact same reason. It takes time. There's no way she can transfer that much money to the new account and get checks and make wire transfers, even if they were willing to overlook how new her account is. It's not gonna happen. I'm really sorry."

I'm aware of how close Jonah's mouth is to mine. Right now, the bottom of my world is falling out beneath me and he's the only thing keeping me steady. I want to be with him forever. I want to say *Yes*.

So, when he ends the call and cups my cheek with his hand, part of me wants to kiss the ever-living daylights out of him to thank him for being my rock, but a louder part whispers, *Look how bad you just messed up again. Look what a burden you are*. I close my eyes and drop my head on his shoulder.

Jonah pulls me into a gigantic bear hug, and I wonder how bad it would be to wear the ring for the rest of the week until he leaves for Boston because I really, really need the emotional support he's giving me right now.

I want to pretend like this can work, and after pretending for so long, my heart doesn't know anything else. What if it could be? What if it already is?

# Chapter Twenty-Nine

I WEAR Grammy's worn golden ring when I work out the next morning. Chief glances at it. "Nice."

"Thanks."

"Crunches."

That's the whole conversation, and then he puts Lindsay and me through a killer workout, as usual. After we're done, Lindsay and I walk with him to his car.

"I'll reserve the farmhouse by the ski resort for your wedding. It gets booked early, so we'll be lucky if there's a date left."

I lean against his car and wipe my face with the bottom of my t-shirt. The chill air feels good on my hot skin. "I'm not ready to set a date."

"You won't ever be ready, so I'm setting one for you. You can change it or cancel it." He whips out his phone and pulls up some website. When I see the pictures, I have to admit that it's my dream wedding venue.

Someone's turned an old barn into a reception center with guest rooms, and it's here in Sugar Creek. There are huge windows that overlook a meadow, and you can see St. Ambrose Peak in the background. "You want the first or second weekend in

October. I'll see what I can do." Chief slips his phone in his pocket. "I know them."

"It's really not necessary."

"You'll feel differently in a few months, and then it will be booked." Chief pops open his car door. "Is this a double wedding, Lindsay?"

Her eyes widen. "Okay. Just in case. You said we can cancel or change the date?"

Chief nods and slips into his car. "Am I telling Jake, or is this a surprise?"

Lindsay darts a glance at me. "Let's keep it a surprise. I don't know if I like him yet."

Chief huffs. "You're both lying to yourselves. Of course you like him, Lindsay, and Brie, you want to set a date. You're just scared. You can both thank me next year by making me the best man." He slams the door and drives away.

"Tough love," I say. "You get used to him."

Lindsay and I walk through the December air to our cabin. My muscles burn, but my head is clear. "I'm going to hop next door for a sec before I shower."

Lindsay grabs my arm. "Is Chief usually right?"

"Always. Why? Do you need someone to tell you that you like Jake?"

"Yes. No. I'm so confused." Lindsay lets go. "Is this love? Do I love him? I admire his good qualities. I've seen the good that he does, but he never lets me see the *real* him. He's always putting on an act. I only catch glimpses of his potential when he lets down his guard and has no idea that I'm watching." She sighs. "I expected it to be more fun to fall in love."

I laugh. "Nah. It's all nerves and flutters and stress. *Being* in love is way more fun than *falling* in love."

Lindsay pushes open the door. "Maybe Jake is right. We should skip the dating part and go straight to the girlfriend part."

I'm not sure how to respond, since Jonah and I actually did

that, so she takes my silence the wrong way. Lindsay laughs awkwardly. "But no one does that."

I knock on Jonah's door. "Right. No one does that."

Even though it's seven in the morning, Jake whips the door open. "What's up?"

"I need a minute with Jonah."

"Alone time, lover boy!" Jake yells. He looks over my shoulder. "Lindsay? Wait up!" He jogs across the clearing without waiting for an answer.

I cross their living room and watch Jonah dicing vegetables for an omelet or frittata or something. He glances over. "Brie." His eyes drop to the ring on my left hand, and his knife drops on the cutting board. He smiles and leans against the counter. "Hey."

"Can we talk real quick? I know you and Jake are working extra-long hours this week."

He rinses his hands in the sink and dries them. He's wearing a short sleeve black t-shirt under his apron, and his hair isn't styled yet. He's got on some flannel pajama pants and leather slippers. He looks perfect.

Jonah prompts me because I'm gawking at his awesomeness. "I'm listening."

I slide onto one of the bar stools at the kitchen counter. "I'm sorry things have been so up and down the last day or two. I hate to be *that* girl, you know, but then last night Lindsay and Jake made another assumption, and I couldn't let them down, even though we hadn't had a chance to talk. She and Jake are barely starting out, and I can't kill their fledgling romance."

He flashes me a blinding grin. "Right. I'm glad we're talking now."

"I don't know how quickly I can commit to a *Yes*."

Jonah glances down at my hand. "*Probably* is great for now."

I hold it up and wiggle the fingers. "Is that all right with you? I don't want to be unfair to you, but I'd love to go back to what we were doing."

His brow furrows. "You mean the theoretical, hypothetical junk?"

I laugh. "Hey, yes. Something like that while I'm deciding." I play with the edge of the cutting board. "You started it."

He shrugs. "I'm an idiot. We've established that."

"No, you're not. You respect my boundaries, so I can tell the truth, and I value the way that you also have integrity. You're willing to wait and give me the time and space I need instead of rushing me." I take a deep breath. "And I really appreciated your help last night."

Jonah reaches across the counter and takes my hand. "So, you want to keep testing our recipe? We already know it works." His thumb skims lightly over my skin.

My breath hitches. "I thought I'd wear my grammy's ring, but maybe we could back off on the make-outs. I can't think straight when you kiss me."

A slow grin breaks across Jonah's face. "I'm thinking crooked right now because I want to kiss you." His gaze rakes over me slowly and settles on my lips, and heat flares in his eyes.

I let go of his hands. "If we go back to the original plan and you don't break up with me until you leave for Boston, we could also help Lindsay and Jake."

Jonah scrubs a hand over his face. "So, my choices are break up now or break up on Friday? How about not at all? That would help *me*. A lot."

His brown eyes are pools of chocolate sadness. I feel like I killed his puppy, burned his brisket, and cancelled Christmas. "I don't like the idea, either, but... Tommy is always going to be my dad. If you can find a way around that..."

His gaze searches my face. "I'll take the delay, if this week is all I have, but I hate the idea of scratching the recipe completely when it works so well. Give it a chance."

"Again, Tommy. He can ruin your career, too, and I've already given up cooking." My throat feels tight. "I've cooked meals for the president of the United States to eat on Air Force One. I've cooked for four-star generals in Europe. I've cooked for queens and prime ministers as well as airmen in mess halls, and I loved it all. Tommy took that from me."

Jonah's eyes are filled with so much understanding and sympathy that I keep rambling. "You know what it's like to obsess over flavors and herbs and ingredients, and now I make sexy spreadsheets instead."

He's still giving me some fiery compassion with a side of smolder, and there's no way I will last a week without kissing Jonah. I clear my throat. "We should spend as little time together as possible. It's crunch time for you and Jake, plus I know you're still working on your restaurant concept." And I can think better when my hormones aren't fully activated.

Jonah rounds the kitchen counter. "But you want to show Lindsay how it's done, right, girlfriend?"

"Right," I answer hesitantly. "Why does this feel like a trap?"

Jonah grins and advances toward me. "Is it just kissing that's off-limits or all PDA?"

I eye his snug black t-shirt and pajama pants, slung low on his hips. We are way too comfortable with each other, and I hope I won't regret this, but I still say, "Just kissing, I guess."

"So, PDA is back on the menu." He settles his hands on my hips and tugs me off the bar stool. "I've missed you since last night."

My hands land on his chest, and my heart races. "See? My brain stopped working. Now. Completely blank."

Jake slams the door open.

"Knock!" Jonah yells. "Why don't you ever knock?"

"I live here." Jake leans against the wall. "What are we doing?"

"Having a moment."

Jake groans and hides himself in the refrigerator, rummaging loudly for ingredients.

I wrap my arms around Jonah's neck. "I'm going back to my cabin to call Nick, then we'll probably call my loan company as soon as they open, and my bank, and yeah. Basically, Nick and I are going to spend all day dealing with the bank fraud from last night."

"I'm sorry." Jonah's arms wrap around me, and I barely resist crying. I'm lost in the circle of his strong embrace. This is what I need. Someone to help me through the week.

And what if we can find a way to make it last longer?

I tip my head up to gaze at him and whisper, "Thank you."

He rests his forehead against mine and threads our fingers together. He spins Grammy's ring, which is still a little loose. "I want to do so much more. No more test batches. I'm ready for the real deal."

I nod. "But thanks for what you are doing. Thanks for waiting."

His eyes drop to my lips. "You're killing me."

"It's hard for me, too," I say softly.

He groans when I let go.

I head back toward my cabin without kissing him goodbye.

Jake slams the refrigerator. "What's hard? I missed something."

I'm at the door when Jonah answers. "Love, bro. Love is hard."

# Chapter Thirty

WHILE JONAH TESTS recipes all week, he also finds ways to test my tolerance for affection. Now, this is the man who memorized the consent policy, so none of it is inappropriate—it's impressively creative.

First, he and Jake need me and Lindsay to taste things all the time, so I'm constantly in their cabin all week.

Second, he needs a sous chef, someone to help chop vegetables and help sauté and make sauces, and he has to reach around me to get something or check to see how the food looks or taste the seasoning, and that turns into a hug. Every. Single. Time.

And third, he has to go over every single ingredient that Tommy Fuller might throw at him, and he wants my ideas, since I'm a trained chef, too. He spreads the papers all over the counter, and he's got his hand on the small of my back, since *that's* okay, and this conversation goes on and on and on, since the possible combinations are endless.

He's got to lean across the counter to point, and his cheek brushes mine when we look at the papers, and he still smells like that stupid pine aftershave.

Everything I do to put distance between us backfires. I wear more lotion than usual to avoid smelling his pine lumberjack scent, but then he wraps his arms around me and leans close to take deep breaths, and asks, "Why do you always smell like peppermint?"

"Shampoo and body wash and lotion."

He groans. "I do not need that visual."

I go back to stirring my sauce and try not to think about Jonah shaving or how smooth or stubbly his cheek might be at the moment. He leans forward and dips a clean spoon in the sauce to taste it and takes advantage of the moment to press his cheek against mine.

Medium-smooth-to-stubbly. That's how Jonah's cheek feels. It must be late afternoon.

I'm not sure if we are ever *not* touching for the entire week. I have to hand it to the man. His ability to improvise has improved.

And he never does reach my limit for PDA.

Jake's on board with Jonah's strategies, of course, and he uses them on Lindsay, but with far less success. She doesn't know how to cook with him, she works in our cabin, and she backs away when he gets too close.

But she will eat his food, and she always picks his dish over Jonah's. Every. Single. Time.

When Thursday night rolls around, I give Chief my ticket to go on some super romantic ski date that Jonah had planned. Chief has a night off from driving the North Pole Express train, so I tell him that they can go have some bro-bonding time on the lantern-lit cross-country skiing trail, and I stay home to finally finish my book.

Tomorrow is Friday, and it's breakup day. Or not. It's D-Day. Decision Day. There's no way I'm going to subject myself to the most romantic date ever on the eve of our breakup, if there is one, or let myself get carried away by emotion and make a rash decision.

But even that backfires. After Lindsay comes home, Jonah pounds up the stairs and slams open my bedroom door. His cheeks are flushed, and he's still wearing most of his gear.

I push off my stomach and sit on the edge of my bed. "What's wrong?"

Jonah tears off his Red Sox beanie, unzips his parka, and drops them both on the floor. "Did you reserve a wedding venue for next fall?"

I stare at him. He's dead serious, and I can't read his expression. "Chief reserved the local farmhouse for sometime in October, I believe."

His dark eyes flash, and he steps closer. "I've never wanted to kiss you more than I do right now."

I've never wanted to kiss him more than I do as he advances toward me. I swallow and lean against the headboard. "Close the door, and I'll explain."

Jonah kicks his parka out of the way and collapses in the chintz chair in the corner. I hate my own no-kissing rule, but I'm going to keep it, or my heart will never survive if we do break up.

"Where are Jake and Lindsay? Can they hear us?"

He nods toward the closed door. "They are down on the couch. What does this have to do with them?"

I tilt my head against the wall. "You can't repeat this."

Jonah edges forward to the edge of the seat. "Fine."

"Chief reserved it for a double wedding for Lindsay and me."

Jonah's eyes widen. "You're kidding."

I shake my head. "She wants it to be a surprise for Jake."

He drops his head in his hands. "Do you know what you're doing to me? First, you wear that ring, then you set a wedding date."

"You weren't supposed to know." I scoot around the edge of the bed and take Jonah's hands.

He immediately tugs me onto his lap. "Chief tells me everything."

I squirm to settle into his arms, and his ski pants rustle beneath me. "This doesn't change the fact that Tommy Fuller is my dad, and he's practically a member of your family. Chief didn't know that when he made the wedding reservation."

"But you didn't tell Chief *No*. You let him do that." Jonah rubs his hand up and down my back and rests his chin on my head. "That got my hopes up."

"Chief said we could cancel or change the reservation. It was just..."

Jonah puts his finger on my lips. "Don't say it. We both know this is real." He traces the outline of my lips and tips my chin up to look at him. "I'm starting to hate myself for ever telling you this was fake, but I'm starting to hate Tommy even more, even though I love the guy."

"I don't want you to regret this when it's over," I say, even though I will. "I'm trying and trying to think of ways around the obstacles—"

"What happened to *Probably*?" Jonah asks gruffly in a low and gravelly voice. He pulls me into one of his smothering bear hugs, and I love the feeling of safety in his arms.

But I ruin people's lives. How many times did Mom tell me that? I can't ruin Jonah's life or his career or his relationship with Jake or take him away from his family. "I'm trying," I whisper, and my voice catches as emotions knot in my chest. The harder I try to love Jonah and fight for our relationship, the louder Mom's voice gets.

*If it wasn't for you...*

*You were a mistake.*

*I could have done so much more with my life if I hadn't had you.*

*Do you have any idea how much I sacrificed for you?*

I try to silence the voices. Jonah doesn't see me that way. Does he? Should he?

We sit that way, snuggling in the oversize armchair, for a few minutes, and it's easier and easier to believe that Jonah loves me as the heat grows between us. I can't resist the pull much longer when Jake pounds on my door. He pushes it open. "Hey, lovebirds, are you coming downstairs?"

Jonah sighs.

"What? I knocked."

"But then you *wait* for people to tell you to come in."

Jake looks at us cuddling in the chair. "Like I've never seen that before. Are you watching the show with us or not?"

"*Not.* We've got an early morning, and you're not watching it, either. Last day to prep for the show tomorrow."

I slip off Jonah's lap. "I'll see you tomorrow."

"Tomorrow." He leaves with a long look backward that has enough heat to sear any steak.

I check Jonah's private calendar, and it has "Break Up" scheduled in pink, his color for events with just him and me, for lunch. There's something new since last time I checked—an emoji of a red heart, the one broken in two with ragged edges. *Ouch.*

*I'm with you, J-Dog.*

But lunch comes and goes without a word. Jonah texts me instead of coming over, and I wonder if he's going to break up over the phone.

**Jonah**: Got some great recipes for the new restaurant.
**Me**: Good. You're going to win.
**Jonah**: If Jake gets the salt right.
**Me**: (laughing face emoji)

And that's it. They don't bring us lunch. He doesn't need me to be his sous chef today. We aren't going over the list of possible ingredients or menu items again.

I check Jonah's calendar. Maybe he doesn't use it.

Oh, he does use it. "Break Up" has been rescheduled to dinner time.

Lindsay and I don't hear anything from the twins until it's

almost time to leave for the play. Jake rushes into our cabin. "Are you ready?"

Jonah follows him in. "My fault. I burned everything and had to go to the store. Sorry. My mind isn't in the game today." He levels a gaze at me.

My heart stops.

Lindsay's unaware of the tension between us. "We were trying to decide where Brie should move now that she doesn't have anywhere to live. She says the current options are Boulder, Los Angeles, or a new apartment in Boston. She is leaning toward Boulder, but I want her to crash on my couch until she decides. I mean, a long-distance engagement would be so hard, and you'll both be in New York."

Jonah's brooding stare deepens. "You're moving?"

I can't find any solutions. I want to believe this relationship could work, but if it doesn't... "My landlord wants to sell to his backup buyer. I have to be out by Wednesday."

He and Jake are both glaring at me now. They speak at the same time.

"Why not New York?"

"You'd actually move to Boulder?"

I answer the easier question. "Boulder is a firm *Maybe*."

Jonah scoffs.

I don't need to get defensive, but I do. "I ran it past Nick and Luke. Nick said I could work from home, and Luke says there is space in the Boulder office."

A muscle ticks in Jonah's jaw. "Nick approved that?"

Jake actually cracks his knuckles like a Neanderthal. "He didn't approve it with either of us. Lindsay's right. That's too far to commute and see each other on weekends."

Lindsay notices the tension now. "Brie's staying with me after we leave Sugar Creek, right, Brie? At least until New Year's. I wish I had two bedrooms, but I have a comfy couch."

I nod. "Right. I won't move until after the holidays, and only if I can't find another solution." I catch Jonah's eye. "I'm trying. I'm looking around."

He folds his arms across his chest. "That's only two weeks away. That's not much time to decide on something so drastic."

And I know we're not talking about apartments. Jonah doesn't come right out with what he wants to say. He hides his worries inside another concern.

Jake whacks him on the chest. "Dude, did you leave the broiler on?"

"No idea." Jonah stares at me. "Luke knows, too?"

"You left the broiler on. I can smell it from here." Jake races out of the cabin.

"Nothing's final. Just looking at possibilities." I walk to the front door to put on my shoes. Jonah's wearing his *Deck the Halls* Christmas sweater. "Looks like you dressed up for tonight."

He holds up a piece of plastic mistletoe. "I went all out." He tosses the mistletoe on the bench by the door. "We should eat, if there's anything left."

There isn't. It's charcoal.

"They have snacks at the theater," Jake says as we slip into the SUV. "Sorry about dinner." He glances at Jonah. "You're totally off your game. Are you nervous about tomorrow? You don't usually get this worked up."

Jonah looks at me. "I've got a lot on my mind."

We pull up to the community center. A decent amount of snow is coming down, and it's a cool evening. Jonah casually slips an arm around me, and I wonder if it's the last time he'll do that.

Because I don't want to hold him back. I don't want to ask him to sacrifice for me, like my mom had to. I don't want to be a burden he resents later after the honeymoon phase wears off. I couldn't bear that heartache.

I know what it's like to be resented by the person you love most in the world, and I'll never do that again.

We enter the playhouse, and memories of watching Christmas movies flood me. *White Christmas* is playing, and a bright-eyed teenager escorts us to our seats. We've barely arrived in time to make the curtain, and there's no time to grab popcorn or anything to eat.

"Isn't this cozy?" Jake asks.

"Boy, girl, boy, girl," Jonah replies half-heartedly, with a side glance at me.

My stomach sinks. This was Mom's favorite movie, and I've never seen the play version of it. She could quote the lines by heart. How long has it been since I watched it?

Twelve years, but I still remember it. Sometimes, I forget her. I don't miss her, then I realize that I should.

My eyes cloud over, but no one sees because the lights go down, the music comes up, and the play starts. It's opening night, and the energy is vibrant.

Everyone else laughs at all the right places, but I feel heavier and heavier as the play goes on. It's about sisters and a fake engagement, and here I am, part of a fake engagement, but I'm all alone. No sister. No family.

At least I have friends. I have Jonah for now.

But I have to move to avoid Tommy Fuller, and he's moving to Boston, where Jonah's family lives. He's coming to Jonah's Christmas dinner, so I can't go.

Once again, my mom's decisions are taking away everything I love. So are my dad's choices.

But mine? My choice to fight for what I want? How can I do that when it means asking Jonah to leave his family behind? How can I ask him to spend Christmas Day alone with me, so we can avoid the man who wants nothing to do with me?

My temper rises. It's so unfair. If it were anything else, I would fight so hard for this relationship. But this? Asking Jonah to give up everything and risk his career?

And I realize I'm starting to make up my mind. I know what I'm going to have to do.

I've already lost the money I put down on my townhome, and I'm going to have to start all over again. It might as well be in

Boulder or a place where Tommy doesn't own restaurants. That rules out Los Angeles, come to think of it. I guess that means I'm moving to Colorado after New Year's.

Here we go again. Christmas in another place next year, as usual.

I've missed almost all of the first half of the play while I thought about my mom and my move and how none of this is right. I'm angry and sad and a thousand other emotions as we file out to the foyer during intermission, and the twins line up to buy snacks.

I'm not prepared for Jonah to hand me a tub of popcorn and a package of Red Vines. "It's not much of a dinner."

It's something my mom would say, and the shock wipes every other thought and emotion away. "What?"

"It's not much." His face is serious, and my stomach somersaults. This is when he's going to break up with me. It's on his calendar. Or he knows I will.

We have to decide before he leaves tomorrow morning.

I panic and set the popcorn and licorice down on the glass countertop behind me. I can't breathe.

Jonah grabs my hands and pulls me off to one side. "Hey, what's wrong?"

It's not usually hard for me to talk, but it takes me a second. Once I start, I can't stop. "That's my mom's favorite meal. Crazy, right? She was a chef and all that, but she was too tired to cook at home. It was all she could do to pop a bag of microwave popcorn, pour it in a bowl, and call it dinner." I laugh. "She used to say that, too. *It's not much, but it's the best I can do.* That pretty much sums up my childhood. It wasn't much."

I have to clench my jaw to keep from crying. "Is it weird that I remember the last meal we had together before she died? We watched *White Christmas* because it was her favorite and we watched it every year, and we had popcorn and licorice for dinner during the movie, then she went to work at Pappy's and never came back."

Jonah wraps me in a hug, and the tears are flowing now. The lights blink on and off a few times, so we know we have a few minutes to get back to our seats. Now that I've started, the emotions won't stop. "She never cooked for me. She cooked for everyone else, but never for me. She was too tired. It wasn't her fault."

Then I lose it. I opened the emotional floodgate before, and it starts to overflow. "I've blamed her my whole life." For some reason, with Jonah's unconditional and unquestioning love, even knowing that this might be temporary, I'm finally able to forgive her. "It wasn't her fault. She did her best. She was a single mom, you know, and her dad died right before she met Tommy, and then she got pregnant with me. I was a mistake."

Jonah grips me so protectively and gazes at me so tenderly that I can hardly breathe. "Don't ever say that."

I shake my head. "No, I was. She once told me that her mom changed once her dad died, and she had no one. Grammy pulled out of that depression after a few years of grieving, but I think that's *why* my mom got pregnant with me, you know? She was so alone at first when her dad died, and then Tommy moved to L.A. right after they got married, and she was alone again. He moved for a temporary job and never came back, and she had to work to provide for all of us—her mom, herself, and me. Grammy had never had a job, so my mom did what she could, and that should have been enough for me."

"Hey." Jonah rubs my back. "I would have loved licorice for dinner when I was a kid. I would have been so jealous of you, if you'd told me that. But, Brie, you are not a mistake."

I laugh through my tears. "She did better than I thought."

Jonah dips his head down to catch my eye. "She did great because you turned out great."

I can't respond. I can't tell him that I'm not a mistake.

He tugs me closer. "It must be hard to watch this show."

I tip my head up to look at Jonah. "Yeah."

My heart tries to beat out of my chest as emotions overwhelm me. I feel lighter because I told him so much, and I'm still heavy from the hurting, and so, so scared to lose him.

Like I lost her. Like I lose everyone.

"I'll cook for you as long as you'll let me," Jonah says in a low and husky voice. "Like, as long as we both shall live."

A dam breaks inside me. I grab his face and pull it down to mine, then I'm kissing him like *he's* dinner. Something aches inside me, but when Jonah responds and pours himself into the kiss, I'm complete.

I wrap my arms around his neck. He backs me up against the counter, and his arms trap me. I see him steady the popcorn, and I don't care if a few other patrons are streaming past us to find their seats. This urgency inside me can only be answered by Jonah.

It's been building all week, and it's a relief to finally kiss him again. Jonah's lips brush over mine frantically again and again, then the pressure deepens, and I wonder why we ever stopped kissing. This is obviously right, and he's my person.

Jake slaps him on the shoulder. "See you inside, bro."

Jonah's arms slip around my waist and pull me closer, lifting me off my feet. The lights blink on and off faster, and our time is ending.

Desperation glues me to him, and he has to be the one to end the kiss. We're both breathing hard. Jonah reaches past me to grab the popcorn bucket and licorice. "Can I buy you dinner?"

I wipe my eyes when I realize there are some tears there.

We sneak down the aisle. The play starts as we trip across everyone's knees to get to our seats.

Jake pounds Jonah on the back as we sit down. Jonah sets the popcorn bucket in my lap and drapes an arm around me. He holds me tight for the rest of the play, and when we get home, I check his personal calendar.

The "Break Up" item has been deleted.

That means I'll have to do it.

# Chapter Thirty-One

JAKE SLAMS OPEN the door of the gym a little after five thirty in the morning. We've barely started warming up.

"We're leaving."

Chief nods to him, and Lindsay waves from the treadmill. "Good luck! See you on Monday."

I sit up. "Goodbye."

Chief turns off his *Grinch* soundtrack. "Where's Jonah?"

Jonah appears in the doorway of the gym. He's wearing his Red Sox hoodie with a pair of dark wash jeans that fit his legs and thighs perfectly. His eyes flick to mine, and he takes in my form-fitting workout clothes. The same heat that burned between us last night flares again.

Jonah swallows. "Can I say goodbye to Brie alone?"

Jake stares at the sweatshirt, then blocks him. "Not if you're going to be an idiot."

Chief crosses the gym and folds his arms across his chest. "Is there a problem, Jake?"

"There better not be." Jake glares at his brother.

"He's leaving," I say. "I gave him back the hoodie for good luck."

Jake scoffs.

Jonah shoulders past his twin. "I need some alone time with Brie."

"Sure." I grab my water bottle, and we head down toward the lake, even though it's still dark and there are no fires. "It's freezing. Let's go to my cabin." We change course, and Jake and Chief and Lindsay watch us from the doorway of the gym.

"You better be making out!" Jake yells. "And nurturing your romance!"

As soon as we're inside my cabin, I reach for his Red Sox hoodie to warm up, but it's not there.

Jonah's wearing it, along with his Red Sox beanie. He sinks into a cushion on the far end of the sectional couch. "It's Saturday."

"It is." I flop in my usual spot in the middle of the couch, shivering. Jonah stretches to peel off his hoodie, and I see a sliver of abs underneath.

That is not helping with this breakup. The tight black t-shirt that shows off his washboard abs isn't helping, either. Jonah eyes my exercise bra and leggings, then tosses me the still-warm sweatshirt with his man scent on it. "You look cold."

I toss it back. "I'm good."

Jonah levels a gaze at me. "You're cold." His eyes drop to my bare stomach and shoulders and back up to my face, and then his gaze settles on my lips.

I'm pretty sure we're both thinking of a way to warm each other up, but Jake is waiting in the car or the gym or somewhere, and we have a painful conversation to get out of the way.

"I'm fine." I throw the hoodie back at him and grab a blanket instead. "I can't keep it if we break up."

Jonah shoves the hoodie in a wad next to him. "Is that what you want?"

I've known this was coming all along, in a way. Nothing will change who my father is. "Right. That was our deal."

Jonah's jaw clenches, and he nods. "Consider it done."

I want to hear him say the actual words, but I'm too stunned.

He really did it, and it's over that fast. He didn't try to talk me out of it or anything. I hate how much he respects me. I hate his integrity. I'm getting madder and madder at him for doing what I asked when someone pounds on the door.

"Not now," Jonah yells.

I hate this abrupt change when last night was perfect and almost magical. I want to tell him all my reasons and beg him to find an answer.

Jonah moves closer and sits beside me on the couch. There are dark circles beneath his eyes and worry lines around his eyes. "I was up all night after you gave me back my hoodie."

"Me, too." I want to take his hands, but I don't have that right anymore. "I don't see any way for us to have a relationship without asking you to pull out of the restaurant with Jake or quit the family business or us never going to your family's house on holidays. What would be the point of having grandkids if they couldn't know their grandparents?"

Jonah scrubs a hand down his face. "I know."

His answer guts me. I scan his face. "You do?"

He blows out a deep breath. "I had a lot of time to think last night. I don't know what else to do, Brie. I would take on any challenge for you. My entire family would. We love you." His jaw tightens. "Let me help you. Please. We can uninvite Tommy from Christmas Eve and Christmas dinner. Even if he blacklists us or causes trouble for Pappy and my dad's restaurants."

I see it happening. He's trying to sacrifice for me. He's trying to let his entire family sacrifice without asking them. "I want so much to let you do that, but I'd never ask you to choose, and you'd end up miserable if you gave up so much or if your family did. How selfish would I be?"

Jonah drapes an arm on the couch behind me and leans over, his eyes flashing. His voice is dangerously low. "You're asking me to walk away and leave you alone, and that feels even more selfish. It's just wrong."

Jake knocks, then slams open the door. "Come on, lovebirds. Alone time is over. We're going to be late."

"Dude." Jonah looks over and raises his voice. "We just broke off our engagement. I don't care if we're ten minutes late."

Jake gapes at him. "Don't be stupid. Brie, tell him he's stupid. Is he serious?"

My emotions finally engage. *I'm not engaged*. It was just a trial run, and it's done.

"He's serious." I take off Grammy's ring, pry open Jonah's hand, and shove the ring into his palm. "I don't want it back. I just...can't."

Jonah's arm slides off the couch, and he stares at his open palm. "What am I supposed to do with this?"

"Consider it a souvenir." I wrap his fingers around it, which is a mistake.

Jonah tugs my hand to his chest, and my grammy's ring peeks out between his fingers.

Jake smirks. "Is this a *break* or a breakup?"

I tear my hand away. The ring has too many memories of Jonah. It's not Grammy's ring anymore. I'd always think of him if I saw it.

Jonah reluctantly slips the ring into his pocket. "A breakup. The real thing. My call, not hers, so don't blame her or think she messed something up or text Mom before I can. This is all on me."

"Of course it is. It always is, and she doesn't want to marry someone dumb anyway." Jake pulls me off the couch and hugs me.

I'm touched by Jake's sarcasm. He only lashes out like this when he's hurting a lot, and Jake never wants to believe that Jonah and I are *really* fighting. Call it PTSD from Danny and Patricia's divorce.

Jake glares at Jonah over my shoulder but talks to me. "I'm going to miss you. You can marry Danny or Nick. Luke's weird, and Matt's too young for you."

Ouch. He's going too far today.

Jonah's jaw tightens. "She's not going to marry a Butler."

I tear myself out of Jake's smothering hug, but he slings an arm around my shoulders protectively. "Brie can marry anyone she wants next year. Chief says he has the venue reserved, but the groom is still to be determined. I vote for Nick."

Wow. Just wow.

Jonah shoves Jake away from me. He grabs his hoodie from the couch and tosses it to Jake. "Take my sweatshirt to the car, and I'll meet you there. I have to get my coat."

Jake catches it. "Fine, but you're making a huge mistake." He storms out of the cabin and leaves me with Jonah.

It's almost six o'clock now. It's dark outside and the sun won't rise for a couple more hours. Only the under-cabinet lights are on.

I stand in the middle of the living room, and my arms hang loosely at my sides. I feel broken and unlovable. I hoped for too much—for a solution. I drop my eyes to the carpet. I never should have allowed something to start that I knew would end like this.

I'm alone. I'll always be alone. Friends come and go, and it's best to move around so I don't expect permanence in my life.

"Brie." My name comes out in Jonah's choked voice.

I don't look up. This breakup was *my* idea, no matter what he told Jake. He's trying to protect me, but we both know that he's respecting my choice, and it's the right one. I'll never ask anyone to live the way I live or hurt the way I hurt. I'm never going to ask him to leave his family, so I can have one.

But part of me wishes he would fight me on this.

"Good luck." I glance up.

That's a mistake. Jonah's eyes plead with me, and I feel empty and incomplete. I back away.

Jonah watches every step I take. "Are you going to be okay? Because I'm not okay walking into Tommy's studio like we're still friends when I know what he's really like and what he's costing me."

I nod because I agree, not because I'm okay. I'm not going to tell him that I'm fine, because I'm not. I turn my back and walk up the stairs to the loft. "Goodbye."

"Brie," Jonah calls again urgently. "This doesn't have to be so final. We'll figure out a way around this. I'm going to miss you so much. Too much."

I pause halfway up the stairs, but I don't turn around. I've had a lifetime to think, and a lifetime of people leaving my life when things get hard.

"This was the plan," he pleads. "You said I had to do this."

I turn around and run my hands along the smooth wood banister. "I know. Thanks for following through."

He jams his hands in his jean pockets, and his right hand fidgets with Grammy's ring. "So... This is what you want? Final answer? Because it's not what I want."

I can't answer his question honestly, but it will only hurt us both more if I tell him the truth—if I tell him how much I love him. I have to press my lips together for a moment before I can answer in a steady voice. "No regrets, remember? I'm moving to Boulder anyway."

Jonah's eyes flick to mine. "You're really doing that?"

He seems to be holding his breath, hoping, like I am, that I will say something else.

*But I can't.* "I'm not going back to the Boston office, especially if Tommy moves there." No one sticks around, so it's easier to be the person who moves.

His shoulders droop, and his eyes drop to the floor, and my heart drops along with them. Jonah stares at me and walks slowly to the cabin door, his eyes never leaving mine. "I'm not ever going to see you again?"

I shake my head. "Not unless you visit Luke."

Jonah shoves open the door, and a blast of cold air enters the cabin. "I hate losing you."

"Just don't lose on Monday." I wave. "You've got this competition in the bag." My heart is breaking, but I want the best for him. This isn't fair to him or me, but I don't want him and Jake to lose because of it.

I've hurt him enough.

He scoffs. "My whole world just went dark, and I don't know which way is up or down. I burned dinner twice yesterday, because I could only think of you."

My voice catches in my throat. "Then forget me."

Jonah's dark brown eyes lock onto mine. "Never. How can I stop thinking about the best thing that's ever happened to me?"

My pulse pounds in my chest. I have so many things I want to say, but I'm afraid they'll make things worse if I tell him how I really feel. I smile weakly. "Thank you. Thanks for trying. Thanks for everything."

Jonah's voice is raw and ragged as he says, "I'll always love you, Brie," and he disappears in the dark morning air.

And my heart shatters into a thousand pieces.

# Chapter Thirty-Two

I SEARCH my bedroom until my eyes land on my battered old suitcase. Yes. *Pack. Move. Escape.* Don't leave room for emotion.

That's what Mom always did.

I toss the suitcase on my bed, unzip it with maybe a little too much force, and start tossing clothes inside.

Lindsay pounds up the stairs and stands in the doorway to my room. "Jake's pretty upset."

Chief pushes his way past her and falls into the chintz armchair. "He's not the only one." He covers his face with one hand.

"Jonah broke up with me." Candy cane pajamas go into the suitcase. The *Deck the Halls* sweater. My workout clothes. Pants. Tops. "Cancel the venue. Wedding's off." It was never on, but I'm not telling them.

Chief wipes his eyes and gives me a hard look. "So, you're running away."

"I'm moving to Boulder. Yes."

He laughs. "Typical. Of course you're moving again. That's what you do. You run. I warned Jonah."

"Hey." I slam the lid of my suitcase closed. "He broke it off."

It's easy to blame him, but it's not fair. "It's my fault we didn't work out. He was just the one who said the words."

Chief pushes out of the chair. "I don't see you trying to fix anything. If it's your fault, you can fix it."

"There's nothing we can fix. It's unfixable." I'm unfixable.

*You're the problem*, Mom always said. *You drove him away. If I didn't have a kid, maybe these boyfriends would stick around.*

But even her last-ditch efforts to trot out her cute little daughter couldn't save her relationships. They still broke up with Mom, and then she blamed me. They still left us. Everyone leaves.

Like Jonah just left. Because it's me. There's something wrong with me, and I'm not worth loving or fighting for.

"Earth to Brie. Pity party is over." Chief glares at me. "I trained you better than this. We don't quit because it's hard, and we don't blame other people when it's our mistake."

Lindsay glances down at her phone. "You're not going to cancel the farmhouse are you, Chief?"

He looks at her. "Why?"

"Jake is texting and driving."

Chief checks his phone and types something. "I told him to pull over or stop texting."

"Jake's worried you'll cancel the venue and then they'll need it." She reads another text. "Jake says that his family is good at arguing, and Jonah and Brie will make up quickly. They always do."

Chief snorts. "He's right."

Lindsay slips the phone in her pocket. "Jake probably owes you some money for not taking you seriously, Brie. Also, I'm sorry about your breakup. I liked you and Jonah together. You were good for him."

I smile. "You're getting the idea, bestie. I told you that you were ready to train Jake on your own."

"But why would I want to?" She flips her ponytail over her shoulder.

"Oh no." Chief holds open the door. "Downstairs. If we're doing Jake and Jonah drama instead of my workout, I want breakfast."

I lug the suitcase off my bed and roll it toward the door. "It's not drama." They stare at me. "I am hungry. Fine, let's eat."

Chief's accusations pound in my head. *We don't quit when it's hard. We don't blame others when it's our mistake.*

I keep telling myself that I won't fall into my mom's bad habits, but what am I doing right now? Blaming Jonah for leaving when I told him to go?

We head downstairs, and I carry my suitcase the whole way. It was awkward to have three of us watching me fold and pack my underwear anyway when all I want to do is lay on my bed and sob.

Once I roll my suitcase to the front door, I grab a cutting board and attack an onion, because that's how I feel, while Chief starts cracking eggs and Lindsay gets out a pan.

"I didn't mean to be dismissive." Chief adds some water and whips the eggs with a fork. "I'm emotionally invested in your relationship, too. This is the first time I've liked anyone you've dated."

I snort. "That's a lot of words from you, especially this early in the morning."

Chief smiles. "I've got to look out for you. I already paid the deposit for the wedding, and I'm not going to let you and Jonah sabotage yourselves, or you and Jake, Lindsay."

Lindsay grates some cheese. "Jake's texting again."

Chief grabs his phone and calls. "Am I on speakerphone? Jake. Hang up and drive. If you text one more time, I'm calling Highway Patrol."

He puts down the fork. "Don't tell me Jonah's driving. I can smell a lie a mile away."

Chief pauses, then his voice ratchets up a notch. "What do you mean, *you're* too upset to drive? Jonah's the one who had the breakup. Pull over, switch places, and don't text us again. We both know Jonah's in no shape to drive. Jonah, call me tonight." Chief ends the call.

A minute later my pocket buzzes, and I know we broke up for real this time, because my texts are exploding. I wipe my hands on the Santa Claus tea towel and pull out my phone.

**Jonah**: I hate this.

"Hey, Chief." I wave my phone. "Jonah's texting, so I think we're good. I think Jake is driving."

Chief grunts and mutters something under his breath that sounds like, "Too upset to drive?"

My phone buzzes again. Jonah's been busy now that he's in the passenger seat. He must have told his family what happened.

**Mrs. Butler**: Call me, sweetie.
**Mr. Butler**: Pappy wants to call you.
**Jonah**: I hate this even more now.
**Jake**: My brother is an idiot. Don't cancel the wedding, even though you can do better.
**Luke**: Jonah says you're serious about moving here. I'll see if I can find an apartment by me. Andie says hi. If you want to play any games online, we'll send you the link.
**Jonah**: I hate keeping my promises.
**Nick**: Jonah is mad at me for approving the work from home. You didn't tell me you were using it to move to Colorado.
**Danny**: We need to talk about Jonah.
**Jonah**: I'm always going to hate this.
**Matt**: Jonah's pretty broken up about losing you.
**Mrs. Butler**: Jonah should have talked to me before making any major life decisions. No one should make a major life decision at 6 a.m.
**Mrs. Butler**: Are you calling me about Jonah?
**Mr. Butler**: Are you calling Pappy?

I'm too restless, and we didn't work out this morning. I slide the phone back in my pocket without answering any texts. "Can we leave for Boston after breakfast, Lindsay? I need to pack my apartment. I have to be out by Wednesday anyway, and you were going to the show on Monday, right?"

"Running," Chief mutters. "Marathon runner."

"Like you have room to talk. You left the Air Force and you're hiding up here in Vermont. You can run with me. Move to Colorado. They have railroads there, too."

Chief slams down the bacon. "No. I'm not running. I chose a place to put down roots, and I thought you did, too. Now, one thing happens, and you relocate. I'm not going to follow you."

My phone rings. It's Mrs. Butler. I silence the call. "I lost my townhome. I lost my boyfriend. I lost my savings, and I might lose my job." I take a deep breath. "I'm strategically relocating and starting over. Yes, I'm running. What else can I do?"

Lindsay takes the knife out of my hand. "Stay where you have friends." She pushes me out of the way and begins to chop a bell pepper.

I rest my weight against the counter. "I can't see him. I can't hang out with you and Jake and have to be around him."

Lindsay sets the pepper aside and starts on some scallions. "Jake's right. You're really good at fighting. I like listening to you and Chief argue, and I bet you and Jonah will be back together by tonight."

Chief and I look at each other and laugh. "You're weird, Lindsay." I tug her into a side-arm hug. "That must be why we get along."

She hugs me with the arm that doesn't hold a knife, then finishes chopping the scallions. "We can leave for Boston after breakfast. Maybe you'll get a chance to argue face-to-face with Jonah."

"We already did that, and we broke up."

My phone buzzes again.

Lindsay points at it. "Then you can argue with Mrs. Butler."

Chief cranks up the heat and pours some garlic-infused olive oil into the skillet. "Will you answer it? She's going to call until you do, and you're not a coward. You're a fighter."

Lindsay nods. "A good fighter."

I press the button and walk away from them. It's starting to smell good, and my stomach rumbles.

"Hello?"

"Brie?"

"Yes."

Mrs. Butler clears her throat. "Thank goodness."

I wander back upstairs and flop in my chintz chair. There's a lake house Santa on a sign that says *Who's been Nautical?* hanging in my room. I stare at it while I wait for her.

Oh. *Nautical. Naughty.* I finally get the pun.

"Sweetie."

"Hi, Mrs. Butler."

She sighs. "You're still uncomfortable calling me *Mom*."

I'm not sure how to respond. "Jonah broke our engagement." So now I have to break up with his mom, too.

Her voice catches. "I'm not sure what I did wrong with my boys. I'm a therapist and my boys are old enough to be married by now and none of them are, and one of them is divorced and I'm a therapist. A licensed marriage therapist."

"Right."

She continues. "I have a good marriage with their father. I show them how happy we are, and I model conflict, and I don't think that's hurt them."

"No. Jake says your family is very good at arguing and making up quickly. He's proud of your arguing."

Her voice wobbles. "Thank you, Brie. That means a lot to me to hear you validate my conflict skills."

"Sure." It's really weird to be complimented for telling her that she's good at arguing, but whatever.

Mrs. Butler didn't call to listen or yell at me. I guess she called to talk. "But I thought Jonah was different. He's so much like his father, you know—"

She waits for me while I stare at nautical Santa some more.

"Right." I have no idea what Mr. Butler is like outside of work, but I'll go with it.

"—and you seem like you know how to bring him out of his shell, and the boys are all so accomplished in every other facet of their lives, but they just work too hard to prove themselves. Am I making sense? You can't prove how much you love someone. You can't win at a relationship. It's not a competition, but that's all my boys know how to do. Compete."

I kick my feet onto the bed. "This is the strangest breakup I've ever had, Mrs. Butler."

"Maggie. I told you. I'm either *Maggie* or I'm *Mom*, and you have some issues about using the appellation *Mother*, so we're going to go with *Maggie*."

I'm in the Twilight Zone now. "Maggie, sure, that makes sense. Your boys are competitive superstars and all that, but no worries. The boys see how much you love their father, and they want what you have. They yearn for it, in fact, and they do try, but the reason none of them are married yet comes down to one simple thing."

Maggie gasps. "What? Tell me what I'm missing."

"Their personalities. They're kind of clueless. They're good men, amazing men, and they're going to make the best and kindest of husbands and fathers, but they're low on the emotional intelligence scale. No offense. It's a genetic thing, and I don't know where your husband ranks—"

She interrupts. "Low. Sub-par. Off the scales low."

I laugh at her honesty, even though this conversation is ripping the hole in my heart even wider. "So, they don't have any natural instincts, and they might always need some emotion coaching from their wives or girlfriends. They need schemas. Routines. I gave Jonah a recipe, and he gave it to Jake."

Maggie lets out a long sigh. "Oh. That's what you did that worked, until Jonah blew it with you."

"It was me—" I start to protest, but she cuts me off.

"It was Jonah, sweetie. Let's not lie to each other. It's always Jonah. I love my boys, but their dad has the emotional intelligence of a third grader when it comes to romantic relationships. Bless him. He can run a restaurant empire and has a killer instinct for negotiation and who to trust, but he has no idea what to buy me for Valentine's Day." She sighs. "That's another story that I'll tell you once you and Jonah get married. Short version: you make a wish list at the jeweler's, and he just buys you something you both know you'll love. Sure, there's no surprise, but everyone is happy, and he feels like a success."

I remember Lindsay's initial assessment of Jake's antics as the emotional equivalent of a grade schooler and stifle a laugh. "I'm going to hang up, but thanks for calling, Maggie. I'm sorry to disappoint you, I really am, and Jonah's great. It is one hundred percent my issues and not about him. You don't have to worry about him." My voice chokes up. "I'm already jealous of the girl he does marry."

"Don't hang up!" Her voice hurts my ear because it's so loud. "I called Jonah and had a conversation. A much shorter one than we're having, obviously, because he's his father's son, and he's on Tommy's set today. He said it's fine if I stay in contact with you, so I'll be texting you from time to time. Don't tell Danny, but Patricia and I text every now and then."

I'm not sure how to respond. "Thanks."

"You never leave the Butler family, sweetie." She laughs. "Well, *we* never leave you alone. You've probably gathered that already." She hangs up.

And I'm mad because I have a lump in my throat at the idea of belonging to a family. I want so fiercely to never be alone that my throat burns.

I hate the idea of her texting me every now and then, because it will remind me that other people have families. It will remind me of Jonah and how much I wanted to belong to him.

But I love the idea of belonging somewhere, even if it's sideways and adjacent and almost and hypothetical.

And then Pappy calls.

# Chapter Thirty-Three

I SILENCE my phone and go downstairs to make myself an omelet. A girl's gotta eat.

Especially after a breakup.

Chief washes the cutting board, and Lindsay cleans the countertop.

I'm sprinkling cheese on top of the almost-done eggs when my phone buzzes. My heart catches. I let it go to voicemail. Cold eggs aren't worth eating.

The phone buzzes again when I'm halfway through eating my omelet, and I let it go to voicemail again. I've cleaned my plate, and I don't have any more excuses the third time my phone buzzes.

Chief levels a commanding gaze at me. "Answer it."

I answer it. "Hey."

"Brie. This is Pappy. About time you answered. Boy, have we got a lot to talk about. I'll start. You comfortable?"

"Hang on." I put a hand over the microphone. "When will you be ready to leave, Lindsay?"

"Take your time. I'll wash the dishes and pack."

I uncover the microphone. "Hey, Pappy, I'm about to leave

for Boston. Can I talk to you when we get back? I've got to clean up and finish packing. You know."

Pappy's gravelly voice booms from my phone. "I know when you're trying to avoid a difficult conversation because I worked with your mother, and I practically raised you."

He did. Mom started working there after the divorce, and I've known Pappy since forever.

There's a heavy silence. I sigh. "Give me four hours. Three and a half. I'll be back in Boston before you know it."

"Text me your address, and I'll stop by with Mary."

I'm dreading this, but Pappy is a force of nature, and I can avoid him as much as I can avoid the next Nor'easter storm. "So, Jonah told you?"

"Yes, he told me, and Jake and everyone in the family told me. This isn't right. I changed your diapers. You should be a Butler."

"You're not responsible for me." I won't be a burden to him, either. "I'll text you my address as soon as I hang up."

Because he's relentless. I know that about Pappy.

"Text me *now* and then I'll hang up. I know how cell phones work. You can do it at the same time. If you hang up, I'm never getting that address and who knows if you'll pick up the line again."

I text him my address.

"All right. See you at noon. I'll be waiting." Pappy ends the call.

I set the phone on the counter. I'm emotionally exhausted.

Chief folds his arms. "Sounds like he knows you as well as I do."

I shake my head. "He knows me like a father, if I had one. He's pretty much the only father figure I ever had."

Chief pulls up a stool. "Why don't you know your father?"

"We're not going there. That topic is off-limits."

Chief shrugs. "I can't help thinking that your running all the time has something to do with the fact that you won't talk about your parents."

I smile. "You should've been a shrink. Love you. I've got to run." I slug him in the shoulder. "See you for Christmas?"

"Call me tonight," Chief says. "I'll give you an update after I talk to Jonah."

I grab my Yankees hoodie and slip it on, just to make a point. "Since when do you and I talk girl talk?"

Chief pulls me into a hug. "Since you got unengaged. That is not happening on my watch."

I start to pull away, but he holds me tight and looks at me seriously. "You saved me when my ex-wife cheated on me, and I'm returning the favor. I'm all about protecting your heart and your happiness, and I'm not letting you walk away from Jonah, not until you tell me what's really going on."

"I think you used up all your words for the whole day in one go."

"You wish." Chief grimaces. "What did you break that needs to be fixed?"

The tears start to flow, and I can't stop them. Chief pulls me into a hug while I cry. My stomach shakes, and my whole body is weak from emotion overload. Finally, the sobs subside. "I can't be selfish. He wants to give up too much to be with me, and I won't let him. I'm not worth it. I can't handle marrying Jonah if he resents me and rejects me afterward."

Lindsay wheels her suitcase out of the bedroom. "Why would he resent you?"

"Long story." My stomach stutters as I draw a deep breath. "Tommy Fuller is my dad, and he's never acknowledged me."

Chief glares at me, and Lindsay gasps. "I'm never watching that show with you again," Chief growls.

"So, yeah, short story, that's why I went into accounting. That's why I don't work as a chef. That's why I can't live in New York or Boston or in Jonah's world."

Lindsay crushes me in a hug this time. "That's lame."

"It is." And the tears start all over again.

Chief points at me. "So, Jonah wants to be with you, and you won't let him?"

My chin quivers. "It's for his sake. He's protecting me, and I'm protecting him, and this is the best thing for both of us." Especially when he realizes that I'm a mistake.

Chief shakes his head. "Fix it. Fix this." He grabs my phone off the counter. "Now."

I hold the phone in my shaking hand. I've been through every emotion in the last twenty-four hours.

"How much do you love him?" Chief asks.

"That's not the question." I set the phone back on the counter.

Chief picks up my phone. "That's the question I'm asking you. If you love him like I think you do, and if you're the woman I think you are, nothing will stop you. Not even the lies your mom told you."

I cover my face with both hands as emotion washes over me. I slowly regain control and lower my hands. Lindsay shoves a tissue into one fist, and Chief pushes my phone into the other. Before I can think, I send a text.

**Me**: Jonah, can we talk? I love you, and I want to be with you.

My hands shake as I lock the screen. "He's probably in his meeting right now. I won't see him until tonight, and I don't know if he can—"

My phone buzzes.

**Jonah**: I'm driving up there right now, girlfriend. Jake will cover me here.
**Jonah**: (heart emoji)
**Jonah**: (GIF of silly happy dancing penguin)
**Jonah**: I love you, Brie.

I type frantically.

**Me**: No, don't leave. I'm packed. Lindsay and I are leaving now.
**Jonah**: I'll meet you at your place. I'll take an extra-long lunch break.
**Me**: Is that okay with Tommy?
**Jonah**: If it's not, I don't have to go back.
**Me**: You can't quit the show.
**Jonah**: Watch me.

# Chapter Thirty-Four

LINDSAY ASKS me for advice about Jake and dating and relationships the whole way down to Boston. *Three hours plus.* I don't have any time to think because I'm talking the whole time.

But I prefer that. I give her really long answers to simple questions, because my heart is pounding, and I can't sustain this level of emotional overload for much longer.

Jonah wants to give up everything for me. He's willing to walk away from the *Santa Snack Smack Down* without a moment's hesitation, and I don't doubt he's willing to do a lot more than that.

No one's ever sacrificed for me, and I don't know how to accept his gift.

The trees are flocked white with snow as we drive through Vermont and New Hampshire. The roads are clear, but a light snow falls as we drive. We're getting close to home, so I wrap up the gab session. "My work here is done. I'm transferring the Bro Fund to you, since Jake is still going to need it, and I'm always here for some Girlfriend Guidance."

Lindsay falls silent. "Thanks. Just a couple more questions? I know you're hurting from the breakup, and I'm sorry if this is a bad time, but... You're getting back together, right?"

"I hope so. I think so. I have no idea." I laugh. "I love the questions. They keep me distracted from this mad race down to Jonah and Boston and the terrifying future I'm trying to face. Ask away."

She smiles sheepishly. "Even after this amazing month I've had with Jake, I still doubt myself, like *How can I trust my feelings?* How well do I know Jake? How well do I really know anyone when I come right down to it?"

I'm about to answer when Lindsay asks more rapid-fire questions. "You and Jonah looked so close last night at the play. I never would have guessed you were having any trouble. That scares me, too, like the closer I get to a guy maybe the faster he'll run away. But that kiss looked epic. Was it?"

She waits for me to answer this time. I take a deep breath. "Emotional intimacy before physical intimacy, right? I shared some really personal things last night, and Jonah was there for me, and I got swept up."

"So, it was as hot as it looked?"

I see the exit sign, and relief washes over me. "Yeah. Maybe the hottest kiss of my life because we had just connected on this emotional level." I stop talking as the memory washes over me, and Lindsay is silent for a moment, too. "But for every high in our relationship, there's a low. Honestly, I'm scared to feel so loved." I glance at her. "Is that weird?"

Lindsay smiles sadly. "It's weird that I understand you. Like, after so long, how can I believe that *he* really loves me when no one else ever has?"

A weight lifts off my chest, a weight I realize was still there. "Exactly. When I felt so loved by him, then I wanted to break up the next day. It shouldn't make sense, but..."

"But strong emotions are terrifying, and it's so much easier to stay numb and not risk anything," Lindsay finishes for me. "Thanks, Brie. This has been really helpful."

And at that moment, I know something's shifted. I've found my first best friend for life, someone I want to risk things for. I want to stay in Boston, not just for Jonah, but also for Lindsay now.

But I push down the emotion and put on the blinker. "Your car is still at my townhouse, right?"

She nods.

I turn onto my street. "Cool. Good luck. Thanks for the offer. If I can crash with you after Wednesday, that would save me."

Lindsay gasps.

"What?"

She points at the front of my brownstone—well, the place I had dreamed I would call my own.

My heart nearly stops. I park while Lindsay gives me a running commentary. "Jake. Jonah. That's Matt, right. Oh, he's hot. Those must be Jake's parents, but who are the old people?"

I turn off the car. "Pappy and Mary."

"Oh. I've heard of them. They're legends." Lindsay pokes me. "You have to get out. They're waiting."

"I don't have to do anything."

Lindsay unlocks the doors. "But the Butlers' superstrength is arguing, remember?" She opens her door. "Come on. Go fight for your man."

I drop my head to the steering wheel, and it honks. I whip my head up, and they're all laughing except Jonah.

I pop open my door. The Butler clan is bunched in a group a few feet away, and my heart nearly explodes with hope at the sight of the family that I want to belong to.

Jake waves. "Hey, Brie."

I close my door and lock the car. "I thought you were covering for Jonah at the *Smack Down*."

Jonah leans against the wall of my townhouse with his hands awkwardly at his side. "I asked him to come."

"No way was I going to miss this."

Matt knocks Jake on the back of the head. "Shut up and let Jonah talk. This is his moment."

Jake knocks Matt on the back of the head. "Don't interrupt me. I'm his twin. We share everything."

Pappy knocks them both on the back of the head. "Matt, don't talk to your brother that way. Jake, you don't share everything. You don't share his girl. Hi, Brie. You look very good as always."

Jonah grins. "Sorry."

"Why are you sorry? She looks very beautiful, and you should be telling her that. No wonder you're not married yet. What do I always tell Mary first thing in the morning and every day? I tell her, *Mary, you look beautiful,* and boom, I have a wife. I have eight kids. I have what? Fifty-two grandkids and how many great-grandchildren? What have you got? An engagement ring hanging around your neck like an albatross and no wife. So, you should be telling Brie that she looks beautiful."

Jonah looks around at our audience instead of me. "You look very beautiful."

Pappy knocks Jonah on the back of the head. "And smile like you mean it and stand respectful-like."

Jonah pushes off the wall and comes over to me. He takes my hand and lowers his voice. "It's really good to see you." He swallows. "I didn't think I'd ever see you again." His grip on my hands tightens, and his eyes soften. "You look amazing, Brie."

Warmth explodes inside my chest, and even though it seems like Jonah's forgiving me, I'm still nervous. "It's good to see you, too, Jonah."

"See? There. Was that so hard to be honest? That's better, Joey."

Mrs. Butler. Maggie, I mean, rushes forward, and Jake and the brothers swarm him from the other side. Jonah locks eyes with me and slowly unzips his parka. Maggie tugs at one sleeve, and Jake pulls the other. They grab his coat and race back to the safety of the sidewalk. Jake steps in a huge puddle of ice water along the way, but just laughs when it also splashes Danny and Nick.

Jonah's gaze never wavers as he drops to one knee in the gray slush of the snowy parking lot. I stare at him and my nerves jitter even more.

He's wearing a tuxedo. "When did you have time to change? How long have you been gone from your meeting?" I drink in the sight of Jonah in a perfectly fitted black suit with a black bow tie. His dark hair and dark eyes look even more dramatic, but it's the longing in his eyes that does me in.

And those dang dimples in his cheeks.

"The flowers," Maggie whispers, and I glance over. She whacks her husband in the chest, and he produces a bouquet of grocery store blooms from behind his back. Jake grabs them like an Olympic torch and races to hand them to Jonah.

"What are you doing?" My voice squeaks on the last word.

"I know," Maggie whispers loudly. "That suit is Armani."

Jonah keeps his gaze locked on me. "Brie—"

"It's seven degrees out here, and your knees... You're kneeling in a slush puddle in the parking lot next to my beater car, and—"

Jonah stands, tosses the bouquet onto the roof of my car, and kisses me. His whole family whoops and hollers, but I lose track of the count when they get past ten. Jonah cups my face with a hand on each side, then one arm wraps around my waist as he draws me into an embrace.

I try to ask him between kisses. "Are—You—Proposing—Again?"

Jonah presses his lips to mine over and over. "Marry me?" And then he's kissing me hungrily again. When we finally break apart, our chests heaving, I take the bouquet off the top of my car.

"Yes, Jonah."

He grabs me and swings me around. Luckily, there's no one parked on the other side of my car. Snow and slush fly everywhere. "Your suit," I say. "You're going to ruin it."

"I knew I liked her." Maggie sniffs, and Lindsay hands her a tissue.

Jonah sets me down, then pulls me over to the sidewalk. "You don't have to keep asking," I whisper.

"I'll keep asking until I get the answer I want." Jonah winks at me.

Then we're on the sidewalk, and Maggie hugs me, then everyone piles on, and we're a huddle of hugs. Jonah's on the outside of the circle, and I fight to draw him inside. I catch Lindsay's eye as she watches us awkwardly from beneath the overhang.

Jake notices, and he pulls her into the group hug. When everyone lets go, my flowers are wilted and crushed, and I toss them in the nearby garbage can.

"I'll get you more," Jonah promises. "Every week for the rest of our lives."

"Thank you." A fierce determination rises in me. Nothing and no one will stop me from being loved. Not my mom. Not my dad. No one.

Jonah's willing to risk everything. He's willing to give up his cooking competition with all the publicity and sales it will bring. Even Jake is willing to sacrifice for me, and I'm going to accept the gifts this family is offering me.

Because Jonah must have told them what's at stake, or they wouldn't be here in this show of support.

And then Jonah's phone rings. "Hang on. It's Tommy." He gives the phone the evil eye before answering. "Jonah here." He grimaces at the phone and winks at me. Long pause. "What do you mean the show's cancelled?"

# Chapter Thirty-Five

PAPPY LEADS everyone to the door of my apartment. "It's cold. Let's go inside." So, I fumble for my keys and unlock the door. We don't fit on my tiny sofa and the one chair, so the men stand, and Mary and Lindsay and I sit.

Jonah stays outside on his phone call.

When I take off my coat, Jake huffs. "Yankees." He looks around my apartment. "Where's that hoodie?"

"Jonah was wearing it," Matt says.

Nick shakes his head. "But he changed into the tuxedo."

"I threw it in his car," Danny says. "Along with his jeans."

Jonah walks inside, and everyone turns to him expectantly.

"So, are you fired or what?" Pappy asks.

Jonah's brow furrows. "No. Crazy thing. Jake and I took the first Covid tests, then left early for lunch."

"With no plan to ever return," Jake mutters.

Matt rolls his hand in the air. "Get on with it, bro."

Jonah looks at Jake. "One of the teams failed. They have Covid. No symptoms, but yeah, both of them."

Jake groans. "So, no show? He's cancelling?"

Jonah looks around, and I motion to him. He squeezes himself onto the couch, and I'm happy to curl up beside him to make room. Jonah scrubs a hand down his face. "Or Tommy needs a second team." He looks down at me. "I pitched a crazy idea to him."

Jake grins. "Are you thinking what I'm thinking?" He leans over and bumps his fist against Jonah's.

"Yep." Jonah looks around my crowded living room until he finds Matt. "Can you compete with us? If you'll be Jake's sous chef, and Brie will be my sous chef, Tommy will owe us big time."

Jonah smirks at me. *Smirks.* Jonah. He's a combination of angry and cocky and John Wayne riding into the sunset. "He's desperate." Jonah grins even wider, like he's happy to see Tommy's show go up in flames, and I love that he's so loyal to me.

And that gives me the courage to face this thing that my mom's warned me against my whole life. A fierce fire erupts inside me. I nod my head. "Let's do it." I'll brave anything for Jonah, and yeah. Revenge might not be bad, either.

He shifts on the crowded sofa and reaches behind me to rest an arm along the back. "Are you sure? Tommy thinks he has to cancel. This is a long shot."

Then I notice a chain dangling around the neck of Jonah's tuxedo. Pappy wasn't joking.

Jonah really is wearing my grammy's ring on a thick metal necklace, and the silver chain and gold ring lie perfectly on the black t-shirt. It has the bad boy vibe to match Jake's haircut and Tommy's personality.

Jonah wore it for the taping of the preliminary stuff today. He wore it for the whole world to see, not knowing if I'd even watch the show.

I shake my head because this guy keeps giving me more reasons to love him, and I can't take it. I want to run into his arms and kiss him and never let go. I want my ring back. "I've never been more sure."

Jonah grins. "Matty? You in? Come on, Tommy's waiting. We'll fill you in on the way."

"Brie and I should be the new team. The twins never compete

alone." Matt winks at me. "You know you want to."

Mary shoos the boys out of my townhouse. "Of course she does not. She's going to cook with her husband, not you."

"We're not married yet," Jonah interrupts.

Mary shrugs. "Same difference. Everybody out. Yes, Matt will do it. We help each other out in this family, and Tommy needs us. Put your coat back on, Brie. Nice to meet you, Lacey."

"Lindsay," Jake corrects her. "She works in accounting with Nick."

Lindsay stands. "Oh, are we all leaving?"

Mary raises an eyebrow. "You work with Nick?" She takes in Lindsay's supermodel stature and appearance.

"But she's with me." Jake slings an arm around Lindsay's shoulders. "Right, babe?"

Lindsay shrugs his arm off her shoulders. "I don't cook. Matt's your sous chef."

Matt grins. "You can cook with me."

Jake takes both her shoulders and turns her to face him. He looks at her directly and speaks slowly and distinctly. "When I say *You're with me*, I mean that we're dating, and I don't want you to date anyone else. I don't mean that you're *literally* driving to the same location that I am this very second."

Lindsay blinks, then she smiles an outrageously flirty smile. "So, you're saying we're together?"

Jake heaves a huge sigh of relief. "Yes, when I say *You're with me*, I'm saying *We're together*. We've spent almost every single moment together for the last month, so I would hope we're together by now."

She places a hand on his chest, and Jake flashes his smoldering gaze. Her flirty smile turns adorably, insincerely pouty. "But you've never asked."

He groans. "I've asked so many times. What did you think I meant when I asked, 'Right, babe?'"

Pappy opens the door. "Jake, that is not the way you ask a mature woman to go steady with you."

Matt snorts. "No one goes steady, Gramps."

"And Jonah, I didn't hear you set a date to marry your girlfriend, yet." Pappy ushers everyone outside, including me. "The grandkids don't make themselves."

It's still seven degrees and humid, and it's a good thing, because Pappy's comment makes my cheeks flush bright red. My nostrils freeze shut the first time I try to draw a breath, so I shut my mouth and decide not to respond to Pappy, after all. Jake grabs Lindsay, hugs her, and says, "You know you want to date me."

She pushes him away and says, "You owe me at least fifty dollars for that one, bro." She unlocks her car with her key fob, hops in, and drives away.

"See you on Monday," Jake yells after her. He turns to us after her car leaves the parking lot. "She's so in love with me."

"Keep telling yourself that," Matt says.

Jake whacks his brother in the chest and presses a button on his key fob. His electric SUV whirrs and clicks, warning us all that it's on, and Matt hops in the car. "Is that your way of trying to butter me up to cook with you?"

"You know you want to." Jake pops open his door and runs a hand through his hair. "See you on set. Tommy loves my new 'do." The black SUV peels out of my parking lot, spitting snow and ice as it disappears.

Jonah jingles a set of keys in his hands. "I brought my Tesla, too, if you want a ride."

Pappy tilts his head. "Yes, she would love one. Brie, answer him like a lady."

I laugh and wrap my coat around myself. Pappy never changes. "Yes, I would love a ride. Thank you."

"I'm getting in the car," Mary yells. "It's too cold to breathe without getting icicles in my lungs."

Pappy waves at Mary and unlocks their mini-SUV. He turns to me with a fierce, all-knowing glare. "You gonna talk to me now that everyone else is gone?"

# Chapter Thirty-Six

I'M HUDDLING in the cold. "Tommy Fuller is my dad." I blurt it out. "I don't know if you ever guessed that or if my mom told you, but I can't meet him or go on set with him. That's why Jonah broke up with me. To protect me."

Pappy looks like I slapped him. "No, she did not tell me." He steps back and folds his arms. Tears fill his eyes. "She told me your dad died, and she was four months pregnant and needed a job."

"Well, my mom lied. He was dead to her, so she was telling you her version of the truth. They got divorced." I bite my lip, and Jonah's arm wraps around my waist. "She always believed her version of the truth, but there was sometimes a gap between the real, honest-to-goodness truth and the way she saw things. There was *the* truth and *her* truth."

Pappy nods. "Yeah. I figured that out about her, too. Good chef, though."

Mary honks the horn.

Pappy waves at the car. "Not now!" he yells, then moves forward and grabs me in a bone-crushing hug. "Oh, Brie, sweetie. Your mom was like a daughter to me. A very troubled daughter, but a daughter, nonetheless." He pulls back and looks me in the eye. "You didn't inherit her propensity to bend the truth, if you know what I mean, and I was very grateful for that. Not so many mood swings or so much drama. You can at least thank Tommy for that part of your genetics. You're like a granddaughter to me, so don't worry about him." Then he hugs me again.

"Everyone you meet is like a daughter to you," I grumble into his shoulder, and I feel him shake with laughter.

"True, true." He pulls back. "But I never forgave myself after your mother died working at my restaurant. You never should have joined the Air Force. You should have moved to Boston when I opened my new restaurant."

"You tell me that every year in your Christmas letter." I swallow. I had to run. I couldn't accept his offer. I didn't deserve it, because I don't miss my mom the way he thinks I do.

Jonah stands off to the side with his hands jammed in his pockets again. "We gotta go, Pappy."

Pappy won't let go of me. "I've worried about you for twelve years, and all I had was a Christmas card from you every year, and then I finally think you're taken care of and you're gonna marry my boy, Jonah, and then he goes and messes everything up by breaking up with you—"

"It wasn't Jonah," I interrupt. "It was me. He's protecting me."

"—and I need to know you're going to be okay. I need to know this is going to work between you two."

Jonah snugs me into his side. "This works."

I nod. "Like a dream."

Pappy narrows his eyes like an F.B.I. investigator, then his face crumples. "It better, because if your mom hadn't been working at my place, she wouldn't have stayed late when I asked her to, she wouldn't have been in that car crash at three a.m., and you would still have a mom." Pappy's lip trembles. "It's my fault she died, it's my fault you don't have a family, and I've got to make sure you and Jonah are solid, so you have a family again."

Tears are contagious. Once Pappy starts, I do, too.

Mary honks twice this time. She unrolls the window. "Jonah

and Brie are due on set." She rolls up the window and honks a third time for good measure.

I can't help laughing, even if some tears are freezing on my cheeks. I hate talking about the night Mom died. "It's never your fault when other people make bad choices." I glance at Jonah, because I'm paraphrasing something he said to me a few days ago. "You're not responsible for me. Any of you."

Pappy shrugs. "Fine. Jonah is now. Get back on set, both of you. I don't want to see either of you until you're serious and you've set a date for the wedding."

Jonah glances at me and shoves his keys in his pocket. "Hey, Gramps, it's not that simple. We have no idea how Tommy will react when she meets him. Give it some time."

Pappy tromps across the parking lot toward his car. "You love her?"

Jonah glances at me. "So much."

"Then it's that simple. You can't protect her if you're not with her. You can't be with her if you don't marry her. So, get married already." Pappy glares at both of us and yells at his car. "I'm coming already, Mary. Turn the heater on. I love you but stop with the honking."

Jonah grabs his phone, reads the screen, and jams it back in his pocket. "I'm sorry. My family is crazy, and Jake is freaking out, and Tommy wants an answer now." He takes two steps toward me. "Are you ready for this?" His gaze travels over my face. "I love you so much."

I can feel every nose hair when I breathe in and out. I shiver. "I'm ready for all of it. All of the crazy, but can we make up inside the car?"

"Brie." Jonah's voice is low and rumbly as he brushes the tears off my cheeks. "This is killing me. You need a really long hug. I need to hug you even more, but you're right. It's freezing."

He takes my hand, and we run toward a pearl white Tesla SUV. He's got his parka zipped up again, and I'm struck by how low pressure this guy is. I've seen him compete on TV. I know he owns restaurants and works as an executive chef, but he's not trying to push his own agenda right now. He's not in a rush to get back to the set.

He's giving me the reins, and he trusts me. I really am the most important thing in his entire world right now, and I'll take it. I've never been important to anyone before, not like this. I need someone to lean on, someone to support me and help me through the first meeting with my dad and all of the fallout.

Jonah pops open the passenger side door and waits for me to get inside. I go up on my tiptoes and wrap my arms around his neck. I never want to stop hugging him, but it's freezing, and everyone is waiting for us to arrive at Tommy's set.

I dip down and slip into the leather seat. Jonah studies my face for a long moment, then closes the door.

Once he's inside, Jonah starts the car, then turns to me with a serious expression. "Were you serious back there when you told Pappy..." He chokes up. "This is real. That wasn't a *Maybe* or hypothetical or anything?"

I rest a hand on his leg. "I want my ring back."

Jonah shakes his head and turns on the *Grinch* soundtrack. He puts a hand on the back of my seat and reverses out of the parking lot. He glances down at me and lifts the chain around his neck. "No way. You said this was mine. You can get a new one."

"You know you want to," I say in a sing-song voice, imitating Matt.

Jonah grins, then he heaves a deep, shuddering breath. "This has been the best and worst day of my life."

"Me, too," I whisper. "I'm serious. You're not responsible to make up for my mom's mistakes."

*Neither are you.* A voice drifts into my mind, and it's so quiet that I wonder if I heard it. But I hold onto that feeling.

Jonah puts the SUV into drive, and we glide down the street. The shadow of my fears and the breakup hover over us, and I want to live in the sunshine of our future.

Jonah glances over from the road. "I'm serious when I say that it's not an obligation. Is it selfish if I want to take all of your problems and keep them for myself so you never hurt again?"

My heart cracks open even wider. I snuggle into the leather seats and turn on the seat warmer. I can't handle the serious conversation anymore. "Not selfish at all. Take them all, but I'm on to you. I know what you've been doing."

"What?" he asks innocently. He's still grinning from ear to ear, and he glances over at me again. "I mean, what, *babe*?"

I swat his shoulder. "Stop, or there's no way I'm going on set with you."

He presses his lips together, and there's absolute silence until I break it.

"This whole *Let's try it on* thing. First you were like, *Let's try being engaged*, and then you were like, *How about we see what that ring looks like on your finger? A*nd when I tried to break up, you're like *Let's change that No into a Maybe*, and now when I freak out in the parking lot, you'll probably say, *Just come inside the building and you don't have to actually meet your dad. You can work with the producers*."

Jonah laughs. "You know my secret sauce."

I slug his shoulder a little harder, but still playfully. It feels so good to be with him, like everything is right again. "You've been cooking up a recipe of your own without telling me. How many times do you think I'll fall for that?"

Jonah turns onto a side street. "Until our golden anniversary?" He slows down and pulls into a parking space. "You were the one who set a wedding date *just in case* we need it." His arm brushes my leg as he twists to reach into the backseat. He turns around with his knife kit and a bundle of clothes. "I'm not the only one exploiting this theoretical angle."

I draw a deep breath. "I've wanted to meet my dad yet dreaded this my whole life."

Jonah instantly gets serious again. He reaches up and tucks a stray hair behind my ear. "I'm here for you. We're in this together, if you want me, or you can walk away again." He hands me his keys. "If you aren't ready to meet your dad."

Jonah opens his door, and the keys are heavy in my hand.

"Hang on." I slip out of the car and toss the keys back to him. "No way. I said I was going to do this. I said this was real."

Jonah grins and slings the knife kit over his shoulder. He reaches back inside the car, then stands and tosses me a navy-blue blob. "You're going to need this." He slams his car door shut.

"What is it?" I hug the blob to my chest as we run through the thickening snowfall toward the industrial building ahead.

Jonah grabs my hand to help me over an icy spot. "My Red Sox hoodie. You can't go on camera wearing your Yankees gear."

He lets go once we reach the sidewalk. I unwrap the blue blob and hold up the oversized sweatshirt with the crimson "B" emblazoned on it.

"Just try it on." Jonah winks. "You know you want to."

And as much as I love my Yankees, I don't hesitate. I rip my sweatshirt off in the freezing parking lot and slip Jonah's hoodie over my head. Even though Jonah's still wearing Grammy's ring around his neck, I finally feel at peace again, like we never broke up or doubted our future.

# Chapter Thirty-Seven

JONAH GRABS my hand again as we near the warehouse door. "You want to try this back on, too?" He holds up our intertwined hands. He's got sleek black gloves on, and I'm wearing cream mittens.

I shake my head. "You're relentless with the PDA." But I hold on tight because I'm terrified to meet my dad.

"You know you want to," Jonah whispers in an annoying imitation of Matt, and I slug his shoulder.

Jonah stops us before we go inside and turns to face me. "I know you're overwhelmed right now and not sure of anything."

My throat closes with emotion. I didn't even know that myself, because the day has been such a whirlwind. "Yes. I'm freaking out on the inside."

Jonah nods. "I'm not going to take advantage of that to press for anything you can't give, but there's no way I'm going to leave you alone when you need me."

I nod, but I can't form a coherent sentence. This is all so new. We're just back together, and we can't take time to define anything right now or right here.

Jonah's eyes soften. "Everything changes when we walk

through those doors. I'm going into competition mode, and you..."

"I've got this." I swallow. "I won't let you down."

Jonah brushes a snowflake off my cheek. "I'm not worried about winning. Let me know what you need when we're in there. You come first. Remember that." His fingers linger on my cheek. "I hope you need me, because I will always want to be with you."

When I don't pull away, he hugs me tight, and I hug him back for all I'm worth. "I need you," I say into his shoulder. "So much."

He grabs my hand and pushes open the gray metal door. "Let's go win."

And like that, he's changed. There's a swagger in his step, and a smirk on his face. He looks more like Jake and his brothers than I've ever seen. He leads me along the hallway, and a thrill of excitement wars with the pit of dread in my stomach.

We reach some office, and I'm scared to go inside. I stall for time.

"So, I'm wearing a hoodie and space buns with leggings. If I'd known I was going to be on TV, I might have dressed up."

Jonah cups my cheek. "You look amazing."

I can't take the tension. "That sounds like something Pappy would tell you to say."

Jonah's eyes rake over my face. "Oh, no, *babe*, this is all me."

And that does it. The tension is gone, and I laugh. How does Jonah know exactly what to say and do when I'm freaking out? "I'm warning you, boyfriend... If you call me *babe* one more time."

Jonah threads our hands together. "Let's go, girlfriend."

The door to the office pops open, and I'm relieved to find a woman standing there, impatiently tapping her foot. She eyes the wet patches on Jonah's knees and his tuxedo. "Welcome back, Mr. Butler." She stares unapologetically at the Red Sox hoodie and my space buns. "Are *you* the one we're waiting for?"

"She is. That's us." Jonah tightens his grip on my hand, and we go inside. Someone eventually leads Jonah to a green room where he can change out of his tuxedo, while the grouchy lady has me take a Covid test. By the time the test result comes back—negative— Jonah is back, too, and he looks even better than he did in that tux.

He's switched the formal attire for jeans and his signature black t-shirt. He reaches back to run a hand through his hair. As his arm stretches backward, his biceps bulge where the t-shirt hits his arm. The guy needs a sweater, even if he is going to be cooking. It's December. Cover those muscles.

Some lawyer in a suit walks in and shoves some papers at me. Jonah stiffens beside me, but I start signing them.

"Chad."

"Jonah."

I glance up, and they're glaring at each other.

Jonah lets out a long breath. "How's the wife and kid?"

Chad takes the first contract and slides another paper across the table to me. "Estranged. Your brother is drawing up the divorce papers for her."

Jonah leans forward in his chair. "Oh. Like you did for Patty."

Chad grunts. "She asked me to. What was I supposed to do?"

"Maybe not sleep with her?"

Chad slams his hands on the table and stands, but just then the door opens. Jake, Matt, and a bunch of other people stream into the room. There are two other sets of contestants, and they ignore me, so I ignore them.

My heart pounds. "I'm not ready for this," I whisper.

Jonah grabs my hand and laces our fingers together.

"All right." A short, stocky man with sandy blond hair and pale green eyes charges into the room. *My dad.* Tommy Fuller. "All clear on the Covid tests?" He doesn't wait to hear the results. "Where's my new team?"

All eyes swivel to me and Jonah at the table in the back. Tommy stares. He blinks and stares some more.

Chad grabs my paperwork. "We're all clear here, boss. Non-disclosures and contracts signed. Do you need anything else from me?"

Tommy shakes his head. He grabs the paperwork from Chad. "Let's see. You all met Matt Butler. Our other new sous chef is... Brie Santoro?"

I nod. "Yes."

"Wow," he says, and I'm not sure what to make of that. He probably thinks I have guts to come face him or maybe he's wondering how I got past security. The grouchy lady slides a clipboard in front of him, and he clears his throat. "First thing. Anybody have a problem with the change in teams?"

The other chefs smirk at us. They must know we have a huge disadvantage. They've prepped and cooked together. Jake and Jonah know all of each other's ideas and secrets, and they're working with sous chefs who have no experience getting ready for this competition.

"No complaints here," a beefy man says. The other contestants nod.

"No worries." A team with two women give each other a fist bump.

Meanwhile, Tommy scans my paperwork. "You're twenty-eight?"

I nod. "Yeah, is there some minimum age requirement to compete?"

"No, no. Nothing like that." He hands the papers back to Chad. "I'll walk you out. Hang tight, everyone." The lawyer glares at Jonah as he leaves, and Jake and Matt join in the hate fest. Tommy, on the other hand, can't keep his eyes off me, and I am terrified that he's going to call security or something.

The contestants all sit in awkward silence for a few minutes. Tommy's grouchy assistant lady whispers to someone else about the schedule and how behind they are, and "What is Tommy doing now?" I get the sense that it's not typical for him to wander out of meetings like this, but I'm grateful because it's giving me a minute for my heart rate to go down.

Tommy returns and rubs his hands. "Everybody grab a chair, and let's get back to work." His gaze meets mine again, and he starts going over the rules and how things will play out.

I'm fascinated. So, this is my dad. He exudes charisma. He owns the room, but I can see why I'm so short. He looks taller on TV.

A wave of emotion washes over me. Looking into his eyes feels like looking into a mirror. I wonder if he feels it, too, because he avoids eye contact with me. At one point he's going around and introducing each of the contestants to the other chefs in the room, but he saves me for last, of course, and then has to ask me what my name is again.

I barely hide my anger. "Brie Santoro."

Tommy drops his clipboard and sits on the edge of the table behind him. He's been pretty friendly, digging for information, and making up nicknames for anyone who doesn't already have one, so this isn't entirely unexpected. "I knew a Santoro in New York."

I shrug. "There are a lot of Santoros in New York."

Tommy rubs his hands together and leans forward. "Sure, sure. You have her look, though, and she cooked, too."

I nod. "Aria Santoro. She was a classically trained chef. We worked in Pappy's kitchen." I can't believe him. He was married to her, and he won't even say her name.

Tommy whistles. "That's the one." He looks around the room at the beefy guy and his sous chef, the team with two women, the grumpy woman, and everyone else. "Brace yourselves. Pappy had a Michelin Star in New York. She'll be tough competition, if this lady cooks like her mom and knows any of those recipes."

I don't know what to make of his breezy comment. He's so casual. *Yeah, hey, I knew your mom once,* and then he whips out this compliment.

For the woman he wanted to throw in jail.

I want to yell at him, "Look at me. Look at my eyes. You have to know I'm your kid." But I don't. I let go of Jonah's hand and fold my arms across my chest. At least he's letting me compete, which is more than I expected, in some ways.

"This is gonna be our best show ever, the *Santa Snack Smack Down*." Tommy's back into his cheery, TV host persona. He grins as he looks at each team. "We've got some old rivals, some scores to settle, and for the first time ever, we've got the twins competing head-to-head."

One of the other women, who sports a spiky black high top to rival Chief's, grins over her shoulder at us. "You came back."

Jake grins at her. "So did you."

"And another fun twist viewers will love—Jonah and Brie are engaged." Jake tips his chair back and leans against the wall.

"Really?" the same woman asks. She eyes Jonah. "I'm surprised you landed yourself a bride, Killer." Then she winks at me, and I'm starting to feel like I'm part of this family of bickering celebrity chefs now. I think she's going to be my favorite.

"Play nice, HomeRun," Tommy says, laughing. Then he leans over to Jake in a loud stage whisper and asks, "Come on, Jake, is Jonah really engaged? I mean, how did he land himself someone like her?"

Tommy glances at me, and a wave of emotion flashes across his face so fast that I almost don't catch it because everyone else is still laughing. He likes the Butlers. Maybe he's going to warn Jonah later or try to break us up.

Jake puts his arms behind his head. "True story. You can tell they're engaged because she's wearing the Red Sox hoodie. When she's mad at him, she wears the Yankees hoodie. I know you like nicknames, so here's another fun fact—we call her *Shrimp*."

I pretend to groan and glare at Jake. "Not that nickname. I will get you later."

Tommy's eyes light up. "Well, Shrimp here has good taste. I like the Yankees."

A beefy man claps me on the shoulders. "You can't be all bad if you like the Yankees."

Tommy leans over to Jonah. "But seriously, Jonah. Engaged?" He chuckles.

Jonah glances over at me. Why doesn't anyone believe we're really engaged when we're finally not faking? I squeeze his hand and laugh. "Yeah, I wore the Red Sox shirt today, so I guess Jonah and I are still engaged." It feels unreal, too good to be true.

Jonah tugs my ringless hand onto his leg. "I keep her ring safe while we cook. In fact, I'm trying to convince her to let me keep it all the time. It belonged to her grammy, so I wear it over my heart to keep Brie close to me." He lifts the necklace off his black t-shirt, and the gold ring slides to the bottom of the chain.

A few of the crew members say, "Aww," quietly, and I melt a little inside.

Tommy smiles, glances down at his clipboard on the table, then does a quick doubletake. His gaze snaps to Jonah, and his eyes zero in on the ring. He leans over to peer at Jonah's chain, then his eyes widen. For the first time, his body stills. I hadn't realized that he's always in motion until he stopped moving. "That design... That's Mama Emmy's ring."

I'm not prepared to hear her name. He really knew her. Part of me always thought my mom was lying or something, making up stories about him to make herself seem important. It seems like something she would do—say that a famous celebrity chef once knew her.

But he does know her, even if he won't acknowledge me.

Even though I have his eyes.

"Brie?" Jonah asks.

I nod. "Yeah, that was her ring. She passed ten years ago. It's Jonah's ring now." I sit on the edge of my chair to be closer to him.

Tommy leans a hand on the table at the front of the room. "I'm sorry to hear that. Brie's mom and I go way back."

I glare at him. That is such an understatement. He picks up his clipboard and rifles through his notes, then glances around at the other contestants. "I knew her grandma." He clears his throat.

"But I don't know Shrimp here, so you don't have to worry. In fact, I talked with Chad a few minutes ago. I'm bringing in experts to judge your dishes blind this time, so it will be completely fair."

Everyone whispers. This is a huge curveball. We've all planned our dishes to suit Tommy's taste. He's always one of the judges.

A woman with dark brown hair snorts. "Too bad about that, Meatloaf. There goes your advantage."

"Save it for the show," the beefy man says. "I'm not scared of you, PopTart."

The smack talk flies around me, but for once, I don't have any desire to join in. My dad doesn't want me. Right there, in front of everyone, he said he has no connection to me. He didn't claim me or acknowledge me. He blew me off.

Jonah wraps an arm around me and leans down to whisper in my ear. "You sure you're okay?"

"I'm fine, if you are," I whisper back, gazing up at him. Someone wants me. Someone loves me. Maybe not my dad, but Jonah does, and I'm not going to back down or back away from this relationship.

"Never better." His dark brown eyes light with a fire, and Jonah threads his fingers through mine.

Jake knocks on the table. "Hey, lovebirds. You're missing the details. You're going to lose while you're whispering sweet nothings in each other's ears."

Tommy motions to an assistant. "Get a camera in here now." He folds his arms across his chest, and we all wait.

A woman with a camera appears in the doorway. Tommy points at us. "I want footage."

"Of what?" the camerawoman asks. "All the contestants? This meeting? You?"

Tommy gestures around the room. "Everyone."

Jake smirks. "He especially wants shots of the lovebirds, but I don't know why. They spend all their time making out, and then

Jonah gets distracted. He burned the meal twice yesterday. Let's just say it's a guarantee that they're going to lose."

Or he wants footage to prove that I violated some court order that I don't even know about, but now I'm just paranoid. If he wanted to kick me out, he would have. I try to relax and act like no one's there, even though the camerawoman is uncomfortably close.

Jonah tightens his arm around my shoulders. "Nah, man. I heard every word Tommy said. I'm totally focused. You worry about yourself and Matt. Right, Brie?"

This is the side of Jonah that I knew existed, but never saw. He's got his game on, and he's hyper focused. He's still acting chill, but I can feel the electricity in the air. He's actually more comfortable in front of a camera, which I never would have guessed.

Tommy looks at me to answer Jonah's question. "Right. We've got this in the bag, no matter which sauce Jake makes—his bland one or the super-salty variety." I wink at him, because that's what the Butlers do.

And I'm one of them now, or I will be.

Jake pretends to die, like I've shot him through the heart with an arrow or something. "Oooh, Brie. You cut me deep. I thought we were friends."

Tommy nods in approval. "Let's see if you cook as well as you talk, Shrimp."

I relax even more. I'm getting used to the camera in my face, and I've never had a hard time with the teasing kind of trash talk. We're in my wheelhouse now.

"Oh, she's way better," Jake warns the other contestants. "She's gonna be tough to beat."

"No hard feelings," Matt says to me. "I hope I'm still your favorite brother after we win."

"You were never my favorite brother." I smile at him. "It's always going to be Luke. Don't tell Danny." I fake a panicked look. "Oh, did I say that on camera? You know I love all of you."

Tommy laughs and gestures to the camerawoman to get some angle, I don't know what. When I glance at him, there's something like real affection in his expression, but as soon as he catches me watching him, the expression vanishes.

Jonah sighs. "Give it up, guys. Brie and I are unbeatable. You know we bounce back from everything."

Jake and Matt glance at each other and shrug. "Until now." Matt leans his chair back to match Jake's casual posture.

"First time for everything." Jake gives Matt a fist bump.

I feel bad for the other two teams who sit in their seats, ignored now. Tommy and the camerawoman don't pay them any attention, despite what Tommy said about filming all of us.

Tommy laughs. "Why haven't I ever had you guys compete *against* each other before? This is money."

Matt snorts. "Because Jonah never had a super-hot chef girlfriend before."

"Super hot? Now you're my favorite brother again, Matty." I blow him a kiss, and most of the room laughs. Two of the other contestants eye me with distaste. They must be the ones with the grudge.

Tommy locks eyes with me, and suddenly I have his attention. "Where *have* you been hiding?" He makes it sound playful, but there's something more behind it.

I tug at the bottom of Jonah's hoodie. "In the Air Force."

Tommy nods. "Good idea. They've got some talented chefs winning culinary competitions." He looks at an assistant. "Why haven't we done that? We'll do a military-themed show next. One team from each branch of the service. I love it."

Then he's back to explaining the rules and what shots they need to get today. When he's finished, he asks for questions. I hate to draw attention to myself, because despite the bantering, I feel invisible. My dad doesn't want me. He doesn't even want me to think that he might like who I am. He won't acknowledge me, but here I am. For Jonah.

I raise my hand. "My knife kit is packed because—"

"Use mine." Tommy cuts me off in a gruff tone of voice.

Everyone in the room turns to stare at me. Not only is Tommy famous for his privacy and his courtesy, but he's also remarkably careful with his knives. Everyone knows the way he obsesses about them. He's done entire shows to teach people how to slice an onion, but he spent just as long teaching people how to clean and sharpen their knives.

"I'm left-handed," I start again.

Tommy waves away my concern. He's telling his assistant where to find the knives instead of looking at me. "Sure, sure. So am I. We're developing a knife set for chefs that are left-handed. Should work for ambidextrous chefs. You can use my prototype and tell me how it works. Any other questions?"

The other chefs turn around, and a couple of them glare at me again.

They seem to think Tommy likes me or is giving me special treatment, but it couldn't be further from the truth. He's gone out of his way to prove how little he thinks of me, and yet... Here he is, doing me a huge favor, something he's never done for another contestant. I don't know what to make of him.

Except I do. Mom always said he was all about money. He cared more about his career than about us, and he wouldn't even pay child support. So, I suppose I shouldn't be surprised that he's trying to promote his products on this show. He's probably never had a leftie before, and he's just using me.

Tommy dismisses us, and we spend the rest of the afternoon and evening with the camera crew.

Jonah's in his element. He's got an easy, quiet confidence, so different from Jake's noisy personality. Jonah knows his craft, and he's at the top of his game. Most of Tommy's staff know him from previous competitions, and everyone respects him.

He's decisive and intelligent. We're touring the kitchen where we'll cook on Monday, and he's taking everything in. We're whispering about what we see, making notes, and Jonah misses nothing.

He's a different person, and I'm falling deeper in love every second. I love seeing him do what he was born to do. There's no way I would ever ask him to leave this behind.

But the question eating at me, now that I've met my dad, is whether this is too good to be true. Can it really be this easy, after all these years of worry and all the warnings from my grammy?

# Chapter Thirty-Eight

I HOP on the hostess's counter at Pappy's restaurant. It's early Sunday morning, and no one is around yet. "Who's judging?"

Jonah rests a hand on either side of me, then leans over to answer me. "He typically picks among the same five or six judges. I'm not sure why he decided not to judge this time, except for the obvious. He's never done that before he met you."

Jonah makes my heart race, but we have to be professional today, so I don't kiss him immediately. "You mean he can't judge his own daughter."

Jonah nods.

"See. I'm already messing things up for you and Jake." And it's even worse because it's more proof that Tommy knows he's my dad, but won't actually say anything about it.

Jonah tucks a stray hair behind my ear. "Blind judging is better. You're helping us." He dips his head down to nuzzle my neck.

I'm still trying to be professional, so I talk over the very distracting nuzzling. "I've watched every episode of every show he's ever made."

Jonah moves to the other side of my neck, and I keep talking.

Look at me. So focused. "I should know this. It's Christmas. It's Boston. Who will be available, and what do they like to eat?"

Jonah groans and buries his head in the hollow of my neck. "Do we have to work?"

I cradle his cheeks with my hands and pull his head off my shoulder. "I'm not going to ruin anything for you."

Jonah sighs. "Fine. Name a style of cooking, and I get a kiss for every judge in Boston I can think of who matches your criteria." He drops his hands to my hips. "I think our list will be longer than Jake's because I'm way more motivated to think of answers."

I haven't had this much fun in years, even though that game doesn't last long. I hop off the counter. Pretty soon we've got sketch pads, and we're brainstorming which appetizers and entrées and desserts to make—with very motivating questions and rewards, of course.

"If one of us makes the biscuits, the other person can make the gravy and dumplings. It's a Christmas meal, so I'm thinking of comfort food."

"Cornbread stuffing."

"Takes too long."

Jonah and I have thrown out the notes he wrote with Jake and are coming up with our own. Before we know it, Pappy and Mary arrive an hour early. We head into the kitchen and hunch over a counter with papers strewn all around.

Pappy hugs me. "Where's the ring?"

Jonah holds up the chain around his neck.

"Still wearing the albatross." Pappy shakes his head. "You two are killing your parents. You understand that, right, Joey? Your mom's going to have a heart attack if you don't get that ring back on her finger, and your father will never forgive you if he doesn't have grandchildren by next Christmas."

Jonah and I exchange an uneasy glance. "No pressure," he mutters. "We'll set a date when we're ready, Gramps, and I want to buy Brie her own ring."

Mary hugs me. "They're fine. Stop with the obscure poetry

references. No one reads *The Rime of the Ancient Mariner.*" She grabs the notes. "You can't serve veal with that."

"They won't ask you to prepare veal in that amount of time." Pappy grabs the notes from Mary. "Everyone reads *The Rime of the Ancient Mariner.* It's a classic. I should recite it at your wedding."

Jonah grabs our notes from them. "There is no way I would hand you the microphone at my wedding."

"But Brie would." Pappy winks at me. "You know it's actually a wedding poem. The narrator is talking to a wedding guest."

"Fair point," Mary concedes.

"So, what do you think Tommy will throw at us?" I try to get Pappy and Mary back on track, since we have so little time to prepare. Also, there will be no albatrosses or mariners at my wedding when it *does* happen.

"Matt and Jake won't forgive me if you win because I helped you." Pappy grins widely. "Then again, they didn't ask my opinion, so, their loss." He shrugs. "And I mean that literally." He winks. "Their loss."

It's the best hour of my life. I've forgotten how exciting it is to put a meal together in my head. We all argue, and I love watching Jonah push back. He comes alive when he talks about food, taking charge of the conversation, making snap decisions, and acting more confident than I've ever seen.

We leave so Pappy and Mary can open for the day. We've only got one day to prepare. It's been almost five years since I cooked professionally, and I've missed this. I feel like I'm home again, and cooking with Jonah adds something new to our relationship.

Which I'm still worried about. It was too easy yesterday. My mom and grammy went to great lengths to avoid Tommy and warned me never to meet him.

And then *nothing*. I'm confused, but it's also frightening. I'm walking on eggshells, not sure why Tommy was so dangerous or why my mom insisted that I never meet him.

I just believed her. I still feel panic rising in my chest at the idea. Meeting him meant losing Mom. The one time she went to his studio I almost got put into foster care, so when I thought about him, I just felt sheer terror.

We have to wake up at five o'clock to get ready for the taping tomorrow morning. We've got to be at Tommy's kitchen studio by six-thirty a.m.

Jake and Matt are practicing at Matt's restaurant, the one he bought from Jake and Jonah, the one that Jake knows like the back of his hand, the one with high-end stoves and every possible ingredient and kitchen tool.

Jonah and I take our notes back to the Butlers' enormous home in a posh Boston suburb. I'm shaping meatballs with ground chicken. We're really hoping we don't have to use that protein, but anything could happen.

Jonah's making a carbonara sauce, and it doesn't smell quite right. I turn to him. "I want barbecue on this instead of Italian."

He doesn't miss a beat. "Sure thing, girlfriend." Jonah turns off the sauce and searches for another pan. He grabs a bunch of spices and starts mixing a sauce. Jonah glances at the timer on the stove. "We don't really have enough time left for the sauce to simmer, but we'll get more flavor punch from barbecue."

"Nothing says Merry Christmas like Bourbon meatballs." I wash my hands and start to sear the meatballs. By the time I have the moisture locked in, Jonah has the beginnings of a barbecue sauce. He slathers it on the meatballs, and the sauce pops and sizzles as it hits the hot pan.

We stand side by side as he spoons the sauce over the meatballs, our arms brushing against each other. I take the meatballs and shove the pan in the oven. We're timing ourselves tonight, and Jonah won't give me a single extra second.

Not without making me pay for it, anyway.

But he's intense and in the zone, so I'm taking it as seriously as he does. Even if I don't mind paying his penalties for going over.

"What do you want me to do with these noodles, Chef?" I ask. "We cooked them to go with the pasta sauce."

"Change of plans. Make a broccoli slaw and save the noodles for something else."

I love his decisiveness. "On it." I rinse the pasta with cold water to set it, slide it in the fridge, and start shredding vegetables for the slaw.

He's in constant motion when he cooks, and his brain works just as quickly. "The meatballs would be a good appetizer."

I dip a spoon in the barbecue sauce. "That's killer, Killer. Are we making sliders or tacos or a bánh mì sandwich or what?"

"What." He grins, and we work until the timer goes off. We grab some dishes, and I plate the meatballs while he reaches around me to scoop the slaw on the plate. He grimaces. "We needed some mango or citrus in this."

He sets down his bowl and spoon, then his hands rest on either side of the counter, trapping me. I turn around and run my fingers up his forearms. My favorite part of him.

Except his brain and his heart and his goodness, of course. But I do love those muscles and veins.

We've been racing to beat a timer, and a thrill of adrenaline surges through me. The barbecue sauce smells amazing, like honey and lemon and chipotle and maybe a hint of garlic.

It's the smell of love.

Jonah bends down, his eyes twinkling. "Let's sample the appetizer."

I take in his black apron, his wavy brown hair, and the biceps peeking out where his t-shirt bunches on his upper arms. He looks better than dinner, but I'm also worried about disappointing him tomorrow. I've never competed on television or cooked under such strict time guidelines. "I don't want the food to get cold."

His eyes flash. "There's plenty of heat in the kitchen."

I wrap my arms around him and wish I were taller, or he were shorter. I run a hand along his shoulders and down to his biceps. "I thought you didn't like to eat cold appetizers."

Jonah grins. "I'll make an exception for you."

Mr. Butler clears his throat. "Did I hear the timer go off?"

Jonah groans and his arm slides down around my shoulder. "You're like Pavlovian dogs. You hear the timer and come running."

I smile uneasily at Mr. Butler, whose eyes are misty. "You and Jonah look so natural cooking together."

"Dad." Jonah grabs a plate and shoves it at him. "Do not cry until you try our food, then you can cry with joy."

Mr. Butler sniffs. "I'm so happy for you, Joey. Good to see you again, Brie."

I nod. It's only been a day since the parking lot proposal, but Mr. Butler acts like I'm his long-lost daughter.

I find that ironic.

Mrs. Butler wanders into the room. *Maggie*, not Mrs. Butler. "Appetizers? I thought you were working on entrées."

"Brie doesn't like my carbonara."

"Hi, sweetie." Maggie crushes me in a hug and holds me in a vise grip. "Are you fighting again?" she whispers. "Is the sauce a symbol of deeper disagreement? You can tell me."

I pat her shoulder and tear myself out of her hug. "We don't argue all the time, despite what Jake says. I'm Italian, and he's Irish. Whose carbonara do you think I'm gonna like?" I take my plate. "But his barbecue..." I slide into a seat at the table. "That's why I love him."

Jonah flashes me a lopsided grin and sits next to me. "So, you *do* love me?"

I nudge his shoulder. "You know I do, but I might love this sauce more."

I lean over for a quick kiss. Mmmm. A mesquite make-out might be in our future.

Maggie pulls the plate toward herself. "As long as you're not hiding your feelings in your food."

Mr. Butler takes a bite. "Of course they're hiding their feelings in their food. What do you think comfort food is for?"

"This is good." Maggie wipes the rest of the sauce with her slaw and glances at the pot on the stove. "Your romance is maturing, and I love to see the way you work together."

Jonah reaches for her empty plate. "This sauce is not a metaphor for our engagement, Mom."

She smiles sheepishly. "Fine. Do you have more? Not that I'm expressing a desire for your relationship to continue or pressuring you to set a wedding date. I'm just hungry."

Jonah grins at me and rolls his eyes. "When your mother is a therapist, every conversation is a metaphor for your emotions." He goes to the counter to scrape more out of the pan. "There you go. Brie wanted a different sauce, and I listened and made this just for her. Read all you want into that metaphor for our relationship."

Now Maggie's eyes are glistening at the edges. "Oh, Brie, you've changed him. He's ready for marriage. He is. He'll do anything for you."

"He made her a mesquite sauce instead of carbonara." Mr. Butler holds up his plate for seconds. "He must be head over heels in love."

"Stop with the sarcasm." Maggie whacks him in the chest. "It's symbolic, and it's romantic."

"Barbecue is romantic?" Mr. Butler rubs his chest. "You've never opened a barbecue restaurant, Jonah."

He and Jonah grin at each other. "Not *yet*, Dad."

"It'll be crowded on Valentine's, because everyone associates meat with love." He pulls Maggie into a hug and tries to steal the last bite from her plate, but she dodges him.

"I love these meatballs," she says. "Almost as much as I love you. Like Jonah and Brie clearly love each other."

Jonah nudges me. Again, am I on his football team or engaged to him? But roughhousing is the second love language in this household, after food.

Mr. Butler takes the plates to the sink. "Brie loves his sauce more than him. I'm telling you. Barbecue. What's in this anyway?"

I see why she thinks Jonah and his dad are so alike. They're practically allergic to discussing emotions. Jonah starts listing ingredients, and just like that, the mushy emotional moment is over.

If you can't beat 'em... You talk about food instead of feelings. I clear my plate from the table. "Would meatballs be a weird choice for Christmas dinner? Mustard and mesquite are not traditional holiday flavors."

"It's weird for some people, but not for others," Mr. Butler says. "And it's not weird for an appetizer."

We hurry to clean the kitchen before Jake gets back. I only have one loose end before the competition. It's a big one. It's the excuse Jonah used to rope me into the fake engagement in the first place, so I'm forever grateful for it. "Thanks again, Mr. Butler, for the contribution to the food banks. The donations arrive on Tuesday, regardless of who wins or loses."

He waves a hand. "We should do it every year. In fact, we have enough extra produce and food from my restaurants that we should be donating to those food banks year-round."

I'm touched. "It makes a huge difference to have fresh produce instead of canned goods."

After we clean up, Jonah drives me back to my townhouse, and he walks me to the door. It's closer to two or three degrees outside, now that it's evening.

Jonah bends over to hug me. "See you tomorrow." His voice tickles my ear.

I shiver. "Thanks. I needed the distraction. I haven't stopped to think all day."

He tugs me closer, even though we're human popsicles. "Do you want to talk about Tommy?"

I shake my head. "I told you he didn't want me." I bite my lip to stop from crying.

Jonah's eyes dart to my mouth, but he swallows and shakes his head as we huddle beside my door. "You don't know that. Give it time."

"I do know. I've always known. It's different to experience it, though."

Jonah puts a finger beneath my chin and gently tilts my head up. His gaze is gentle, but intense. Intensely gentle. Fiercely loyal. *Loving*.

"I'll always want you."

A raw feeling erupts inside, the fear that I'm not worth loving. "Goodnight." I push open my door.

Jonah watches me with his dark brown puppy dog eyes. "Are you okay?"

How can I tell him that all the love in the world will never fill this hole? I inconvenienced my mom by the mere fact of my birth, and my dad can't be bothered to acknowledge me.

*I'm a mistake, and I'm flawed, and people leave.*

Jonah tugs me back into a hug. "You're not okay, and you don't have to talk about it. I love you, and I'm here for you. Step five of your recipe, remember?"

I lean into the hug.

"I'm going to stick around," Jonah whispers. He runs his hands up and down my back, pressing me closer.

I lay my head on his chest. "So, what, the oven is preheated, and you're just going to let it run indefinitely? You might burn out." What if he doesn't have the patience to wait for me to deal with my issues?

Jonah rests his chin on top of my head. "Nah. Ask Jake. I can leave the broiler on as long as I have to."

Then he gazes at me with so much heat in his eyes that I'm surprised I don't burn to a crisp. Even though I'm torn up about my dad's rejection, I believe him. "Until our golden anniversary?"

"Hey." Jonah pulls back to look at me, and his expression is gentler now. "For as long as we both shall live. We've already been over that."

It's hard to feel it, though, sometimes, even through the fierce love I have for Jonah. The old whispers come back to haunt me, and I shove them aside. "Thanks, boyfriend."

Jonah kisses my cheek. "You're amazing. Let's put Jake and Matt in their place and show your dad what he's missing tomorrow."

"Yeah." That sparks a fire in me. Like the Grinch's heart expanding, except it's my temper that grows three sizes right then. How can Tommy dismiss me without even giving me a chance? I'm going to make him regret it. I'm going to show him what kind of relationship he could have had, if he'd gotten to know me.

I'm going to win that competition.

# Chapter Thirty-Nine

GOING to bed early doesn't help. I don't really sleep because I'm so wired. I've spent half of my life desperately wishing my dad wanted me, then the other half resenting him. And there's a lot of fear mixed in there. This morning I feel all of the emotions at the same time.

I crawl out of bed in the pitch black and sneak down to the bathroom to avoid waking Lindsay. I wind my hair into two tight space buns, apply makeup that would make Lindsay proud, and pull on a simple black Henley and jeans with some Keds. The casual look was fine for the pickup shots and B-roll, and it should be good again today. *Professional.* But not too flashy. It's my job not to outshine Jonah. I'm the sous chef. Today is all about him.

I arrive at the studio, and I'm both pumped and terrified. The emotions feel a lot alike. I sit in my car, not sure if I want to face my dad. I was able to avoid him for most of the day on Saturday, but there's no escape today.

We're filming in a winter wonderland.

I take a deep breath and step into the icy air. I want to be with Jonah more than anything, and I have to face my dad to figure out my future.

So here goes.

Jonah's already there, and he shows me into a green room. I slip a candy-cane-striped apron over my head—because wearing *all* black only looks good on the Butler boys—and I'm ready to cook.

He's got a crisp, double-breasted black chef's coat instead of an apron. Grammy's gold ring rests on his chest, still hanging from his silver chain. His chestnut brown hair is perfectly styled, with the waves rolling back from his forehead. Colleen couldn't have done it better herself.

He looks hot. There's no other way to say it. Like, get me a poster and hang it in my room. Now I see why he and Jake have a huge following on social media.

They're man candy.

A producer goes over final instructions with us. When we go out to mill around with the other contestants, Jake stands beside Matt with his arms crossed. They barely acknowledge us. Jake's hair is tousled on top, and the sides are smooth. The high-top blends into his stubble perfectly, and he looks good, too.

And Matt is just as hot as his brothers. The camera is going to love him. It's his first cooking competition, too, and he looks a little jittery, like me.

Everyone is so different from Saturday. The level of tension is times ten. Times a thousand. I feel like I'm about to sled down Mount Everest face first without any brakes.

Even Jonah looks nervous. "Are you okay?" I ask.

He plays with Grammy's ring, dangling on his tough guy chain. "I've never competed *against* Jake before."

"Sure, you have. You compete against him every day. We've got this." I want to wrap an arm around his waist, but I'm trying to keep this professional.

He's still rattled. "It feels wrong."

Matthew and Jake stare at us. "Let's concentrate on the other chefs, and we'll worry about them when we get to the final round."

Jonah shakes his head. "I'm worried about the food, not the

competition." His face clears, and it's like he's back in the zone. "Let's check out what they've got for us."

We wander over to the enormous pantry that lines one wall of the kitchen area where we'll film the *Santa Snack Smack Down*. We lower our voices and start strategizing. Jonah's right. The jitters calm themselves.

I'm going to need all the self-control I ever learned in the military to face my father, after his rejection on Saturday, and Jonah's going to have to take on his twin.

The crew takes us out of the arena and back into the green room. They get a bunch of shots of the celebrity chefs walking in and out. The sous chefs stand around and wait.

Matt and I nod to acknowledge each other, but that's it.

We're fifteen minutes away from starting. The audience fills in, and the celebrity chefs come back. It's weird to think of Jake and Jonah as celebrities, but they are. They have bios on Tommy's website with other chefs who have competed in his shows, and people follow their careers.

Tommy Fuller rushes in with ten minutes left. Four people are trailing behind him, and I know who I got my organizational skills from—my mother, not him. I expect something from him. A glance. Some kind of acknowledgment, but I get nothing.

"Alright, what's up, brother?" He clasps hands with Jonah, then the other chefs. He's in performance mode. This is the Tommy Fuller I'm used to seeing on TV, the one who has a nickname for every chef. "Thanks for coming, Killer. Still love that haircut. Just as sexy as J-Dog said."

I've figured out that Jonah is *Killer*, and Jake must be *J-Man*. Tommy pulls a three-hundred-pound man into a hug. "What's up, Meatloaf?" He hugs a seriously intimidating woman next. "Homerun. Ready to knock it out of the park again?"

The puns and jokes are starting. The cameras are rolling. We are on, even if the show hasn't technically started.

My new favorite trash-talking bestie smirks at the other contestants. "You know it."

Tommy gives her a fist bump. "Love you, sister."

She glares at both Jake and Jonah, but grins at me. I nod my head back in acknowledgment. Women gotta stick together.

Because I remember her. She lost to them by one point, and that was an awesome episode—no wonder Tommy wanted her back. She will be tough to beat.

But yeah, I still want to beat her.

"PopTart! Gonna make the flavors pop?"

The dark-haired woman smirks at us. "I'm going to toast these kids."

Jonah and Jake grin back at her. I know the twins have competed against her a few times, too.

Tommy's looking at the head chefs and not paying attention to the sous chefs who will assist. "Thanks. This is going to be epic. Our ratings will be through the *rooftop*, especially with all of you cooking."

Everyone groans. Jake nudges his shoulder. "You're already starting with the puns?"

I dare to look at my dad. "Keep up, Jake. He started a long time ago. Or did you miss all the introductions?"

Tommy laughs at me, a surprised natural laugh, and grins at me. "You ain't seen nothin' yet, Shrimp." He rubs his hands. "Alright, let's do this. Any questions before we go out there?"

*No one.* Tommy turns around. "Roman and Felix will be commentating, as usual, and I'll be tasting along with our mystery judges." He winks. "Don't forget to make a plate for me. No way am I giving *that* up."

The other sous chefs step forward, but I hang back in the shadows of the scaffolding in the enormous unfinished room backstage. There's only five minutes left before we begin.

The producers line us up and prepare more shots of us entering as teams.

"Three minutes."

We all strut into the kitchen arena when the producer gives us the signal, but I'm shaking. Jonah grabs my hand. "I love you, girl-friend. We got this."

There's a camera in my face, but I try to act natural. "Love you more than mesquite," I say.

"What's that?" Jake asks. "Sweet nothings? Because you know what you're walking away with today?"

"Nothing." Matt finishes the punchline, and the brothers fist bump.

Of course, Tommy has put our mini kitchen directly across from Jake and Matt, so we are directly in their line of sight while we're cooking and vice versa.

Jonah doesn't trash talk back, and he probably never does. Jake probably does all the talking for both of them when they compete.

So, I step up again. "That's fine, Jakey. You keep up the smack talk, and we'll let our food do the talking."

Jake sets out his knife kit. He grins and glances over at me. "Oh, yeah? And what is it going to say?"

Jonah interrupts before Jake or Matt can cut to a punchline. "It says your fryer isn't turned on, and you didn't check your oven, either."

Jake swears, and Matt checks all the appliances in their kitchen. Since it's Matt's first time, he doesn't know the basic routine. Meatloaf and Homerun glare at Jonah for tipping his brothers off, but Tommy nods approvingly at the gesture of sportsmanship.

Especially since it was couched in smack talk, Tommy's specialty.

Then I realize where I get it from. The way I always have a quick comeback?

I get that from my dad.

I'm flooded with a feeling of belonging, because I understand parts of myself I never did before, but it also stings, because I'll never know how much more I'm like my dad.

And I want to get to know him. If I let down my guard, I

would admit that I like him and that everyone on set likes him. He's funny and warm and nice and... I wish he wanted to get to know me, too. But I can't admit that, so I put on my Bronx face and get ready to cook.

Tommy starts his intro. "Welcome to the first ever *Santa Snack Smack Down*! We got a tip that Santa is heading to Boston first on his Christmas Eve rounds, so we're serving up some gourmet snacks to help him on his route around the world."

I'm still getting used to the lights and the set and the audience and the cameras. I can't let Jonah down. He and Jake need this money for their restaurant, and winning would mean double donations for the food bank.

"Let's see what appetizer the elf pulls out of Santa's sack." A beautifully dressed woman in an elf costume reaches into an over-sized Santa sack. I'm surprised that she's so tastefully attired. This isn't some skimpy costume. It's cute and family friendly and one less reason to resent Tommy.

I'm disappointed. I want some rage to fuel me right now. He's been way too nice to everyone so far.

"Santa wants an appetizer with turmeric! Three-two-one-go!"

Jonah looks at me, laser focused. He's in charge, decisive, no hesitation. "Pappy's tomato soup."

I nod. "Sure, Chef. You want me to use the turmeric in Mary's curry cream swirl?"

Jonah's already in motion. "Yeah. We'll add a crostini on top."

"Parmesan? Asiago?"

"Both." Jonah's mouth tilts in a half grin as he rushes over to the pantry. "And fry some chickpeas, then roll them in the curry powder you make for the crema swirl."

We're both on it, running to get ingredients. I hear people yelling around me. "Behind you! On your back! Coming around!" My heart races as I thread through the other chefs to get ingredients and get back to my station.

Once we're back, Jonah makes the soup, and I make the crema

swirl. I worked in Pappy's kitchen, so I know exactly what Jonah wants me to do.

I'm completely in the zone, watching the timer, but in the back of my mind I'm worried about something else. I've watched enough of these shows that I know how important it is to get the audience on my side.

That's how you get invited back to these shows. That's how you get a following online and sell products and bring people into your restaurant. Win or lose, that's what matters—the audience.

And Jonah's quiet. Across the way, Jake does all the talking at his workstation. Felix asks him, "What have you got for us, Chef?"

"Chicken noodle curry soup."

Jonah's head snaps up. They tested that recipe together, and it's good.

Tommy wanders around, staring mysteriously, taking clean spoons and tasting sauces without reacting, and trying to psych us out. Felix comes over to us, and I know I have to chat him up, even if I'm the sous chef. Jonah's too quiet.

Felix starts asking questions. "Tell me about this crema."

"It's crème fraiche with turmeric and a curry blend," I say as I mix the spices and thin the crème fraiche, so I can drizzle it into the soup.

Felix turns to Jonah. "Are those red peppers you're adding to the tomato soup?"

Jonah does okay with his answers, but he's not as charismatic as Jake. Tommy watches me shred some cheese for the parmesan-asiago crostini crisp, so I call him out. "Hey, Chef, do you want to know why I'm smiling?"

Tommy takes the bait. "Sure."

I finish shredding the cheese, shove it aside, and start chopping a tomato to top the soup. "Because I know something you don't know."

He grins and watches me chopping. "What is that?"

"I'm not right-handed."

Tommy full on laughs. He's famous for his crazy knife skills and diatribes about right-handed people. He loves being a leftie. "Yeah, I'm not right-handed either." He pounds the cutting board next to me. "She gets it, people, am I right? And look at that knife she's using." He winks at me as the camera zooms in on his signature, emblazoned on the knife I'm using.

Yes, I just gave him a free shout out for his new knife set, and no one can resist a *Princess Bride* reference.

The audience roars and whoops and cheers. Jonah feeds on their energy and starts talking to Felix more naturally about the spices that will go on the fried chickpeas.

Tommy tastes my crema and groans. "Bury me in that sauce!"

The audience goes crazy again, and I grin at him before I catch myself. I'm not supposed to like him or share inside jokes with him, but it's like I have an inside track to his brain. The two of us have the audience eating out of the palm of our hands, figuratively.

Tommy loves me right now, and even if it's just because I'm selling his knives and making his audience laugh, for one short moment, he approves of me. Yeah, I resent that he's all about money, and it's only because he's using me, but still. He doesn't hate me, and it feels amazing.

Jonah and I plate our appetizer course with twelve seconds to spare as Jonah wipes the plates with a cloth. We've got a bowl of red pepper-tomato soup with a curry crema swirl, topped with a garlic parmesan-asiago crostini crisp and fried curry chickpeas. We leave the arena while assistants clear the dishes and counters. We can't even watch the judging from our green room, since there are multiple rounds. We just have to sit and wait to find out our fate.

Single elimination. One loss, and we're out.

# Chapter Forty

MEATLOAF GETS ELIMINATED, so it's us and Jake and Matt against Homerun, my new bestie with the snarky attitude, and PopTart. We wait for the assistants to reset the kitchens, and Jake comes over to give us a fist bump. "Bold choice, bro."

"That was some ultimate comfort food." Jonah tugs Jake and Matt into a hug as a camerawoman walks up to them. "You're looking good out there."

"You look decent, too," Matt says.

"But not as good as this new hairdo," Jake says, rubbing his mostly bald head, and we hear laughs that must be Lindsay and the Butlers in the audience.

Tommy's right—the ratings are going to be ridiculous with two brothers taking on a twin, and Homerun and PopTart are insanely good at what they do.

The lady elf draws Santa's Christmas wish for his entrée dish out of the oversized sack. "Sourdough bread and jalapeños."

Jonah and I huddle. "Those barbecue meatballs," Jonah says immediately. "Use the bread to make the meatballs and put the jalapeños in the sauce."

"No." My gut instinct kicks in. "Something lighter. Every-one's going to go heavy with meat. What if we go vegetarian?"

Jonah stares at me. Seconds tick by, and I try not to panic. Everyone else rushes over to the pantry.

He grins. "You're right. No one wants a heavy meal on Christmas Eve." We put our heads together. "It's more about making the meal flow. Judges consider that."

We know it at the same time. "Should we?"

"Yeah. Might as well."

Felix is in my face. "What have we got here, Chef?"

"Grilled cheese."

Tommy's right behind him. "No protein?"

I turn to the audience. "Cheese has protein in it. Where are my vegetarians?" Some audience members whistle and clap, and Tommy salutes me.

Jonah and I run to grab a gray tub together. I toss in the jalapeños. He's already got the sourdough, butter, mayonnaise, and onion powder.

I grab apricots and meet him in front of the cheeses. He tosses in white cheddar, Gruyere, smoked gouda, Monterey Jack, Manchego, and then his hand lands on the brie.

I nod. "For sure."

I'm shredding cheese again, like I did last round, except this time I'm also slicing the brie, or spooning out gobs of goo, and prepping the cheese mixture. Jonah makes apricot jam, then he mixes the butter, mayo, onion powder, and Manchego cheese. I slice the bread, slather the mixture, and start toasting the bread.

"Slaw," he says.

I run for cabbage and broccoli. "Which citrus, Chef?"

"Pineapple!" he yells.

Felix loves the way we interact, finishing each other's sentences, handing ingredients back and forth, working side-by-side, leaning across each other. Jonah presses a kiss on the side of my cheek when he reaches across me to grab the jalapeños, like it's the most natural thing in the world.

Because it is. We love each other, and we let it show.

The audience goes crazy. I smile at Jonah, then look back at my cutting board. I have a knife in my hand, and I have to stay focused, but the next time I reach across his workstation for the pineapple, I wrap one arm around his waist as I lean, and someone in the audience wolf-whistles.

They love us.

So do the cameras. I've come alive under the pressure. I feel at home in the arena with the audience and the lights. It's like I was meant to do this my whole life.

We shred the ingredients and get the pineapple-cabbage-broccoli slaw marinating with jalapeño and lemon, then we slather a thin layer of fresh apricot preserves on the toasted bread and cook the grilled cheese.

I plate the slaw, he slides the sandwiches on the dishes and wipes the rims with a cloth, and the timer buzzes.

Tommy turns to the audience. "Who thinks they should be able to hear the judges?"

The crowd whistles.

Tommy nods to us. You never know what kind of twist he'll throw at the contestants. "Head back to your green rooms, and you can listen, but no cameras."

Tommy and the other judges taste our food last. He narrates as they sample the grilled cheese. We took a huge risk. Is it too easy and simple?

But then the jalapeño-apricot jam hits their tongues. Tommy moans. "What is this witchcraft? Everyone knows brie is my favorite cheese."

Jonah glances at me when Tommy says that, but we've got cameras all around us.

*Did Tommy know my mom was pregnant before or after they decided to divorce? Did he help pick my name?* I shake it off. I've got to stay focused.

"The fresh jam should make the sandwich soggy, but they've retained a perfect crispness," one judge says.

Another judge complains, "The pineapple slaw seems like an afterthought."

That's it. We're toast.

Then the third judge comments. "The jalapeño note in the slaw pairs perfectly with the hint of heat in the apricot preserves and gives the bite some texture at the same time."

We wait for scores. It could go either way—one bad note from one judge could sink us.

A producer signals to us, and Jonah lets out a deep breath beside me. We're through to the next round. Homerun has fouled out, and it's just PopTart left with us and Jake.

The lady elf comes out to draw the dessert challenge out of the huge sack, and my nerves are jangling. I'm pumped. We've had a minute to use the bathroom while they cleaned the stations, but I'm ready to go again.

Winning feels good. Halfway there, and this is the hardest round. Jake and Jonah are known for their desserts.

"Santa wants sesame and chocolate for dessert."

The audience groans. It sounds disgusting, and Tommy laughs his signature evil chuckle. He's known for the hard combos he throws at chefs.

Jonah and I huddle at our workstation. I'm stumped, but he is the dessert guy. "Gingerbread, obviously. It's Christmas."

I nod. We'd agreed that we had to do sugar cookies or gingerbread, if there was any way.

"Or fudge or miso caramel..."

He shakes his head. He's already moving to the pantry wall. "Sesame-ginger cookies. We'll use tahini."

I follow him and grab spices. "On it."

He's still thinking. "How about a white chocolate coating?" He lowers his voice. "Jake will go for milk chocolate, and PopTart will go dark. I want to stand out."

I nod and grab everything he needs. "Sounds great. I can dip the cookies. They will barely have time to cool, but I think we can pull it off."

He grabs ingredients off the shelves and fills our oversized gray tub. "Use the blast chiller." He stops with his hand on the cinnamon. "White chocolate ice cream."

I scramble for ingredients. "There's no way we have time."

"Push it."

We only have half an hour. Then an idea hits me.

"Boyfriend."

"Yeah." He glances over, his arms full of cream and sugar.

I love sesame, and my gut instinct tells me that I inherited my dad's palette. He's liked my sauces and cooking. He's gotta love sesame, too, and if we can nail this, we can win this round. Even if he's not handing out points on a score card, Tommy's comments still hold weight with the judges.

"Sesame-ginger ice cream, not white chocolate."

He stops everything and stares at me for a second. "Do it."

In that instant, I know again that we have something real. There's nothing hypothetical left anymore. Jonah trusts me with his professional reputation. He trusts my instincts as an equal, as a chef, as a competitor. I'm not just his sous chef—I'm his partner, and he's willing to take huge risks, round after round, by listening to me.

I've never been so attracted to him as I am right now.

I mix the ice cream base as quickly as I can. "Hey, boyfriend." Jonah turns, eyebrows furrowed, then his eyes light up. I feed Jonah a taste of it. His eyes twinkle as he licks the spoon, his gaze locked with mine, and I'm sure the cameras are getting this shot of us.

He tweaks the flavors and makes them stronger, then I run the mixture to the ice cream machine. It'll be a soft serve consistency in twenty minutes when we have to serve it, if I'm lucky.

I run back to Jonah, who's sliding the cookies into the oven. I melt the white chocolate. "What do you want in here? Tahini? Ginger? Or both?"

"Both. Light touch."

Felix comes over. "Whoa. Are you making dinner or dessert?"

"Is there a difference on Christmas Eve?" I add a small

amount of tahini to my white chocolate and hope it won't ruin the texture. "Cookies *are* dinner for Santa."

The audience whoops again, and Felix moves on to bug someone else. Tommy comes over and dips a spoon in my white chocolate coating. I wait to see if he thinks the flavor is too strong. We lock eyes, and I almost dare him to say something, but he doesn't react.

I taste it and add more tahini. Toasted sesame paste? Yes, please. I can't go wrong.

Tommy arches an eyebrow. "Bold move, Santoro. Big flavors for a tiny chef."

He's trash talking. I know it. I know him. I can't tell how, but I trust my instincts. I taste the chocolate and add even more tahini. "That's why Pappy calls me Shrimp."

Tommy laughs. Everyone who watches these shows knows Pappy and his restaurants. They trust him and ought to trust me if I throw his name out there.

He takes another clean spoon and tastes the chocolate again. He smiles before he can hide his reaction. "Wow. I'm calling you Jumbo Shrimp. That's a bold flavor."

He can't psych me out. I saw that he loved it, so I leave the chocolate mixture alone. The cookies will mellow out a little after they bake, and they need this flavor punch.

Jonah takes out the cookies. I throw the soft ice cream in the blast chiller. We dip the cookies in the white chocolate-tahini mixture, sprinkle sesame seeds on the shiny chocolate, and chill them. I use two spoons to make oval quenelles of ice cream as Jonah slides the cookies onto each plate.

Time buzzes, and I look up. Tommy is sweating almost as much as Jonah and I are. I didn't realize how close we came to not finishing.

Jake and Matt have exquisitely decorated shortbread cookies with sesame seeds in them. Colored sesame seeds replace the traditional sprinkles. Melted chocolate covers the sesame flavor, though, and PopTart's toffee has the same issue. There are sesame seeds in it, but they're not the star. There's no clear sesame flavor —the chocolate overrides everything.

Which, honestly, seems like a good idea in a way. It's neutral. Let the chocolate shine. It's Christmas Eve, after all—or it will be when people watch this show.

But I have something to prove, and I'm not playing it safe. If Jonah's willing to risk everything, so am I.

Jonah grabs my hand. "Remember Chief's hummus," he whispers in my ear.

I shiver as his breath tickles my neck. I'm not sure if the cameras caught that, but I couldn't stop myself. I'm feeling closer to him than I ever have, because we're sharing the thing we both love—cooking.

"It was delicious with Colleen's gingerbread cookies." He snugs his arm around my waist, and I decide that I trust him. "We got this."

Too late now, if I don't. I'm in it to win it. All of it. *For as long as we both shall live.*

"What do you think?" Tommy asks the audience. "Should we let them watch the judging this time?"

Some of the audience boos and some of the audience cheers. Tommy decides that the Christmas Spirit is high enough to let us watch this round of judging from our green room.

The judges are expressionless as they consider our soft serve ice cream and white-chocolate-covered ginger-tahini cookies. We dipped the cookies so that half is covered, and the other half is exposed.

The judges pick up the cookie, holding it with the undipped half, and dunk it into the ice cream. Tommy takes a bite, then the others do.

I'm holding my breath.

"It's a lot of sesame flavor," Tommy starts. He's been critiquing the food, but not giving scores.

"But the ginger is just as strong," another judge argues. "My question is whether the chocolate is the star or an afterthought."

Again with the *afterthought*. That judge is not my favorite.

Another judge chimes in. "The ice cream cuts the flavors. It's meant to be eaten together. Sure, if I ate the cookie alone, it might be overpowering with that punch of fresh ginger in the cookie."

The third judge speaks up. "The tahini in the ice cream is light enough to enhance the flavor, not overwhelm it."

Then the first judge surprises me. "The creaminess of both the dairy and white chocolate coating tame the heat."

That almost sounds like she liked it. Maybe I like her after all. As an afterthought.

"They definitely got the memo from Santa about sesame," Tommy says.

I hope that's a good thing. It's the only note he's given us, but I'm hopeful, despite his poker face. I still want to prove myself to him. The judges write their scores on their cards.

"This is tight," Tommy says as he reads the final scores. "I'm sorry, PopTart, the twins just edged you out."

We're through to the next round—the final round.

# Chapter Forty-One

IT'S JUST us against Jake and Matt. The tension is palpable as we wait for the crew to reset the kitchens. Jake makes small talk with Matt for the cameras, but Jonah gets quiet. I have to admit it's a sexy kind of quiet, like a tiger about to pounce, so I wrap an arm around his waist and let him scheme. Or worry. Or brood. Whatever he's doing.

Tommy ushers us back into the arena to cook. We've got a few minutes before it's time to start the last round. The audience is there, just waiting for us to win them over. I see Lindsay, and my mind starts turning.

This competition is all about image, win or lose, so I've got to draw Jonah out and cut the building tension. His shoulders are creeping up, and he's working those adorable dimples in his cheeks. The ones that come out when he's really happy or super anxious. "Ready for some payback, boyfriend?" I ask.

He blinks, then turns and gazes down. He answers me with a sexy smirk and so much smolder. So. Much. Smolder. "You know it, *babe*."

My cheeks blush furiously. He is going to pay for that *babe* later, but we've got our own payback to worry about right now.

Jake grins at us. He loves competing. "Payback for which

thing, lovebirds?" He runs his hands through his hair. "I can't wait to see you with a buzz cut, bro. You, too, Brie."

A muscle pops in Jonah's jaw, then he's back to the sexy smirk. "I don't think so."

Tommy comes over. "What's this?"

"Winner gets to choose the other one's new hairstyle." Jake points at Jonah. "He's gonna be bald next time you see him."

That's exactly the barb Jonah needs. "No way. Ask Jake how he got that new flat top."

Tommy laughs. "I heard something about two hundred push-ups."

I look at the audience. "Who wants to see some push-ups?"

Lindsay whistles, and Nick and Danny whoop.

I feign deafness. "I can't hear you."

The audience roars, and Nick and Danny start a chant. "Push-ups! Push-ups! Push-ups!"

Tommy folds his arms across his chest. He should be the one to say this kind of thing, but I've taken over without asking. I arch an eyebrow at him, and Tommy nods appreciatively.

As if that's the permission they need, Jake, Jonah, and Matt drop and execute some perfect push-ups, and the audience goes wild. I hope all the single women at home will go crazy over them, too. They stand, brush off their hands, and head over to a sink nearby.

"I'm so ready for payback," Jake says. "Are we gonna do this?"

"Not so fast." The kitchen crew is still cleaning. "I think the audience needs to hear *why* Jonah wants payback."

Jonah looks at me. He doesn't know why.

I laugh casually. "Wasn't it something about the Rosie Hot Springs in Sugar Creek, Vermont?"

"Oh, yeah?" Tommy looks between Jake and Jonah. "So, this is some kind of grudge match?"

Jake shakes his head. "Oh, man, we do not need to go there. Thanks for bringing that up, Brie."

"Yeah, we can go there." Jonah grins. "Jake wasn't happy

about losing the push-up bet and having to shave his head, so he shoved me into the hot springs."

"Hey, that was falling with style," Jake protests. "You have clumsy feet. I just helped you get started." He pinwheels his arms, imitating Jonah's fall.

The audience laughs.

"So, Jake, I'm wondering why you helped Jonah *get started* when he still had his shoes and clothes on," I say. The laughs in the audience turn to boos.

"Or why you ran away immediately after," Jonah adds.

Jake holds up his hands. "I was chasing a cute girl." He squints into the bright lights. "That one, there in the audience."

The cameras swing to face the crowd, and Lindsay blushes.

I glance over, and the kitchen still isn't ready for the final round, but I want to get the pressure off my friend. "Speaking of Sugar Creek, we did our practicing for this competition in a tiny cabin kitchen up by St. Ambrose Bay."

Tommy turns to me. "How small is Sugar Creek? I haven't heard of it."

He's eating up the whole "small town" angle and the idea of us prepping on normal stoves. That makes us *relatable*. He starts interrogating Jake and Jonah, like they are the underdog chefs of the competition, not celebrity chef royalty whose parents own twelve or fifteen or however many restaurants in three major cities.

I keep feeding Tommy these lines and helping him with the show, stalling for time until the kitchens are ready again. It's not at all what I meant to do. I'm here to show him up and show him what he's missing. Instead, we work seamlessly together, almost like we share a brain. I'm just trying to calm my nerves and make Jonah look good, but this kind of thing comes naturally to me.

What can I say? I guess I'm my father's daughter.

Even if it hurts that we're so alike. I tamp down the emotion.

The lady elf comes out, and this is it. The last round of the competition. I try to channel Grammy and Mom and all my

Christmas magic. They taught me to cook before Pappy did. They did their best with what they had—I want to do the same here.

I'm overwhelmed. It's too much pressure. Jonah rubs my back. "Relax and have fun."

But he's still got his sexy tiger focus on, and no way am I letting up on the intensity, either.

Tommy rubs his hands together. "Santa's tired of the same old cookies and milk. He wants something different this year. Let's see which ingredient he wants for his drink and snack."

The elf reads her line. "Santa says anything with cayenne will do the trick!"

Tommy grins. "This is it. The final round. Whip up Santa's Snack for our Christmas Eve *Smack Down*. Three-two-one. Go!"

Jonah and I huddle again with a camera in our cozy little circle. His brown eyes are dark with concentration, and there are worry lines around them. "We can't do chocolate-cayenne. Everyone knows that's our brand's signature drink."

Felix is in our face. "Your brother has already started, and he says he's dedicating this win to Lindsay. Who are you cooking for?"

Jonah looks at me. "Brie? This win is yours."

I glance at Tommy. "Since we're making drinks, I'm going to remind you all not to drink and drive tonight." Even though it's December twelfth, I know people will watch this on Christmas Eve.

The clock is ticking, but Jonah isn't worried. He's thinking, so I'm going to take this time. "A drunk driver killed my mom on her way home from work after a holiday party, so I'm dedicating this win to her. This one's for you." I hit my chest with a fist twice and point to heaven. "Love you, Mom."

And I do, however imperfect she was. Jonah wraps an arm around my waist.

Tommy blinks. "Your mom passed?"

I look directly into the camera. "She did. Call an Uber or a Lyft or something. Good things happen when your hands are free to do something other than drive. Right, Jake?" I yell across to him.

"Right, Brie! Take a cab if you're drinking." He blows an air kiss to the audience. "Both my hands will be free on the way home, Linz, if you want to ride with me."

The cameras are trying to find Lindsay, and when they find her, it's gold. First of all, she's gorgeous, and second of all, she's blushing. She waves back to Jake, and Tommy looks at me like I'm the best thing he's ever seen.

Even though I've just dedicated this competition to my mom. I don't get him.

"Got it." Jonah pulls me down. "Popcorn. Your mom."

I nod. "Yeah?"

"Let's put the cayenne in the popcorn *and* a drink."

"Something warm—"

"But not literally warm—"

"—like lime and coconut and—"

"Beach Santa. Nautical and Nice."

We scramble together to the shelves. He grabs spices and I grab popcorn. "Mom would love you so much, Chef."

"I love *you* so much, Brie."

It's so natural that I almost forget he just said that on national television. "Back atcha."

And I mean it. I've never meant it more.

I grab the blender, and he starts the spice mix. We work like crazy. When time is up, we have a spicy tropical drink with a cayenne-lime popcorn-nut mix on the side.

It's a huge risk, again, but my mouth waters. The spices on the nuts and popcorn are addicting. There's heat from the cayenne and a bunch of other complex flavors. Cumin, paprika, thyme, oregano, garlic, and even a tiny hint of sugar mixed with the salt.

Then the drink has just enough coconut to cool down the cayenne and lime. We've added a little pineapple to bring back the flavors from the slaw we made in the second round.

This meal comes full circle now, and I'm incredibly proud of Jonah.

We wait for the assistants to clear our mess, and I glance over at Jake and Matt. They're exhausted, too, and their drink is gorgeous.

They've gone with the signature dark chocolate cayenne drink, a cayenne whipped cream, and some spicy nuts on the side.

Tommy laughs. "You guys think a lot alike."

Jonah sizes up Jake's cup and saucer, and a hint of sadness flits across his face.

I hate that they're not competing together. I hate that Jake feels left behind because Jonah is with me. I'm still not sure what the future holds for Jonah and me or Jake and Jonah's relationship after this competition. Some of my euphoria drains.

Then Tommy switches things up again. "Who thinks they should meet the judges in person this time?"

We stay in the kitchen arena waiting for the judges to come out. Meanwhile, Jonah reaches over to fist bump his brothers. "Good luck, bro."

Matt does the same. "Good luck, man."

Jake grins and gives Jonah a fist bump. He rubs the sexy curls on top and the bald sides of his head. "Ready for your new haircut?"

"You know you want it," Matt says.

I roll my eyes. "If we win, you owe us a swim in the hot springs, Jakey."

Jake bows. "Gladly. You just want to see me in my swim trunks again, babe."

I roll my eyes even more dramatically and put a hand on Jonah's chest. "Not when I've got *this*. Remind me which twin won the push-up competition?"

Tommy loves the smack talk. The show is called a *Smack Down*, after all, and it's all good-natured. Then, as the judges file in, he turns to me instead of Jonah, and his face gets serious. "You want to tell us about this woman that you dedicated your efforts to?"

I hate him for asking me. My eyes mist over. He knows her. How dare he? He could at least use her name.

Jonah wraps an arm around my waist. "We're dedicating our win to Brie's mother, who was a professional chef, like her daughter. She was a good woman and an amazing cook. She worked for my grandfather, so we have her to thank for introducing us, in a way."

I bite my lip. "Her name was Aria Santoro." I've got to pull this together for Jonah and for the show. "I told *Killer* that she was too tired to cook meals for me herself, since she spent all her time as a chef cooking for everyone else. Our favorite meal to make together was popcorn. It's still my favorite dinner and snack."

Tommy's taken aback but recovers quickly. He's a pro. "Yeah, I get that." The other judges nod. "It's a lot of work to cook for everyone else."

"We call this our Nautical and Nice snack," Jonah says, as he serves our snack to the judges.

They toss back a handful of our popcorn and nut mixture, then sip the tropical drink we've invented.

"Ridiculous," Tommy says. He shakes his head and takes another handful. He sips the drink again.

The other judges drain their drinks before making any comments.

"I'm seeing Santa on a beach after he's done delivering his presents," one judge says.

"The perfect way to end his long night."

Tommy tosses another handful in his mouth. "If that's dinner at your house, I want to eat with you." He finishes the drink, then seems to remember that he's judging, or commenting at least. "It's hot and cold at the same time, like my last girlfriend."

The audience laughs. "Sorry, Monica. I'm joking. She knows I love her."

Someone whisks the dishes away and serves Jake's drink. Matt glances over at me and gives me a thumbs up. The cameras are probably paying attention to Jake and Jonah right now, so I mouth, "Good luck," again.

The judges sip the hot chocolate and taste the nuts. Tommy's eyes roll back in his head. "Are you trying to kill me, boys?" He shakes his head. "I'm glad I don't have to decide."

The judges break down the flavor profile and minute differences between our drink and Jake's. It takes them an excruciatingly long amount of time to write the scores.

Finally, Tommy holds the final scores. He stares at them. "I love the Butler boys. Who loves the Butler boys?"

The audience claps and screams, and Lindsay's voice is one of the loudest. "These are the highest scores we've had on any of my shows, and they've earned them. If you're at home, I'm telling you, watch out. Santa's going to be zooming tonight! He's had a killer meal, and he's ready to fly."

I've never competed before, and I already feel like I've won. I did it. I survived. We got high scores, and I didn't mess up in front of the cameras. The adrenaline from competing is addicting, and I see why the twins have done this so many times.

Tommy really draws this out, and I'm dying while I wait to hear who won.

He finally calls the name.

# Chapter Forty-Two

"J-Dog, the Killer Chef. Jonah Butler."

The audience goes crazy. I don't think—I act. I throw my arms around Jonah's neck and kiss him like I never have before, cameras or not. The heat's been building between us all day. All weekend. My pulse races with the euphoria of winning.

I vaguely hear Matt and Jake counting. "One, two, three, four..."

Jonah eagerly cups the back of my head and holds the kiss well past six seconds.

I savor the feel of his lips on mine again, and then he buries his head in my neck. "We did it," I whisper. He tastes vaguely like chili and lime and coconut and home.

Jonah lifts the ring on his chain to his lips and kisses it. "For you, Brie. I'd do anything for you."

My heart nearly stops at the intensity in his eyes. I peel myself off him, because Tommy's waiting.

Tommy claps him on the shoulder. "Congratulations, man. I guess you're even for the hot springs now. That was some killer cooking, and your high score was well deserved."

Jonah grabs my hand, and grins from ear to ear. "Call your ride share, Jake. Time to pack up and head home."

Jake looks out into the audience, as if he's searching for Lindsay, but he comes over and nudges Jonah's shoulder with his. "By one point, bro. I need a rematch."

"We can arrange that." Tommy rubs his hands. "I like Boston."

I'm trying to fade into the background, but Jonah won't let me. He tugs me forward when I try to step away, even though Matt is hugging Jonah.

The whole brother versus brother thing is golden. "Tell me about Matt's hair." Tommy grins. "Now that he's lost, is he getting a flat top, too?"

Jake grabs Matt around the shoulders. "I've got buzzers at home. Say the word, Joey. I'll hold him, and you do the honors."

Matt unwinds Jake's arm. "No way. Hey, bro, that drink is genius. Can I have some?"

Jonah nods. Matt goes over to the workspace where some of the tropical drink still sits in the blender.

Tommy's still interviewing Jonah. "Tell us about your new restaurant. What are you going to do with fifty thousand dollars startup money?"

Jonah looks at me. "I'm thinking about a barbecue concept."

Jake and Matt both react with shock, and I love that.

Tommy doesn't miss a beat. "Barbecue. That's a departure from the other Butler restaurants."

Jonah smiles. He hasn't stopped smiling, and his whole personality lights up when he smiles like that. "Maybe I'll work on it with my girlfriend this time, instead of my twin. We'll have to negotiate on that one." Jake stares at Jonah, but recovers quickly for the cameras, and my stomach drops. I don't want to cause a rift between them, even if I love the idea of working with Jonah again.

I excuse myself and slip away to the green room to change out of my splattered candy cane apron. I'm exhausted, physically and emotionally, but Mr. and Mrs. Butler are there to hug me. I can't process everything that's going on.

I feel like I'm on top of the world, but I also want to be alone to sleep and cry. I woke up at five o'clock and we've been taping for hours, but I still have to go home to pack my apartment.

Mr. Butler hugs me. "You doubled the donations. I couldn't be prouder if you were my own daughter. When are you going to call me Dad?"

"It's Jim." Maggie hits his shoulder. "She doesn't use the traditional parental monikers. We're so proud, sweetie." She pulls me into a hug.

And I feel a surge of belonging. I get to be part of Pappy and Jim and Maggie's family. "Thanks. It was a blast."

"We'll see you soon." Maggie tugs Jim out of the green room, and they leave.

I stuff my dirty apron into a crumpled plastic grocery store bag and wait for Jonah.

He's got paperwork to fill out and interviews to do. I curl up on a couch and try to sleep. Finally, he finds me, and we can leave.

"Tommy asked where you were."

The worst is over. I met my dad. I faced him.

Kinda.

"I was trying to sleep. I'm so tired. I'm ready to crash."

Jonah's dimples are working overtime. "Me, too." He doesn't push the issue, and I love him for that. "He says you blew him away. He asked you to swing by and say goodbye on our way out."

So I thread my fingers through Jonah's, and we head down the hall to an office. Tommy looks up. "Hey there, Jumbo Shrimp. Nicely done today. How come you've never competed before?"

"I switched from cooking to accounting."

He recoils. "That's just wrong with your kind of talent. You ought to be on the circuit with these guys. We gotta get you on another show."

So, I'm just a ratings machine to him? Yeah, that tracks. "Thanks. Hey, I had an early morning, so we're going to head, unless you need anything else."

Tommy fiddles with the papers on his makeshift desk. "How'd you like the knives?"

"They were great. Thanks for letting me use them. They ought to sell well." Again, he's all about money, just like Mom said.

Tommy stands and pulls Jonah into a hug, clapping him on the back. "Great show, Killer. See you for Christmas."

"Can't wait." Jonah hugs him back.

Tommy and I stare at each other. I have the feeling that he's the hugging type. So am I. But I've just met him, and I have years of resentment festering. Hopefully, I'm hiding it. This is Jonah's work, his colleague. I smile and offer him a fist bump. "Great show."

Tommy bumps my extended fist. "Yeah, great show. Thanks for bailing us out at the last second."

"Sure thing. Couldn't let Jake have the win." I grin and turn toward the door.

"Are you going to be there?" Tommy asks. "With your boyfriend, I mean, on Christmas Eve? At the Butlers'?"

Jonah and I stop in the doorway. I turn around. "I guess. We haven't talked about it."

Tommy flashes me a smile that doesn't quite reach his eyes. "I guess I'll see you then. You did great today."

"Right. Thanks." Jonah and I leave his office and head out into the parking lot.

And that's it. I met my biological father, just like I wanted all these years, and the pain of that disappointment blunts the euphoria of our win.

Tommy doesn't want me. He won't acknowledge our relationship, and I'm nothing more than another person on the street to him. Worst of all, it confirms something I've secretly feared my whole life— I'm unlovable.

If my own dad doesn't want me, why would anybody else? Why would Jonah?

Jonah unlocks his car and opens the passenger side door for

me. I turn to stare at the blocky industrial building, and he pulls me into a hug. "We did it. We won, but more importantly, you showed up and didn't get arrested."

I laugh a little, but it's not funny to me.

Jonah continues. "We can move to New York. We can stay in Boston. We can do anything, and you never have to be afraid of paparazzi or lawsuits or anything else." His eyes light with excitement. "You could even cook professionally again." He draws me close. "And we can set a wedding date."

This is it. This is what I wanted, what I fought for, the reason I showed up and won this competition, and yet I feel unsettled after that parting conversation with Tommy.

I'm tiptoeing across a minefield of eggshells, still unsure of my destination on the other side, and today's encounter with my dad only moved the goalpost that much farther. Twelve more days.

I'd almost be glad if he'd yelled at me or showed some emotion. *Any* emotion. His total lack of acknowledgment hurts more than some outburst or anger.

But I already know he doesn't love me.

"Hey, you just got quiet again." Jonah kisses the top of my head. "Not what a guy wants to hear when he proposes. Again. Kind of. Did you even hear me ask if we can set a date?"

I look up, and Jonah's spinning the ring on Grammy's chain. I smile. "You only have to ask me to marry you once. I told you that about kissing, too, boyfriend. You ask once and get a lifetime *Yes*."

Jonah presses a quick kiss to my lips, and I duck inside the car where I can't feel the wind cut through me. "So, no wedding date yet. I can keep asking about that one?"

He looks more nervous than he did waiting to hear who won that last round. His eyes hold so much worry that you'd never believe he just won the competition of his career. I reach for his hand. "Yes. *Please* keep asking, but today was rough. Amazing, but wow. Tommy doesn't want me in his life as a daughter, and that..." I clench my jaw. "That was a hard blow to take. He had a chance, back there, to say something. *Anything*. We were alone.

Pretty much everyone had gone home, and he didn't say anything. I'm just reeling, and I need to get my head on straight again. I love you, Jonah, and I'm sorry to keep asking for time, but..."

"No, take your time, girlfriend. I'm so sorry. That must have hurt so much." Jonah straightens with his hand on the door. I can tell he has no idea what to say. He shuts my door, then slides into his seat a moment later and turns on the car.

The *Grinch* soundtrack blares from his premium speakers, and he shuts it off. "I'd like to deck your dad instead of decking the halls."

I grin, but my heart is rapidly shrinking three sizes. I didn't know it could go the other direction. That doesn't happen in the *Grinch* story. His expands, but not mine. Not today.

"Anything I say will sound trite or stupid or... Gah." Jonah scrubs a hand down his face. "I just love you, and anyone who doesn't want to spend every second of eternity with you is an idiot." He reaches over and laces his fingers through mine as the heater kicks on and the fan begins to blow freezing cold air in our faces. "I've waited a long time for someone who understands me and puts up with the way I can't express myself. I've bumbled and said the wrong things and messed up, and you've given me chance after chance. So... Step five. I'm here." He sighs. "You believe me that I want to be in your life, for the rest of your life, right? Forever, Brie."

"Absolutely. Me, too." I nod, and guilt washes over me. For the first time in our relationship, I lied to Jonah.

I mean, it's the truth—kind of. I do believe him even though it's hard to believe that anyone would want to spend the rest of their life with me if my own father doesn't, and my own mother thought I held her back. But I know Jonah does. He's proven that over and over and over.

The thing is this—I desperately want to be with him, too, but can I ever make Jonah happy or be the woman he deserves? Or will I just be a burden to him?

# Chapter Forty-Three

I PACK and put everything into storage on Tuesday. I had never unpacked half of my boxes, so it's not that bad. Jonah insists on helping me, and I'm living a dream. I'm afraid this can't last, because good things always end in my life, but I'm going to enjoy it as long as it does.

The ring seems to hang heavier and heavier around Jonah's neck, though, the longer I don't set a date for the wedding. He plays with it all the time now, and I'm starting to think that he's never going to take it off.

Which makes me love him even more and makes me worry about talking to my dad even more. I'm imagining all sorts of catastrophic scenes in my head for Christmas Eve, trying to explain the total lack of disaster when I met Tommy, and each one ends with Jonah dumping me because I've ruined his career and his life.

Meanwhile, I can't find a place to live in January, so I'm crashing on Lindsay's couch for the foreseeable future.

She's kind of down. Jake flirted with her at the taping, but then hasn't reached out since then.

I explained that she left without congratulating him, and he had specifically invited her to drive home with him.

Lindsay shakes her head. "But he lost. And he wasn't serious. That was just for the show."

I am starting to think that the only thing keeping Jake and Lindsay apart is, well—Jake and Lindsay. They're great when they hang out casually, but they're too scared or proud to just talk things out—*looking at you Lindsay*—or they bluster, then don't follow through. *Hello, Jake. That's on you.*

Someone pounds on our door early on Friday morning. Lindsay and I have already worked out, showered, and are just cleaning up breakfast.

"It's Jonah. He probably wants to celebrate your win again." Lindsay smiles and turns around to put some dishes away in a cupboard. "If you know what I mean."

I grin and pull the door open, and Jake nearly flattens me on his way inside.

"Hey! You learned how to knock!" I say with false cheerfulness. I glance around, but Jonah's nowhere. Jake's alone, which happens...never.

"Where is she?" Jake growls. He spots Lindsay in the kitchen and storms over, his eyes flashing. "Well," he demands.

Lindsay closes the cupboard. "Is there a reason for this man-tantrum?"

Jake glowers. "Who is he?"

She pivots to face him. "Who?"

"The groom." Jake folds his arms across his chest. "You called me out for cheating on my girlfriend, but you've been stringing me along this whole time?"

Lindsay puts a hand on his chest to push past him. She and I exchange a glance, and I know she's as confused as I am.

"Do you want to sit down?" I ask Jake.

"No." He narrows his eyes. "I want answers."

I pat the seat cushion next to me. "Stand down, soldier, and start over."

Jake paces in front of us. "My mom asked me to call that farmhouse place in Sugar Creek to pay for the wedding."

I freeze. "Thanks, Jake. You didn't have to—" I really don't want him to. I'm not ready for that kind of pressure. Not until after Christmas Eve.

"—and they couldn't find the paperwork. Some mistake. They only had the brides' names. *Brides*. Plural."

Lindsay turns to me with wide eyes. "Oh no."

Jake gets in her face. "Oh, yes, Linz. Oh, yes."

I'm trying to figure out how this happened. "Does Jonah know you called?"

He scoffs. "No, my parents wanted to surprise him."

Of course, it's a surprise. That sounds like Maggie. Just a little passive-aggressive push toward the altar. It'll probably be our Christmas present or something, along with my wedding gown.

Lindsay plays with her ponytail. "What names did they have?"

Jake levels a gaze at her. "You know the names."

I stand. "We don't know the names. Tell us." We're facing him two-on-one, a veritable wall of bridezillas, but he doesn't back down.

"They didn't have a Butler wedding listed. Just Brie and Lindsay. You have no idea how long we had to dig to even find that, because Chief set it up. Is he the groom?"

Before I can stop Jake from doing something he regrets... He does something he's going to regret. "Is that what's going on with those early morning workouts? First Brie and Jonah hook up at work before anyone else gets there, and now Lindsay and Chief?"

I drop onto the couch. "You already owe me your entire life savings, and you'd owe me your first-born child, but... I don't want it. Not cool, Jake."

Lindsay's face flushes. "I'm sorry. I don't understand. Do you want to spell that out for me? What, exactly, do you think I did, and just how low is your opinion of me?" She steps closer to him. "Brie and Jonah never 'hooked up,' as you call it, at work. They talked, okay? And if I *talk* to Chief when I work out, what is your problem?"

Jake closes the distance between them, and they are both red-faced and furious now. "My problem is your hypocrisy. You've been making plans to marry someone else while you've been flirting with me the way you have for the last month? I was going to break up with my girlfriend. I only kissed you after I found out she cheated on me." His chest heaves. "She cheated first. I'm not that kind of guy. I thought I was free when I kissed you."

Lindsay cocks a hip and puts a hand on her waist. "You talk one way in public and act another in private, just like you did that day."

Jake's mouth drops open. "You're calling *me* the hypocrite?"

I sigh. "Hey, I'm hearing some hostility. It sounds like you've had a misunderstanding or two. How about we start over with a clean slate? Can we ask clarifying questions?" Maggie would laugh if she heard me, but I have more pity for what her life is like.

Jake's jaw clenches. "I don't understand why you'd do that, Linz. Why would you reserve a wedding date unless you were engaged?"

Lindsay's face flushes. "I figured you'd want to get married with your twin, if, by some miracle, we were still dating next year."

His face changes instantly. "*I'm* the groom?"

Lindsay rolls her eyes. "*Was.* You can cancel the reservation for a double wedding since there was obviously a mix-up."

Jake's shock doesn't last long. He grins as he grabs Lindsay by both arms. "I accept."

"I didn't ask."

He shakes his head and wraps one arm around her shoulders. "Oh, no, babe. My parents already paid in full. No refunds."

Lindsay tilts her head up, and her voice sounds breathless. "Even though you thought I was marrying someone else?"

Jake nods and wraps his other arm around her waist. "I want you to be happy with anyone you pick, but I want you to pick me."

Finally. I leave the couch and go get a drink of water, just to have something to do.

Lindsay sways into him and puts a hand on his chest. "You have a hard time asking for what you want."

Jake draws her close. "You need to hear the exact words?"

Lindsay gazes up at him, and I feel like a third wheel. Her voice is breathy. "Or I could tell you how annoying you are, and that you're really impulsive."

Jake leans down. "I need someone to balance me out. I'm losing Jonah to Brie and barbecue. The position is open, babe."

"Again, not asking. *Telling*." Lindsay runs a hand through his hair and rubs the smooth sides of his head. "You're also annoyingly sexy."

Jake grins. "That's what I hear. You know you are, too."

"Annoying or sexy?" Lindsay asks in a sultry voice.

I do not want to witness this. I look around the open space, but there's nowhere to go to leave them alone. I've been sleeping on the couch, and the kitchen opens into the living room.

"I've had my eye on you for three years," Jake whispers, and his gaze rakes her body up and down. "What do you need me to say, Lindsay? I'm crazy about you. You get me like no one else does. This last month—"

His voice chokes up, and I know I have to get out of here at any cost, whether or not I can think of an excuse.

"I've gotta..." I slip down the hallway toward the bathroom and text Jonah.

**Me**: Jake and Lindsay. Happening now.
**Jonah**: ?
**Me**: (kissy face emoji)
**Jonah**: (confetti)
**Me**: So, Lindsay and I might have scheduled a double

wedding without telling you.

**Jonah**: (mind blown emoji) (hearts) I'm in. Let's do it.

The kissing sounds subside in a few minutes, and Jake hollers, "Brie!"

I walk casually down the hallway. "What's up?"

Jake's fingers are tangled with Lindsay's. "We're going ring shopping. Do you want to come and get a matching set? It'll be cool."

"We are?" Lindsay lets go of his hand. "You haven't proposed."

He grins. "You know you want to, babe."

Her brow contracts. "Want to what? I don't hear a question."

Jake grabs her coat and a pair of shoes from the hall closet. "You know you want to kiss my face, buy a ring, and marry me in October. You know." He pushes her gently onto the couch, and he's trying to jam shoes onto her feet.

Lindsay laughs. "Right now?"

He checks his phone. "Jeweler opens in fifteen minutes, and it's a fifteen-minute drive, so yeah. Let's go." He glances up at me. "You're texting Jonah to meet us there, right?"

I sit beside Lindsay. "You really want to marry this tornado?"

Lindsay bites her lip. "I don't know." She looks at me. "Do I?"

Jake freezes with her shoe halfway on her left foot. When he looks up, his eyes plead with her. "Babe? Yes, you do. We've had some good talks. I haven't tried to kiss you once before today, and I've told you things I've never told anyone, not even my mom. You feel it, too, right?" He sits on the floor and the shoe drops from his hand.

Lindsay leans forward and rests a hand on his shoulder. "How do I know you're not rushing into this because your twin is getting married? What if you regret it and we end up like Danny and Patricia? I haven't dated very much. How do I know you're the right one?"

Jake covers her hand with his fingers. "I've dated enough for both of us." He winks. "I'm not rushing into this, because I've been slowly falling in love with you for almost a thousand days, Linz, and I don't want to wait any longer to tell you how much I care. You can take your time." Jake swallows. "You can date other guys, if that's what you need. Just remember that I'll be slowly dying on the inside while you do." He flops on the floor and pretends to writhe in agony.

"Way to ruin the beginning of a beautiful sentiment," Lindsay says. "Like you have the patience to wait."

Jake stands. "No, seriously. Why did you tell Chief to make it a double wedding?" He's completely serious now. I see the vulnerability in his face, and I hope Lindsay hears the raw tone in his voice.

She looks at the carpet, and her voice comes out in a whisper. "Because I've been fighting my feelings for you for three years, too."

Jake whoops, then starts dancing around the couch and chanting in a sing-song voice. "You know you want to. You know you want to."

I know she wants to. I know she's scared and has no other relationships to compare with this one. I know it's sudden.

But I've seen her growing closer and closer to Jake for the last month. I've stumbled on the ends of some pretty personal conversations, and I know they're doing fine with the emotional intimacy stuff.

I've seen her and Jake at work for the last three months before this. I know Jake and Jonah and their family, and I trust them. And she has ten months before the wedding.

Lindsay looks at me, a question in her eyes.

"You know you want to, Lindsay." I smile at her. "Chief knows it. We all know it except you. Twins. Best friends. Double wedding. Jake needs a Christmas miracle, remember? That's you. No one else will put up with him."

Lindsay considers me for a long moment. I hate that she's so smart and beautiful and kind and insecure, but she is.

I shrug. "Tell Jake I'm wrong. Tell him you *don't* want to."

She rolls her eyes, and a smile breaks across her face. "Fine." She slips on her boots, and Jake's there with her coat in a millisecond. "I'm tired of pretending like I don't see how awesome you are, Jake, but you already have such a big ego…"

Jake grabs her by the waist and kisses her hard. "You know you want to marry me."

Lindsay laughs. "That is the least romantic proposal—"

He interrupts her. "Oh, you're going to have the most embarrassing public proposal as soon as we buy that ring. Social media, livestream, whatever you want. As romantic as I can make it, babe."

"We're going *Instagram* official? You must be serious." Lindsay is completely unfazed by his antics, and that's why they are perfect for each other.

Jake's already snapping a selfie of them and writing a caption. "*Save the date. October 2023.* That should freak out my followers."

She shakes her head and motions to me. "You're coming, right? Twins and best friends do everything together."

I bite my lip. Am I ready for this step? "I don't know."

Jake stops celebrating. "What do you mean?"

I swallow. "I already have a ring. Jonah and me. We're good."

Jake levels a searching gaze at me. "Are you? Because I don't see you *wearing* your ring."

Lindsay grabs Jake's hand. "Leave her alone."

"I'm texting Jonah anyway," Jake says. "Just in case *he* wants a ring. You realize he'll need one, too, when you get married?"

The reality freaks me out, but I nod. "Go ahead. I'll text him and see if he wants a ring to match yours."

Jake leaves reluctantly as Lindsay tugs him out the door. I draw a deep breath and grab my phone. I close my eyes and remember how it feels when Jonah holds me, how patient he's been, how much I love him. I open my eyes and start to type on my phone.

357

**Me**: Jake and Lindsay are buying rings.
**Jonah**: What? They haven't even dated.
**Me**: Jake's counting the last month and the last three years.
**Jonah**: I can't judge. Look at us.
**Me**: Exactly. He wants to know if you want to get matching rings for the double wedding.
**Jonah**: Wedding? Did you really just say that?
**Me**: Technically, I typed it.

Three dots bounce, and I stare at my phone. Am I really committing to this? I love Jonah, and I need him in my life, but I don't feel ready to get married. Jonah's answer doesn't force me into anything, of course, because he knows me so well.

**Jonah**: I want to go, but only if you do.

I stare at my phone for a couple minutes. I do have to decide eventually.

**Jonah**: Brie? Jake's pinging me. Should I drive there to meet him?

I swallow. I'm still not ready to fully commit to a wedding date, but I don't want to lose Jonah. He can't wait for me forever, and I promised myself to be the fighter that Lindsay and Chief and Jake think I am. The woman that Jonah deserves. Maybe I can commit to a wedding. Maybe.

**Me**: It wouldn't hurt to try one on. You know, "just try it out."

Jonah texts back immediately with a heart emoji: On my way.

# Chapter Forty-Four

RING SHOPPING DOESN'T GO WELL. I forget that I have my Yankees hoodie on, so Jake freaks out when I show up and Jonah looks seriously rattled. "Burn that thing," Jake says. "You live in Boston now."

I swallow. "But aren't we all moving to New York?"

"Are we?" Jonah wraps me in a hug, and we aren't much help to Jake and Lindsay after that.

Lindsay tries on all the rings, since I already have my grammy's ring and I don't want anything else, but she can't decide on any of them.

Jonah half-heartedly shops with Jake, but their tastes are nothing alike. He still insists that he gets to keep Grammy Emmy's ring, and I have to find a new one, but I'm fighting him on that now. Watching him wear that ring over his heart has only made me want it for my wedding band even more, no matter what I said before.

He's poured all the love in his heart into that ring, and I want *that* on my hand.

Jonah talks me into at least getting our finger sizes measured, but neither of us walks out with a ring or anything on order.

The next week is a blur of Jake and Lindsay PDA. There's

nothing worse than a couple who's just fallen in love. They're certainly worse than Jonah and I ever were, almost like they're determined to win the PDA war, because, with twins, everything is a competition.

And they win easily. I snuggle into Jonah's side on Lindsay's couch while we watch a show together, but Jake and Lindsay are inseparable. That is, you cannot see a sliver of daylight between them. Now that their walls are down, and they've both admitted they're crazy about each other, they're making Jonah and me crazy.

And we're the ones who are actually engaged. They're newly-engageds, barely starting to date, and it's painful to be around. "We were never like that," Jonah whispers as he leans down to nuzzle my neck.

Jake snorts. "I heard that, and no, you were not like us. You were so much worse. Still are."

I'm happy to let Jonah win that battle, because I still can't believe anyone could love me this long or last through the ups and downs we've had.

But I'm trying to believe, and it feels better every day, like maybe I have something to offer. Jonah is happy all the time, and why can't it always be like this? Maybe I'm not a burden. Maybe I make his life easier and better and happier. I can't shut down the voices of the past as easily as that, because believe me, I've done years of therapy and tried, but I am trying so, so hard to show up for him, and Jonah is making it so, so easy to believe that I'm enough.

I even have that stupid bell from the North Pole train ride in my jean pocket most days, as if that's not desperate or cheesy enough.

Finally, it's Saturday, the afternoon of Christmas Eve. I'm over at the Butlers' house, because it's actually easier to be there than at Lindsay's condo, even with Maggie hovering and Jim puttering around the house.

I decide to make crescent rolls for dinner, so we're rolling out the dough together. Jonah pats the round of roll dough. "I like this recipe."

I spin the rolling pin across the pillow-soft dough. "My grammy taught me how to make rolls."

Jonah plays with the ring around his neck. It's his favorite toy. He spins it absent-mindedly. "Wanna show me how it's done?"

I bump him aside with my hip. I'm five foot two, and he's probably six feet. It doesn't do much. He's a brick wall.

I put my hands on his hips and shove. He goes nowhere.

"Do you want to learn or not?"

Jonah grins down at me. "I want a hands-on demonstration." He tucks my arms around his own.

"I can't see over you. How am I supposed to guide your hands?"

Jonah slips an arm around my waist and tugs me into his side. "Fine. I'll watch instead." He tucks me in front of him and rests his chin on my head.

My back presses into his stomach and chest. He leans an arm on either side of the counter around me and lowers his mouth to whisper in my ear. "I already preheated the oven."

I smirk up at him. "We both know that *your* oven is on permanent broil."

He grins back. "True."

"You can turn your *parents'* oven off. They raise for two hours before we bake them." I smooth the round circle of dough. "But you already know that."

He glances at his parents' high-end double-oven. It's stone cold. "I was speaking metaphorically."

I nudge his shoulder. "Roll out the dough, slather it with butter, and cut it into triangles."

"Mmm-hmm." His arms trap my shoulders, so I can hardly maneuver the pizza cutter to make a series of even cuts.

I roll one wedge over and over until it's a crescent, then place it on a waiting cookie sheet.

"Can I try?" Jonah's deep voice tickles my ear. He leans

forward and his hands cover mine. His arms rest on my hips as he curls the dough over and over to form a roll.

"You got it. Now do it twenty-two more times," I say.

Jonah locks eyes with me as he winds the dough. His chin brushes the top of my head, then my shoulder as he reaches for the cookie sheet.

"Twenty-one." My voice comes out a little breathy.

"Why did you want to make rolls anyway?" Jonah's cheek presses against mine as he leans over to shape another roll. "I'm not complaining. It's my favorite Christmas present already."

I shift to face him. His warm brown eyes glitter with desire, and my heart pounds in my chest. He's holding back, but just barely, like his restraint might snap at any second. When he bends over to wind the next roll, he's practically hugging me.

I wipe my flour-dusted hands on my apron. "The way to a man's heart, you know…"

He grins, and this time his lips brush my cheek as he places the next roll on the cookie sheet.

"Also, I don't have any money. I'm sorry I couldn't buy you a real gift. Making rolls is the only present I have. I'm giving you my grammy's roll recipe for Christmas."

Jonah freezes. "What do you mean?"

I turn around and start twisting rolls. "The bank fraud. New credit cards take seven to ten business days. It's the holidays, so it looks like it's going to be the full ten days, and mail is slow. I was hoping to get it today."

Jonah covers my hand and turns me to face him. "You haven't had any access to your new bank account for the last two weeks?"

I bite my lip. "Lindsay insisted on sharing her groceries, and I've been careful, so I haven't had to fill my gas tank."

Something like a growl comes out of Jonah's throat. "Why won't you let me take care of you, Brie?" He cups my face, and he gazes at me fiercely and tenderly at the same time. "Is that why you don't smell like peppermint anymore?"

I can't believe *that's* the question that makes me want to cry. "You noticed?"

"Did you run out of shampoo and bodywash and lotion a few days ago?"

I nod.

"That explains it." He straightens and finishes turning the rolls as quickly and efficiently as a professional chef can. "We're going shopping. There's got to be some drugstore or supermarket. I don't care if it's a gas station. I'm going to spoil my girlfriend on Christmas Eve. Let's go buy you whatever you want."

I fight back tears. "Thanks, Jonah. I haven't really thought about Christmas presents. I never got many."

"You will today." Jonah grabs me, and there's flour all over both of us now. I see the pent-up desire in his eyes, like going this long without a kiss is too much because we're at his parents' house and it's been half an hour or something. He crushes me in a hug. "I'm sorry you haven't had your cards or any cash, but there's nothing I love more than your recipes. That's the best Christmas present I could ask for."

"I'll get my coat," I whisper into his shoulder. "The rolls have to rise anyway."

We drive around until we find a drugstore that's still open this late in the afternoon. The parking lot is insane, but we circle and circle until we get a spot. Jonah tugs me inside, and his grip on my hand is iron-clad.

He scores a small red shopping cart from someone who's leaving, and we wander until we find the shampoo aisle. Jonah turns to me. "What do you want?"

I shrug. There's a bunch of peppermint, and it's on sale since it's Christmas Eve.

"How about this?" Jonah loads a million bottles, then he gets the same amount of bodywash.

I put a hand on his arm. "Hey, there are other scents. I don't have to smell like peppermint year-round, and Christmas will be over tomorrow."

"Christmas never ends, because you mean Christmas to me." He says it matter-of-factly.

My heart melts faster than Frosty the Snowman in the Bahamas. "Thanks."

He's not even watching me melt. He's loading bottles of clearance-priced candy cane lotion into the cart now. "The Butler men spoil their women. You should have seen Danny when he and Patty were married. Even now, he pays her a ridiculous amount of alimony."

And I remember what Danny told us. Something about not putting up walls like he and Patty did. I didn't really pay attention, since we weren't really engaged, but his advice slams into me in the drugstore aisle. Am I still shutting him out by refusing to set a date? Are my fears still louder than my fierce, fierce love? I have to take down my walls before it's too late.

Jonah lights up. "Nail clippers!" He tosses ten pairs in the shopping cart.

I'm in the middle of an epiphany about Jonah and love and relationships, but that sidetracks me. "Why so many pairs?"

He bends down to grab something else from a bottom shelf. "My dad says true love means never having to look for a pair of nail clippers." He shrugs and turns to grin at me. "He keeps every drawer in the house stocked with nail clippers for my mom, so I want to get you some for your new apartment. Do you need some for your purse?"

I nod. "Sure." That's the moment that I decide that I'm going to marry him. It's when he tells me that true love means making sure that I can always find a pair of nail clippers, and he's buying me ten pairs, and I know he loves me so much he wants to make sure I never suffer from another hangnail.

Like, for sure, for sure. This is *love*. I know it in my nails. It's dumb. He says he's going to spoil me, then he buys nail clippers.

I'm a total goner.

Jonah is still down on his haunches, completely unaware of the epiphany I'm having. "My mom always cries during

Christmas movies." He grabs an eight-pack of pocket-size tissue packs, tosses it in the grocery cart, and stands. "Are you a crier?"

I wrap my arms around him. "Yes." He has no idea what's going on, but there's some jazzy electronic version of "Deck the Halls" playing, and I remember our matching Christmas sweaters. "I want to marry you next October in Sugar Creek. You pick the date. I want to wear matching Christmas sweaters every year for the rest of our lives. I want to give your parents as many grandbabies as we can handle."

He's got this gob smacked look, like Rudolph ran over him, then a lopsided grin breaks out.

I press my lips to his. Jonah's hands cup both sides of my face, and he responds eagerly. I cling to him, and I don't care if anyone can see us. I savor Jonah's pine scent as he pulls me closer.

I'm done living my life in fear. I won't let my mom's fears or my biological dad's failings keep me away from the man I love any longer, not in any way. No one has ever cared about me like this before, and I'm never letting him go.

I slide my hands up Jonah's chest, even if we're both wearing puffy parkas. He's got his Red Sox beanie on, but I wrap a hand around the back of his neck to play with the hair poking out. He starts to pull away, but I coax his lips into another kiss and another. My nerves explode, and I can't wait to get home and cuddle on the couch with a cup of cocoa and my fiancé, the man I intend to marry.

"Brie." Jonah whispers my name in a ragged, throaty voice. "I love you."

"I love you, too, Jonah." I untangle myself from him. "But I changed my mind. I want my ring back."

He clutches at his parka. "It's mine now. We can get you a new one, but there's no way I'm giving up Grammy's ring. I've been carrying my hope for you over my heart for weeks now." He chokes up. "No way."

I'm too happy to fight him on this one. "Hey, I've got nail clippers and a Red Sox hoodie. I don't need Grammy's ring."

Seeing it around his neck makes me feel more loved than wearing it could.

I try to steer the tiny cart toward the checkout counter, but Jonah finds more and more things to buy me until the cart overflows. The woman working there doesn't bat an eye as she rings up container after container of bodywash—until she gets to an oversized plush. "You got kids?"

"Not yet." Jonah winks at her. "But a guy can hope. We're getting married."

The woman's face lights up. Her boredom vanishes, and she really looks at us for the first time. "Hey, you're that chef on TV. Don't you have a show tonight or something?"

Jonah grabs me. "We do. We're heading home to watch it, too. How long is your shift?"

She finishes bagging my haul. "Too long."

He taps his phone to the card reader. "Thanks for working on Christmas Eve."

She smiles. "It was worth it to meet a celebrity." She looks undecided.

Jonah hands me the bags. "Brie is pretty amazing. Do you want a picture with her? I can take it."

The woman laughs. "How about one with both of you? My kids won't believe this. They watch those *Smack Down* shows all the time. It's our thing to do on Sunday nights when I don't have to work. They love cooking shows."

Jonah wraps an arm around each of us and takes a selfie. "Can I post this?"

The woman's eyes widen. "Sure."

Jonah posts it to his social media while the photo sends to her phone. "Merry Christmas." He pulls a hundred-dollar bill out of his wallet. "Make sure you get your kids something from us, okay? Some nice groceries or a plush or whatever Santa needs to fill their stockings."

The woman's eyes fill with tears. "Wow. Thanks. Merry Christmas to both of you, too."

We walk out of the drugstore, and I'm more deeply in love with Jonah than ever. "You are ridiculous. You're kind and thoughtful and humble and super hot, plus you cook like a beast. You've been more than patient with me, and when I think I'm empty and at my lowest, you fill me to overflowing with your love."

Jonah unlocks his Tesla, then leans over to kiss me. "Mutual, I'm sure."

And I'm so happy that I can almost forget I'm about to spend the rest of the night with the father who abandoned me at birth and rejected me two weeks ago. *Almost.*

But no matter what happens tonight, I choose Jonah and true love and hope. He bought me nail clippers, after all. Things are serious now.

# Chapter Forty-Five

JONAH DROPS me and my mountain of personal care products off at Lindsay's condo. I hug him. "Thanks for the early Christmas present."

He follows me in. "I'll wait." His eyes follow me as I stack the bags along the edge of Lindsay's living room, and I love it. Now that I've torn down the last wall between us, neither of us wants to be away from the other for a second.

"I'm gonna change, and then can I catch a ride back with you?"

Jonah nods slowly, his eyes never leaving my face.

I dig through my suitcase to find a cute outfit and race into the bathroom. I pull on a red and black ruffled buffalo check skirt that hits my legs about knee length. It pulls to a knot on one side, so the ruffle drapes perfectly. I pair it with a simple black turtleneck on top and a pair of black knee-high boots on the bottom.

Jonah's eyes widen appreciatively. "It's too bad that outfit is so cute."

"Why?" I grab my purse and head toward the door.

He tosses me his Red Sox hoodie from the couch. "Because no one will see it under this."

I catch the hoodie and slip it on. It almost matches my ruffle skirt, and the black turtleneck pokes out the top.

Jonah pulls me into a hug. "Now you look amazing." He kisses me long enough to mess up both my lipstick and my hair, and then we leave for his parents' formal Christmas Eve dinner.

Jonah opens a compartment in his car before we start driving. "These nail clippers are yours." He opens another compartment. "And these are mine."

He puts a hand on the back of my seat and reverses out of the parking lot.

"His and hers nail clippers, and I'm moving into your car. This is real commitment, Killer."

Jonah grins and shifts from *reverse* to *drive*. "Yep."

We arrive at his parents' home, and I've pretty much fixed my hair and makeup in the car. Jonah takes me by the hand, and we sneak upstairs through the oversized garage. I can't believe how many cars there are or how many people live here.

We tiptoe past the great room and all the people, and he leads me to his parents' industrial double ovens. "Time to preheat, literally." He turns on the ovens, then lounges against the marble countertop.

I put a hand on his chest. "What should we do while we wait?"

His hands drop to my hips, and he tugs me to him. "I have a few ideas."

Before we get very far, though, I hear some brothers in the background. We stop kissing, and Jonah drapes an arm around my shoulder. "Luke! Did you wait to catch the very last flight out of Boulder or the second-to-last flight?"

Matt slugs Jonah in the shoulder. "Knock it off. At least he came."

"For what? Two days?" Nick claps Luke on the back. "Tonight and tomorrow, then home again?"

I wave. "Hey, Luke. It's good to meet you in person."

Luke waves back. "Hey."

He's obviously as talkative as Jonah.

"Brie? Can I talk to you?" It's Danny.

I glance at Jonah. "Sure. It'll take the oven a few more minutes to warm up." I thread my fingers through Jonah's and tug him along with me because part of my body has to be touching part of his at all times now.

"What's up?" Jonah says as we follow Danny to the front room. It's one of those formal living rooms that no one sits in. Right now it's filled with an oversized Christmas tree that nearly touches the ceiling. The huge tree sparkles in the center of the darkened room, and the windows look out over the snow-draped neighborhood. Christmas lights twinkle from every roof.

"Go ahead and sit down." Danny has a stack of papers and a couple pens. He glances at his watch, his phone, and the door. "Hang on."

Jonah and I turn our heads in time to see a car pull up. Tommy Fuller hops out.

"I thought Chief was coming down for Christmas," Jonah says. "I forgot about Tommy."

I stare at him. "Seriously. You forgot?"

Jonah tugs me closer on the couch. "I have someone else on my mind." He leans over to kiss me, and we're still making out when the front door slams. We break apart but sit shoulder to shoulder with no space between us. Jonah's arm draws circles on my shoulder, and I slip an arm around his waist.

Tommy's standing at the entrance to the formal living room. He waves. "Hey there, Killer. Shrimp. Good to see you again."

Jonah nods. "Chef."

I wave. "Hey."

No one talks.

Danny points to a chair, and Tommy perches on the edge of an armchair across from us. The Christmas tree is in between us, but we can see each other around it, because that's how big the formal living room is. Tommy rubs his hands together. "It smells delicious."

Jonah nods and clenches his jaw.

I shrug. "Thank you?"

Danny clears his throat. "Brie, we have a couple of items of legal business before dinner. Is that okay?"

Jonah's grip on my shoulder tightens. "I'm staying."

Danny looks at Tommy, who nods. My heart starts thumping. Am I in trouble for something? For being born? Does he want me to promise never to tell anyone that we're related?

Yells and laughs float in from the great room. "Tommy couldn't ask me to write the non-disclosures and other documents for his *Smack Down*, since the twins were competing, but he asked me to consult on a personal matter."

Here it comes. I brace myself for the worst.

Jonah reaches for my free hand, and I feel protected in the circle of his arms. "Yeah, we saw Chad. Our favorite person."

Danny levels a gaze at me, but before he can say anything, Jonah holds up a hand. "Hold up. Whatever you think she did, she didn't. She was innocent. It was her mom."

Tommy stares at him. "Excuse me?"

"Brie and I go together, and my family stands behind her. If you want to drag up the past, you're going to have to take on Pappy and the entire Butler family." Jonah shoots Danny a look of pure venom. "And we'll hire Chad to represent us and fight you, Dan Man."

Danny's jaw clenches. "Hear me out first."

Jonah arches an eyebrow. "We're not signing any more non-disclosures or whatever. I don't know why you're worried. Brie's not going to go tell the world that Tommy has a kid."

Danny lets out a long breath. "Okay, can we start there? Do you have any brothers or sisters, Brie?"

I roll my eyes. "No."

"Did your mother ever remarry?"

Jonah threads his fingers through mine. "We don't have to put up with this interrogation. She didn't do anything wrong. She didn't ask to have him for her father."

Tommy scoots forward on his chair. "What's with the hostility, Butler? I thought we were friends."

Jonah glares at him. "Yeah, until you broke my fiancée's heart two weeks ago. That's how you treat your daughter? Don't even get me started on the last almost thirty years of neglect."

"Whoa." Danny stands up. "Dial it back, bro. How about you step into the kitchen and let me handle this?"

"How about you—"

I put a hand on Jonah's arm and interrupt him quickly. "Look, Tommy. Danny. Cut to the chase, alright? What's the problem? I'm going to marry Jonah, and you're going to have to deal with that and with seeing us around. I won't advertise our relationship, since that's what you want, and you don't have to invite Jonah back onto any of your shows, but we're not going away."

Tommy's eyes widen, and he takes a deep breath. "Wow. You're so much like your mom, and not. And so much like me, and not. I don't know what to say."

"How about you say, *Merry Christmas*, and we all go watch the show and have some dinner and keep sweeping this under the rug like you have been?" Jonah tries to smile.

Tommy hangs his head and stares at the carpet. It's silent for a long minute. His gaze snaps to Jonah, and his eyes drop to the ring on his chest, then back up to Jonah. "You want to know what my problem is? I've got no problem with my daughter marrying you."

Emotions rise in my chest when he says that. *My daughter.*

"My problem with you, Butler, is exactly what you just said." And now Tommy looks angry and sad at the same time, and I'm scared. "The part about keeping things quiet. I don't want that. I don't need that. I need a daughter."

He glances over at me, and I have no idea what reaction he's getting. I'm too shocked.

Jonah's not. He's firing back. "You gave up that right when you walked away and divorced her mom and tried to arrest her."

Tommy shrugs. "I never knew I had a daughter until two weeks ago."

Jonah sinks back into the couch beside me, and we look at each other. My mind is whirling with so many thoughts and feelings that I don't know where to begin.

"Let me try this one more time," Danny says. "My client, Mr. Fuller, believes there is a previously undisclosed relationship between himself and you, Brie. He believes he is your father."

"Well, yeah. Duh." I say. "Of course he is."

Tommy puts his hands over his eyes and starts crying. That's when it hits me. He's not lying. And that means... He's telling the truth.

He never knew about me. He never rejected me.

He wants to claim me as his daughter. Jonah brushes my cheek. "You're crying."

I rush off the couch, tug Tommy off his chair, and pull him into a hug. He bends over and clings to my neck. "I never knew, baby girl. I never knew. She divorced me. How would I know?"

The tears come faster, because Mom always said that he divorced her, and Mom bent a lot of truths. How much of what she told me about my dad is a lie?

"I wish I'd have known sooner." Tommy pulls back and wipes his eyes. His pale, green eyes that look just like mine.

"Me, too," I whisper.

He puts his hands on my shoulders and studies my face. "You look just like her, but you got my eyes."

I nod. "And your personality. I drove Mom crazy. A leftie."

Tommy laughs, a genuine belly laugh, and wipes his eyes. I return to the couch and snuggle into Jonah's side again, and a timer beeps. "Can you grab the rolls out of the oven?" Jonah asks.

Danny slams his papers on the coffee table. "Seriously?" He winks at me. "You think that's all a lawyer is good for?" But he leaves for the kitchen.

Tommy gazes at me in wonder. "I can't believe I have a kid.

Aria was... Well, you grew up with her. You probably know. I won't speak ill of the dead."

I nod. "It's fine. You wouldn't believe how much I've spent on therapy."

Tommy throws back his head and roars with laughter. "I love you, kid. I love you already. You take after your old man, I can tell you that. We're going to get along, if you'll call off your attack dog."

I put a hand on Jonah's knee. "We're good, right, Killer?"

Jonah nods. "Ish. So, what happened? I want answers, and if Brie won't ask..."

I sigh. "He might be a little protective. We haven't been engaged that long."

Tommy waves a hand. "No, I get it. I look like a deadbeat." He leans back in his chair and blows out a long breath. "In the spirit of Christmas and charity, I will say this. I loved your mother more than she loved me. She was a beautiful woman like you."

"Thanks, Dad."

Tommy chokes up and covers his eyes. I rummage in my purse for one of those mini-packages of tissues that Jonah bought me at the drugstore and pull one out. I hand it to Tommy, who wipes his eyes. "I thought I was the luckiest guy to get to date her. All the guys at the culinary institute were crazy about her, but then she started asking me to do things to *prove* how much I loved her."

I nod. "I hear you."

He shrugs. "So we hardly dated, then we were about to graduate, and all of a sudden, she asked me to make a choice. Marry her or lose her forever. She was ready to move on, if I wouldn't commit. I couldn't lose her, so we got married, but I had this gig in California for a few months, and I couldn't lose that either. She was so mad."

I laugh. "Yeah, I might have her temper."

Jonah bumps my shoulder with his. "Toned way down."

Tommy wads the tissue in his hand. "So, we get married, short honeymoon, I'm off to L.A., and she's mad that I'm not calling all the time, but I'm working sixteen-hour days, and I don't want to wake her up at three a.m. when I finish my shifts. I wake up earlier and earlier to talk to her, but I'm falling asleep at work, and I can't keep it up, so I have to make a choice, and I choose to keep my job so I can provide for her."

I draw a deep breath. "I bet that didn't go over well."

He rubs his hands together. "After a few months of that, she mails me divorce papers. I mean, I just landed this big show, and I tell her to wait, but she starts yelling at me, and I hardly recognize her. Things were just starting to take off, but she was already done with me."

Danny comes back in the living room with a plate of hot crescent rolls. "Never say I didn't do anything for you." We each take one.

"Is that a double negative or a triple negative?" Jonah asks, and Danny whacks him in the arm.

"Anyhow," Tommy continues, as if he can't finish his story fast enough. "I sign the papers, mail them back, divorce is final. Fastest marriage and divorce in history, right, and I'm devastated. My heart is breaking, I feel like a failure, and I'm worried because I don't even know her anymore and maybe something is really wrong, but I can't do anything about it. I'm not there."

He sets down the roll and covers his eyes. "Her dad had only died a year before, and her mom couldn't find a job. We were so young, but I wanted to take care of her with all my heart. It was hard, you know, long distance, and we were poor."

He needs a minute, so it's my turn to talk. "That sounds really hard, but you know what's soft?" I tear off a piece of the warm, buttery roll and take a bite. "This is Grammy Emmy's recipe."

Tommy smiles appreciatively at my joke, but then he hangs his head and his shoulders shake. "I should've been there for your grandma. I worried so much about her. About both of them. For years, I worried, and I never stopped caring." He chokes up again. "I didn't ever understand what I did wrong. I wanted to provide, and I was finally starting to make enough money for them to move out with me. I mean, maybe the pregnancy hormones and the grief and all her stress made it too much."

How can I explain my mom to him? "Mom's story was different. You know she always had her own version of the truth. You picked your career over her. Money was more important than family. You abandoned her. But really, I think you wouldn't play her games or let her control you, and she knew you never would, so she kept looking for someone else. She was always looking for something better and never finding it. I'm so sorry she hurt you."

Tommy stares at the carpet. "Thank you. I'm sorry about so many things. Sorry I didn't know about you. Sorry I signed the divorce papers without more of a fight. Sorry I didn't know she needed child support. I never even knew she came to my studio. I get so many crazies, and security never told me about her. Who knew she was the one person telling the truth?"

I sigh. "She said she went to the police station, and they detained her for hours. She threatened to put me into foster care." Now I'm the one whose shoulders shake. "Because she couldn't handle me or afford me, and I didn't carry my own weight."

Tommy's face turns a blotchy red. "Oh, yeah?"

"But I did the dishes. I did the laundry. I did all of my homework. I took care of Grammy. I cleaned the house. I hardly played with friends. I remember thinking, *What else am I supposed to do? Why can't I ever please you? How come I'm never enough?*"

Tommy moves to the edge of his chair. "You're enough for me, baby girl."

I bite my lip and try to swallow back the emotions swirling inside. I've waited twenty-eight years to be good enough for a parent, and Tommy wipes away my hurt with one sentence.

He catches my eye. "I wasn't enough for her, either. She asked for money once, after the divorce. She called when I won my first big competition and said I owed her something, even though we had no alimony agreement or anything. I sent her half and that was that. I thought of moving back to New York, but..." He trails off, and a wave of sorrow seems to crash over him. "Fifteen grand, and no thank you note. Nothing. She changed her number, and I never heard from her again. That's probably around the time you were born."

I fight my anger. "That's the reason I moved so often? That's why I never had Christmas in the same place twice? Just to spite you and hide me?"

Tommy shakes his head. "I have no idea. I'm sure she loved you in her own way, but I'm sorry, kid. I wish I could've raised you."

Tommy and I share this bond—Mom loved us both, at times, and he understands how it feels to keep hoping and hurting at the same time. I jump out of my seat and hug my dad again. *I have a dad.*

The anger, grief, love, hope, curiosity, and excitement are all too much. Jonah takes two tissues out of the package. He hands me one, and I see him wipe the edge of his eye with the other as I hold Tommy and the tears stream down my face. Down all of our faces.

Danny returns and settles into a chair. "I put in the second tray of rolls and forgot to set a timer."

Jonah blows out a long breath and pushes the nearly empty tissue pack into my hand. "You're okay with me, Tommy. Stay for dinner. Come to the wedding. I'll gotta run, though. I'll be right back."

"Sure, sure. Don't burn Grammy's rolls," Tommy mutters over my shoulder. I sit down again, and we stare at each other. "One look at you, and I heard your name, and I knew..."

I sniffle. "She must have still loved you a little. Everyone knows brie is your favorite cheese."

Tommy wipes a hand across his eyes and pushes the papers toward me. "Yeah. I don't know. Anyway, I asked Danny to draw up some stuff as soon as I knew you were mine. "

*I'm his.* My dad's voice catches when he says that. The most powerful sense of belonging sweeps over me, and I'm whole in places I didn't realize were broken.

I pick up the papers and hug them to my chest. "Yes. We'll sort everything out later, but yes. Come to the wedding. I need a dad to give me away."

We look at each other through misty eyes.

"This is gonna be awesome," Tommy says. "I have a kid, and wow. She's a leftie, and she can cook."

"One question." I let go of the papers enough to tug at the sleeve of Jonah's hoodie. "Why didn't you say something earlier?"

Tommy grins. "My lawyer advised me to wait until the show airs, so I couldn't get sued for having my daughter compete. Technically, I didn't know I had a daughter until tonight." He winks. "So I can't get sued." His face sobers. "That was the longest two weeks of my life."

I swallow. "I'm so relieved to know the truth. Mom's passed away, and her side of the story is gone, but I'm grateful that I get the rest of my life with you. It was kind of lonely after Grammy died. I had no one."

Tommy chokes up again. "Yeah, I've had no one for a while, too, but now we've got each other."

"And you've got the entire Butler family."

Tommy's eyes shoot to Danny. Danny offers him another roll. "Don't even think about trying to skip family dinners. You're invited for life."

Tommy covers his eyes with one hand. Slowly, he nods. He uncovers his eyes. "This is the best Christmas present I've ever gotten. A daughter. A wonderful, beautiful daughter." And then he breaks down and cries. Really cries.

So do I.

# Chapter Forty-Six

Tommy holds up a hand. "Hang on, Killer. I've got a present for you and Brie." He looks at Danny. "You wanna explain?"

Danny holds up his hands. "What? The lawyer finally gets to talk?"

"Shut up and talk," Jonah says with a grin.

"You know that's not possible." Danny grabs the papers. "Acknowledging you. Will. Power of attorney. Trust fund. Way too generous. He's spoiling you, Brie. Offer to work for him. Blah, blah." Danny hands me the stack. "Dinner's almost ready, so you can read it over the next few days. As your lawyer, I advise you to sign it, because as Tommy's lawyer, I did a killer good job of drawing up the papers. No typos."

Jonah huffs. "Dude, you can't be our lawyer and his at the same time."

"Watch me." Danny smacks Jonah on the back of the head and runs away.

"Real mature!" Jonah yells, and lunges after him. He comes back to kiss me, then races off down the hall.

"Boys!" Maggie shrieks. "I'm carrying the ham!"

Tommy and I laugh. "There's one more thing."

379

"Jonah!" I holler. "Get back here."

And he saunters down the hall with another roll in his hand. "These are way better than you said. You should have warned me. I don't care about eating anything else for dinner." He unrolls a piece of the crescent roll and pops it in his mouth. "What's up, girlfriend?"

Tommy grins as Jonah settles beside me on the couch. "Merry Christmas, Jonah." He digs in his pocket and produces a shiny, golden band.

Jonah swallows, then his mouth drops open. "What the...? It matches." He slips the chain over his neck.

I scoot to the edge of the couch and stare at the ring in Tommy's hand. "No way."

It's Grandpa's ring. "Grammy never told me where that was. I never thought about it. I-I..." I stammer and can't believe what I'm seeing.

Tommy offers it to Jonah. "If you want matching rings for your wedding, you can have it."

I stare at him. "You kept it all these years, even though you were divorced?"

Tommy drops the ring in Jonah's hand. "Yeah. I almost think I married your mother to take care of your grammy more than her, and your grammy is the one who gave me this ring to wear. You know?"

I nod and gaze at the twinkling lights on the Christmas tree. "I'm sorry she didn't tell you about me. She held grudges and she was protective of the people she loved. Fiercely protective. I'm sorry she hurt you."

Tommy waves off my apology. "It's not your job to carry her mistakes."

"Brie thinks she's a mistake. You can guess how well I take it when she says that." Jonah undoes the clasp on his chain and slips my grandpa's ring on. My grandparents' two wedding rings dangle on his chest.

"They look good together," Tommy says gruffly, as Jonah slips the chain back around his neck. "You kids look good together. And don't you ever say that again, kid. You are no mistake. You are my Christmas miracle."

"Even though my birthday is in March?" I duck out of the way when Jonah tries to whack my shoulder, and Tommy and Jonah and I meet in the hallway for another hug. I can't get my fill of this.

But it's time to fill our stomachs.

"Stop making out and come eat," Jake shouts down the hall.

"We're not making out in front of Brie's dad, you goon." Jonah yells back.

Jake runs down the hall. "Brie has a dad?" He spots Tommy. "What? Tommy is her dad? Way to keep another secret, you dork."

Jonah grabs Jake in a headlock while he's still in shock. "You don't know everything about me."

Jake grunts from beneath his arm. "That is wicked. No way."

Then Tommy grabs Jonah to help Jake, since we're all family now, and I can't let it be two against one, if Jonah is outnumbered. We wrestle our way to the dining room where Maggie sighs. "Every year. Every year I say *Formal dinner* and then it's like this. Just one dinner. Is that too much to ask?"

"Yes." Her boys answer in unison, and I assume that she asks this question every year. I wink at her, and she smiles back.

Dinner is everything you'd expect from a Christmas Eve meal cooked by a family of chefs. The crescent rolls are perfect—golden brown on top, buttery and crispy on the bottom, and light as a cloud in the middle. Maggie and Jim serve a maple-glazed ham with a cinnamon-apple compote and roasted sweet potatoes. Danny makes a fresh spinach salad with goat cheese, glazed walnuts, pickled beets, persimmons, and a mustard vinaigrette.

Matt wilts spinach but adds white beans and bacon to the lemon and garlic. Jake and Lindsay make a decadent macaroni and cheese casserole with breadcrumbs toasted on top and at least four kinds of cheese.

Luke makes his mom's famous crockpot hot cocoa, since he just arrived and that's the easiest thing to do, and Chief helps set the table when he gets here from Sugar Creek. Nick roasts the golden potatoes with rosemary, but then mashes some red potatoes, too, with the peels. Tommy brings a variety of appetizers in from his car, but he keeps going back to the kitchen counter to get another roll. "I remember these," he says with a grin. "Your grandma knew how to cook."

As if that's not enough, Jim makes an apple and pecan-stuffed pork tenderloin topped with apple butter and cherry-cranberry sauce, and Maggie serves green beans, "So there's something green on your plate. Color matters."

"This meal's too heavy," Jonah whispers to me. "Too much green already if you ask me."

"Nothing vegetarian," I answer. "Spinach doesn't count."

I giggle, and Jonah grins. We already have our own inside joke, and we might even have our own Christmas traditions starting. I'm warm inside. I've never had many Christmas traditions, other than watching *White Christmas*.

Someone turns on the *Santa Snack Smack Down*, and Maggie serves everyone steaming cups of her crockpot hot cocoa, but Jonah offers to make me tea. "You can use your new mug."

"Too late," I tell him. "I'm addicted to the cocoa, and you, and your family."

He sets down the Shrimply In Love mug and stalks toward me. We claim the darkest, most private love seat while everyone else settles around the great room to watch the final, edited version of the show. It's weird to see myself on TV. They've made us look good and sound funny. Tommy played up the twin rivalry, and the whole show is a huge hit.

Everyone congratulates Jonah, and I wonder if it's weird for Jake to have his twin outshine him. Matt gets a lot of ribbing about his hair, and Nick and Danny drag him down the hallway toward the bathroom, threatening to shave his head.

Jake's a little quiet.

I don't want to downplay Jonah's victory, but I need to find a way for Jake and Jonah to get back to the way they were before dating and engagements and cooking shows put barriers between them.

*Repair effort.* Mrs. Butler's words float back to me from Thanksgiving. Or was it Pappy? Someone. But the twins can't kiss and make up.

What's the equivalent?

Later that night, after games and talking and more rough-housing between the brothers, Jake makes some Cajun popcorn as a tribute to Jonah's victory. "You were brilliant, Joey. I salute you and Brie. That was a solid win."

We're all ready for another snack by this time, so Jonah whips up the coconut lime drinks, and we all settle in with our late-night snack. The lights are low and a fire burns in the enormous hearth at one end. Another Christmas tree towers over the great room.

Tommy waves goodbye. "I'll be back tomorrow for leftovers." He grins at me. "Let me know what you think of that offer."

Everyone looks at me curiously. Jonah threads his fingers through mine as we sit on the couch together. "Sure. I'll talk about it with Jonah."

Tommy waves again, and he's gone. Maggie and Jim walk him to the door and never come back.

I snuggle into Jonah's side, content and truly peaceful for the first time in my life. The room is quiet as we all stare into the fire or watch the twinkling lights on the tree.

"What offer?" Chief asks.

I tilt my head and rest my cheek on Jonah's shoulder. He's pensive, not at all cocky or gloating, like he might be after his win. I care about Jonah, and I can see that today, on what could be the happiest day of his life, he's aching a little inside, because he had to beat his best friend and brother to win.

"Tommy offered me a job," I say. "Long story." I'll save it for tomorrow or the day after Christmas. I don't want to disrupt the mellow mood in the room with my drama.

"Whoa. Are you going to take it?" Jake asks.

I glance at Jonah. "I don't know. We have to decide where we'll live—Boston or New York." I want to push Jonah to talk about the restaurant with Jake, but it's not my place.

"Or Boulder," Luke says hopefully.

Chief has no qualms about asking questions. "So, what's up with the restaurant that Jake and Jonah were going to open?"

The quiet that felt peaceful before? It's deadly silent now.

"Jake and I need to figure that out," Jonah says.

Jake stretches and drapes an arm around Lindsay. "It's fine if you want to bail. You can't handle working with my awesomeness. I get it." He smirks. "Stay here in Boston, if that's what you want."

I hear Jake's hurt and know he's trying to cover it up with bravado. I decide to jump into the conversation after all. "Or you could stay here, Jakey boy. This town might be big enough for the two of you."

Jake laughs. "Barbecue?"

"Yeah." Jonah moves to the edge of the couch. "Remember that amazing brisket we had in Boulder?" That's all it takes. Jonah doesn't do well with theoreticals. He likes real world examples.

Jake sits up. "You're kidding. What was in that?"

Jonah grins. "Mesquite—"

Jake scoots forward to the edge of his seat. "—smoke—"

Jonah's starting to get excited. "—maybe honey or brown sugar..."

Jake stands and starts pacing. "Nah, not too sweet, that's where everyone goes wrong."

Nick and Danny groan. "Here we go," Luke mutters.

Jake rounds on him. "Hey. You are not stealing Jonah again. Boston is fine, but not Boulder. We already opened a restaurant there."

Luke holds up his hands. "I didn't say anything. It's just... Does every conversation have to be about food?"

Jonah and Jake and Matt say, "Yes," at the same time.

"Sorry, Luke," I say. "You and I can talk about *Pokémon Go* while they discuss ingredients."

He puts away his phone. *Busted.* I saw what he was doing during dinner.

Jonah looks over at me. "Where are we opening our restaurant?"

Jake leans back casually, too casually. "Whose restaurant? Yours, mine, ours, or hers?"

Jonah shrugs. Chief levels a gaze at me, and I know what he's thinking even though he hasn't said anything.

Nick pops another handful of Cajun popcorn in his mouth. "Tommy is established in New York. Man, I can't believe you have that connection. You should use it."

"Unless he moves to Boston," Danny said. "He's seriously considering it."

"We'll see," Jonah says noncommittally. I love that he knows that I don't want to explain Tommy to everyone yet. I want a few hours to process what happened.

The lights are dim, some upbeat Christmas music plays in the background, and Jonah and Jake are talking to each other about the ultimate test of twin loyalty.

Not the cooking competition—that was nothing compared to this choice. The restaurant. Jonah picked me over Jake. He's getting married and moving forward. He's talking about pulling out or starting over with a new concept with me instead. Whether Jake moves *with* him or *away* from him could hinge on this conversation.

Then it hits me. "Open side-by-side restaurants. Stay in Boston, Jake. You know you want to."

He can't admit I'm right that easily. Jake relaxes into the couch, resting one leg on his knee and pulling Lindsay closer. "Give me one good reason to stay."

I tug Jonah back from the edge of the couch and point to the two of us. "Side by side. Like milk and cookies for Santa. You can open restaurants next door to each other. Twin restaurants."

"Because having a twin means always having a friend," Luke says in a sing-song voice.

Jake slugs him. "It's true, bro. It's not just twins. It's brothers. We all have your back."

"I have your back literally." Danny grabs him in a headlock.

Luke elbows him in the ribs, hard, then rolls his eyes. "Whatever." But a tiny grin tugs at the side of his mouth and those Butler dimples pop in both cheeks, just like they do when Jonah is fighting a smile.

Jake and Jonah can move forward together, but on their own, and I can stay here, where my dad is going to live, close to Chief, and have Christmas in the same place next year.

I put a hand on Jonah's chest. His nice, chiseled chest. That distracts me for a moment. He knows it and leans in with a grin. Jonah pushes up the sleeves of his sweater, just above the wrist, so I can see the veins in his forearms, too. He knows all my weaknesses by now.

I keep talking while he kisses my cheek. "Twin restaurants. You can each have your own but have them together."

Chief gets it. "Like Cookies and Cream."

Then Nick chimes in. "Milk and Sugar.

And Luke has the worst idea. "Tea and Sympathy."

Jake scoffs. "No one's going to eat at a restaurant called Sympathy. Give me a break. I'll have a side of mesquite pity with that."

Luke gets out his phone again. "Fine. Peanut Butter and Jelly."

Jake says, "Bacon and Eggs."

Jonah stops kissing me long enough to say, "I'll open *Bacon* and you open *Eggs*."

Jake shakes his head. "No way, man. I want the restaurant that's bacon-themed. Eggs? That's, like, breakfast only."

Lindsay and I laugh because Jake eats a lot of eggs. He's the one always cooking an omelet or making a frittata.

"Come and fight me for the rights to *Bacon*." Jonah's starting to get into it. I have some pity for Luke. If he doesn't care about food, he must not ever feel like he fits into the family. Jonah leaves the couch, and Jake leaves Lindsay's side. They meet in the middle of the great room, like they're about to have a boxing match. Jonah shoves Jake's shoulder with his own. "I'll open *Fish* and you open *Chips*."

Jake grunts and puts up his fists. "An entire potato-themed restaurant?"

"I like potatoes. Potatoes are trending," Luke says.

Everyone stares at him. Jake drops his fists, and Jonah shakes his head. Danny grabs Luke's phone and turns off whichever video game he's been playing. "What world do you live in? I love you, buddy, but I don't think we live on the same planet."

Luke shrugs. "Potatoes are awesome. I'd go to that restaurant."

"*Sweet* and *Sour*," Jonah says. I doubt he listened to the potato argument. He has that look on his face, the same look that he gets while he's cooking.

"Which one of you is sweet and which one is sour?" Danny asks.

Nick starts to say, "Jonah for sure is—"

"Don't answer that," Jonah says. "*Cream* and *Sugar*. We're known for our desserts."

Matt leaves his chair. "*Salt* and *Pepper*. I can see that."

Jonah snorts. "Jake would definitely own *Salt*."

"Are you insulting my sauces again?" Jake pretends to be insulted.

"No way." Matt grins. "It's because *you're* salty all the time, as well as your food."

Jake tries to put Matt in a headlock, and they wrestle around Jonah, who ignores them. Jonah shakes his head. "None of those sound like barbecue. *Pepper*, maybe, but not *Salt*. It depends on which kind of pepper, right? Chipotle pepper and black pepper are totally different flavor profiles."

And that's the end of the peace and quiet. Nick turns off the music, Luke goes to bed, and the rest of us brainstorm side-by-side restaurant concepts with the twins for the next two hours, well past midnight.

I've never been happier.

I'm in love, and I've found two new families: the Butlers and my dad. I have a best friend who needs me, and Lindsay looks like she's on her way to finding love with a great guy who needs her as much as she needs him.

Jonah is the guy I never knew I needed, and he's a package deal. He comes with Jake and four other brothers and two over-involved parents and as overwhelming as it all is, I'm not going to ask him to pull away. I'm going to face my past, so they can stay together. I'm going to do it with Jonah and my dad at my side, and maybe I can make new memories to replace the painful old ones.

I have everything I asked Santa for, and more.

But then Jonah has one more surprise for me the next morning.

A charcuterie board.

"I know it's a cheesy gift," he says.

"Oh yeah. What would you pair that cheese with?" Jake asks. "A heaping side dish of PDA?"

"Dude, butter boards are trending," Luke says. "No one makes charcuterie boards anymore."

Everyone stares at him.

"What? I have Pinterest. I have friends. I eat food." Luke's sitting near me, and he lowers his voice. "Goat cheese makes a good base, too. Sprinkle some herbs, and—" He looks up and notices his family listening.

"Dude." Jake crosses the room and slaps him on the back. "You've been holding out on us."

"Luke *does* like food," Matt says. "You've been cooking, haven't you? Admit it. You know you like to cook. Tell the truth."

Luke glances at me. "Anyway. I'm glad you're part of the family."

"I love you, too, Luke." I pull him into a sidearm hug, and his neck reddens.

Jake steals the wooden charcuterie or butter board, whichever it is, and tries to hit Danny with it. Maggie and Jim yell for them to stop. Nick steals Jake's candy cane while he's running around, and I have a vision of what growing up with five brothers was like for Jonah.

And then Chief challenges Jonah to a push-up rematch, and I have to join in, and it's the best Christmas morning of my life. I hope to spend Christmas here at the Butlers' every year for the rest of my life, paired with the perfect match for me.

Even if he's cheesy. Even if he bought me a "Shrimply in Love" mug for my tea.

Jonah hands me a hand-knitted stocking with a dozen red roses and twenty more pairs of nail clippers. "For our new house someday," Jonah says with a twinkle in his eye. He sets the stocking aside and tugs me to him. "I can't wait to find our own place."

"I can help with that," Maggie says. "Jim, find them a place. Anna said she's getting a place on Mill Street."

Jim opens a real estate tab on his phone's browser. "Mill Street is too far. We can't have the grandkids living that far away."

"It depends on which part of Mill Street. Here's one on Marsh Street, or there's this one on Somerset. That would make a good Christmas present."

Jonah shakes his head. "I didn't mean we had to find one right now."

"Thank you," I say softly, pulling Jonah aside from the vigorous real estate debate developing. "That's a lot of drawers in one house."

He grins. "His and hers, remember?"

Chief promises to confirm our wedding date with his friend, Laraine, at the reception center. *October Sixth*. The first weekend of fall leaves. We're going back to Sugar Creek to get married because Jonah makes sure that I always have what I need, and I want to make sure that he knows this relationship is real.

It felt real from the beginning, and if I said anything else, I was lying to myself. I want to make sure there's nothing temporary or hypothetical anymore. I want this to be permanent as soon as it can be. I want to marry him.

I even ask Maggie and Lindsay to shop for wedding dresses online with me, and that distracts Maggie from house hunting. "Dresses. We can look at dresses. Are you Dior or Armani?"

"Armani is the right answer," Danny whispers loudly. "Ma never wears Dior if she can help it."

Maggie swats his shoulder. "I'm not a snob. Don't make her think I'm a snob." She looks at me tentatively. "But if you don't mind Armani..."

"I don't mind Armani," I say, laughing. "Luke! Jonah's wearing our rings, we've set a date, and your parents are paying for a designer wedding. Is that official enough for you?" I bump his shoulder.

Luke grins. "Yeah. Am I invited?"

Jonah wraps an arm around my waist. "You've got to play at our wedding. Right, Jake?"

Jake glances up from his phone. "There are twin homes. Or we could get townhouses next to each other."

Lindsay wraps her arm around his. "Luke's band. Focus, Jake. We've moved on to wedding dresses."

Jake looks around, disoriented. He's still shopping for homes. "Sorry, babe. I was making you a sexy spreadsheet." He kisses her cheek. "Extra Christmas present for my accountant."

He winks, and Lindsay blushes.

"I want one of your sexy spreadsheets," Jonah mutters in my ear. "Jake steals all my ideas."

Jake locks the phone and slips it in his pocket. "Yeah, Lukey, we want you to play at our wedding for sure. No one else. When are we buying rings, Brie? Lindsay's been shopping for a week, and I don't think she'll ever decide."

"Dresses," Lindsay prompts. "Focus."

"Decide," he shoots back at her. "I can't propose until you pick a ring. Do you want me to make a spreadsheet for that, too?" Jake turns the full force of his attention on her, though, wrapping his arms around her back and kissing her so long that Matt stops counting.

"Let's get those matching rings," I say, when they finally stop. "Jonah's never giving mine back."

Jonah looks up from his dad's phone. His parents are huddled around him, looking at the closest home in his price range in one tab and wedding dresses in another and wedding rings in a third. "Is this going to be a thing? Do we have to have our kids at the same time and whatever?" Jonah asks.

Jake shrugs. "Pretty much, yeah. You okay with that?"

Jonah shrugs. "Ask Brie. She's the boss." He winks at me.

Nick and Matt laugh.

"I'm never going to be a mess like them," Luke says. "No offense, Brie and Lindsay, but love's not for me."

Danny catches my eye. "They all say that, then *boom*!"

"Never gonna be me. I'm impervious." Luke waves his hands like there's a forcefield around him. "Software engineer. We repel women."

"You're such a dork," Matt says.

Jonah slings an arm around my shoulders. "You're really okay with all this crazy?"

"More than okay. Lindsay warned me this would happen when I started working for you."

Jake looks up from his phone. "She did? What did she say? We can get a showing on these two houses tomorrow. They're on the same street." He glances at Lindsay. "After we shop for dresses, babe. I'm listening, I swear."

She kisses him. "Thanks."

I slip my arm through Jonah's. "Lindsay warned me about the Butler brothers. One hit, and I wouldn't be able to stay away. Sure enough, I'm addicted."

Jake grins and puts his phone away. He moves Lindsay in front of him and wraps his arms around her. "You loved me all along."

Luke and Danny look away from the over-the-top PDA, but Nick and Matt grin at us. Chief looks pensive, almost sad, but his steady gaze tells me that he's proud of me for not running away. Maggie and Jim are wiping their eyes and getting ready to make down payments on enormous homes for their grandbabies. "It has to have a yard so they can get a dog."

"And throw a football."

Jake and Jonah look at each other. Jonah rolls his eyes, and Jake tips his chin up in a nod. We're surrounded by brothers and parents, and we're never getting away. Tommy is coming over in a few hours, then we're meeting Anna and all the cousins at Pappy's restaurant for a huge Christmas dinner tonight.

So, even if it feels like the twins are going their separate ways, at least they're doing it together, side by side, with the women they love, and cocooned by family.

Maybe even literally side by side, if Maggie and Jim can find the right houses for sale.

Jonah pulls me into a hug, and his breath tickles my cheek. "Should we tell them how things really started? It's a good story."

I lean back onto his chest, and he rests his chin on my head. "Sure."

"Really?" Jonah gazes down at me. "When? Now?"

"On our golden anniversary."

# Epilogue

I ONLY HAVE one person left to invite to the wedding: Danny's ex, Patricia. I've connected with my dad, and Jonah and Jake are tight. It feels like the right thing to do. Maggie is still grieving the divorce, and I don't want my wedding day to hurt her.

"Patty's like a daughter to me," Maggie says as she texts the contact info over. "I still love her, two years after the divorce. Don't tell Danny, but I still text her."

Everyone still texts her, but no one tells each other that. I'm the only one who knows that they all secretly keep in touch with her, and there's no way I'm leaving her out of the wedding.

I text Danny first.

**Me**: Can I invite Patty to the wedding for your mom?
**Danny**: Yeah. She won't come.
**Me**: Thanks. I'm sorry things ended like that for you.
**Danny**: Thanks.

Jonah thinks I'm crazy, too, even though he secretly texts Patty on her birthday and on holidays. I agree, but I can't shake the whispers that Patty was like me. *Alone. Not much family. Moves around a lot.*

393

Once I get his okay, I send Patty a text.

**Me**: This is Jonah Butler's fiancée, Brie. I want you to come to our wedding on October 6ᵗʰ. I know it's short notice, but I'm calling to talk you into it.

I give her a minute to read it, then I call to follow up. She picks up on the first ring. "Patty here."

I jump right in. "Hey, this is Brie Santoro. Can I book you a cabin in Vermont next week? I want you at our wedding."

She fires right back. "Danny's not okay with that."

"I asked him. He's fine."

I like her. She keeps arguing. "He's lying."

"He said you wouldn't come."

She's silent. "Thanks for trying. It means a lot."

"Sure. I think he misses you. He told Jonah not to mess up with me the way he messed up with you."

She's quiet again. "Yeah, he did mess up."

I'm not going to convince her, but I tried. "You have my contact info. We're friends now. You can change your mind anytime. You know the Butlers will pay for everything."

She laughs dryly. "I can't get them to stop paying for things. Yes, they're very generous."

I hear a noise in the background. *Crying*. "Are you alright?"

Something crashes to the ground, but she lies. "I'm fine."

I'm really worried. "You're not fine. What was that?"

She sounds panicked. "Listen, I'm gonna hang up, and it's nothing personal. I wish you and Jonah all the best. He's a great guy. My favorite, honestly, of all the brothers. Don't tell Jake."

"I won't tell Jake, of course, but please tell me what that noise was. I heard a baby crying."

She sighs. "Would you believe me if I said I was babysitting?"

"Way to sell it. No, I'm not going to believe that now."

She tries anyway. "I'm babysitting."

I send a Facetime request. A woman with perfect porcelain

skin answers. Thick black hair frames a heart-shaped face. She smiles hesitantly. "This is between you and me?"

I hear her worry and vulnerability. "I promise."

She holds up the phone, and I see a baby in a highchair behind her. She's the exact image of Patty. "Danny doesn't know," she says. "I tried to tell him when we were separating, but he accused me of sleeping around, so I stopped talking to him."

I'm gob smacked. I'm also in a really awkward position. "You have to tell him."

"I know." She collapses at the table, opens an applesauce packet, and hands it to the toddler. The crying stops. "I've been worried for two years, ever since my daughter was born, like this is too good to be true."

"She's beautiful," I say. "I want one."

"You get one after your wedding." She smiles sadly. "I promise I'll tell Danny by then, if he'll listen."

"How do I know you won't change phone numbers or move so I can never find you again?" That's what my mom did to my dad, and no way am I letting that beautiful baby grow up without her father, especially when Danny is so awesome.

"If I text Danny now that I want to talk later, is that good?"

I get a group text a second later.

**Patty**: Hey, Daniel. I'm including Brie on this text thread because she invited me to Jonah's wedding, and you should know that I accepted her invitation. I'd like to see you and talk.
**Danny**: Okay. Ma will be glad to see you. Everyone will. Are we talking about something bad?
**Danny**: Hi, Brie.
**Me**: Hi, Danny.
**Patty**: Nothing bad.
**Danny**: I'm fine if you need more alimony again or whatever. You know that, right? You don't have to go through Chad.

**Patty**: Stop worrying. I'll see you when we get to Sugar Creek. Thanks for the invite, Brie.
**Me**: Thanks for accepting. See you next week.


"I promise you that I'll follow through," Patty continues. "Danny's got my alimony. He can always find me. If I say I'll do something, I'll do it."

"I like you. See you next week. The whole family's going to rent rooms together, and I think they're full, but there's a cute set of cabins by the lake. It's not more than five minutes from the farm. We arrive on Saturday afternoon, but I can get you a cabin as soon as you want one."

She pauses. "Okay. I'm in Manchester. I can pack this weekend and drive up there, too. I'll take next week off work. What do we wear?"

"I'll send you info on the wedding, the cabin reservation, everything you need. Thanks, Patty. This is going to mean a lot to Jonah and Maggie and everyone. They all love you."

"Sure." She lets out a deep breath. "I knew this had to happen. Thanks for helping me face Danny."

"You never leave the Butler family," I say. "I tried, and they reeled me back in."

Patty laughs. "That's the truth. I left them, but they don't leave me alone."

I wonder what that means, but I let it go. I have my suspicions. Everyone still texts her, after all, and it sounds like Maggie and Jim might be supplementing her alimony with gifts of their own. I'm glad that I've got a new sister-in-law, even if technically she's an ex, and I'm not married to Jonah yet. "See you in Sugar Creek." We hang up, and I drop onto the couch. The Butlers have a grandbaby that they don't know about.

Next week is going to be epic. Emotions off the charts. I've got three days to get ready. My suitcases are almost packed to return to Sugar Creek. Jake and Jonah and all the boys are picking up their suits from the Armani store. Even Luke flies into town tomorrow.

Excuse me. *Boutique.* The Giorgio Armani Boutique, where the stylists know my fiancé and his family by name. It's weird, but my dad also has an account there.

I guess I won't wear space buns on my wedding day, since I have a couture wedding gown. Maybe Colleen can curl my hair again or something.

Jonah knocks, and I open the door of my apartment. There's not much furniture left. We're moving after the wedding and whirlwind foodie tour of Europe with Jake and Lindsay, and most of my boxes are already over at the new house.

Jonah drapes his suit over the edge of the couch. "The Emporio wants to decorate our new place."

I freak out. "How many thousand dollars are in that bag? Hang it up."

He slips it into my coat closet. "Dad's happy to pay. Tommy's trying to split it with him." He wraps an arm around my waist. "Everyone's so shocked that I'm finally getting married that they'll pay anything to get me off their hands."

I lean into him. "You're such a big-head celebrity that everyone wants to sponsor you."

Jonah brushes a loose hair behind my ear. "No, Tommy wants to spoil you, since you won't let him pay you a salary. He's trying to talk my dad into going fifty-fifty on our house."

I run my hands along the smooth black sheet that covers the clothes. "I feel bad that I turned down that offer to work with him."

"You spend plenty of time helping him get organized." Jonah kisses me slowly, then more and more eagerly until the back of my legs hit the couch. He grabs my face, so we keep kissing, and he climbs over the back of the couch and tries to pull me down onto his lap. "I need you more."

I walk around the couch to join him. "We're really doing this? Opening a restaurant together, just like Pappy and Mary?"

He grins. "You're the big deal now. Everyone wants to know what Tommy Fuller's daughter is like and whether she can cook as well as her dad."

I tuck my legs beneath me on the couch. "What do you tell them?"

Jonah grabs the remote. "You're better. I tell them to come try the new restaurant and see for themselves." He turns on the TV. "Let's rewatch our episode again. I love the shocked look on Jake's face when he realizes he lost. Never gets old."

I settle into his lap. "Aren't we supposed to be doing something? Weddings are a lot of work."

Jonah shifts my weight to snuggle better. "Nah. I've got this whole work-life balance thing figured out. My company psychologist banned me from work for a month and look how that turned out."

"Yeah, now we're both workaholics."

Our *Santa Snack Smack Down* plays in the background while we work on perfecting our chemistry.

"Oh!" Jonah tips me off his lap and onto the couch. "Dad said I'm supposed to get you a wedding present, and I wanted to do that before we left for Vermont and Europe and the new home in Belmont."

"That makes us sound so ridiculous, like we're fancy or elite or something we're not."

Jonah grins. "Fake it 'til you make it. Worked with you."

"More like fake it so you can make out." I tuck myself into his side. "You tricked me."

"You know you love it." He pulls out a light teal box with a white ribbon on top. "Jake got a matching set for Lindsay. They're not completely identical. Yours is white gold and hers is rose gold."

"Lindsay finally decided what she wants?" I can't open the box. For some reason, Jonah's gesture has knocked me off my feet.

Maybe because rings are real. I can see his love wrapped around my finger now as well as hanging over his heart.

Jonah grins. "It only took eight months. Jake's been sweating it, but yeah, we ordered these sets a few weeks ago and they finally came in." He lifts the lid off the box and spills the new rings into the palm of my hand. "There's a row of diamonds inset, so the dough won't get into the ring, and the engagement ring fits right into the wedding band. You know you're never getting Grammy's ring back."

He wears the chain with my grandma's and grandpa's rings every day. People comment on social media, and it's his new trademark. I've seen a couple other chefs wearing their wedding rings on their necklaces when they compete, now, too.

"I know." I close my hand around the rings, then throw my arms around his neck. "I love them."

"Should we try them out?" he asks and there are crinkly lines around the edges of his warm brown eyes.

I hold out my hand, and Jonah slides the wedding band on first, then the engagement ring.

He blows out a long breath. "They fit."

"You fit. This fits." I gesture between us. "You and me together. Am I supposed to get you a groom's gift? I've never gotten married before, and neither has my dad. No one tells me these things."

Jonah grins and takes another light teal box out of his pocket. "Got you covered."

"I can't wait to see what I got you."

He opens the box slowly. "Me, neither. You engraved a mushy message or our initials. I don't remember. Lindsay and Jake helped with that part."

He lifts the lid and pushes through the tissue paper. There's a tiny teal bag inside the box. He pulls at the strings to open, and a miniature silver pocket knife falls into his palm.

I stare at the ridiculous object. "I should have gotten you a set of chef's knives or a new Red Sox hoodie, since you are never, ever getting this one back."

"Nah. Your dad will get me a knife set, and I don't want my

hoodie back. It looks too good on you." He gazes appreciatively at the oversized sweatshirt dangling from my wrists and adjusts the hood, so it lays flat on my back.

I snuggle up to Jonah. "You're sure?"

"I'm sure. We can get matching hoodies." He unfolds the pieces and shows me the gift I guess I got him. "You don't understand how awesome this thing is. Nail file. Tweezers. Scissors."

I do understand. It's the ultimate nail care set. "You're going to carry this everywhere with you, right?"

He slips it into his pocket. "Everywhere."

"And you'll always know I love you. Wherever we go, wherever we are, my love will be with you."

"Because I can trim my nails." His gaze burns, a broiling look that caresses my features and sets my pulse racing. "See how much you love me?"

I'm still overwhelmed by how deeply this man loves me and always has. "You've been sure of that from the start, haven't you?"

He drapes an arm around the back of the couch and leans down to look me in the eye. "I was never wrong about you and me. That was always a good idea. It just took you a while to acknowledge that I was right."

I love it that he's able to lighten up and tease me more and more. My conversation with Patty floats back into my mind. "And what about the grandbabies for our parents?" I tap his chest. His lean, hard, muscled chest. He wears these black t-shirts more often, just for me. I gaze up at him with a look I know he can't refuse. "I'm not getting any younger, and you're almost thirty-one, so I'm good with starting soon. Honeymoon baby."

He swallows. "I'll talk to Jake."

"No, I'll talk to Lindsay."

I love the panicked look in his eyes. Lindsay has Jake wrapped around her finger, and Jonah knows it. And since Lindsay is my best friend...

Jonah squirms on the couch. "We should at least give birth to the new restaurant first."

"Fine. Tell Jake that he and Lindsay have three months before... You know." I relax onto his chest. "I want a Butler baby. You've got some fine genetics. You know you want one, too."

Jonah's neck flushes bright red. "Thanks. Yeah. I mean, of course I do. You've got great genetics, too. Tommy Fuller genes."

I love him even more when he's flustered, but I cuddle into his side to help him recover from the shock and embarrassment of baby-making talk. "Do you know the moment I first fell in love with you without even knowing it?"

He relaxes now, too, and turns off the TV. "Tell me the whole story."

I shrug. "Pappy's kitchen. He went on and on about how to treat women, lectured the wait staff, and bragged about his grandsons. I watched the way my mom's boyfriends treated her, and these Butler boys seemed too good to be true."

"And when you met us?"

"You definitely seemed too good to be true." I run my hands along his neck and toy with the hair that is growing long again. "Chief has an appointment with you and Colleen in two days."

Jonah nods drowsily. "Is that why you agreed to my ridiculous idea of the fake engagement? I couldn't get up my nerve to ask you out, so it seemed like a great way to get a girlfriend without risking rejection."

"Free-range chicken," I tease him. I rest my head on his chest, and I hear his heart beating for me. Just for me. "A fake engagement was a perfect way to prove to myself all the things that were wrong with you, so I wouldn't fall for you."

Jonah looks like he's about to fall asleep. "Since I couldn't *actually* be a nice guy."

I'm okay with a power cuddle nap on the couch. "But I couldn't find a single thing wrong with you. You're not too good to be true. You're too good for me." It's still how I feel after all these months of dating and engagement and wedding planning, but I've quieted those other lies that told me I wasn't worthy of him.

Jonah gazes at me with wonder. "There's no way I'm ever going to feel like I'm everything you deserve."

I shrug. I've thought about this a lot. "Love isn't about what you deserve. It's about giving, and I don't expect you to be everything or do everything or know everything. No one can. That's why I have my dad and your family and Lindsay and my Amazon app and Kindle Unlimited books and that adorable hypothetical future baby—"

"—that we are not even going to start trying for until after the wedding and Europe and the restaurant opens, but she has your eyes and my dark hair."

I laugh. "Right. Except it's a boy with your deep brown eyes and my organizational skills, not yours."

He leans down to kiss me. "I don't know. A girl that looks like you sounds better." And he looks like he's ready to go make that baby right then.

"Since we're waiting to try until after marriage, maybe we should put a pin in this conversation."

He leans back and runs a hand through his hair. "One more week."

I press a kiss to his mouth. "Stop worrying. You don't have to be everything to be everything to *me*, Jonah."

His eyes glisten with something like tears, and he scrubs a hand across them. "I love you, Brie. I never knew I could care about someone so much it hurts."

I lace my fingers through his. "I love you, too, Jonah, and I'm not going anywhere unless it's with you and you have your nail clippers."

Jonah laughs, wipes a hand across his eyes, and we get back to establishing our work-life balance.

And by that, I mean kissing each other like we are the world to each other, because we are. He's my whole universe.

# Acknowledgments

This book was so much fun to write. I love cooking and I love Christmas, so it was two of my favorite things. Speaking of two of my favorite things: I love twins!

My first *Thank You* goes to David and Daniel Reynolds, a set of fraternal twins that I knew growing up. David gave me a ton of helpful insights into the life of a twin.

I can't begin to list all the sets of twins I've known. Some are identical; others are not. One set that I grew up with still works together in their profession, just like Jonah and Jake.

I have an amazing brother, who let me live at his place when we were both young, single, and dating. He had three or four guys who were also his roommates (it was a large house—I can't remember how many guys there were), so I got to hang out and feel what it would be like to have a bunch of brothers. Thanks to the Bell brothers, the Whettens, and all the other guys who played Halo until three a.m.

About that Six Second Kiss. It's a real thing. *Try it.* Drs. John and Julie Gottman are my love gurus. I read their books and follow them on social media. They say the Six Second Kiss is a "kiss with potential," and it is.

I've also got to acknowledge Noel Perrin, who took me to a country store in Vermont and introduced me to real maple syrup and real Vermont farmers. He was a professor at the small college in New Hampshire that I attended, and he went out of his way to make sure I had the real New England experience.

As did Rachelle and David Ostler. Thanks for road trips to

waffle houses and antique stores, long rides through winding New Hampshire roads, and the many trips to Lyme Pond. I couldn't have imagined Sugar Creek without you.

Thank you to the people of New England and to all the friends I made there.

I love cooking, and I've learned some of my best recipes from my mom, Sara Hacken, and my aunt, Susie Jensen. Thanks to them for the roll, gingersnap, and crockpot hot cocoa recipes. Susie's hot fudge sauce is amazing, but you're going to have to wait for another book to get that recipe...

Funny thing about that roll recipe. My mom learned to make those rolls in the late Sixties in Sacramento, California....from my friend, Paula Bergeson's grandmother, Pauline Broadbent! Ms. Broadbent was on a one-woman crusade to change the world, one roll recipe at a time, and she succeeded.

Thanks, too, to Dan and Natalie Hemmert for sharing their love of cooking with me. I'm inspired by Colton Soelburg and Joseph McRae and the many other chefs who spend countless hours, cook on holidays and weekends, and stay up all hours of the night, so the rest of us can enjoy a night out. Colton is the inspiration for Jonah's comment that every meal is a work of art.

God is the source of all my ideas and inspiration, and I acknowledge his help with writing this book.

Many thanks, too, to my editors, Michele Paige Holmes and Lorie Humpherys, as well as my proofreaders and beta readers, Sara Hacken and Marianne Siegmund. Big thanks to Heather B. Moore of Precision Editing.

And there's my husband, who listens to me read every single chapter out loud. He's my very own cinnamon roll hero, and I only know about romantic love because of him.

And to my kids—screen time is over. I finished my edits. Put *Minecraft* and *Animal Crossing* away. I love you. Homeschool is back in session...until the next deadline.

# Jim's Cranberry-Cherry Sauce Recipe

10 ounces of frozen cherries
12 ounces of fresh cranberries
A handful of blueberries (optional)
Juice and zest of one orange
¼ teaspoon cinnamon (or more)
1 cup brown sugar

Jim's a simple guy, and this is a simple recipe. Dump everything in a pan and let it simmer. It'll take about ten-fifteen minutes to thicken, depending on how much juice was in your orange and whether you toss in some blueberries, too.

Jim smashes the cranberries and cherries against the side of the pan while the sauce cooks. He leaves a few for texture, but otherwise, he waits until they're soft and then attacks them with his spoon. You can add a pinch of salt if you feel like it.

Also, he picks through his cranberries before he starts the sauce to throw away any white ones or mushy ones. You can refrigerate the sauce and keep it for a week, if it lasts that long. Hello, leftovers.

# Grammy's Roll Recipe

1 tablespoon yeast (active dry yeast)
½ cup sugar
1 tsp salt
1 cup hot water from the tap
½ cup butter (one stick) melted
3 eggs, well beaten
4 cups flour

Stir together yeast, sugar, salt, and **one** of the cups of flour. Add water and mix until yeast is dissolved. Add butter, then eggs, and mix until smooth.

If you have a mixer that can handle it, slowly add the other three cups of flour. Otherwise, place the remaining flour in a bowl and make a well in the middle. Pour liquid mixture into the flour and mix until all the flour is combined.

It's going to be sticky. You did it right. Don't add extra flour. Trust me. I live in the Rocky Mountains, and I still don't add extra flour to compensate for the high elevation. This is what makes the rolls fluffy and magical. Cover the dough with a cloth and let rise for two hours.

Melt another stick or two of butter, then grease your hands.

Punch down the dough and plop the dough out of the bowl. Roll it into a circle on a buttery surface. I use one of those plastic cookie cutter mats, but your counter will work just fine.

Spoon or pour a bunch of that melted butter all over the dough, then spread it out with a spoon or a pastry brush.

Here's the fun part. Cut the circle in half. And again. And again. And again. I use a plastic pizza cutter, or you could use a knife. They should look like one-two inch pizza slices. Now you start at the wide end of the wedge and roll the dough until you have a crescent.

Once you've rolled all the dough, brush the tops with butter. Again. I'm telling you. Cover your cookie sheet or tray and let the rolls rise for another two hours. It's worth the time it takes.

Bake your rolls at 400 degrees for about ten minutes. You know your oven best, and it depends on how wide you cut your rolls. Watch for the tops to brown. Use the middle rack so the bottoms of the rolls get crispy and golden brown, too.

And then, you know, if you want, when they come out of the oven, you can slather the tops with butter *again*. I usually skip that part and go straight to eating them.

*You can double or triple this recipe. Grammy used to quadruple it, feed everyone in the apartment building, and still have leftovers for the next three days.*

# Jonah's Cajun Popcorn Recipe

**Cajun spice mix:** Mix these together. Jonah uses a small whisk to break up any clumps.

 1 ½ tsp smoked paprika
 1 tsp salt
 1 tsp sugar
 1 tsp basil
 1 tsp cumin
 1 tsp garlic powder
 1 tsp onion powder
 1 tsp dried oregano
 1 tsp dried thyme leaves
 1 tsp turmeric
 ½ tsp black pepper (more or less, to taste)
 ½ tsp cayenne (more or less, to taste)

¼ cup butter, melted and browned (or more. Lots more.)

½ cup of kernels or 2 bags of microwave popcorn

Pop some popcorn: air popper, on the stove, microwave bag—however you want.

Jonah browns his butter by melting it on the stove and waiting for the butter to caramelize. When the butter puffs up and the foam turns brown, wait a few seconds for the salt at the bottom to toast. Then, you're golden. Literally.

Coat the popcorn with butter and toss it. Don't add salt—that's what the Cajun spice is for.

After you butter your popcorn, sprinkle Jonah's secret spice mixture on it. He adds about a tablespoon and a half for that much popcorn, but you can add as much or as little as you want.

If you want more heat, you can increase the black pepper and cayenne to ¾ tsp each or 1 teaspoon each. If it's too hot for you, add less cayenne and black pepper next time.

The spice mix works well with roasted potatoes. Cut some Yukon Golds or red potatoes into the size you want, toss them in olive oil, and cover them with the Cajun mix, then roast them your usual way. Jonah cuts the potato at an angle to get triangle-shaped pieces that are about an inch long-ish and wide-ish and a cool wedge shape. But you do you.

Next, he cranks the oven to 425 degrees, covers the potatoes, and roasts them for 20 minutes. When the timer goes off, he takes off the foil and roasts the potatoes for another 15 minutes.

Here's the tricky part. Flip the wedges gently with your spatula, so the other sides get toasty and golden, too. You can't really see with the spice rub on the potato, but it'll work. Now give them another 7-9 minutes. It depends on what size you cut the potatoes and how crispy you want them.

And, let's be honest, Jonah has a convection oven. He actually sets his temp to 400 degrees and the times are 16 minutes, 12 minutes, and 7 minutes for him with his equipment, but you know your oven best.

The best step of any recipe is always the last one—just ask Jonah how that boyfriend recipe is working out... The last step? Enjoy immediately and often.

# Colleen's Gingersnap Recipe

¾ cup shortening or butter—your call
1 cup brown sugar
1 egg
¼ cup molasses
2¼ cups flour
2 teaspoons baking soda
1 teaspoon ginger (see note on spices)
1 teaspoon cinnamon
¾ teaspoon cloves
¼ teaspoon salt
A bowl of granulated white sugar

Cream shortening (or butter) and brown sugar. Mix in the egg, then the molasses. Now add everything else except that bowl of granulated white sugar.

Colleen doesn't have time to chill the dough, so she skips that step, even though most people chill their gingersnap dough. She doesn't bother, and her cookies are famous, so—your call. Just preheat the oven now, baby. Why wait for this goodness?

Colleen uses a small cookie scoop to make balls. You can make balls in your hand or use spoons, or whatever, just make sure you roll them in a bowl full of granulated white sugar.

Colleen tells her friends to bake the cookies for eight minutes at 375 degrees to make sure they are crispy, but she cooks hers at the lower heat of 350 degrees for ten minutes or so. She likes her cookies a little softer, and so do her friends.

Recap: bake dough ten minutes at 350° for softer cookies or bake for eight minutes at 375° for crispy gingersnaps.

That's it! But why are hers so special?

Colleen buys her spices online from a store called Penzey's. Their spices are purer and pack a flavor punch. She's never told any of her neighbors, so they buy the blander spices at the grocery store, and none of their cookies ever taste like hers. But now you're in on the secret—Vietnamese Cinnamon!

It's not the recipe that makes this cookie special, it's the ingredients.

Also, Colleen doesn't level her teaspoons. They are generous and rounded. Maybe not on the cloves, but yes to extra cinnamon and ginger.

When Colleen is feeling extra fancy, she adds crystallized ginger bits, but that's only for special occasions. She's not a fancy person.

One more thing. The cookies taste even better when they've cooled for a bit, rather than serving them hot. They age well, because then you can really taste those spices.

One last, last thing. Colleen uses butter to get a softer, yummier ginger cookie, but she tells her friends to use shortening to make crispy gingersnaps... And no one understands why their cookies don't turn out as well as hers.

# Chief's Hummus Recipe

2 15-ounce cans of chickpeas
¼ cup tahini
¼ cup olive oil
Juice of one lemon, plus more to taste
¼ cup water or more to thin the hummus
2 garlic cloves, peeled
1 teaspoon salt
½ teaspoon cumin or paprika or more to taste
Paprika to sprinkle on top (smoked or sweet, whichever
you like)
Extra olive oil

Juice the lemon.

Pro tip: knead it on the counter first. Chief rolls the lemon under his palm to soften it up and get more juice, then uses one of those yellow squeezy things that catches most of the seeds. He gets a different amount of juice from every lemon, so you have to taste your hummus and see how strong you want your lemon flavor to be.

Then he makes a mixture of all the liquids: lemon juice, olive oil, some water, and that glumpy tahini stuff. It's like natural peanut butter. You have to stir it first, and it's messy, but worth it. Drain and rinse your chickpeas and toss them in a food processor. Add the garlic cloves, salt, and whichever spice you like: cumin or paprika or smoked paprika. Chief uses cumin. Colleen adds cracked black pepper, but that's why he brings his own hummus now. You can try it both ways.

Pulse the mixture ten times and scrape it down, then add the wet ingredients and let the food pro run until it looks like hummus. Taste it and see if you want more salt or cumin or lemon or anything, and then it's done. Here's the best part.

Put the hummus in your serving dish and sprinkle lots of paprika. Like, so much. Make it look like Christmas—lots of red on top. Then drizzle a generous amount of olive oil back and forth across the top. If you start eating and the paprika or olive oil runs out, do it again!

# Maggie's Crockpot Hot Cocoa Recipe

Maggie always has a few crockpots of these ridiculously rich and creamy cocoas on the counter for Christmas Eve.

- 1 can sweetened condensed milk
- 2 cups heavy cream
- 5 cups milk
- 1 teaspoon vanilla
- 12-ounce bag of chocolate chips—white/vanilla, dark, milk, mint, or a mixture

Add everything to a crockpot and whisk it together. The chocolate chips will be kind of clumpy at the bottom. Turn the heat onto "Low" and stir every half an hour for the next two hours until it's melted and warm. Turn the heat to "warm" after it's all melty and smooth. Maggie pops over and whisks it anytime it separates.

If you want a cocoa that's slightly less rich, adjust the milk/cream ratio. Try six cups of milk and one and a half cups of cream. I don't know why you'd do that, but some people do. You can also leave the sweetened condensed milk out, but again, why?

You can add an entire bag of white chocolate/vanilla chips, a bag of dark 60% or semi-sweet chips, or go for full milk chocolate. Sometimes Maggie mixes half semi-sweet and half milk chocolate. Don't worry if the bag is only ten ounces or eleven and a half. Close enough. Or toss in an extra handful of chocolate chips.

Maggie's secret ingredient? She only buys Guittard chocolate, but you can use your favorite brand or whatever's on sale.

Add toppings and leave them on the counter by the mugs and spoons:

Crushed candy cane
Mini chocolate chips or white chocolate chips
Candy canes to stir
Whipped cream for the top
Cocoa powder
Cinnamon
Nutmeg (use a grinder for the freshest)
Marshmallows
Flavor shots, like salted caramel, if you have Torani syrups
in your grocery store
If not, buy a bottle of caramel sauce to drizzle on top
Chocolate syrup
Flavored creamers
Red hots, sprinkles
Andes Mint chips

## Also by Lisa H. Catmull

**The Jane Austen Vacation Club Series**

You never know what might happen when you take a trip to the Jane Austen Vacation Club...

**The Victorian Grand Tour Series**

Fall in love with a chivalrous gentleman and adventurous ladies traveling around Europe in the Victorian Grand Tour series.

**An Autumn Kiss**

Three authors, three short stories,

all swoony romance.

# About the Author

Lisa Catmull is the author of contemporary clean and wholesome romances as well as novels set in the Victorian era. Lisa's books have been nominated for Swoony, RONE, and Whitney awards.

She earned a Bachelor of Art in English from Dartmouth College in New Hampshire and a Master of Education in Elementary Education from Utah State University in Logan, Utah.

Lisa taught Middle School English and History for seven years before pursuing screenwriting and writing. She currently lives between a canyon and a lake in Utah with her husband, two cats, and two rambunctious children.

amazon.com/~/e/B08R5F1SMY

instagram.com/lisa_h_catmull

tiktok.com/@authorlisacatmull

facebook.com/authorLisaCatmull

goodreads.com/lisacatmull

twitter.com/LisaHCatmull

youtube.com/lisacatmull

pinterest.com/lcatmull

bookbub.com/profile/lisa-h-catmull

linkedin.com/in/lisa-catmull-368896209

# Want more of Sugar Creek?

### The White Christmas Lie
### By Amey Ziegler

Chapter One

Two thousand dollars. Coco Poverly needed two thousand more dollars to buy Aunt Deb the perfect Christmas present. The shipping deadline—December fifteenth—for the professional bread slicer, was only two weeks away. In desperation, she agreed to wear a giant white chef's toque and coat, large enough to use as a sail, to dab the finishing touches on a Christmas-themed wedding cake.

The bride preparing for her nuptials in the grand Laurent Mansion up the snow-covered walk from the gatehouse, insisted the catering staff wear the chef uniform instead of the usual black long-sleeved T-shirt with Sugar Creek Catering embroidered over the heart.

Yeah, she was one of *those* kind of brides.

Somehow, Coco got suckered into assisting Megan with the

rest of the food.

At a table set inside the stone walls of the gatehouse, Coco rolled her eyes and, using a spoon, stuffed another mushroom with cream cheese and truffle oil before spreading delicate orange orbs of caviar on top. Kristy and Megan hired her for desserts, not for cooking. Baking and cooking were two separate things. One of them Coco was good at. The other...well, let's just say she wasn't making those mushrooms look appetizing.

She was a baker not a mushroom-stuffer.

Her fingers were covered in the white mess. Without thinking, she took a lick off the back knuckle of her thumb.

"Cooocooo."

Coco hated that her name sounded like baking chocolate when drawn out in Megan's annoying nasally voice. Coco's face burned at being caught.

Megan, Kristy's daughter, leaned over the plastic table and slapped her hand. "Now go wash your hands." She took the mushroom in question and tossed it into the trash. "No licking. And you should be using gloves."

Coco glanced to the other sous-chefs in the kitchen, standing over rented, hot propane stoves, singing along to Christmas oldies on the radio. "I didn't touch the mushroom after I licked my finger." She held up her cream-cheesed-covered hands. "I was planning on washing my hands anyway."

Although the December chill blew around outside, where uniformed valets parked cars up and down the brick drive, the heat was on overdrive in the gatehouse, set up as a staging area. The bride wanted the menu freshly made on site, but she didn't want the stench of cooking in the house.

Megan cocked her hip and placed a gloved hand on her waist. "If you won't wear gloves, you should probably leave." Megan didn't own the business. Her mom was the one cutting the check.

Coco rolled her eyes. Leave. That's what she was hoping to do ever since she finished the cake.

All around Coco, the rest of the catering staff hunched over the rented professional ovens and ranges near the front, cooking asparagus, rolls, gravy, and chicken. The smells of roasting, frying, and baking filled the room.

"I'm happy to go," she murmured under her breath. But she needed the overtime cash.

Humming a Christmas tune, Coco crossed to the bathrooms near the rear of the gatehouse to wash her hands. On her way, she stopped to admire the view.

Two French doors perfectly framed the sprawling, red brick, Georgian revival mansion covered in snow upon the hill. A wreath tied with a red bow decorated each of the many lighted windows of the two stories. Along with white lights, lining the rooftop and windows, decorative lanterns lit the garden shrubs, as dusk approached around four.

She paused, inhaling the view with a cleansing breath. The peaceful scene contrasted with the hustle and bustle of the preparations for the wedding behind her. What would it be like to be in that house, surrounded by well-heeled, well-connected guests? She'd heard about the mansion for years, but she'd never been inside. Mostly, it sat vacant, used only occasionally by the family —for as long as she could remember.

"Look at these mushrooms. They're all ugly. Did fill these with a shovel? You are, like, the worst at this." Megan's pitchy voice carried across the room. "I'm telling my mom." She threw down her gloves and marched out of the room.

Kristy strode into the room. "What is going on?" Her long, gray-blonde ponytail flipped over her shoulder, and she wore a purple long sleeved shirt. Why she was exempt from the ugly chef coat escaped Coco. Her face we red from the heat in the gatehouse.

"She's is doing a terrible job." Megan picked up the platter Coco had worked on. "Look at these mushrooms."

Coco's face flushed at the accusation. "I was hired to finish the piping on the cake, not stuff mushrooms." She finished the cake hours ago.

"And she refuses to wear gloves." She put on her gloves with a smug smile.

Megan's whiney voice grated on Coco's nerves. "If we could put the mixture into a pastry bag, I could pipe them. They would look prettier and be easier to do." That's what she did at the bakery to fill anything.

Folding her arms across her chest, Megan twisted her face into a sneer. "Maybe if you weren't so clumsy with the spoon, you wouldn't have to use a bag." When Megan scowled, she had the jowls of pit bull. "Get back to work." Seeing people had stopped to watch the drama, she clapped her gloved hands with the crinkle of plastic. "We're on a time crunch, people."

Just because her mom owned the business, Megan thought she was the boss. After washing her hands, Coco rolled her eyes and went back to the mushroom table, smelling the sweet scent of her aunt's cake sitting behind her. Oh, how she'd rather be working in the Sweet Suite Bakery, her day job, rather than here.

Megan barked orders to others then turned to Coco. "You're not working."

This was so not worth a measly hourly wage.

Coco unbuttoned the coat and removed the hat. "You know what? I'm done. Sign me out." She could find some other less painful to pay for Aunt Deb's Christmas present.

"Where are you going?" Kristy picked up the clipboard.

Laying the uniform on a chair, Coco wiped her hands on a nearby towel. "I finished my end of the deal. I only stayed the extra hours to help out. But I'm outta here. Good night." Her chest rose and fell with the confrontation.

Megan dropped her jaw. "You can't quit."

"Watch me." Coco hated overbearing bosses. Who did they think she was? Throwing her coat over her, she grabbed her purse and keys and stepped out into the cold wintery air. The crisp breeze felt good on her hot face. The overcast sky matched the color of the snow—white-gray. Only a few minutes remained before sunset. She marched a few steps before she heard someone speak.

"Excuse me."

Coco turned.

A blonde woman in a fur coat blew by her with the scent of designer perfume. She held a small, silver-wrapped gift. "Do you have a pen?"

"Maybe in my purse."

The blonde stamped her feet in the cold while Coco dug through her purse. "I cannot believe I forgot to write my name on the gift tag." The woman was a little younger than Coco's twenty-three years and wore heavy eyeliner, enough lipstick to last her all winter, and her blond hair was perfectly set in place. "After driving all this way from Concord, you would've thought I'd noticed."

Concord, New Hampshire? She doubted that. Concord, Massachusetts? Mostly likely. Rumor had it that the bride was from a well-connected family in Boston. Why she chose to get married on the outskirts of Sugar Creek, Vermont was such a mystery. Sugar Creek was beautiful in every season, but it wasn't huge—only about twenty thousand people lived on the banks of Lake Champlain. Mostly the maple trees and the skiing kept jobs in town.

Coco shook her head. When she got married, whenever that would happen, she didn't want to inconvenience her family and friends and make them drive over four hours just to see her wed. At last, at the bottom of the purse, she found a pen. "Here you go."

With too-white teeth, the woman forced a smile and took the pen, settling a rose gold clutch on a brick wall. "I didn't want to come to this wedding anyway."

"Oh?" Coco watched her scrawl Silvia Patterson on the tag near the bow. She couldn't imagine not wanting to go to such a grand event.

Silvia threw down the pen, picking up her clutch. "My

parents made me come. I'm supposed to be at a party in Montreal, but no, I had to come here and represent the family. So now I can't leave until tomorrow morning." She picked up the gift. "My parents spend the winter in their house in Barbados. They go every winter, no exceptions." She rolled her eyes. "What I wouldn't pay to be on my way to Canada right now. Tatum Fast is at my friend's house party, playing in four hours. A grammy winner is playing at a party where I'm invited." She jabbed a thumb toward the house. "And I have to go to this boring wedding where I don't even know anyone. All by myself."

"That's such a shame." Coco picked up the pen Silvia left on the wall. After the scene she just left, she wanted to get far away, put her feet up, or take a bath. "Too bad you can't get someone else to drop off the present—talk to the guests, schmooze, sign the guest registry—and then you could be on your way. Your parents would never know."

Silvia's eyes lit up. "You're brilliant." She ran her gaze over Coco's body. "You're about my size. Although it's hard to tell with your coat on. Tell you what. I have another outfit in the car. Why don't you wear my dress and run this up to the house? You'd only need to be there long enough to sign the guestbook and drop off the present and talk to a few guests. You can stay for food, drinks—whatever." She wiggled her fingers. "You would introduce yourself as me. It's been ages since I've seen any of these people. Nobody would know what I look like. If my parents asked anyone, they'd say I was here."

"What wait?" Coco wasn't volunteering for the job. Opening her mouth, Coco glanced around at the manicured and snow-covered sprawling garden. "I'm not going in there pretending to be you."

"Listen." Silvia opened her clutch. "I'll pay you."

Raising her eyebrows, Coco leaned in. Now here was a reason to go. Her heart pattered in her chest. "How much?"

"I've got five hundred in cash, and I can Venmo you another five hundred when I get Wi-Fi. Here, I'll go get my other dress."

Coco scratched her neck. Did it grow suddenly hotter? She looked at the fist of green Silvia held out. A thousand dollars! Half of what she needed for Aunt Deb's gift. Money was so tight. She wasn't sure she would ever get enough cash to pay for Aunt Deb's bread slicer. Coco would do anything she could do to make her aunt's life better. But now this woman was practically throwing money at her. Wasn't this some sort of Christmas miracle? She'd be a fool to not to take it. Coco bit her lip. Should she go? What had she got to lose? "Okay."

"Perfect!" A huge grin spread across Silvia's perfectly painted lips. "I'll be back." She bounded down the brick sidewalk.

Fingering the bills, Coco glanced to the mansion. Guests gathered en masse toward the main front door. Would anyone notice she didn't belong?

Silvia returned with a satiny top and skirt. "You'll look so nice in this ensemble."

Yeah right! Coco ran her fingers the softness of the fabric. It felt heavy and rich. "I'll look like a scarecrow with my hair like this." She stroked the top of her hair which was held up with a claw clip. "You know, you can put lipstick on a pig, but she'll still be a pig." She was a country girl through and through and would never look as sophisticated as Silvia or anyone else from that elite crowd.

Silvia tilted her head and laughed. "You seem like a nice girl. Why would you be so mean to yourself?"

Floored by her frankness, Coco took a step back. A large part of her humor was making digs at herself.

"You really shouldn't say anything about yourself that you wouldn't say about someone else." Silvia gave her a half smile. "Who was it that said, if you can't say something nice, don't say anything at all? Doesn't that apply to ourselves?"

Coco recovered her humor. "If I did that, I wouldn't have much to say, and I definitely wouldn't be as funny."

"You're so strange." Shaking her head, Silvia dropped small, zippered bag into her hand. "And here's something for your face."

424

Silvia shrugged. "I have plenty. My dad owns a cosmetics company."

"Is it obvious I don't normally use makeup?" Coco would feel goofy walking into an event with her sweaty face.

Silvia pursed her lips and *tsked*. "There you go, dissing yourself again. You need to stop it. You're beautiful."

Coco opened her mouth to object.

Silvia waved a dismissive hand. "Don't worry. You'll figure it out." She ran a hand down front of her cloak. "Ta-ta! I must be off. I feel so much better. You've lightened my burden, and I couldn't be happier." Stepping closer, she clutched Coco's hand with manicured nails. "And just a warning." Her smile dropped, and her voice grew more serious. "If you take my money and tell anyone you aren't Silvia, I'll find out and send my lawyers to ruin you." She smiled again, squishing her blue eyes. "Ta-ta!" Silvia retreated toward the cars.

Coco gulped staring after her. Silvia didn't seem like a person who gave threats wantonly. Perhaps she should run after her and give her back her cash. But she opened her fist to the crisp bills that could help Aunt Deb.

Staring at the line of imported cars driving up the brick drive, waiting for valets to open their car doors, Coco huffed. Could she really slip in, drop off the present, and be Silvia for the evening? Who would ever find out? Coco certainly wouldn't tell anyone. This would be the easiest thousand dollars she'd ever made. The bread slicer was practically under the Christmas tree!

To enjoy a bit of quiet from the hustle and bustle of the wedding preparations inside, Preston Laurent stood in the snow-covered gardens in the back of his family's estate. He hadn't been to Sugar Creek since he was a little boy. He didn't particularly relish being here now. Turning, he went inside to face the music and the noise. Of course he couldn't really see it well. He broke his glasses on the trip up from New Jersey and wouldn't get another pair for forty-eight hours. Most of what he saw was blurs of light and color. The music was nice, though. A string quartet played classical music in a distant room.

The wedding filled the nearly the bottom floor of the twenty-thousand square foot mansion with people. He'd been up since before daybreak to supervise the tents set-up and direct workers.

His grandfather's interior decorator picked out the theme of the seasonal decor months ago, but Lisel wanted all the decor to reflect her wedding colors—silver and champaign pink. She insisted on the giant forty-foot fir tree nestled in the neck of the two-story spiral staircase to greet people in the foyer. Trying to find a forty-foot tree in a small town in Vermont was no easy task. He had one flown in from Boston.

He shook his head. When he got married, if he ever did, he would never want one as ridiculously lavish as this one. But Lisel was an old friend of the Laurent family, and this wedding would be one of the last events his family held before Preston sold the property after the New Year. His was tasked to oversee all the preparations for the sale—a job he wished he could do from New Jersey where he finished grad school, rather than from the empty house, built in 1905.

Older houses always needed maintenance, and his grandfather, was tired of holding onto the old property and was ready to move on.

The wedding planner waved to him in the hall. "I'm so glad I caught you." She puffed, out of breath. A few strands of hair had fallen from her bun, and she looked like she needed to get off those heels.

"What's wrong?"

"The bride is worried people will come late and walk in the middle of the procession going through the foyer." She tucked in her shirt. "She wants someone stationed at each of the entrances to make sure people don't ruin her ceremony."

"Such a specific request." He had once went late to a wedding in Boston because traffic was horrific on April 19—Patriot's Day. People flooded the streets wearing tricorn hats.

The wedding planner's eyes bugged out. "You have no idea what this woman is capable of coming up with. She needed matching hosiery, which no one will ever see, for her bridesmaids, and the gifts! She insisted everyone wrap their gifts in pink or silver so they'd match." She threw her hands into the air. "But I'm out of staff. Brutus was sick with the stomach flu. Marlin had a flat tire. Peter didn't check in at all. No one is left. Do you have someone employed here, a valet, or a housekeeper even, who could lend a hand?"

He'd never kept a valet, although the idea intrigued him. And the housekeeper was off for the weekend. "I'll watch the front door. Put your mind at ease. No one will interrupt the procession."

The woman let out a sigh that could've blown out a candle in the Old North Church in Boston. She swept back her hair, but it fell right back into her face. Wrinkles smoothed across her brow. She looked years younger. "Just stay there until they're all clear of the foyer."

"I will. No problem." He flashed his best smile.

"Thank you! I have to go check on the catering. We'll be eating in about an hour." She stomped off, her pumps clacking on the black and white marble floors.

Guests filled the great salon at the front of the house. He aways loved the abundance of windows along the front of the house, although the wreaths partially blocked the fading sun.

The blazing house was packed.

He hired movers for the wedding. All the furniture was either moved to the sides if it was too heavy to store on the other floors, making way for two hundred or so chairs, each covered with pink and silver bows.

Was he a little sad to sell this property? He checked his feelings. Fifty years ago, his grandfather had a terrible experience in Sugar Creek—one that he would never forget, yet, one he never shared with Preston. Papa Roland could never live here—in fact, he hadn't been back in those years. So sell, he must.

Earlier that day, Preston opened the double pocket doors to the study—the adjoining room—to accommodate all the guests. Now, minutes before the start of the wedding, hundreds of people gathered in those two rooms all facing the study.

The fuzzy outline of the pastor stood in front of a grand fireplace, shifting nervously.

Preston checked his watch. He'd better get to the front door quickly. The wedding was about to start.

cf86f028-2c87-425c-96b3-4c44946bb07dR01